Graphic Novels by Kurt Amacker

Art by J.C. Grande

Art by Karl Slominski

With Dani Filth
Art by Montgomery Borror

With Jyrki 69 and Marc Moorash
Art by Various

The Landmark Graphic Novel Returns in 2016

VLAD DRACULA
DEAD SOULS
ERZSÉBET BÁTHORY
RESURRECTION

"A fascinating debut that delivers..."
—Alan Moore (*Watchmen*)

Written by Kurt Amacker and Illustrated by Montgomery Borror
Introduction by Dani Filth

Featuring Expanded "Author's Cut" Story, New Art by
Montgomery Borror, Cover by Dan Brereton, and
Introduction by Dani Filth of Cradle of Filth

BLOODY OCTOBER

by Kurt Amacker

DARK NOTES PRESS

Bloody October
By Kurt Amacker

First Printing – First Edition

ISBN13 - 978-0-9915712-7-7
Published in the United States of America by Dark Notes Press, LLC

Lord Chaz appears courtesy of Three Lords Entertainment, LLC
For tours, visit www.LordChaz.com
Maven Lore appears courtesy of Dark Awakenings
For custom fangs, visit www.DarkAwakenings.com

Cover by Tim Lattie and Fletch Boogie

websites:
www.DarkNotesPress.com
www.KurtAmacker.com
DARK NOTES PRESS

With Deepest Thanks...

As my first novel, *Bloody October* benefited from the counsel, support, and boundless encouragement of the many wonderful and talented people in my life. I cannot thank all of them enough. Reviving the raucous heyday of the New Orleans goth scene in the late 1990s was both thrilling and heartbreaking. It was a pleasure to remember all of the people, places, and events that helped make me who I am, and who led me to write this book. And, it was both terrifying and heartbreaking to examine where else things might have ended. Jason Castaing is not me. He is who I might have become without all of the people who have stood by me over the years. With that, I would like to thank, in no particular order:

The Amacker Family, the United States Marine Corps, Graham Hayes, Olivia Hunt, Kimberly Caron Hirsius, Drake Mefestta, Maven Lore, Lord Chaz, Dr. Tim Peterson, Alan Moore, Dani Filth and Cradle of Filth, Jyrki 69 and The 69 Eyes, Tim Lattie, Fletch Boogie, Shades Casanova and Shadow Reborn, Michael Gunn, Mange Voorhees, Elizabeth Lesher, Destiny Adcock, Lisa Watson, Katie Picone, Mary Pappas, Sarah Manowitz, Dana Fairchild, Marc Moorash, Holly Taylor, Brad Richard, Anne Gisleson, Richmond Eustis, Blake Bailey, Jim Fitzmorris, and everyone else who believed.

Thanks to the staff and crew at:

Spitfire, CONtraflow, Fear Fete, Comicpalooza, More Fun Comics, BSI Comics, Media Underground, Wyatt's Comics and Cards, Hammond Horror Festival, The Black Syndicate, Bar Redux, One Eye'd Jacks, The Howlin' Wolf, and NOLA Drink N' Draw.

Above all, I wish to thank my wife, Sabrina Amacker, without whom none of this would be possible.

Chapter 1

Friday, September 12, 1997

To say that I knew John Devereux in those early days would imply that I understood him as I would come to, in time. True, I had known him and called him my friend for nearly two years by that afternoon. Much had changed after that first night on the road back from Baton Rouge. The man I had met in the corner of the dim nightclub wore clothes that I would charitably call "out of date." His gray suits and parted hair bespoke of an office executive who hadn't left the house since the 1960s. But, since making my acquaintance, he had purchased enough black clothes to outfit a funeral parlor. And, he, like me, dressed that way at night when we darted and dashed through the nightclubs and dive bars of the lower French Quarter.

That early September evening, he wore one of his old suits, and looked every bit the part of someone wearing his grandfather's clothes. When I called and woke him, I suggested he avoid dressing "the part." He knew what I meant, but, speaking through the last haze of sleep into the phone, he wanted to know why. I only told him that I would explain in person. We met at the Rue Café on Magazine Street at around five. I suggested a table near the picture window that faced the street. With the sun's light fading, but present, he reluctantly complied. I ordered two cups of coffee and returned to the table to sit.

John rested his cigarette next to mine in the ashtray. The smoke and the steam from his mug rose in front of him, briefly clouding the space between us. His fedora rested next to my elbow. Through the great window to our right, I could see the end of the day's traffic trickle by outside. The New Orleans summer had given way to the earliest days of autumn, in air if not in date. The cool weather had reached the city a few weeks earlier than usual.

"These will kill me one day," I said, picking up my own cigarette.

"I'm just lucky," he replied.

John winked as he took another drag. That afternoon, only minutes before, I'd put off quitting for another year. Part of me wanted to keep up with John's appetite for liquor and the endless chain of cigarettes that he smoked. He lived exactly how he wanted to because he could. I sometimes tried, but I could never compete.

"You could at least, you know, pretend to restrain yourself around me. Not all of us are like you." As far as we knew, no one else was like him.

"Jason, does it really bother you that much?" he asked. He held up the half-smoked butt for a second, and looked down at my own smoldering in the ashtray.

"No," I said. "I'm quitting next year."

"I suppose we'll talk about it then," he said.

"What are friends for?" I asked.

Before knowing me, my friend had kept his secrets well. He'd asked me to reintroduce him to the world, even if it only meant the bars, restaurants, and local characters near his house in the lower Quarter. His request seemed odd at first. But, I took it in stride and we took to the town, leaving an endless string of gothic bars, empty glasses, and smoked cigarettes in our wake.

After meeting me, we still kept his greatest secret.

But, word had crept away from us gradually—the "V-word," of course—either through drunken half-admissions or his noted aversion to daylight. We never said it, but others did. Most people laughed at the idea, but a few believed it.

"Sometimes, he comes out during the day," I would argue. And when he did, he stank of sunscreen and always wore a hat. Nevertheless, he had been seen in the shops and cafés near his home often enough. That alone quieted the worst of the rumors.

Still, the stories swirled from his home on Barracks down the street and through the bars like so much music and smoke. It stood to reason, then, that a passel of corseted girls and would-be blood junkies hung all over him in search of the truth—and when he could make them like him. They ignored his denials and continued asking. He seemed to enjoy the company of the girls, but John had sworn off relationships decades before I knew him. His resolve eventually gave way, though, and his reputation as a minor lothario gradually emerged. The rumors enlarged a handful of trysts into grand affairs, replete with a vampiric super-villain, swooning heroines, and a supporting cast of lovable drunks and nightclub divas. As with the other stories about him, he largely ignored them.

I enjoyed the odd one-night-wonder myself, but I envied the ease with which John met women. I was rarely privy to anything more than the meeting, though, and certainly no particulars worth transcribing.

Whenever I asked about the interim, before we'd met, he would only grumble "Maria," and wave his hand. I'd pieced together bits of the story—she'd died in the 1950s, but of what he would never say. I suspected cancer, but never asked. A few others might have come and gone remained alone for much of the past forty years—until he asked me to reintroduce him to the world.

"So, why did you get me out of bed at this ungodly hour?" he asked.

Without a word, I dropped the manila envelope I'd concealed in my jacket. The thick packet clattered to the floor beneath the table.

"You dropped—" he said, as I shook my head slightly. "What?"

I leaned across and lowered my face. John and I could read each other better than anyone, and he knew I meant to play it cool. He moved in, and his eyes gleamed cool and hard. He knew when to get serious, and it had kept him alive for a long time. I drew a yellow Post-It note from my breast pocket and passed it to him. "Read," I whispered. As his eyes jetted back and forth, I heard his voice in my mind speaking the words.

Pick up the envelope and hide it in your jacket. Go into the men's room with the envelope and act like you're using one of the stalls. Open the envelope and look at the pictures. Look at them for as long as you need to. She was one of yours. While you're gone, I'm going to leave. Come to my apartment in one hour. Flush the pictures and this note. I've got more copies.

John nodded. After only a second, he bumped his cigarettes off the table with a clumsy elbow. Leaning over to pick them up, he quickly shoved the envelope into his gray sports coat. Standing up, he walked to the men's room and looked back at me for half a second. I jerked my eyes at the door next to him. He waited for a moment in front of a corkboard cluttered with advertisements for art galleries, concerts, and anything else you could imagine. I pushed my black glasses back up from the end of my nose. He nodded slightly and pushed the narrow wooden door open with his shoulder.

With a handful of cocktail napkins, I dried the sweat forming on my bald head. I grabbed my jacket, my notebook, and my smokes and walked out of the coffee shop on to Magazine Street. The fading September sun continued its slow descent across the New Orleans sky, with Halloween just beyond it. In a city ruled by history and its dead, I knew that more of both would lie before us—me and John, the only real vampire I knew.

I walked between the cars waiting in traffic like nothing had happened—a lone man in black, crossing from one side of the street to the next.

***

Let's just get all this out in the open.

In a city and a decade full of people that wanted to be vampires, John was the only real one either of us knew of. We'd never met any others. According to him, he'd stopped aging at about thirty and started drinking blood. If he went without it, he told me, the hunger never ended. He'd even grown fangs. My friend was an accident of fate or nature or a trial experiment conducted by whatever you think of as God—a prototype or a pilot aired once and never spoken of again. As far as I knew, he'd just happened. And, though he needed to drink blood, he could—and did—eat or drink whatever else he wanted. He wasn't allergic or opposed to crosses, silver, or garlic. In fact, he ate tons of the latter in the Italian food he frequently gorged himself on (and Mexican, and the piles of fried seafood and chicken available throughout the city). And, he gained weight from none of it. He really didn't like sunlight, but it didn't set him on fire. If he had to get up early for some reason, it took a dozen hits of the snooze button on his alarm clock. It's not easy to wake up when your body tells you not to go outside until dark.

He was immortal, though he'd never tested the limits of that.

I met him at a bar in Baton Rouge, and then saved him from a car accident almost immediately thereafter. That was 1995, and I was a journalism student at a liberal arts college in Uptown New Orleans—a boy in black given away by grateful parents to academia. Two years later, that September, I was something of a journalist for the gamut of free weeklies that cluttered the coffee shops and bookstores of New Orleans. Editorials, humor pieces, movie reviews, and low-level muckraking—I wrote anything they asked, and submitted everything I could think of. It was all quick and dirty, written fast and for an easy couple of bucks. The editors called me "the holy trinity" because I was good, fast, and cheap. I'd never once asked for a raise or negotiated a higher rate. I'd earned a reputation as a guy that could fill a rag overnight, even writing under other names to disguise my output.

The gothic scene had taken over the American musical underground. I was part of it, but I had largely avoided writing about it. You can't keep many friends if you write about their top ten most embarrassing bar moments from the night before. But, a perfect storm happened around that time, especially in New Orleans—one of vampire novels, horror movies, and a retro music movement of moody baritones, synthesizer beats, and macabre verses.

"Goths" they called us for short, though we were the least likely group to raise a sword against Rome or anyone else. It was hard to think of violence when you were too busy lighting clove cigarettes and examining outfits at vintage clothing shops.

It was the perfect time for John to venture outside of his home, where he'd long secluded himself.

Ten years before, barely anyone outside of New York, Los Angeles, or London knew what a goth was or who the hell listened to Bauhaus. That band had broken up in 1982, when most of the current black-clad mob wore diapers. But that year, whispers of a reunion circulated through the bars and clubs, as the smoke from cloves mingled with beats by the Sisters of Mercy, the Cure, and Siouxsie and the Banshees.

"Goth is Back!" all the music magazines said. I was right there to see it.

Back then, they didn't really have books with names like *What is Goth?* that explained the order of things. A Germanic barbarian tribe's name was once insultingly appropriated for a style of medieval architecture during the Renaissance. The style of architecture's name was kindly appropriated for a genre of supernatural literature in the 1800s. Then, the style of literature's name was used to describe some horror movies in the early part of the century. Finally, the description of those horror movies was, in turn, applied to a bunch of moody British rock bands in the 1970s and '80s. Those bands and the handful of black-clad punks that preferred them over the Sex Pistols faded to ash grey amidst a few burning embers—whispers of secret nightclubs in New York and Los Angeles—until the early 1990s, when everyone realized they were worth keeping around.

I had always liked vampire stories and preferred black clothes. I didn't just want to wear it. I wanted to live it. When I found the music that catered to that kind of thing, I knew which road I'd travel. My parents saw it too, and they begged me to leave home for college—to go anywhere that would keep me out of the French Quarter for four years. I'd realize the error of my ways, they told me in so many kitchen table arguments over meals growing cold. After much haranguing, we finally agreed upon the aforementioned liberal arts institution, which, like so many subjects in this narrative, will remain safely anonymous. But off I went, determined to become a journalist and tell the world all the true stories fit to print.

That's why I'm writing about John. Whatever the papers, the police, true crime TV, or the rumors say now, he was my friend. I want to tell the truth.

Chapter 2

Friday, September 15, 1995

The night I met John, I attended a club night in Baton Rouge. With the handful of the capital city's black-clad denizens and a few visitors from New Orleans, I tried to drink away the boredom. The music sounded the same—The Sisters of Mercy, then Christian Death, then Siouxsie and the Banshees, then Bauhaus, then Joy Division, and so it went. On the inside, it felt akin to New Orleans. The same five types of people you met at a goth bar lined the bar and crowded the dance floor. A few vampire dandies sat among young men with black leather jackets and band t-shirts. Between them mixed the club girls, thin and their hair woven with neon and crowned with useless goggles. And there I sat at the end, wearing my usual boredom in the form of black jeans and a suit jacket over, yes, a band shirt. The lights burned low, and the smoke swirled just the same. Baton Rouge always seemed like a nice change of pace before you walked through the barroom doors. But when you arrived, it felt like you'd made reservations at a new and second location of a restaurant you loved—similar on the surface, but without a soul behind the wheel or fire in the engine. And in New Orleans, you could always leave and come back. Bars dotted the streets, and patrons ran from one to the other—dodging cars and trailing shadows, cast by the lights of so many signs and open doors. The city could do that for you—stay open and stay awake for you, even when no one else would.

In Baton Rouge, you walked outside and saw the dark of night and locked doors and dim windows. Only closed businesses surrounded the one goth night (which was probably a neighborhood pub or a gay bar the other six days of the week). I'd made my way there on a promise from Serenity—a girl I'd met the weekend before at a bar in my own city. I would visit, and she would invite me back to her apartment after a few drinks. I'd called her the day before and confirmed. She'd answered and said yes, and hissed her last few words as she bid me come hither and good-bye. When I made up a reason to call her back the next day, she didn't answer. I drove to our state's capital anyway, spurred on by my good faith in her word.

That night, I sat at the bar—most recently dubbed "The Catacomb"—and watched the lithe black forms swirl across the dance floor. Serenity never arrived, despite my best efforts to stare at the door and will her there. I looked from corner to corner in search of her, or a reasonable facsimile. I didn't spend much time worrying about sex. Or rather, I'd given up worrying about it. Women largely ignored me. At a gangly six feet tall, with no hair and a notably simple wardrobe, I didn't exactly attract them in droves. I'd enjoyed my few experiences dating and screwing around, but not enough to make either a fulltime pursuit.

College men wanted—in their words to me, at least—"pussy, beer, weed, and video games." I had little experience with the first three, and no interest in the fourth. But, liquor had blossomed into a healthy interest, though one I could barely afford. A student budget kept me relatively sober, and I remembered as much as I glanced at the plastic cup before me. It was cheaper and weaker than I would've liked.

I wrote for the school newspaper. I went to class. And at the end of every day, I went home and studied. I'd finagled enough money out of my parents for a cheap apartment near campus. The rest of my income consisted of student loans and odd jobs I worked during the summer. I moved through the days quietly and without incident, mostly trying not to offend anyone.

A trip to Baton Rouge counted as a significant expense then, and I silently cursed Serenity for leading me on, canceling, or whatever she'd done. I scanned the room once more, and no eyes met mine. But in the corner, sat a man dressed formally and wholly out of place. He wore a tan suite, and a light blue shirt with no tie. He had dark, reddish-brown hair, brushed into a part. He stubbed out a cigarette, as he stared straight ahead—not at me, but past me. Rather than looking, he seemed to remember something. I imagined a story of some other day playing in his mind. On a chance, I pointed at myself and mouthed the word, "Me?" in his direction. He shook his head, still twisting the dead cigarette into the tray.

Goth clubs always had a handful of curious outsiders. Some arrived firmly in-the-know. Others walked in simply looking for a drink, because any bar would do. Some adventurous sorts had heard media whispers of hidden BDSM dungeons and promiscuous women in black (if only). But, I suspected the man in the corner already knew about the Catacomb, and had arrived there on purpose. As I considered him, he stood and walked towards the bar. When he reached the space next to me, he stopped.

"I apologize for staring," he said. "May I buy you a drink?"

Momentarily confused, I replied, "Uh, sure."

"You drink Scotch?" he asked. I nodded and said that I did. Glancing at the plastic cup in front of me, I knew what I'd drank didn't count as Scotch and barely counted as whiskey. Feeling slightly embarrassed, I nudged it away so that I could block it with my other elbow. The man held up two fingers to the bartender—a husky young man, also bald but with a goatee, wearing a black work shirt. He placed two glasses—not cups—in front of us. He turned and retrieved a bottle from the top shelf across from me, behind the bar. I didn't recognize the label, but it looked expensive. As a naïve college student relatively unschooled in premium whiskey, I decided not to inquire.

The bartender filled both glasses halfway with the dark amber fluid and then left us. The man who'd bought me the drink leaned back and raised his glass. I lifted mine and touched it to the edge of his.

"Cheers," he said, smiling. His lips twitched and hesitated. He'd forced the expression, but I did not know why. I returned the word and took a sip. Sharp brown fire filled my mouth, and I swallowed gently. I'd had the good stuff before, but not in a long time.

"What's this for?" I asked.

"I was staring in your direction, though I confess not at you, at least initially," he said. "It seemed rude. And, I was coming here anyway. And also, this." He held up his left hand and waved it.

"Southpaw?" I said.

"I saw you drinking with your left," he said. "It caught my attention."

My father was left-handed, and so was his father before him. It wasn't something I thought about often, except when I had to drive. The stick shift on my car constantly reminded me.

"Yeah, lefties," I said. "I'm glad there's another member of the tribe here."

"What are you here for?" he asked. It almost sounded like an inquiry about a prison sentence, and I laughed. "I apologize, but I don't understand this bar," he said. The formality of his tone and the slightly outdated vocabulary threw me off for a moment. Plenty of assholes in the goth scene would feign courtly manners and even

British accents. People in fake fangs and long coats (younger than me) had called me "my lord" more than once. But, the man's demeanor seemed honest enough.

"I was supposed to meet a girl," I said. I explained the situation with Serenity in as few words as possible, and he nodded as if he understood. Part of him seemed quietly confused. Though he seemed older than me by more than a decade, I pegged him at no later than his early 30s. Over the edge of my glass, I looked him up and down. He stood slightly taller than me. He'd draped the tan sports coat over his arm. On the bar, he'd laid a matching fedora I'd failed to notice. He looked like a young man wearing his grandfather's suit. My new friend was no goth. I could tell that much. Finally, I extended my hand and introduced myself.

"Jason," I said. He nodded and shook my hand.

"John," he said, when his eyes met mine.

He asked about my family, where I went to school, if I came to Baton Rouge often, and any other question one stranger might ask another. We talked there until the club closed at two. He bought us a couple of more rounds. He never ran a tab, and always paid with cash as soon as the plastic cups hit the bar. Whenever I asked him anything about himself, he directed the conversation back to me.

As the lights rose, John held his hand above his eyes and squinted for a second. The bartenders began to usher everyone out, and I excused myself to go to the bathroom. He nodded, and appeared to wait. I thought that once I emerged, I would bid him good-bye and drive back to New Orleans. Perhaps I would see him again one day, or perhaps never again. Meeting people in bars carried that risk, as Serenity had proven once more. When I walked out of the men's room, the spot where he'd rested his elbow on the bar was empty—no John, no hat, and an empty glass. Walking quickly to the exit, I expected to see him outside. I reached the second doorway at the end of a dingy corridor. The floodlights surrounding the parking lot shined bright around the dark and scattered forms of the club-goers. Some walked to their cars. Some walked out of the parking lot and into the street. I figured a few would find a diner and eat, while the lucky ones would head home and fuck someone. I would do neither, I thought, as I watched them leave. My car's CD player would serenade me on an otherwise quiet ride home.

A black Cadillac—old, but polished and maintained as if it were new—roared and sped out of the parking lot. A few stumbling goths jumped out of its way as it veered past them. Turning right sharply, it rounded one of the floodlights and drove away towards I-10 East.

I never asked John where he'd come from.

Looking towards my own black car, I walked straight across the parking lot. I wanted to eat out, but I couldn't afford it. I wanted to fuck Serenity, but I couldn't find her. Even if I could, she clearly had no interest in me. I would drive back to New Orleans, eat at home, and then have a cheap drink before falling asleep.

With each step, I wondered about John. I couldn't understand what happened. He'd spent two hours of the evening buying me drinks and asking me every polite question that a person could—where I was from, where I grew up, where I went to school, what sort of music I liked, and a hundred others. He'd asked me each one as if checking them off a list. And then, he'd left without saying a word.

Before I took my keys out of my pocket, I stood by the dirty black Volvo I'd driven there and stared at the night sky and the distant river beneath it.

***

The Mission U.K. played in my car as I sped towards New Orleans. I tapped the steering wheel and sang along to keep myself awake. A bit of drinking and a late night a few towns over suddenly felt like a bad combination. I mentally replayed my conversation with John as I drove. After running through it a hundred times, I still had no idea what to think.

Out loud, I said to myself, "Maybe he was just lonely. You ever think of that?"

I considered my schedule for the next few days of class, writing, and sitting in my apartment studying. I had enough to do, but no one to talk to. I wrote well enough, but I didn't love it. I had no idea what came after college. The future stretched out before me, and I couldn't even figure out what I wanted from it.

I'd had those moments—alone and dark—in my dorm room during my first year of college. A high school girlfriend had broken up with me on Christmas Eve, and the one anchor of my old life had drifted into the distance. I'd passed like a ghost through the next two years of school—and my apartment and my car stood as my only real move towards adulthood. Having "my own place" seemed like a start, but to nothing in particular. The bored nights I'd spent corking a bottle of cheap whiskey with my thumb continued, and only the bed I laid upon changed. I didn't really need my old girlfriend. I needed something or someone to tell me what to do next. I didn't cry. I couldn't.

Those thoughts flashed through my memory like a movie trailer for the darkest time in my life.

Then, I saw the black Cadillac half-a-mile ahead of me, turned on its top. A small orange flame burned from beneath the hood and was spreading to the grass around it.

Slowing down to see more clearly, I pushed my glasses back up my nose and leaned forward. The scene grew larger as I leaned forward and squinted. The dark shape of a man—John, I immediately realized—extended from the upturned window, not limp, though, and unsubdued by the wreck. His arms flailed and grabbed at the earth around him, finding nothing to grip.

I slowed down even more, as cars and trucks ignored the speed limit and weaved around my Volvo. Headlights flashed and a horn blared behind me, but I continued pushing the brake pedal before pulling behind the wreck and turning off the ignition. Throwing open the door, it occurred to me that no one else had stopped. John was still on the ground. Dirt covered his face, and streaks of blood trickled from the top of his head. Yelling an uncountable string of "Fucks!" I ran to my car's trunk, nearly dropping my keys in the process. After opening it, I dug through three years of textbooks and dirty clothes. Under a loose spare tire, I found a small fire extinguisher I kept. I ran over without closing the trunk, and unpinned the metal tab from atop the red canister.

He looked up at me as though he was glancing over a newspaper, and said, "Would you mind lending me a hand?"

"Your car is on fire," I said, stepping over him. Gripping the base of the extinguisher with one hand and squeezing the top of the other, I sprayed the white foam and the growing flames near the hood. As the fire hissed and died, I looked back at John. He still lay on the ground, but now white flecks of the extinguisher's foam dotted his face. With one hand, he wiped his eyes. Then propping himself up on one elbow, he waited.

Steam and smoke plumed all around us. I dropped the extinguisher and thought to slump against the car, my heart pounding. Before I could rest, I saw a pickup truck with enough lights to shame Christmas pull up behind my Volvo. "Damn it," John said, and raised his hand. "Come on!" he said.

"I don't think I'm supposed to move you," I said. "Shouldn't we wait for—?" The truck's doors opened and two men stepped out, though I could see nothing of their faces.

"Now!" John said.

Confused, I took both of his hands in mine and pulled. After a second of struggle, he kicked free of the wreckage pinning him. He crawled out the rest of the way and stood, dusting himself off. The wreck had torn his shirt and left him dusted with soot and flecks of blood. He appeared otherwise unharmed. "Let's go," he said, walking to the passenger side of my car.

"Wait!" I said, stepping after him. Wordlessly, he opened the passenger door and entered the vehicle. As I walked to the driver's side, he hit the horn. The men from the truck drew closer.

Wearing a purple polo shirt and a red baseball cap, the shorter of the two spat a mouthful of tobacco juice across the white line of the separating the Interstate from the shoulder.

"Y'all okay?" he asked.

Before I could answer, John rolled down the passenger window and yelled, "We're fine! Let's go!"

Shrugging, I said, "I guess we're fine. I'm going to get him to a hospital." I slammed the trunk closed and got in the car. John reached into his pocket and withdrew a handkerchief.

He wiped the blood from across his eyes and said, "For future reference, when I say we need to go, we go."

I turned on the ignition and pulled on to the interstate before speaking. In the rearview mirror, I saw the men turn to each other. One removed his cap while the other held his arms out. He slapped his sides, and they walked back towards their truck.

"Okay, what happened back there?" I asked. "How are you not dead? And what the fuck are you doing about your car?"

"Leaving it," he said. "It's not mine, anyway."

"You stole that?" I asked, pointing behind me with my thumb.

"No, sir," he said. "It belongs to a friend of mine. I'll get square with him once we reach New Orleans."

"So, you are from there?" I asked. He nodded and stared straight ahead. "Okay, that's good so far. Now, can you tell me why you just walked away from that crash?"

"Why I walked away?" he asked. "Because I wasn't content to lay in a flaming wreck for any longer than I had to."

"How, then, did you walk away? You should be fucking hurt or dead. And, you're not even bleeding anymore," I said. I'd noticed it shortly after we entered. He'd wiped away most of the blood with a handkerchief, and the red trickles had all but ceased.

"That's more complicated," he replied.

***

When he showed me his fangs—how they grew and receded at will—I pulled the car over for the second time that night. I promptly accused him of tricking me. I'd known enough self-proclaimed vampires in my time. They wore fake fangs. Some of them drank blood. A few religiously slept during the day. They lived the life. Only a gray hair or an unhealed wound would reveal them to anyone who already believed. But, I didn't. I'd read the books and seen the late-night cable TV specials. I hadn't entertained the possibility of vampires since the age of thirteen, and I had no intention of changing my mind. I called his fangs "some new trick," and "probably from Europe."

"No, no—I'm quite serious," he said. "This is just what I am. I do not know how it happened. But, I assure you I have lived this way since the 1950s."

"But, you don't kill people?" I asked.

"I will not say that I never have, but typically I do not—and I have not in several decades."

"And you can go out in sunlight?"

"I would prefer not to," he said, "but it does not kill me."

"And you're invulnerable? Like, at the crash?"

"Let's just say that I am sturdier than most," he replied. "But, I haven't tested my limits and I've no plans to do so."

He explained as slowly and carefully as he could, after convincing me to continue driving. He needed to leave the wreck behind, because otherwise he might reveal himself to law enforcement, the medical establishment, the "Army, the Navy, the Marines, the CIA, and whomever else might be interested," as he explained it. I laughed at the joke. He spoke stiffly and with unusual formality, but my new friend could still crack a joke.

I pulled back on to the road and pressed the gas pedal. But, I still didn't believe him.

He had, he explained, crashed after dodging an animal—a coyote, he suspected; or, possibly a fox. The ditch he drove into and some accompanying roots had disagreed with his Cadillac. And with no seatbelt across his chest ("Never wore them."), he'd hit the windshield. It didn't break, so he'd tried to climb out of the window when the fire started. I noticed that he had put on the seatbelt during our ride.

Prior to that night he had ventured out very little, he told me. He lived in the French Quarter, but only left when he absolutely had to do so. One night, on a whim, he stopped at a ramshackle bar on the corner of St. Philip and Bourbon Street, after running an errand. A man he met there had recommended a trip to Baton Rouge, to a place where they might accept an older gentleman with pale skin and vintage clothing. He hadn't understood what sort of bar he might be attending, but he had bought himself a drink and sat down nonetheless.

"Now, what is a goth, exactly?" he asked.

As we drove and drew nearer to New Orleans, I spoke of the music, the history, and the fashion—and the fascination with horror, the occult, and, yes, vampires. John laughed and leaned his head back against the chair.

"Oh Lord, if only they knew," he said. I still didn't believe him.

"Lonely vampire living in the French Quarter? That's original," I said. We passed under the interstate's green signs into Kenner. New Orleans waited a few minutes and miles away, depending on traffic. I asked myself what might happen to John and me after our trip ended.

"No," he said. "I don't judge the situation. I am what I am. But, I prefer to keep my own company most of the time."

"Just not tonight?" I asked. "Looking for a friend or a date?"

"I wanted to be out amongst people. I felt that venturing out into New Orleans might bear consequences. I try not to have many personal connections there. I have my contacts that keep me fed at various clinics, but few friends."

"Is that why you talked to me?" I asked.

"Maybe. You were alone. And, you looked about as excited to be there as I was," he said. "I wanted someone to talk to."

It was true. Were it not for meeting John, I would have left and grumbled Serenity's name all the way back to New Orleans. As it stood, our conversation had continued long into the night and I understood him all the better. I found myself believing him more as he, again, demonstrated the raising and lowering of his fangs for me. With his mouth open, I saw his canines grow down from his gums until they extended a half-inch past the rest of his teeth. They made a slight and sickening "squinch" as they emerged, and I asked him if it hurt. It did not, he explained, any more than the growth of fingernails or hair. Gradually, near the age of thirty-two, they had simply grown in and had never left.

Medical science couldn't explain what he had become, he felt sure. "Vampire" simply worked as the closest applicable term. He invited me to coin another, if I could think of one. I could not. Ever since then, I had believed in John.

As I pulled up to the curb near his house in the French Quarter, he asked if I would join him for dinner the next night. I showed him a look both low and half-cocked. He laughed and explained that he could eat regular food, and often did. And, he offered to cook for me. Given that my collegiate lifestyle meant a diet of delivery pizza and Chinese, I readily accepted.

***

Saturday, September 16, 1995

I arrived at the house on Barracks and Decatur the next day clutching a mid-priced bottle of Pinot Noir. Standing outside of his wrought iron gate, I looked at the sky and the worn brick building above me. I had lived in New Orleans for most of my life, and it always seemed like it held the answer to a mystery just out of reach. Sometimes, in observing the French and Spanish architecture of the city's oldest neighborhoods, I almost glimpsed what my fingers could never touch—a meaning nestled beneath the darkened bars, ghost stories, false vampires, and folklore spun into thin history. The bars just harbored gossipy alcoholics in black. The vampires were just obsessed fans with fake fangs. And, the folklore had simply been repeated enough times that most accepted it as true.

At the center of my city lay a culmination of forgiving alcohol laws, a port city's violent history, and political and civic corruption. The city's reputation as a mecca of gothic intrigue sat atop true horror. It was, at the end of the day, no longer special to me.

And yet, there I stood clutching a bottle of wine outside the home of a real vampire—the only one, to the best of anyone's knowledge. It felt as if John validated all I had ever hoped for in the earlier days of my youth. He stood as the answer to so many questions. As the autumn sky darkened, I felt a kind of wonder I'd not known for years.

Looking through the gate, I saw the same black iron bars on all of the windows. The side door a few yards ahead had the same thing. I'd noticed the house before, but the Quarter was full of rich locals who guarded their property like a fortress. You learned to ignore it after a while. I'd never spent a minute wondering who lived there.

I pressed the white button on the black intercom and waited.

"Come in," his voice said, rough through the static. The magnetic lock on the gate buzzed. There was a key lock next to it, but it opened anyway. I walked up the driveway. The brick wall of the building next to it towered over his courtyard, with ivy growing up its walls. I passed potted plants, and more ironwork—a garden table with chairs situated to the side, and a bench with a small pedestal, upon which rested an ashtray. He smoked. I remembered our chat at the Catacomb, and how he'd stubbed out his cigarette before approaching me. We had that much in common.

At the end of the drive sat a black Dodge Charger. The Cadillac hadn't been his only car. I reminded myself that the wrecked vehicle belonged to a friend, but I wondered who owned the sleek muscle car, or the house, and everything else. I decided I would run the address at the Clerk of Courts' office the next day. The property's owner would at least be on file there.

I stopped at the side door. It, too, had an outer gate of black iron. I could never begrudge John's insistence on so many layers of protection. He opened the door to greet me before I knocked.

"Hello, Jason," he said. "Won't you come in?"

"Thanks," I replied, holding out the bottle of wine. He pushed open the gate and accepted the gift with one hand. Without looking at it, he tucked it under his arm and turned to walk inside. I followed him down a narrow foyer. Framed posters of flowers, plantations, and streetcars lined his walls. His taste in art matched that of any old New Orleanian. I stopped at the single photograph among the prints. The black and white image showed John seated next to a Mexican (I presumed) woman on a great rock that overlooked the sea. Both of them smiled broadly, and the sun reflected off of his hair. Below them, I read the words "Cancun, 1949" typed into a small brass plate drilled into the frame. Before I could ask him about it, he returned to pull the door shut behind me. Without a word, he motioned for me to follow him. To the left, a narrow kitchen opened. Brown, polished cabinets lined the walls. Forks, knives, spoons, tongs, and other utensils cluttered the green marble counter, standing upright in open jars. On the stove, sat a large pot of boiling water. Steam escaped its top and wafted to a silver vent above the range. A smaller pot sat next to it. Before I could ask what he was cooking, he directed me towards the living room.

Hardwood floors led to great white walls with tall, curtained windows. Bookshelves filled the walls at the opposite end of the room. Earthy cloth and leather volumes lined their shelves. A recliner sat next to a door leading to a hallway, near a side-table overloaded with books and a banker's lamp. A brown leather couch was pushed against the wall in front of a green chest that doubled as a coffee table. I glanced around the room in search of a television, but saw none. An antiquated record player attached to wooden speakers sat atop the bookshelves on the other side of the room.

To my left, a long dining room table with six chairs waited. The crystal chandeliers' light reflected across its mahogany surface. He didn't have a separate room to eat I realized, but the enormous hall he called a living room left more than enough space. And, I wondered how often he even used it.

For a moment, I wondered why I had even come. I imagined myself laid out down his long table with my throat cut, as he stood over me catching the red stream into a goblet. But, it seemed like a lot of work to prepare dinner if he'd planned to kill me. I dismissed the notion, yet still questioned why he had invited me.

"This is it," he said, waving his arm towards the room. His white shirt's rolled up sleeve showed his pale, hairy arm. He wore a white apron and khaki pants with a pair of simple brown loafers. The orange flecks across his apron told me we were having Italian, but I said nothing. A gothic villain my new friend was not. He looked more like an old New Orleanian with family property and enough money to rarely leave the house. "Well, what do you think?" he asked, forcing a smile. It seemed like he rarely entertained guests—and perhaps had forgotten how.

"It's great," I said, walking to join him. "Is this all yours?" I asked, remembering the car—but apparently not my manners. John furrowed his brow and titled his head slightly. I knew then that I shouldn't have asked.

Before I could apologize, he said, "It's a bit complicated." A buzzing sound from the kitchen interrupted us, and he moved past me.

"Excuse me for one moment," he said. From the kitchen, I heard the buzzer stop and then his voice again. "Would you like a drink?" he asked.

"Got any whiskey?" I asked, loud enough for him to hear in the next room. After so many college gatherings with only cheap beer and bum wine, I'd nearly forgotten how to order a drink like an adult.

"Most certainly!" he said.

Moments later, we sat at the table with two tumblers filled with ice and amber liquid in front of us. We touched glasses and sipped. "What is this?" I asked.

I expected a quick joke about my lack of liquor knowledge, but he answered "Basil Hayden," without missing a beat. With the drink in front of him (and in him), John's mood seemed to lighten. And, so did mine.

We drank more, and then dinner followed. We both shoveled plates of spaghetti, marinara, and veal into our mouths. I'd expected something unpronounceable (and perhaps unidentifiable), but he'd more than delivered a dish my college-kid palette could handle. We drank the wine I'd bought as well, which he told me was fine. While we ate, he resumed and repeated his line of questioning from the bar. He again asked about my family, my schooling, my interests, and enough other bits to fill a biography. And once again, whenever I asked about his life, he only shifted the subject back to me. I finally asked him why.

"There's a lot in my history that's difficult to explain," he said. "Some of it I don't even understand myself. I've no desire to overwhelm you."

"So, back at the bar and here, you asked me just about everything you could about my life. Why are you so interested in me? I'm just a student." He sat back silently and put his fingers together in a prayer-like pose in front of his face.

Lowering his hands, he finally said, "I am in need of a companion. A real one—a friend."

"You know I'm not into that, right? I was waiting for a girl in Baton Rouge."

John shook his head, and said, "That's not what I mean." He raised his arms for a moment and looked towards the great hall in which we sat. It seemed so much larger inside than it did outside. "I'm alone here," he said. "I live here in New Orleans, and I have for some time. But, I rarely venture out except to acquire the blood I need from the banks. You must remember that I'm an old man. I don't always understand this city. I'd like to walk the streets again, and make friends, and, you know?" he asked, rolling his hand. I shifted in my seat.

"No, I don't know," I said.

"I'd like to eat in restaurants, and go to bars, and meet women, and feel like I'm still a part of the world," he said. "If you accompany me, it would of course all be at my expense."

I stared at the ceiling, briefly. "So, you just want me to take you out and show you around?"

"Yes."

"You live right off Decatur Street," I said, pointing out the window. "Just go out one night. You haven't been to a bar in decades? There are people with much worse problems out there. Shit. It'd be nice if most of them had that same issue." He shook his head.

"I need someone to guide me," he said. "Introduce me to people. Explain things to me. In turn, and in time, I'll explain as much about myself to you as I can. I know you have questions."

John had manners, he clearly had money, and he could cook excellent Italian cuisine. But, what he wanted seemed as innocent as it did unnecessary. After letting his words tumble in my mind for a few seconds, I realized that it wasn't very different from simply asking me to have a drink with him—an invitation any friend might offer.

"Sure," I said. "We can hang out sometime. I'll introduce you to a few people."

He stood and shook my hand, and thanked me twice. I stood and only nodded.

We cleared the dishes and left them in the kitchen before adjourning to the small garden. He'd brought two cigars, and we puffed away while sipping brandy. Through the iron gate, I could see traffic pass. With the coming of October, the crickets had faded. The air had cooled, and the sounds of the French Quarter's early evening mixed with the trickle of a small gargoyle fountain. I felt a kind of magic then. My more sensible mind blamed the pleasant weather, John's wealth, and the liquor's low buzz. Certainly in New Orleans, the rich and the poor often mingled on the same streets and in the same bars. But, you would always hit a wall. Someone had to drive to his law firm in the CBD in the morning, and the guy next to him had to wash dishes that night. In this case, the gate had opened and I felt welcome.

We sipped and smoked late into the evening. If I believed John's age—about sixty-eight, I gathered—then I knew he would have witnessed much of the twentieth century through adult eyes. I had questions for him, of course. He'd promised to answer some in exchange for my company. I asked the obvious ones first—the Kennedy assassination (sick in bed and missed the announcement); the moon landing (watched it on television like everyone else); and the long, slow birth of rock and roll (didn't like it at first, but came around after the Beatles). There were others, and he answered. But, the detachment with which he spoke—or his distance from the events—momentarily took me aback. He reminded me that, like most people, he'd lived a mostly unremarkable life. Only, his might never end.

"What about wars?" I asked. He puffed on his cigar and then removed it from his lips. "Too young for World War II, and too old for Vietnam. I tried to sign up for the Marines for Korea, but my appendix burst before boot camp. That kept me out." I remembered my father telling me that just about anything could derail an enlistment. Some guys had stayed back for less than that.

Sitting up and waving the cigar, I asked about "the rules."

"What do you mean?" he asked.

"The vampire rules," I said. He looked away for a moment.

"Didn't we discuss this in the car?" he asked.

"I don't remember," I said. "Tell me again."

"I am not afraid of crosses, garlic, silver, or holy water. I do not sleep in a coffin, but I prefer not to be out in the daylight. I can eat normal food, but it just, well," he paused and made a downward gesture with his hand, still clutching the cigar, "it just goes."

I frowned and imagined the indescribable digestive horror.

"You asked," he said. "As far as I know, I haven't aged since the 1950s or so. I don't know if I can't die, because I have not tried to kill myself. A young man shot me several years ago for my wallet, but the wound healed quickly enough."

"Did he get the wallet?" I asked.

"He did not," John said. "The bullet passed through my arm, and it healed fully within two days. I have a difficult time seeing doctors, as you can imagine." He continued, "But obviously, anything can be destroyed. As I said, I've not tested my own limits."

"I wouldn't, either," I said. I looked up and saw the few stars that could shine in the New Orleans night. Light pollution made it difficult to see most of them. "Do you like it?" I asked.

"Being what I am?" I turned in the chair to face him more closely.

"Yeah," I said. "Being a vampire, or however you think of yourself."

He shrugged, and then put the cigar between his lips. The ember glowed brightly. He released the smoke and looked straight ahead, as if he'd never considered the question. I realized that no one had likely asked him in ages, if ever.

"It just is," he said. "You learn to accept your lot in life as normal. I enjoy being alive in the same way that everyone else does."

"Do you like drinking blood?" I asked.

John looked at me with his brow furrowed. He hadn't expected the question, at the very least. At worst, I thought, I'd pissed him off and might see the other side of his gate in a moment—alone and clutching the fading stump of a cigar. After glancing downward for a moment, he looked up at me.

"Yes, I suppose I do," he said. "I might have starved ages ago if I didn't. But, I have learned to control myself." He stood with a faint grunt, and I knew he wouldn't answer anything more. I stood to leave and shook his hand.

"Last question?" I asked. He half-smiled and glanced up at the sky.

"Certainly," he said.

"Last name?"

"Devereux," he said. "And yours?"

"Castaing," I said.

"Well, Jason Castaing," he said, patting me on the shoulder, "welcome to my house."

***

Monday, September 18, 1995

The next Monday, I descended the gray steps inside of City Hall to the Clerk of Courts' Office. After passing rows of boxy computers and countless filing cabinets, I picked one of the terminals and sat down. A group of college students led by a frazzled older professor passed me on their way to the next set of machines. The professor removed her thick glasses and wiped them on a scarf draped over her shoulders.

"Just pick one," she said to the group. I remembered a similar experience in one of my earlier journalism classes. If you wanted to know anything about anyone, you had to know where to find it. Public records and a few minutes of connecting-the-dots, you could tell you more about a person than they might ever volunteer.

The green text glowed across the dark screen. I typed in John's address. After a momentary search, the record filled the screen. The cursor blinked, waiting for my next command.

"Adrian Reynolds," I whispered. The name "John Devereux" appeared nowhere on the property's file. For all I knew, he only rented the house from the same man who owned the flaming Cadillac. Something told me I shouldn't ask. A cursory Internet search revealed dozens of men with the same name. Devereux, Boudreaux, Thibodeaux, and Leblanc were as common around New Orleans as Smith and Jones over in Anytown, USA. I had no other information about him, other than a vague idea that he was born in the mid-1920s.

He hadn't told me everything. But, he had implied that he would not. I wasn't a spy or a cop or even a journalist by then. I'd skipped class just to run the search at City Hall. I could only decide to trust him or not.

***

Thursday, September 21, 1995

When I returned a few nights later, I wanted to ask him a hundred more questions. But, I held off and decided to see how the night went. He wanted to visit a bar down the street from his house. When he named the corner of Decatur and Ursulines, I laughed. It had changed names and ownership repeatedly over the years. Lately, it was the Crypt, but it was always our goth bar—the only dedicated one in New Orleans that had ever lasted. I'd first snuck in the bar at seventeen, and continued to spend what little money I had there on cheap whiskey and cigarettes.

John had read about it in the newspaper, and figured that he might pass unnoticed. He said he wanted to watch people. I thought he probably just wanted to meet a girl.

I told him what to wear.

When I saw him again, he'd dressed himself entirely in black. I stood in his living room, holding the drink he'd poured for me. He turned like a model on a runway, showing a pair of jeans with a dress shirt tucked in. He wore a pair of pointy black cowboy boots. "What do you think?" he asked.

"It'll do," I said. "It's fine. You look like a guy in black."

"And, not a vampire?" he asked.

"No more than anyone else," I said. "That's probably for the best. How obvious do you want to be about it?"

"I'm not sure," he said, walking to the dining area. He lifted his own glass from the table, and sipped the whiskey. "Who would believe me?"

"Lots of people," I said. "Maybe the wrong people."

"What do you mean?" he asked. He sat at the head of the table and gestured for me to sit in the chair to his left. I did, and adjusted the black suit jacket I wore.

"A lot of people want to be vampires," I said. "They're crazy about the whole idea. If they find out what you are, you'll have a bunch of psychotic assholes in fake fangs after you."

He laughed and took another sip of his drink. "They don't know what they're asking for then," he said. "I've no family left alive, and I feel like—"

I cut him off, saying, "An old man in a young man's body."

"But, it has its advantages."

"That's what they want," I said. "All of the other stuff doesn't matter. And, if they find out you're really real then I don't know what'll happen—maybe nothing, but maybe something bad. People are going to want you to bite them. They'll want you to share it."

"That doesn't work," he said. "I can't transmit it."

"I won't ask how you know that," I said.

"Don't."

***

Friday, September 22, 1995

During our first night at the Crypt, we sat at the edge of the bar near the door. Across the room, at the end of its smoky stone corridor, you could see the dance floor and the DJ booth. We talked about much of the same things we already had in Baton Rouge, during the ride back, and at his house. He wanted to know more about the music. He'd never seen people dance like that—without partners, and swaying to the beat across the damp, tiled floor. And, he asked me if they (or we) actually wore black all of the time.

He bought me more than I'd ever had to drink at one time in my life. As soon as the plastic cup neared the bottom, he would wave a few dollars at the bartender. I didn't argue with him. I noticed that, just like in Baton Rouge, he always paid with cash. At the end of the night, he loaded me into the backseat of a taxi. I woke up at home with a twenty in my pocket. He'd put it there so that I could go back to get my car.

And, I believed most of what he told me—that he had isolated himself at the edge of the French Quarter for a few decades, and the world around him was unfamiliar. He didn't have a television, and he didn't read the newspaper. He stayed home during every hurricane. I knew he had left his home at times to pick up his blood. Somehow, he had refused to pay attention to the world changing around him.

I spent the next several weeks, and then months, taking John to bars and restaurants. He always paid, and I didn't argue. John liked the first place well enough, but still seemed confused by the music. The cavernous, hollow wails of Joy Division, The Sisters of Mercy, Bauhaus, and their ilk dominated the playlist in those days. My friend had hidden himself away during the punk years—and goth, new wave, and all that had followed. I promised him a mixed tape, and said that if he remembered the Doors (he did) we could start there.

In time, he learned to tolerate the music. And, more and more black crept into his rather stiff wardrobe. Before, khakis, plaids, white shirts, and a few awful prints crowded his closet. In time, black overtook his life as it had mine.

Our nights drinking among the hoards at the Crypt led into early mornings. I would often forgo sleep and rush Uptown for class. My grades declined a bit, but I didn't care. Journalists barely made any money right out of college. It was too late to change my major, and I assumed I'd tend bar or wait tables like the rest of my friends. When I spent my nights drinking with the only living vampire, giving 110% to "Ethics in Journalism" seemed less important.

And, drink we did. John's seemingly limitless bank account kept us eyes-deep in booze. And with enough in him (he could get drunk, after all), he'd buy drinks for everyone around us. He never uttered the V-word, but somehow the rumors started anyway. An outdated joke or historical reference, or his insistence on leaving by dawn—however it happened, the rumors ran the gambit. Some said John just believed he was a vampire, and that it was an elaborate act. Others whispered that he might be the real thing.

However it happened, there our troubles began.

Chapter 3

Friday, September 12, 1997 – Evening

After I gave John the envelope that September afternoon, I arrived home to my apartment in the Garden District. I leaned forward on the black futon in my living room and smoked my fourth cigarette. A fragile model of Stonehenge gradually formed in the ashtray before me, one smoldering butt at a time. A knock on the door awoke me from my reverie.

When I opened it, John stood there, leaning against the frame. I all but cleared my throat for the usual joke about having to invite him in first. He didn't come over often. We usually met in town. After the first couple of times, he stopped inviting me into his home. I never asked why.

Before I could speak, he gave me a quick wag of his index finger, and said, "Don't. Not tonight." I nodded, before stepping aside.

"Shut the door," he said. I closed it and walked up behind him. He looked over his shoulder again and sighed without opening his mouth. He stood in my living room, staring at the framed Nine Inch Nails tour poster on my wall. I knew he didn't really want to talk about the pictures. "I still can't believe you listen to that noise," he said, cocking his head at the image of Trent Reznor clutching a leg filling a set of fishnet stockings, ending in a worn Army surplus boot.

"I'm a lot younger than you, remember?"

"Yeah. Never could get into that one. Too loud."

Speaking slowly, he said. "Now, we're going to go over this one thing at a time. First, you know that if what happened in those pictures is what I believe happened, that I had nothing to do with it, right?" He turned to face me. I'd never seen him look that serious. But, he didn't seem angry. He looked afraid. I swallowed.

After a second, I said, "I didn't think it was you."

And really, I didn't. John used blood banks, and he paid his contacts well for their silence. He had no reason to kill anyone. But, someone had. The pictures showed a girl lying naked and dead on the bloody floor of a bathroom, at some nameless shit-hole in the Bywater.

"God, I'm so glad you smoke inside," he said. John sat down on the futon and lit a cigarette. It sounded like he was speaking to himself. He began with, "Um, do you—" he pursed his lips and looked around. "Do you have copies of those pictures? Can I see them again?"

I said that I did, and I picked up a second envelope from the small dinner table that sat in the corner. I tossed it next to him. He took them out, and flipped through them twice, as if to make sure they were the same ones.

Looking up, he asked, "Why did you have me meet you at the coffee shop? What if someone had seen these?" I didn't want him to ask that question, but I figured I should just own up to what I'd done.

"Who do you think I got them from? You know that he knows that I can talk to you," I said, tripping over my words. "Not like undercover, or anything. You remember?" John knew bullshit when he heard it. He continued studying the pictures without looking up, his cigarette hanging limply between his lips.

"Jason, what the hell are you getting at?" He dropped the photos and stood up, facing me. "Come on."

"Look, I don't think you did this," I said.

"So, why did you want to meet in public? Why not just call me over here?" he asked.

I sighed, looking down, and said, "Detective Brad was watching us through the window—from across the street. He gave me the pictures. He wanted to see how you'd react." I felt like an asshole.

"Were you wearing a wire?" he asked, furrowing his brow.

"No, of course not, and I didn't want him to overhear us in the first place."

"Right, hence the note," he said, nodding. "He really thinks I might've done this?"

"Well, no," I said. "It's not that he doesn't trust you, but he wants to know for sure. You're a vampire for Christ's sake. He knows that. You're the first person anyone would think of."

John touched his fingertips to his forehead and looked down. He bit his lip. "All right, yes, I should've expected that. We'll work on that some other time. I wish Brad would realize that I'm on his side. What do you propose we do now?"

I walked towards the small room in my apartment that someone called a kitchen. I reached for one of the several half-bottles of liquor sitting next to the coffeemaker. "I need a drink. You?"

"Please," he said, raising his voice from the living room.

In New Orleans, you leaned one of two ways—you either drank more than anyone else in the country, or you did so much at one point that you had to quit. You were either a soldier in the bar wars or a wounded veteran, and everyone understood why you couldn't return to the front. There was no middle road. "Responsible drinking" happened somewhere in between Oz and fucking Never-Neverland.

I filled two glasses with bourbon and ice. "Mixer?" I asked, leaning my head out of the doorway.

"Not today," he mumbled, without looking at me. He'd stopped looking at the photos to stare at the floor. I brought the drink over and sat down next to him.

"What's on your mind?" I asked. He stroked his chin a little, his mouth open. He hadn't shown me his fangs since the first night we met.

"Well, this has just never happened before," he said, thinking aloud more than speaking to me. "People have been attacked, but not that badly—at least not around here." He stood up, drink in hand.

"You think it's another faker?" I asked. John sipped the bourbon and nodded as he swallowed.

"Yeah. You remember. It's not the first time."

***

John had something of an understanding with Detective Brad Simoneaux of the New Orleans Police Department. Behind his back, we called him "Goth Cop Brad." John had long ago shown his fangs to the detective, who believed his story.

In the two years since John reemerged, rumors about him had settled in to a steady beat of four or five stories. Most people didn't believe them, but a few took them seriously. A few people even asked him to bite them. He denied everything. Despite his best efforts, some of those stories had spread outside of the city.

***

Friday, September 27, 1996

There were rumors about vampires in New Orleans all over the country. A year after John and I met, a band of kids from Florida started following a guy named Rick Fremont, who told them he was the real thing. He said he drank blood, and that he'd live forever—and that he'd take them away. I imagined him, and I thought of a Peter Pan piper who took boys and girls to a place from which they'd never return.

We saw five of them that night. None of them were even eighteen. But they were all ready for childhood to end. After pretending to be vampires all over their shit-hole north Florida town—threatening their classmates and frightening the elderly—they drove towards New Orleans. Before they left, he beat his girlfriend's parents to death with a tire iron. As Mr. and Mrs. America lay dying on the bedroom floor, their own daughter and all of her friends lapped up the blood like kittens. They saved some of it in bottles for the trip.

Rick and his merry band of misfits drove a white carpenter's van west for New Orleans, all in hopes that John would protect them. They'd heard the rumors. I suppose if you're a group of vampires in trouble, you find another one like you—an older one—to help. They were kids looking for a different kind of parent.

For most people, though, the stories about John just blended in with the other ones about the city—how it was a haven for the bloodsucking undead. Rick and his crew picked a rumor that had a grain of truth at the center of a snowball of bullshit. They thought he was an "elder vampire." They thought my best friend wore a poet's blouse and snatched women from alleyways and fed on them in his mansion in the French Quarter.

It's hard to imagine someone that way when you've seen his closetful of plaid suits and suspenders.

They didn't have much trouble finding John. Despite rumors to the contrary, New Orleans has never had a large goth scene. The city itself is too small. Nonetheless, they arrived in New Orleans on a Friday, hungry, tired, broke, and nearly out of gas and waited until nightfall. They found the Crypt, where John and I had settled in to drink. We had been there for nearly an hour, and the club had filled with bodies covered in black—velvet, leather, lace, fishnets, and all that renders the weird wonderful. The music played from the dance floor speakers, while black and white horror movies flickered on the televisions. College girls in corsets with dyed hair gossiped and lit clove cigarettes, waiting for eager young men in knee-high boots to buy them rounds of vodka with cranberry juice. The dance floor filled slowly that night, and I'd counted no less than four boys painted up like Brandon Lee in *The Crow*—black lines from their brow, down raven eyes to pale cheeks, with irony mask smiles across their lips. It was as normal as things ever were for me—a Friday night with my friends, and all the promise of the weekend ahead of us. Then, Rick walked in.

John reclined on a threadbare sofa with a drink in his hand. One of the two girls seated next to him looked like Death from *The Sandman* comic—an ankh on her neck, with loops and swirls of black around her eyes, and a little hat atop her coifed hair. I stood by the bar, alone, ordering my third whiskey and soda when I saw the young man in the doorway. I remembered thinking that he looked underage—not that anyone's birthday ever stopped them in that place. He looked like Vlad the Impaler's retarded stepson, only kept alive to keep the old man laughing while the Turks swept through Eastern Europe. I looked the kid up and down as he walked up to John and took a knee, like he wanted to propose to my best friend. He had the whole nine yards of a goth kid dead before his time. His long black hair hung stringy and unwashed, framing a pockmarked face with a scruffy moustache and beard. He wore a top hat and cloak that were one step above something from Count Boudreaux's Halloween SuperStore. He leaned on a prop cane topped with a plastic wolf's head, and he reached out to take John's hand.

Assholes like that were a dime-a-dozen in New Orleans back then, and I'd seen John handle that kind of thing. I had told him it would happen, and probably more than once. I leaned against the bar and his eyes met mine. We smiled as I nodded. He winked and turned to the young man kneeling in front of him.

"Yes, my son?" He used the most serious voice he could muster, but I could see he was trying not to laugh. Rick grabbed his hand and kissed the skull ring John had taken to wearing, while the girls laughed. I remember thinking they were killing the setup. John would tell men and boys like Rick that they had to prove their loyalty before he could turn them. This often ended with the faker outside the club doing a full-on hat-swinging song and dance routine. Or, they'd end up in a garbage heap somewhere looking for fictional car parts. My friend, finally out and about in the world, had grown a sense of humor. But, we didn't know what Rick had done. And, we didn't see the four teenagers looking past the bouncer through the club door, standing outside in the rain—desperate and hungry—and hoping that the stories they'd heard were true. The vampire liked to get creative.

I couldn't hear any of what they said through the music. The DJ switched from The Cure to Concrete Blonde, and a black-and-silver flock rush towards the dance floor. They blocked my view of the scene. Afterward, John told me what happened.

"I killed them," Rick said, just above a whisper. I only saw John sit up and lean forward. He later told me that he hadn't quite heard him, but I think he really wanted to be sure.

"What?" he asked. I saw the humor drain out of his face, his mouth hanging open a little.

"I killed them for you, to prove my loyalty. We're all here now, Master."

John turned to the girls, and said, "Y'all go get drinks on my tab. If the bartender won't let you, tell Jason and I'll get him back later." The two ran over to the bar, next to me. Death laughed, but the other bore a sick frown.

"What's wrong?" I asked. Death turned to me.

"Oh, he's pledging his immortal soul to John or something," she said.

"I got that part. What's wrong?" The other girl looked down a little. Her blonde and red hair blocked my view of her eyes.

"I couldn't totally hear him because of the music," she said, looking up at me. "But, I think he said he killed someone—like, for real." I took a drag on my cigarette and exhaled. She coughed a little, waving away the smoke. I looked over at John and the kid, who still knelt in front of him. As Rick's story turned for the worse, I saw John try to stand about five times. The dirty, wet teenager finally grabbed a chair and pulled it in front my friend. Before he could sit, John rose, knocking his drink from the arm of the couch. The cocktail spilled all over Rick's seat. My friend looked around the room before we both noticed the doorway. The bouncer stood there with his arms crossed. The four teenagers looked past him through the club entrance. They stood in the rain, looking limp and hungry, practically gnawing their tongues for the pain.

Rick stood and stared John in the eyes. My friend extended his hand and gestured for him to kiss the skull ring again. He put his lips on the pewter death's head and then walked out, brushing past the bouncer. John took five quick steps to the bar and leaned next to me.

"I need to talk to you. Meet me in the ladies' room."

The women's restroom at the Crypt was an unofficial meeting room for goth scene business in New Orleans. There, drugs exchanged hands and DJs and scene queens resolved and inflamed petty squabbles and arguments of all shades. The first time I suggested we talk in there, he refused to enter. Now, John walked across the dance floor without looking back at me or the girls. I turned to Death and her friend.

"I think something might be going on. He doesn't usually get like this." Without waiting for her to speak, I followed him.

He stood in the center of the empty bathroom. Flyers for club nights and concerts adorned the walls, and all but one of the stall doors stood open and broken. No one had cleaned the place in weeks. On really good nights, one of the toilets sometimes flooded on to the dance floor.

"What's up?" I asked. John put his left hand on my shoulder.

"I need you to listen to me very carefully," he said.

"Yeah, sure," I said, nodding.

"I think this guy killed somebody. I'm not sure, but it sounds like it happened in Florida—maybe a couple of days ago."

Most of the aspiring vampires we know only alluded to taking victims—or they used donors that voluntarily bled into a wine glass. But in all the time I'd known him, we'd never seen anyone push it that far. He was old, my friend, and I knew he could detect lies and bullshit better than anyone.

I bit my lip, and felt the whiskey's warm glow drain out of me in an instant. It was a hell of a way to lose a buzz. "All right, what do you want me to do?" I asked.

He spoke slowly and deliberately, as if he feared I might misunderstand: "I'm taking them to my place over on Barracks,"

"I know where you live. You think that's a good idea? You barely let me in the place."

"They think I'm going to turn them or—" he paused, waving his other hand, "conduct some kind of ritual. It was all I could think of," he said.

"Clever," I said. "And, what do you want me to do?"

"Go to the Eighth District Station and tell them what's going on."

"The police? Are you serious?"

He held his hands up, and said, "Don't tell them about me, obviously, but just say that I've got them there. Tell them whatever you need to. I'll keep them as long as I can. They won't hurt me."

"Right. Got it. I'm on it." I sounded far surer of myself than I felt.

Calling the cops might've been faster, but I wouldn't have a cell phone for another five years. The payphone on the dance floor all but dared you to waste thirty-five cents. I breezed past Rick where he still waited for John, and then moved past the bar and the bouncer on my way out the door. The other four kids huddled in a group. I counted two boys and two girls. They'd dressed the part, but the rain that trickled over the ledge above them rendered their black clothes and dyed hair limp. One of the girls—short and fat, with a spiked collar around her neck—grabbed my sleeve as I tried to leave. I turned to pull it back, but I saw the look on her face. It wasn't anger. It was despair.

"Please," she said.

"Please, what?" I asked, looking up at the bouncer.

She released my sleeve and said, "Are they coming back? We're really hungry."

I looked up at the balcony and then back at her, and then inside the club. John was talking to Rick there, where we'd sat earlier. He looked in my direction for only a moment. He meant for me to hurry to the police station for help, and I was wasting time.

"Are they?" she asked, again. The tall youth with short brown hair and a Marilyn Manson t-shirt behind her stared with the same hollow, waiting eyes.

"Uh, yeah. I think so," I said, turning away. "Just give them a few minutes," I called over my shoulder, as I walked down Decatur Street to turn onto Governor Nicholls towards the Eighth District Station. Her mouth hung open a bit as she watched me leave.

I wanted to help them right then and there. Rick saw them as acolytes. I just saw a bunch of kids, soaked to the bone and looking for somebody to save them. Quietly, I cursed and buttoned my black sports coat up as I walked, darting underneath the overhangs and signs, and weaving around trashcans and tourists towards Royal Street.

***

The officer on duty was less than helpful.

Take note: should you walk into a police station soaking wet, wearing all black, and sporting a handful of silver rings, they won't believe your story about vampires—even the fake kind. After fifteen minutes of showing them my school ID and my driver's license (and assuring them that I was not, in fact, on drugs), they agreed to send a car over to John's place—without me in it, of course. I walked, through the rain a second time, as fast as I could to the corner of Barracks and Decatur. When I arrived, the cop car was parked outside, alone and empty.

I could see John's black Dodge Charger through the gate and past the courtyard. He always walked to the bar, so that didn't mean anything. The rain slowed to a drizzle.

I imagined a bloody crime scene behind John's door, with Rick Fremont in pieces all over the place. I'd never seen John truly angry, but I could only imagine the consequences. Only a couple of drunks had ever been stupid enough to challenge him. And while he didn't have the ridiculous strength of his cinematic counterparts, he'd shut down both situations quickly. He'd held one drunk's face to the bar, with his wrist pulled behind his own back. He simply stared at the other until the man raised his hands and backed away from us. Someone had taught him how to handle himself, but I never asked. After that, he could walk into any bar on Lower Decatur and drink in peace.

I pushed the buzzer to the intercom. John's voice crackled through the speaker: "Jason, is that you? Are you alone?"

"Yeah, it's me."

"The police are inside. The kids already came and left before they got here," he said. The magnetic lock on the gate vibrated, and I jerked it open and headed through the courtyard. Rain pooled on the benches. Fallen flower petals littered the brick pavement that lined the path. I knew the side door and the gate outside would be unlocked. I reached it, inhaled, and turned the handle.

John sat at the head of his long dining room table, flanked by two police officers on either side of him. The cops looked less than thrilled. I could tell immediately that the female patrolman to John's right didn't believe a word of it. A short black woman in her early thirties, she looked more tired than anything. Looking down at her notepad, she asked, "He said he was a vampire and that he killed a couple in Florida?" Her eyes never looked up at John as she returned the pen to the paper. She was cycling through the motions.

"Yes, that's correct." I knew he would answer tersely for his own sake, but I also knew it wouldn't convince the cops any faster. "He said that he did it for me—to prove his loyalty."

John put a hand up before I could say a word. The other patrolman dropped his head. The young man had hair the same color as John's, and he kept it a bit longer than the military-style cut most of NOPD wore.

"Really, now?" he asked, a half-smile rising on his lips. "And, why?" He dragged out the "y" in the last word for a few seconds. He knew something. John swallowed hard.

"Listen, a few people around here think I'm a vampire—a real one, you know? Rumors get out. I guess he heard it wherever he's from. It's happened before." The cop smiled, and laughed under his breath.

"Yeah, I've heard that before, too," he said. "Rumors, I bet," he said, nodding. "I bet."

Lower Decatur had always had its share of undercover (and not-so-undercover) cops lurking around the bars. Packets of cocaine and prescription medications exchanged hands in bar bathrooms. Junkies flushed needles down the toilets and crammed their empty half-pints of drugstore vodka into the tanks. But, we all knew that NOPD didn't invest much energy in a bunch of white kids scoring and using recreationally. But, I couldn't say I knew their position on the undead. It wasn't something you asked a drunken cop when you buddied up to him next to Sally's bar at four in the morning. If the cop knew about John, then he'd hung around for a while. Maybe we hadn't noticed him, but he'd certainly noticed us.

"And you," he said looking at me, "they say you guys are, you know, together." He laughed. He was fucking with us. This was pretty much the norm with the NOPD. There were good cops, but there were a lot of bad ones in the ranks and always had been. At the time, I thought he wanted money.

The cop looked at his partner, and said, "Yvonne, can we get a minute?" The remark smelled of unofficial seniority—no more rank, but more time.

"Whatever," she said, grabbing her notebook and walking towards the door. "You're on your own, Brad." She looked back at us for a second more before she left, rolling her eyes.

"What the hell is this?" John asked, leaning forward.

He glanced at me. I shrugged as quickly as I could while the cop looked away. John gritted his teeth. I wouldn't have noticed if I hadn't seen it before. The cop unbuttoned the cuff on his shirt and rolled the sleeve up. He turned his arm over to show the tattoo of an ankh on his pale white wrist. Ever since David Bowie and Catherine Deneuve had drawn blood with razor blade ankhs in *The Hunger*, the goth scene had loved the Egyptian symbol. "For immortality," we always said. It was as much of an identifier as a cross was to Christians. The cop knew.

"Y'all think you're so creative, don't you?" he asked. I looked at him closely. At first, I didn't see it. Then, I imagined the face plastered with white makeup, and black smeared across his eyes, lips, and fingernails. I saw fishnet stretched across his chest and vinyl boots that reached his knees. He was a nameless youth in a sea of black that flooded the Crypt every Friday and Saturday. But, as he sat there in John's kitchen, I remembered him—not by his name, but as "Drax" or some made-up bullshit like that. Goths loved to use fake names. And, the cop had blended right in with the rest of us. He wouldn't have been undercover on business. If he had, he'd have kept his mouth shut. But like so many others, he maintained a separate side from the one he showed the rest of the world. "Weekend warriors," we called them. Young professionals, youth pastors, and, yes, police officers would transform themselves once or twice a week. With enough white makeup on your face and the right set of black clothes, you could pass unnoticed.

"Drax?" I asked. "That's you, right?"

The cop smiled, but said nothing. He looked back and forth between us. John grabbed the edge of the table. I think he wanted to leap across it, but he restrained himself. He didn't want to kill anyone, much less a cop. You can outrun a lot when you live forever. But, I couldn't see him moving several decades' worth of clutter into a U-Haul at four in the morning with a dead cop shoved in the back.

There was that, and I didn't want to help him move. It's strange what occurs to you during moments like that.

"Thought I recognized you," I said, crossing my arms.

"Sit the fuck down," the cop said to me, lowering his voice an octave. "I know what you are, John. Always have."

"How?" asked John. He could spin webs of bullshit better than anyone I knew. He had to. But that day, for some reason, he didn't lie to Brad.

"Doesn't matter," he said. "A lot of people in this town claim to be vampires. If someone's telling people they drink blood, you want to know more about them. Someone turns up dead with their throat cut, you know who to talk to. A real one would keep his mouth shut. But, still—the rumors get out and you ask around."

"And what did you hear?" I asked

John looked directly at him and asked, "Yes, what exactly did you hear?"

The cop shrugged. "Like I said, rumors—that you're real, but maybe it's some kind of medical thing. And, you won't talk about it," he said. "Usually, you won't. Now, I have a few questions of my own."

***

Patrolman Brad Simoneaux didn't arrest John that night. Once John explained his condition in agonizing detail, our cop became a lot more helpful. He took John's statement, along with my own. He stuck to our story—that Rick Fremont quite wrongly believed John was an undead fiend that prowled New Orleans bars in search of prey. That wasn't far off from the truth, but John had never killed anyone for dinner after a night at the bar. A few brave souls had asked him to bite their necks or their arms or whatever, but he'd always refused. Rick was just one more fan boy. And, he was more of a killer than John had ever been.

In the days and weeks that followed, we learned so much more. Before the cops could find them, Rick and his crew begged, borrowed, and stole enough cash to gas up the van and head out of town towards Baton Rouge. John and I gave Brad enough information that the Louisiana State Police were able to ID them. They caught up with the whole group in a cheap motel on Perkins Road in our glorious state capital.

By that time, one of the girls was dead. Fremont and the others got hungry. With no money for food, they bled the fattest girl in their group in the motel room bathtub. The State Police and Baton Rouge PD found her bled out at the wrists, the throat, the crooks of her arms and legs, and anywhere else they could find an artery. They'd collected her blood in the motel room ice bucket, and then dipped it out with those cheap plastic water glasses you find next to the sink. Regular people can't drink that much blood without puking. There was plenty left. The officer who testified said the room smelled of cloves, old blood, and a dead seventeen-year-old girl—one young and dumb enough to follow Rick Fremont into oblivion.

About eleven months later, the courts sentenced Rick to life in prison. It turned out that he'd used a fake ID to enter the Crypt. He was only seventeen and as a juvenile, he beat the death penalty. His lackeys were slapped with various charges—accessory to this, aggravated that. Everyone recognized what he'd done. Unable to withstand the charisma of a natural cult leader, a bunch of children had followed another child who thought he was a vampire. One of them watched him murder her parents, and they all watched him cut their friend's throat. If John hadn't confessed—hadn't admitted to the one thing that made him different from every other person on the planet—they might not have caught him. Ever since then, now-Detective Simoneaux was a friend to John. He kept his secrets.

Chapter 4

Friday, September 12, 1997 – Evening

John and I paced in my living room, still looking over the pictures. We were smoking and drinking enough for an entire bar. I stopped walking, took a loud, hissing drag, and stared at him.

"What do you want to do?"

"What does Brad want from me?" We both knew the answer.

"You know what he wants. He wants to know that it's not you. If he believes you, the rest of the police might not come after you. He wants to know you're okay. He wants reassurance, on and off the record, by way of me, that you didn't do it." I picked up one of the pictures from off the table and looked at it again. Brad wanted to know that the poor fucking girl—covered in her own blood, dead in a pool of piss and cheap liquor—hadn't died with John leaning over her. "He wants to know that you haven't snapped. Because, if he can't protect you, every other cop in the city is going to be looking for the 'real vampire.'"

He sat down and made his best no-shit gesture with his hands, the left still holding his last smoldering cigarette. "Of course I didn't, Jason. You know that. What now?

I sat next to him and slapped his knee. "Don't know, pal. There's not exactly a rulebook for dealing with guys like you. I guess they'll investigate. They might want to interview you. Do you have an alibi?" I did everything I could not to close my eyes and grit my teeth.

"When was it?"

"About four days ago," I replied. "The eighth, I guess. Do you remember where you were?"

He smirked, and said, "Actually, yes. I was with a young lady."

Like I said, John had gone on some dates since we started drinking together. He rarely offered any details, and I didn't ask. But, I knew he'd had at least a few girls between the sheets. I doubted that he told them the truth, but I didn't ask about that either. From what I could tell, none of them seemed to last very long.

"Is she still speaking to you?" I asked. He shrugged. I looked at the Nine Inch Nails poster again, with Trent Reznor staring down at his boot. John paused for a moment and looked back at me.

"I think so," he said. His eyes opened a little wider. He looked relieved. He couldn't die, but he didn't want a warrant either. "We'll have to find her."

"I assume you still have her phone number?" I asked, with my back to him, pouring another drink, as I rolled my eyes and said a little prayer.

"Yes. Yes, I do. Let's call her."

***

They'd met one night at the Crypt, when I stayed home to work on an overdue editorial.

She'd sat next to him at the bar and asked for a drink. Her dyed black hair and corseted cleavage had caught his attention. He rarely approached women on his own. But, he had never quite grown accustomed to women that wouldn't wait for an invitation to dance.

She asked about the rumors, of course. He laughed and denied them. She accepted that, but didn't really believe him. John assumed she saw him only as a source for free shots of Chartreuse, and that she would leave when she had her fill. When he excused himself to use the men's room, he expected her to depart in his absence. Instead, she hopped off the barstool. She was short, he recalled, and her feet had dangled above the floor. Her tall, buckled boots hit the ground and she wrapped her arms around him. She only came up to his chest. He looked down, and saw that she bore a goofy smile with her chin planted against him.

Yes, he explained, he'd fucked her that night. No, he hadn't bothered to call her until now. Yes, she was probably mad at him. But, she said he didn't have to.

"They always say that," I replied. "They never mean it."

John begged me to call her first. I only agreed after I switched the television on and popped in a vampire movie at random out of my "Bad" pile—shitty VHS B-movies with fanged freaks and Draculas fighting everyone from Frankenstein to Billy the Kid. John hated movies like that, but he deserved it. I stepped out for a round of Chinese takeout and told John he had to leave the television on.

"You're really going to make me watch this while you get the food?"

"Yep," I said, pulling on my sports coat.

"What if I turn it off? I'll hear you coming up the steps."

"On your honor, as a gentleman, leave the fucking television on. When I get back, you have to tell me how bad it was."

***

I opened the door with bags of food in hand. I saw his middle finger extended before I saw anything else, as if he'd held it up the entire time I'd been gone. Maybe he had.

"I truly despise you," he said. On the screen, I saw someone in a cheap vampire costume fighting someone in a cheaper werewolf mask.

"I love to make you suffer," I said, sitting down and pulling the Chinese food out, box by white-and-red box. "Turn the volume down. Let's get serious."

We called Jenny Dark's cell phone through the night. She'd given John her number before he gave her cab fare and sent her away at dawn. He still had the slip of paper in his wallet. Neither of us had cell phones. We didn't really like the damn things. If I wanted to talk to people on the phone, I'd stay at home. But every time we called her number, it rolled to the same voicemail greeting: "Greetings. This is Jenny Dark. Give me a good reason to use my minutes and I'll call you back. Unpleasant dreams." After a few more drinks and B-movies, we stopped trying. I'd lost count of how many I'd put down, but the bottle was less than half-empty.

Jenny Dark worked at a used clothing store. John remembered that much, and the name—Second Chance, on Magazine Street. It wasn't far from the café where I'd shown him the photos of the dead girl. He wanted to see Jenny there, but with dawn approaching, he needed my help. He asked me to check out Jenny's job as soon as she was supposed to go in—at ten, he thought. I'd run daytime errands for him before, but never to secure an alibi. But, he begged me. He offered the usual favors in return—drinks on him, a steak dinner at Ruth's Chris, a double-date with a couple of girls, and just about anything else he could offer.

"Fuck it. Fine," I said, intending to collect on every promise he'd made.

***

Saturday, September 13, 1997

I slept for about three hours in my bed, leaving John in the living room. I woke up at a quarter after nine and snuck out of my own house—a temporary vampire's lair, lacking only a coffin.

John had written the address of the clothing store on a slip of paper. He'd left it under my keys on the kitchen table. But, I knew the place. I parked in front of Second Chance Used and Vintage Clothes on Magazine Street, prepared for a second-hand bitching-out from Jenny Dark—a rant prepared for John, and peer-reviewed by all of her friends. And, she would deliver it like only a twenty-year-old girl could.

I grabbed the iced coffee I'd bought the night before out of the Volvo's cup holder. I drank the lukewarm remains as I walked into the store. A tiny punk girl in a white tank top stood behind the counter, bent over. As she dug through a laundry basket of old clothes, she looked up.

"Hey," she said.

"Morning."

"Yep, it is," she said, tossing a dress into a box behind her. She didn't seem angry—just preoccupied. I couldn't tell any difference between the clothes in the box and the fashionably thread-worn dresses on the racks. The store looked neat enough—just reflective of the sudden mainstream status punk rock and all its bastard children had enjoyed since 1991. Half of everyone under thirty in those days wanted to be part of a scene, or fight the slow death of one. I looked around the store with its yellow walls, trimmed in red at the top and bottom, with a Ramones poster here, a Danzig poster there, and images from a dozen other bands. They knew their customers, no doubt.

She threw a t-shirt over her shoulder, sinking it into the white plastic basket. "Nice shot," I said. "Throwing those away or something?" I leaned on the counter, and then promptly stood up when I saw the handwritten sign taped to the glass surface: "Do Not Lean On Counter!"

"They're for charity," she said. She sniffed, and then ripped a paper towel from a roll next to me on the counter. She blew her nose with a loud honk, and then mumbled an apology.

"If someone consigns something and it doesn't sell in sixty days, we call them to come get it. If we can't get ahold of them, it goes to charity." She held up the tag on a spaghetti strap black dress. "Every tag has a date. When we do inventory, we pull the ones that have expired." The tag had "7/10/97" written on it in blue ink. Summer killed tourism in the city every year. The bartenders, waiters, baristas, and strippers always took second jobs or hocked their clothes and CD collections to make ends meet. The limp, thin dress hung there from her fingertips—one more casualty in a war the city fought every year, but never quite won.

"Does that mean I'm hired?" I asked, standing up and drawing my elbows off the counter. She rolled her eyes.

"You must really kill at the open mic night," she said, raising her tiny right fist, the dress still hanging from the left.

"Actually, I'm looking for Jenny. I don't know her real name, but she calls herself—"

She held her hand up, and said, "Jenny Dark. I know." She paused and looked at me. "She didn't come in today, and she won't pick up her fucking phone." She'd gone home with John on Monday night.

"Did she come in the rest of the week?"

"Why do you want to know?" she asked, tapping the counter with a ballpoint pen. She pushed her tongue against her cheek to form a skeptical lump.

"She knows my friend, John. He needs to talk to her, but he's—"

"Vampire John? God, what a douche. Why doesn't he get his ass up during the day and come find her himself? I don't care what he says he is. I've seen him in the sun." I raised my hands.

"Wait, I know. Save it for him. He just wants to talk to—"

"She came in Tuesday and said she fucked him. Okay?"

"So, Jenny hasn't been in since then? Was she upset?" I asked. She sighed. I realized that I didn't even know her name. She leaned on the counter. Her face relaxed. I wasn't the one she wanted to yell at.

"I mean, she kept talking about how he basically kicked her out. But, she doesn't even work Wednesday through Friday," she said. "So, I don't know."

"Yeah," I said, looking down. I rubbed my forehead and pushed my glasses back. "I think he likes to sleep alone."

"Whatever. I think she was going to call him. I haven't talked to her since. Is he trying to get in touch with her now? Why did he send you?" I thought I could get on her good side.

"Yeah, actually he tried a few times last night. I was there. He just got her voicemail."

"Well, I don't know then." She reached for a second paper towel and tore it off, wiping her nose again.

"Are you sick?" I asked. She nodded. I remembered my glove compartment, and a pack of generic dicloxy-something or other, with the same active ingredients as the leading cold medicine.

"Hang on a second," I said, as I exited the store. A minute later, I returned with a foil pack with four pills remaining in their plastic bubbles. "There you go." I placed them on the counter in front of her. She picked up the package and read it, smiling crookedly and nodding. I could see the sarcasm she kept at the ready fading from her eyes.

"Thanks," she said. "That's cool of you."

"Take them with a shot of vodka and you'll forget how awful you feel. You might feel a different kind of awful, but it's a start." I really was killing it. She pushed two of the pills out of the pack and put them in her mouth. Reaching behind the counter—and for a moment, I thought she'd taken me seriously—she produced a bottle of generic root beer. She unscrewed the white cap and swallowed the pills with a bubbly swig.

"Going to offer me your handkerchief next?"

"You could use one," I said, "unless you plan to run out of paper towels. Actually, what I really need is to talk to Jenny—seriously. I wouldn't ask if it wasn't important. I'm not just playing errand boy for John."

"Right." She flicked her index finger at me, her thumb up, like a pistol with one bullet.

"You own this place, right? This is your shop?"

"Mmmhmm." She took another sip. Her eyes looked up at me over the bottle.

"So, you know where she lives. You've got all her tax paperwork and stuff. If you give me her address, I can just run over there." The dance was getting tired, the song too long, and I could see her coolness returning. I looked past her, over the counter, and through the picture window that faced Magazine Street, waiting for an answer.

"That would be kind of fucked up," she said, furrowing her brow.

"I know, but listen—John really needs to talk to her. It's important. NOPD might be trying to finger him for something that happened the night they hung out. He just needs an alibi." I didn't know that for a fact. I only had Brad's word to go on, but I didn't want to make the situation sound any less dire. I leaned forward across the counter on my hands, and said, "Just help me, please?"

The NOPD had as much standing with the New Orleans underground as parents, church, and Wal-Mart. They were all about as welcome as Satan at a tent revival. Deserved or not, the police didn't have a great reputation. The punkette behind the counter at the clothing store (that she owned, she reminded me again) believed my story. She, of course, demanded to know why the police wanted John. I waved my hand across the space between us, as if I could magically silence her questions. It was a personal matter, I explained, and not for me the repeat. She accepted that, but would only give me the information if she could take me to Jenny Dark's place herself—and only after Second Chance had closed. I agreed. Before I left, she extended her hand and grabbed mine for a shake—too firm, to prove she could take me. I ignored the gesture and shook back.

"Jason."

"Maureen," she replied. "See you at five."

I'd somehow avoided a parking ticket and moved my car to a residential spot. The white sign's green print said I had two hours, which meant I'd have to move the aging Volvo twice. I walked to a coffee shop a few blocks away from the store. There was the closer one where I'd shown John the pictures. But on top of John's mess, I didn't want her to think I didn't believe her—that I was poised to catch her running out of the store two minutes before closing time, frantically unlocking her bike (I imagined she rode a bike) as I demanded an explanation.

Instead, I took my notebook and my thoughts to the café down the street. It was another location of the same place where I'd met John the day before. The Rue Café's many locations dotted Uptown and the French Quarter. As a Louisiana chain, the locals had mostly embraced it. I was just glad that I could find decent coffee almost anywhere I went. Each had rows of rustic, worn tables crammed in rows with rickety chairs. Students filled the wicker seats with piles of open books and a few laptops. The low shimmer of classical music lent the whole thing a misplaced air of sophistication.

With a white mug of coffee to my left, I began on a list piece about the best places to eat at three in the morning—and how they measured up sober and in the day. Like a drunken lover, sobriety and the sun's harsh rays could reveal the truth about a place. Each bar-and-grill, twenty-four-hour diner, and late-night pizza joint would receive two ratings measured in small cartoon suns and moons.

That day, I knew I'd finish my work before Second Chance closed. I timed it that way, because I planned to drag the vampire out of my living room at four-thirty, kicking and screaming into the daylight. I'd decided I wouldn't go without him.

You could smoke inside back then. After five coffees, a few cigarettes, and several pithy remarks about bad eggs, I drove back to my place. Maureen didn't know I would have John with me. Still on my futon, John answered my suggestion with a muffled groan from under a black comforter pulled over his head. Getting him up took longer than I'd planned. I imagined myself luring him out with a trail of cups of coffee alternating with cigarettes that ended at my car door.

But, he finally stood up and followed me downstairs. He'd put on a white dress shirt and his own black jacket, along with a pair of aviator sunglasses. His fashion sense had finally reached the 1970s. When we reached my car, he opened the back door and launched himself across the seat. I responded by closing the door on his legs (lightly, but with emphasis), which extended out of the car and over the road. He looked up for a second at me.

"All the way in, sunshine," I said, smiling.

"I could kill you, you know?"

"Yeah, but you won't. You don't have any other friends," I said. He sighed loudly and curled up in a ball across the backseat. He slept like that all the way to Maureen's shop.

We parked in front of the store, where Maureen waited at the curb. She did not, I realized, have a bicycle. I threw the passenger door open. She looked into the car, and saw John.

"What the fuck is he doing here?" she asked.

"This is his deal. He needs to talk to Jenny more than I do."

"Has he been like this all day?" She leaned in further, bracing herself with her tiny tattooed arms. I checked out her ink while she stood there—Misfits, Ramones, Bauhaus. I realized we probably had more in common than I'd thought.

"He crashed at my place," I said. "It was that or send him out in the daylight. He's also still probably hung over. We almost killed a bottle last night."

Maureen rolled her eyes and stepped into the car. I looked over my shoulder.

"Aren't you still hung over, buddy?" I asked, laughing. I tapped Maureen on the shoulder and pointed at my sleeping friend, his dark sunglasses now halfway off of his face. He mumbled something before rolling over to face the back of the seat. The sun would fall behind the horizon in a few minutes and he'd snap out of it. The opportunities for mockery dwindled with the passing minutes. He'd need his head on straight to talk to Jenny, anyway.

"I have no idea where I'm going," I said, I glancing at Maureen. She rested her chin in her hand, with an elbow propped on her knee.

"Sounds like an existential crisis. Maybe quit hanging out with guys that pretend to be vampires," she said.

"To Jenny's place, smartass."

"She's Uptown. There's a bunch of apartments on St. Charles near Napoleon." I knew them. They weren't expensive, but they weren't efficiencies either. If Jenny could afford one without a roommate, it meant rich parents.

"Daddy's money?" I asked.

"Came here for school, so probably. I never asked." I drove down Magazine Street towards Napoleon Avenue. I knew how Jenny's story ended, but I asked for more.

Maureen shifted in her seat. If she was smart, she knew the story too. But, she'd never admit how well. "She took a semester off to work and just never really went back." John snored behind us. I reached back and hit him with the back of my hand. He grunted, shifted, and slept silently as we passed Jefferson Avenue. Maureen looked behind us at the cars tailgating us, their lights flashing. She leaned over me, nearly in my lap, to look at the speedometer.

"Why are you only doing twenty?" She moved back to her seat. "You're pissing off everyone behind us."

I cleared my throat, and said, "I'm trying to give John a chance to wake up before we get to Jenny's. This is his problem."

"Yeah, it is. I don't know why you're doing so much."

"I don't, either. Now, what happened to Jenny?"

She rambled on for a minute or two about decisions and work-versus-school. I'd seen it happen before. They come to New Orleans for college. They get a job to earn extra money to drink, dance, and fuck all night. They meet people—interesting, talented, exciting, and all of them working on a screenplay. And to a one, they've all waited tables, or tended bar, or slung coffee for a decade. And, they seem to be doing just fine. The cost of living in New Orleans is low. Leave your money on the dresser and tip your bartenders, but don't cry. She belongs to everyone and it's nothing personal. It never has been. They realize they can survive without a Bachelor's degree in art history here. They feel the pull of the night, as it beckons with curling fingers of smoke to streets made only of bars and back-alleys. They take a semester off—or two, or forever—but just to work. And, they survive. Ten years later, they've either moved to attend a state school back wherever they came from, or they've become a fixture—a pillar of salt, standing behind the same bar for the lifetimes that have passed before them, all in search of an ear and a drink. Or, they sell clothes.

I wasn't judging Jenny Dark. I just knew the story, top to bottom. I'd seen the city eat so many people alive. The lucky ones ended up like Maureen—more than just surviving, and owning something of their own. The truly unlucky ones ended up on a pole dancing long past their twenties for crumpled dollar bills, or as alcoholics, or with needles in their arms. I hoped I wouldn't see Jenny in any of those places.

"Hey," Maureen said, as she snapped her fingers in front of my face. "Wake up. Napoleon's right up here. Turn before all the people behind you get out with handguns." I'd been dreaming and driving, thinking about Jenny and the road she'd chosen and the ones she might still choose.

"Sorry. I just spaced out there for a second."

The sun's last rays faded quickly as I turned the car towards St. Charles Avenue. I glanced at John in the backseat. He sat up and adjusted his sunglasses.

"Hey," he said, leaning forward. "Who's this?"

Maureen looked over her shoulder. "You know, you can ask me. I'm right here." John's decades-old sexism crept in occasionally. I knew he tried with all he had, and he knew to age with the times. But, his old manners resurfaced when he wasn't on guard.

"My apologies," he said, removing his shades. "I'm John." He stuck his hand through the space between our seats. She glanced down at it for only a second, before awkwardly reaching across to shake it. She withdrew quickly to her seat and looked straight ahead.

"I know—John, the vampire. I heard you fucked my friend." I winced. John settled back and put his sunglasses on again.

"Really, I was only half of the equation," he said.

"Whatever." I imagined Maureen balancing on a hellish snowball of resentment rolling downhill with the conversation.

"John, let it go," I said, turning on to St. Charles Avenue. He smiled and leaned forward again.

"Of course. Forgive me if I offended your lady friend," he said. She sighed angrily behind him. After I pulled in front of Jenny Dark's apartment complex, I put my head on the steering wheel.

"All right, children—we're here," I said.

"Gonna turn the car around so help you, Dad?" Maureen asked. She opened the door and jumped out with a sharp laugh—the way only a short punk girl could.

John stood up and out of the backseat, his sunglasses still on his face. He wore them later in the evening than most people ever would. He said he could still see the sun's rays or some bullshit. I think he just thought it looked cool.

"This way," she said, as she opened the wrought iron gate of the apartment complex, flinging it behind her and stepping into the courtyard.

We walked past the benches and great stone planters that littered the courtyard, surrounded by flowering gardens and dangling ivy. The planters sat randomly, almost haphazardly, along the brick path beneath our feet and beneath the many entrances on either side. Heavy oak doors all lead to stairwells, surrounding us in a kind of M.C. Escher reverie. At one of them, our diminutive friend motioned us to walk inside.

There, the three of us silently ascended the steps to Jenny Dark's apartment, ending in a landing of Spanish tiles under flickering fluorescent lights.

We stopped at her apartment. At the frame where the deadbolt once sat firm and secure, splinters shot inward. Someone had kicked in the door.

Chapter 5

Saturday, September 13, 1997 – Evening

I pushed past John and Maureen and walked inside. Jenny Dark lay there dead in the middle of the floor, in a circle of black candles all ablaze. The wax pooled and mingled with her blood. John and Maureen all but fought each other to reach the center of the room where she lay. There, we crouched over her—the first to mourn for Jenny Dark, no longer alive, as the blood around her dried like roses out of water. Clumps and strings of tattered flesh hung at the left side of her throat, where her killer had torn it away.

I whispered, and I could do no more, saying only, "What the fuck?"

"Did you do this? Motherfucker!" Maureen had nearly tackled John, looking straight up at him and holding up her right fist. I imagined that small form fighting for its life in a hundred mosh pits at as many punk shows, knowing that she had to take out the largest of them. If she didn't, she would be fair game for wandering hands.

When John didn't answer, she reared back. With little effort, he stood and raised her up by the collar of her tank top. She dangled a foot from the ground as he held her face to face.

"No, darling," he growled, cocking his head. "I did not."

"Jesus, John," I said, at the edge of yelling. "Put her down. Holy shit, this isn't going to help anything."

He lowered her, and turned his back without another word. He walked a few steps to Jenny Dark. I could hear his cowboy boots connecting with the hardwood floors—heel-toe, heel-toe.

"Stay out of the blood, John. Be careful," I said, walking next to him as he crouched down and looked at her. I laid a hand on his shoulder. "You okay?" He stood back up and turned to Maureen.

"No," he said, flinging his arms out, "of course I didn't. Do you think I could even do something like—" and he pointed at Jenny, but I knew he meant the great, red wound across her throat, "—like that? Do you?" He leaned down, nearly six inches from her face and lowered his fangs. I heard the same wet sound that I did the night we first met.

Maureen started back, and yelled, "Fuck, you're for real!"

"John, enough!" I looked away from Jenny for a moment and over my shoulder at Maureen. "Told you," I said.

She backed up from John with her hands up. Picking up someone her size wasn't much of a challenge to begin with, but John had made his point. All the stories were true, she now understood. I turned to her.

"Anyway, yes he is. And, he's right. Look around. The candles are still lit. The blood's still kind of wet. This just happened. He's been asleep at my place all day. You saw what he was like before the sun went down."

She cleared her throat, and said, "So, okay, there's another vampire out there now?" She circled the ring of candles around Jenny.

"We think someone might be pretending to be one," I said. "Another girl was killed like this on Monday night. That's why we needed Jenny." John turned to face the circle, where I already stood. He crossed his arms.

"Wouldn't be the first time," he said, as he had in my apartment the day before. Quickly and speaking over each other, we told Maureen about Rick Fremont—and the girl who had already died. She remembered from the newspaper. She believed us.

The entire time—mere minutes, passing in our minds as infinity—we paced around the candles encircling Jenny Dark's body. I don't think we meant so much at the time, but it felt like the only funeral we could give her there, that night, with only the three of us to remember her—a coworker, a lover, and me—an acquaintance, at best. Round and round we walked, now facing inward to speak, the rare silence passing between our words, both hurried and solemn. John recounted his short time with her in a tone that betrayed a longing I'd not suspected—how she asked to be with him, and how his bed alone would not suffice. But he couldn't, he told her. He was the only one, and he couldn't pass it to anyone else.

Around we went again, as Maureen told us about Jenny Anderson from Alabama, who came to New Orleans on a scholarship and fell in love with the city. More, she fell in love with its night. And it, unlike John, had refused to let her leave.

Around we went once more, and only minutes had passed, but there was so much more to do. I stopped. They both looked at me and we knew the moment had ended.

"We have to call Brad," I said.

John halted. He turned his head sharply, and said, "Right. Right. Call him."

Maureen's eyes darted between us, and asked, "Who's Brad?"

"Brad Simoneaux," I replied. "Detective with NOPD. He's sort of John's contact."

"I thought you were trying to keep the cops out of this." She bought into that same set of rules. You never called the police. I didn't feel like arguing.

I only looked at her, hard, with my eyes thin and my jaw clenched, and said, "John needed Jenny as an alibi. I didn't say we wouldn't call them if we found a dead body." I took one deep breath and said, "Besides, Brad's a friend. He knows about John."

Maureen only raised an eyebrow and looked at John.

"He is," John said, nodding. I could see she didn't like it. The underground here—the goths, the punks, and all the rest—liked to believe it guarded secrets unbeknownst to the outside world, as if a detailed knowledge of '80s industrial music and a pair of combat boots made you a Freemason. A real vampire living among them was, to someone like Maureen, a secret to be kept from "them."

"Why would you tell them that?" she asked.

"Because of situations like this," he replied. The flies had moved in around Jenny and her drying pool of blood. I looked at both of them.

"Guys," I said, "there is a dead woman on the ground. The longer we argue, the worse it's going to look. I'm calling Brad."

Maureen walked away with her hands up and yelled, "Fuck!" I ignored her and found the white phone on the wall of her kitchenette.

"What do you suggest we do?" I asked, raising my voice towards the den.

"I don't know!" she yelled. Pulling the cord out with me, I saw her turn to face Jenny again. As she spoke, her voice wavered. "We could clean this up and find the motherfucker that did this and show him what it's like!" I could see the tears she held back glinting in her eyes. It had finally set in, really and truly, that Jenny wouldn't return to work the next day or any other. I listened for Brad's voice on the phone.

After four rings, he picked up and said, "Detective Simoneaux. How can I help you?"

I explained. He asked me a couple of questions. I explained more. He told me he would come alone.

***

Brad arrived faster than I'd expected. He knew anything related to John might quickly spiral out of control. Snapping on a pair of rubber gloves, he made the three of us stand in a group near a corner. Kneeling by Jenny Dark, he looked up at us, lightly running his gloved fingertips over the pool of blood. He held up his wet, red digits and stared at them.

"Did you touch anything?" he asked.

"No, other than our feet on the ground. Should you maybe not touch that, either?"

"It's fine," he said. "It's the cost of doing business." Still kneeling, he looked over at the two of us. "You were never here," Brad said. "You especially," he continued, pointing at John with a bloody digit.

"I wasn't?" he asked.

Even I knew what Brad meant. He removed the glove as he stood, before putting his hands on my friend's shoulders. Maureen stood behind them, looking on with her arms crossed. She'd barely spoken a word since Brad arrived.

"No, you weren't," he said, slapping John's shoulders lightly. "I have to call this in. If you can avoid touching anything on your way out, I can say that she called it in alone."

He glanced at Maureen, before looking back at my friend. His hands remained on John's shoulders.

John's eyebrows pointed inward to a scowl, and he asked, "Why weren't we here?"

I walked over and tapped Brad's wrist. My friend wasn't a violent man, but I knew that touching him wouldn't help the situation. "John, he's right."

"Then, you tell me why," he said. Before I could blink, his eyes were at mine.

"Look, calm down," I said, stepping back. He'd never really lose his temper with me, but I had to convince him before the situation worsened. "There are now two dead girls, and you fucked one of them—the one that was supposed to be your alibi."

Brad breezed past us with his arm over Maureen's shoulder, towards the hallway, uttering a quick "Thank you" from over his shoulder. She looked less than thrilled. From the corner of my eye, I saw Brad take out a notebook. Maureen waved her arms a bit as he quickly wrote.

"Yes, I suppose you're right," John said.

Brad looked over, and said, "Do me a favor. Stay in town, but lay low. No drinking, partying, fucking, or fighting until I can get this worked out."

John cocked his head, and snapped, "I hadn't planned to leave, Brad."

I heard him breathe sharply. The entire setup had pushed him near the edge. Truly, he hadn't done anything wrong—but the odds stood against him.

"John, this might not end well," I said.

He winced a bit. I rarely spoke to him so directly. As often as we'd joked, as often as I'd gotten drunk and jumped on his back at the club, I abhorred the thought of losing my friend. I stared at his lips—the same ones that I threatened to kiss when we were drunk and it was funny. But, he wasn't laughing now—and there weren't tables around us full of goth kids to roar at our bastard drunk routine. He wouldn't laugh for a while. And, in Jenny's darkened apartment, her eyeliner still painted on thick over her dead eyes, he couldn't make her laugh again either.

He looked to the hallway quickly, and my eyes followed his. We saw Maureen slap her sides, and our eyes met. John's rolled briefly.

"You're in danger," I said. "You get that, right?"

"Yes. Someone is trying to frame me."

"Or send you one hell of a message," I said. I knew what we were both thinking, right at that moment.

"Rick."

"Rick's in jail," I said. "The rest of them are either in jail, too—or institutionalized or whatever."

"What if he has someone on the outside?"

"Why don't you leave that to Brad? He's the cop," I replied, loudly enough for everyone to hear.

"You're a journalist," John said.

"Bullshit. I write features for a bunch of weeklies."

"Find out what you can," he said, sighing. "Please?" I looked at Brad and Maureen. He closed his notebook as she walked away.

She turned towards the door, and said, "Let's get the hell out of here, please." Brad stopped her with a single hand on her shoulder. Her eyes opened wide with anger.

"You two, head out," he said. "You stay here," he told Maureen. "Find the phone and call 911. I'm going to say I was in the area when you screamed."

"What do you mean?" she asked.

"Not a request," he said. "You two—go."

Chapter 6

Saturday, September 13, 1997 – Night

John and I left. I knew I'd get an earful later from Maureen. John moved to open the passenger door of my car as I turned the key. Then opening drums of the Cure's "One Hundred Years" boomed from the stereo. John put his head in his hands.

"Jesus Christ."

All I could say was, "Yeah."

"Just," he said, turning towards me, "take me home, please. I have to pack." His face looked blank and cold, and he stared straight ahead at nothing.

"What about what Brad said?" I asked.

"Yes, Jason, I heard him. That does not mean I plan to listen. I'm leaving town for a while. I'll stay in a hotel somewhere. There's no way anyone will believe me. They cannot kill me, but they can imprison me. That's not how I plan to spend the rest of my life."

When we arrived at John's house back in the French Quarter, he opened the car door and got out. He walked to my window as I rolled it down. He extended his hand for a shake. I took it and gripped it firmly.

"I'll call you, but I won't tell you where I am," he said. Then he walked away, stopping only once to type in the code to open the magnetic lock. Then, he opened the gate to his courtyard. When he walked inside and closed it behind him, I drove down Barracks Street and thought about the future.

***

I had no way of calling Maureen. I drove back to Jenny Dark's apartment to see if she was still there. As I drove down Rampart Street towards Uptown, I rehearsed my next words to her. Nothing would console her, but I decided to at least save her the cost of a taxi. Outside of Jenny Dark's apartment, NOPD squad cars and an ambulance flashed their lights. Red and blue colored the intersection, splashing against the trees, the cars, and the homes around them. I didn't see Maureen. But if they were still inside, she would be as well.

I waited for two hours on the side street headed towards St. Charles Avenue before she walked through the gate. She looked up and down the street. I honked my horn and flashed my lights, and then leaned to the passenger window and waved. After looking once over her shoulder, she walked towards the car as I pushed the door open. She got in and pulled it shut. Wordlessly, she sniffed. I remembered that she was sick, but I saw tears gathering in her eyes. After a moment, she wiped her face and leaned forward.

"Listen," she said, "Do you want to get a drink or something?"

***

It wasn't quite nine o'clock, and Maureen's idea sounded like the best I'd ever heard. Instead of hitting the Crypt, we opted for the darkest dive on Lower Decatur. The Monastery had stained glass windows throughout, some to the outside and others to nowhere. They stood in sharp contrast with the unholy behavior that went on in the place. The punks drank there, and the bartenders poured heavy and strong for cheap. The establishment's token homeless guy slept in a booth next to the jukebox, while an ancient television mounted in the corner played infomercials above him. The one beer he'd bought sat half-finished on the table, next to a full one donated by an anonymous benefactor. I rarely drank there, but I supposed Maureen did. I asked, and she replied, "I used to—more anyway."

"Gotta grow up sometime, I guess." She wanted rum. I rarely drank the stuff, but she told me Jenny loved it. "Rum for Jenny," I thought, as I ordered two shots. "Dark, and cold, and sweet—just the way the world will remember you."

"Rum for Jenny," I said to Maureen, as I set down the two drinks, "in her memory." She sniffed again, and blew her nose into a bar napkin. I could still see the glisten of tears in her eyes from the television. The gaudy blue light of a news report lit up her face.

"Hey," I said, reaching to touch her wrist. She pulled away and shook her head, then wiped the tears away with the back of her hand.

"To Jenny," she said, raising the shot glass I'd placed in front of her. The edge of mine connected with hers. Then, we drank and I remembered the apartment again—a girl murdered by candlelight. Before I could ask, she waved at the bartender for two more. She immediately bent over the new shot she'd purchased. It sat at the table's edge, precariously full. She placed her lips to the rim of the glass and hissed inward, taking a sip. She grasped it, downing the rest in a single gulp, and slammed the empty glass on the table, upside down. For a minute, I thought about what to say. I decided that, at least for a little while, we should talk about anything but Jenny.

She saw how I'd raised the shot glass, and asked, "You left-handed?"

"Yeah," I said. "So was my dad, and my grandfather. That's part of why John and I started talking. He noticed it."

"He is, too?"

"Yeah," I said. "Southpaws all around. So, you opened the store, what, a couple of years ago?" I asked. I could recall seeing it for the first time in college around the time I met John, but not before that.

"Yeah, in 1995," she said.

"You used to run with this crowd?" I asked, nodding at the room.

"Yeah, I was a fucking street kid. I had the backpack, the dog, and the cardboard sign—like, 'Anything Helps,' you know?"

"What changed?" I asked

She looked down at her empty glass, and said, "I just got tired of it. Sleeping in doorways when you've got a family back home is just bullshit. I called my dad and my sister back in Austin and got enough cash to get on my feet and get the store. I traded in the backpack for a lease and chucked the sign."

"What about the dog?" I asked.

"Dog died," she said, frowning.

"What was his name?"

"Dog. That's what I just said," she replied. She looked at her empty glass for a second, before waving at the bartender for another.

"Shot?" he asked, from across the bar.

"Rocks!" she said, looking back at him. She shifted back to face me. "But, I didn't, you know, sell out or anything. I own my own business, for Christ's sake. You just get tired of begging for change when you know you could do more."

The bartender placed a plastic cup full of rum and ice in front of her, resting on a wet napkin. She looked at the gutter punks along the bar. Silver spikes and studs lined and dotted their tattered hoodies and denim jackets. They'd cut up band t-shirts and turned them into back-patches, affixed with safety pins. They drank. They laughed. Yet another dog laid next to his bedraggled owner, tied to the barstool by a discolored leash. The pooch slept, immune to the voices, the clank and clatter of glass, and the Misfits song blaring around us.

Maureen reached for my cigarettes on the table, and said, "I don't know." She lit one and took a drag. "I guess you never completely leave anything. It's, like, whatever's in your blood. You mind?" She gestured at me with the open pack. I smiled and adjusted my glasses.

"You already took it, so no. I didn't know you smoked."

"Mostly when I drink, or when things are, you know," she said, waving her hand above her head, "like this. I still can't believe that some sick fuck could do that."

"God, I don't know," I said. "I can't say that it's Rick, because he's obviously in prison. But, it might be someone copying him or something."

"Copying a copycat? Rick wanted to be like John, and now this other guy is trying to be like Rick?" she asked, taking another loud drag and exhaling.

"That's one theory. I'm going to check around a little bit, but this is more Brad's deal now. Like I said, I'm not a cop."

Maureen rested her cigarette in the closest ashtray on the bar and looked back at me. She moved to speak, but paused to sip her drink first. I knew the next question. I knew the next several. She wanted to know about John. In a city where men painted themselves silver and stood still for money—and in a place where voodoo temples stood amongst bars and apartment complexes—a real vampire seemed like less than a stretch. New Orleans had a way of making you believe.

The smoke from cheap cigarettes billowed around us, and the music still played from the jukebox while the street kids laughed. As liquors brown and clear splashed into shot-glasses and tumblers filled with ice—cold, gleaming, and rife with possibility—a real vampire sounded like a fine idea. She believed in him, but she still wanted to know how we were friends. I cleared my throat and lit another smoke. I told her about meeting him at the car accident, and explained that, while I hadn't saved his life in any official sense, I'd certainly rescued him. Then, he'd asked me to show him around.

I'd always encouraged him to visit a lab or a university—or a hospital. I wanted to know what he really was, but he'd always seemed uninterested. He had lived through the Depression, several wars, desegregation, and the '80s. John—the man, the vampire—exulted in simply surviving a century in which many hadn't. But, as I explained to Maureen, I was sure he wouldn't feel that way forever. Eventually, he would realize the possibilities he could offer to the world—to science, art, and even religion. A drunkard's wisdom tumbled out as I extolled my friend, for he was simply the most interesting man I had ever known. I mentioned Maria, who had also died, and what little I knew about her. I always chalked up some of his quirks to losing her—understanding that he would eventually lose anyone he cared about.

Maureen and I smoked and drank more, and time rolled forward. I saw Jenny Dark, her arms crossed and her eyes open, fading backward with her eyes closed into a sea of blood—her memories and her final words muffled by the sound of rum pouring into yet another glass. But, as I knew she would, Maureen wanted to know how I planned to help my friend.

"You're, like, a journalist?" she asked.

I shrugged, and said, "Yeah, only like one. I just freelance. I write fluff pieces for a bunch of weeklies and whatever else I can pick up. I've done some low-level investigative stuff, but it's really not much—just phone calls. I've looked into stuff like the garbage pickup or whatever. But, I mean, I have to help John. He's my friend."

"I think you should stay out of it," she said.

"Out of what?" I asked.

She took another sip of her drink, and said, "Out of 'looking into things,' or whatever. You're just going to get yourself in trouble. If John's really a vampire, then he can handle his own problems."

"That actually complicates it more than you would think," I said. "He has trouble going out in the day, for one. And for two, he risks exposing himself even more if he runs around trying to play detective."

"You know half of the goth freaks in the city," she said. "If you hear something out at the Crypt, just call Brad or whoever."

"I thought you hated cops," I replied.

"Better to let them do their job than you get hurt."

"How did that go, by the way? Back at Jenny's?" I asked. I'd wanted to know as soon as I saw her, but I decided to wait until the booze had loosened my tongue.

"Uh, terrible, but better than I expected," she replied, explaining how, yes, Brad asked her to lie and say that she'd gone to check on Jenny alone. He claimed to be "in the neighborhood" when he heard her scream from outside. From there, the other officers on scene questioned her at length. They wanted to know who she was, how she knew "Miss Anderson," and if she'd seen anything else. At that point, she had nothing to lie about. "Before I left, though," she continued, "Brad pulled me aside in the hall."

"And?" I asked.

"He asked me a bunch of stuff about John—a little about you, but mostly him."

"Like what?"

"Well, just the obvious stuff—how I know y'all, and if I knew about John and Jenny or whatever. He seemed really worried that John might leave. He kind of told me to tell you to tell him not to. I said, I mean, I said 'okay,' obviously. But, he repeated it a couple of times until I swore to him and everything. So, I'm telling you," she concluded.

"Too late," I said, rolling my eyes. I sipped my drink.

"He left?"

"You didn't hear it from me," I replied. "Just because he can't die doesn't mean he wants to spend the next several decades in prison."

"Jesus, he's actually for real," she said. "I'm still trying to get my head around that."

"I don't know. I got over it a while back. I figure it's some kind of virus or mutation or something. Maybe he's immune or partially immune to it. Like I said, I don't think he's ever had any tests done, but that's what he seems to think."

I looked down. She'd grabbed my wrist.

"What? Need another drink?"

"No, let's stop talking about John for a while. Let's get out of here," she said, staring directly into my eyes.

I cocked my head towards the door, and asked, "Together?"

"Yep. My place."

I hadn't expected it, but I wasn't going to turn it down.

***

Maureen lived in half of a shotgun house in Mid-City. When we entered, she left the lights off. When the door shut, she shoved me on the couch in her small living room. She jumped on top of me, and landed with a rough kiss.

She unbuttoned my shirt furiously and yanked my pants around my ankles. Kicking her own off, she darted to the shelf in the corner of the room—a peach streak in the darkness with bright red hair, like a lit match. She arrived at a fishbowl full of condoms lifted from a coffee shop or an arts center or a free clinic.

She'd probably stolen it, but I didn't care.

"Just a second," she said, tearing open the foil packet. She rolled the rubber down on me in one fell swoop, before stripping off her tank top over her head. Flinging it into a pile of clothes in a corner, she straddled me and took me inside.

She moved roughly and rhythmically, looking up more often than at me. It felt like she wanted to purge the grief. She didn't want to cry anymore. She wouldn't close the store tomorrow and stay in bed all day. She wanted the sadness, and the tears, and the loss exorcised and out of her.

In New Orleans, back then and even now, we lived like there might not be a tomorrow. Your chances of dying were high. Whether shot in a mugging, caught in a drive-by, swept away by a hurricane, or drunk to death—we all took our lives in our hands. If you survived there long enough, you already knew someone who had died young. If we mourned forever for everyone we'd lost, we'd spend all our time at cemeteries or in church or in an endless series of barroom wakes. All of us drank, smoked, and fucked. And, if the city blessed us with another day—much less a night—we did it all over again.

By the second time we did it, we'd found the bedroom and left our remaining clothes on the floor by the mattress. Of course, she didn't have a bed—only a mattress with blankets. The halogen lamp outside of her window shined through her white tulle curtains, illuminating and enshrouding her pale skin, her tattoos, her small breasts, and her hair, which hung in front of her face as she leaned over me. I could see the rows of books shelved around the room, featuring the usual suspects—Jack Kerouac, William Gibson, Morrison (Jim, not Toni). She hadn't bored me—how could she?—but she intrigued me more as the night passed.

Maureen slid up and down me at a steady beat, until I felt a grip from inside of her—warm and tight, like a hand. She wrapped her thin, slight arms around my neck and buried her face in the pillow behind me. She turned her head slightly to moan in my ear, growling, "Fuck yeah."

She relaxed and laid there next to me, limply cast across my chest. I smiled and laughed through my nose.

"Not yet," I said, wrapping my arm around her waist. She giggled as I rolled her underneath me and climbed on top. She laughed again, but without the edge she'd brandished earlier in the day. She sounded playful and true. I knew the type. Cynicism and a quiet sneer made her more the woman and less the girl. No one truly grew up in New Orleans, but I felt like less of a creep for her efforts.

I entered her again and she gasped, as I whispered, "I'm not done yet."

"Aren't we assertive?" she said. I stopped moving, still inside of her. I looked down at her. She was flushed, but, yes, smiling. "I don't like to show all my cards. I'm usually babysitting John. It's kind of hard to compete."

I said I didn't want to talk about him," she said, rolling her eyes.

"Fair enough." I'd nearly killed the mood. I had a talent for that. But, I still wasn't about to waste the opportunity. "Keep going?" I asked.

She smiled again, and said, "Sure." She'd let me off the hook.

And, I did. And, it was good. It had been a while. I grasped her neck, her shoulders, and her hair and felt myself throb and release. When I'd finished, I rolled over and sighed. She stood up in the light from the window. She looked unsure of what to say, but finally bit her lip and spoke: "Do you want a beer or something?"

I nodded, with my eyes still closed.

She returned with two cans of cheap beer and a pack of cigarettes. She tapped out a single white smoke and offered it to me. I drew it out and leaned forward to the lit match she held.

"Unfiltered," I said, leaning back. I knew we'd get along just fine.

"Yep. I want to die young," she said.

***

Sunday, September 14, 1997

I woke up the next morning to see Maureen standing with her back to me. She pulled up a pair of white panties and jeans all at once, covering her pale ass. She was nothing if not efficient. They were the same clothes she'd removed the night before.

"Double dipping?" I asked.

"No washing machine," she said. "I usually just do them in the fucking bathtub and line dry them. Wearing them twice saves time."

"Fair enough."

We stopped for coffee at the Rue on her way to work. She didn't own a car. But under the circumstances, I happily drove her. I wouldn't condemn someone to taking the streetcar after lying underneath me. And, I wanted it to happen again. Relationships in the city's bar scene followed a reliable pattern—the late-night and drunken hook-up, followed by "just fucking" or "friends with benefits," then "just dating," or in "an open relationship," or a place where "you don't like labels." If that last part worked out for long enough, you might begrudgingly call yourselves boyfriend and girlfriend—until you broke up. Then, you'd repeat that cycle two or three times before one of you finally moved or stopped coming out to the bars. I liked Maureen. I didn't want that for us.

We walked to the front door of her store. The morning's rising sun illuminated the dew left on the cars, newly parked by the shop owners and caffeine addicts that slowly populated the street. New Orleans always looked strangely clean in the early morning—as if it expected to stay that way, and the city's children wouldn't have a party every day before the sun even set. Maureen stood on her toes to kiss me on the cheek, and to wrap her arms around my neck.

"Thanks," she said. As she unlocked the door of the Second Chance, I finally spoke.

"Do you want me to call you later?"

She shrugged, and said only, "Sure," with a lilt in her voice. I don't think she expected me to ask.

***

I decided to wait a few days before I called her. I didn't want to come off as desperate. I had a deadline to meet, anyway. I'd half-written the piece about late-night restaurants the day before, waiting for Maureen to get off of work. It just needed sprucing up before I e-mailed it to my editor. Then, I could start on another thousand words of free-weekly bullshit.

Ordinarily, I left the phone off the hook when I slept. John certainly wouldn't call me during the day. And, my parents and sister had moved near Washington D.C. a couple of years before. My father's career as a Naval officer had finally led to the coveted captaincy—a promotion that necessitated a move closer to the Pentagon in Arlington. If anyone called during the day, they usually wanted to sell me something or "help" me consolidate my considerable student loans.

That night, with John on the road and Maureen on my mind, I left the phone on. I slept in my clothes, face down on my unmade bed after several hours of writing and drinking—a rumpled mass of black sheets, with the ashtray still perched on the corner of the bed.

Chapter 7

Monday, September 15, 1997

Four hours after I fell asleep, at almost three, I thought I heard the phone ring. I slept through it. Then, it rang a few more times. I ignored it. Finally, figuring that maybe John had decided to call, I answered.

"Hello," I grumbled into the black cordless.

"It's Brad. Do you ever pick your phone up?"

"Well obviously. It's the middle of the night. Now, how can I help you, officer?"

"Cut the shit. I need you to meet me, like right now."

***

Plenty of bars in the French Quarter stayed open all night. I stepped out of my Volvo on to the curb, adjusting my jacket as I walked. Brad asked to meet at the Tower off of Bourbon Street. It was named for the Tower of London, and it was mostly a heavy metal joint where tourists went in search of vampires. John and I stopped there once in a while on our way home, but not with any regularity. He hated heavy music, and always complained about the volume of the jukebox. I stepped into the front bar and sat down next to a rough-looking goth leaning over it, his head buried in his arms. He looked like he hadn't left from the night before the night before. I ordered an Abita Amber and rubbed my eyes. I'd woken up on the drive there, but I hadn't brewed a pot of coffee. The skinny, black-haired woman behind the bar passed the beer to me. I sipped it and waited for Brad.

"Jason," mumbled the young man.

I looked at my new bar-mate and realized it was, in fact, Brad. He looked pale and hollow, as if he hadn't slept or bathed in three days. Sweat covered his face and glistened in droplets throughout his short cop-hair. But, I'd only seen him two nights before that. He leaned on his elbow and ran his fingers over his head. I knew that he rarely put on his all-blacks anymore, particularly after making detective.

"Brad?" I asked. "What the fuck happened to you? Are you undercover or something?"

"Um, no. And, I wouldn't be able to tell you if I was," he said. I looked him up and down again.

"You look like shit."

He swallowed and sipped his drink, before grumbling, "Yeah, I've had better nights."

"What happened? Are you sick or something?"

He stared straight ahead at the mirror behind the bar for a moment. Snapping his fingers, he pointed at his empty cup. The bartender rolled her eyes and looked down for a second. Her straight, black bangs shielded her scowl before she sighed. Brad looked over at her and pointed at the cup a second time. I couldn't imagine how long he'd sat there. She must have known he was a cop. Otherwise, he would've been out the door. The girls at the Tower bar didn't put up with that kind of thing, and he knew it.

After she poured the shot, he took a hard sip, and fixed his gaze at me for a second, and said, "John left town, didn't he?"

"What makes you ask?" I knew I probably wouldn't escape without telling the truth, but I still wanted to know. He moved his pale, wet face closer. His breath smelled like he'd been eating shit.

"Don't lie to me. I know he's gone. His car hasn't been there since you found that girl. Did you think I wouldn't check?"

"Brad, you know he didn't do it. And if you know, why does it matter?" I was torturing logic within an inch of its life. Even I knew that the police didn't work that way. He shook his hands in front of his face for a second. I sat there, unsure of what else to say.

"Cut the shit for a second and listen. Do you have internet access?"

"Yeah," I said, thinking of the bulky PC in the corner of my room, settled upon a particleboard corner desk. "It's just dialup, though. It's slow."

"That's fine. Write down this address," he said. He read it off to me as I pulled a pad and pen from my jacket pocket. It was the address of a free site, out of a domain that every college kid had.

"What is it?"

He cleared his throat, and replied, "Listen, you don't have a lot of time. We just found this, and it's probably coming down as soon as we can get in touch with the hosting company. There's no phone number, of-fucking-course."

I sat up on my barstool and stared at the address—all forward slashes and letters around words. Only on the Internet would someone be named "xxRavenSoulxx." And, Brad's dramatic build-ups were legendary. I could remember more than a few. He liked to remind John and me that he had special cop-only information that he could dole out at his leisure.

I sighed, and said, "Great, Brad. What is it?"

"It's Raven Cartwright—the Bywater girl that I showed you."

"Raven?" I asked. There were only a couple of hundred different goth girls named Raven. "Is that her real name?"

"Yeah," he said. "Look at it. Download it or whatever, then forget I told you." He downed his drink, and then stood up as he dug in his pocket. Withdrawing a wad of money, he tossed it on the bar and moved to leave. He looked back at me before speaking again. "You call me the instant he gets back in town. If you don't, I'll know." I raised my hands in mock surrender and mouthed "fine" as he departed.

He muttered, "See ya 'round," as he exited on to Toulouse Street.

I looked at the bartender, and said, "I'm sorry about that. I don't know what's wrong with him." She picked up his empty cup and the money. As she counted it, I could see her holding back a rant she had quietly composed. "Is it enough?" I asked.

"Yeah," she replied. "It wouldn't matter if it wasn't, though. He's a cop. What am I going to do?"

"I don't know. File a complaint or something. How long was he here?"

She looked up for a moment and then turned to put the money in the register. The machine sat amongst so many liquor bottles and cheap horror movie props—skulls, candles, and a model of a swamp monster that raised and lowered its arms when the batteries weren't dead.

Looking over her shoulder, she said, "He was here at the start of my shift. I have no idea how long before that. He would've had to pay the last girl on shift. He looked pretty bad when I came in, though. I haven't seen that guy in ages, but he never looked like that."

"He doesn't come out much. Something's not right," I replied. I remembered how Brad had all but stopped coming to the Crypt or dressing like "one of us" (whatever that meant) around the time he made detective. At some point, the job demanded respectability. He wouldn't gamble his career to hang out with a bunch of drunks and cokeheads. But, I'd just seen him there in his old clothes and acting like he hadn't slept, bathed, or given a damn in a week. I looked back at the bartender and raised one finger. I needed a refill of my own.

***

I pushed my glasses back up as I fumbled with the keys at the door to my apartment. I'd driven home slowly to avoid any inquiring members of law enforcement. With whatever mood Brad was in, I didn't feel like calling him to get me out of lockup on a DUI. Stumbling into my bedroom, I ignored the light switch and then tripped over a pile of clothing. I hit the floor, but then landed against the soft pile on my knees. Looking up, I saw my destination: the desk chair and my computer. After standing again, I took two long steps to the seat and switched on the lamp beside my bed.

I fished the scrap of paper Brad had given me out of my jacket pocket. Once Windows loaded up, I clicked the grey Terminal icon and waited. The beeping and distortion pulsed for a minute as it connected. I clicked on the Netscape icon—a small ship's wheel that promised to take you wherever you wanted to go. I typed in the address Brad had read to me. The website loaded slowly out of a fuzzy pixel haze, and I saw her picture there, smiling beneath a masthead of a suitably arcane font. Scrolling down, I saw images and short journal entries. "Raven's Chamber," the swirled letters proclaimed. The haze parted for a moment. I leaned forward to look at the screen—closer than I already sat.

Just as Brad had promised, it was a website run by our first dead girl.

There she stood, smiling with friends and goth bands. No one had updated the site in months, long before she died. It felt like a morbid placeholder. Anyone who found it would think Raven still lived in New Orleans, very much alive. Briefly, I considered e-mailing her—a good-bye letter to a dead girl. I looked through the images and saw the usual dramatic poses in cemeteries (in black and white, naturally). Scrolling down, I saw her posing in group shots with her friends outside of the Crypt—smiling pale faces, lit cloves, and one fish-netted leg held up by her companions. She was pretty, but she'd followed the dress code—black clothes, dark eyes and lips, and a Betty Paige bob haircut.

Then, I saw her with John.

He had his arm around her, and she held one hand against his chest. It showed two people on a date, if I'd ever seen such a thing in my life.

After saving a copy of the website offline, I began to read her journal entries. Raven Cartwright had moved from Vermont a couple of years ago to attend school. She hadn't dropped out to work. She'd met John on a vampire tour when he happened to be standing outside of his house. The guide pointed him out. In a rare mood, I assumed, John simply laughed at the accusation. But, he stayed to pose for pictures. The tour left, but Raven stayed. From what I could tell, they'd met in the spring, long before the end of the semester and the coming of summer. Then, she'd returned to Vermont for the break. Though she'd written no entries after returning, I counted the dates. She would've returned to New Orleans about three weeks before she died. She and John had only lasted a couple of months and broken up before she left. But, that was par for the course with our crowd.

She didn't seem angry, and she'd written nothing about his condition. A couple of months later, someone found her and cut her throat. Before that happened, she'd fucked my best friend, just like Jenny Dark did only a few days before.

John had never mentioned Raven. He hadn't mentioned Jenny, either, but I thought it was odd he wouldn't tell me about a steady girlfriend. He'd said he wanted to meet women, though, and I knew that he'd proceeded as planned. I'd always just thought it was none of my business.

Part of me hoped he hadn't recognized her in Brad's pictures. If he had, it meant that he'd lied to me.

I laid down on the bed and slept in my clothes again. My glasses still rested on my face. Before I drifted off, I began to rehearse the chat I would have with my friend if and when he finally called. But, I didn't have to wait long. Just before sunrise, my phone rang. I fumbled for the phone. Finally, I picked it up with a hungover "H'llo?"

"Good morning, Jason," he said. The sound of John's voice woke me up immediately, but I couldn't quite summon the ire I'd felt earlier.

"John, where are you?"

"We both know that it's best I don't say," he replied.

I didn't feel like waiting for the right moment, and I blurted out, "Who was Raven?" like I had the answer on Murder Jeopardy. He sighed into the phone, and I waited.

"She was a girl I knew briefly in the spring," he said.

"How well did you 'know' her?" I asked. "In what sense?"

"We were close for a short time."

"So, she was like your girlfriend? Did she know about you and everything?" I asked. I couldn't tell if he was evading me or trying to be polite.

"There was some disagreement on the subject," he said. "But yes, she knew. And, we remained friends after formally parting ways."

"What do you know about her now?"

I stood up, finally. He said that he knew nothing of her whereabouts and left it at that. I told him what I'd found. He went silent again.

I spoke first: "Did you know? When I showed you the pictures?"

He cleared his throat before continuing, "The thought had crossed my mind, but I was simply unable to tell. There was simply…"

"Too much blood," I said. "You know what this means, right?"

"Someone is trying to frame me for killing my ex-lovers."

"Well, it wasn't hard to tell with this one," I said. "There were pictures of you two together on the Internet from a vampire tour."

"Damn that thing," he grumbled. John hated the Internet. We both knew that someone out there could expose him in an instant. Maybe, they already had.

"Who gave the tour you were on?" I asked. "Which guide?"

"The one and only," he said.

"Jesus Christ. Lord-fucking-Chaz." I hit the back of my head against the wall behind me.

***

I hated the ghost tour guides. I hated their top hats, their long coats, their cheap canes, and their fake fangs. I hated that they saw themselves as rogue historians, willing to discuss the supernatural secrets of New Orleans no "real" academic would touch. They'd sprung up a few years before, and one man could claim responsibility for the trend. "Lord" Chaz Howell was, in fact, a minor lord in the legal sense. Unlike most of the pseudo-vampires that called themselves Count Dread or Prince Blood Bat, or whatever, Chaz had claim to a small plot of land in Scotland that lacked both people and property. Rumors pointed to a bog in the middle of nowhere that no would-be Scottish Laird stooped to claim. Chaz found a way to make it his, and even his driver's license bore the title. He had started the ghost tour thing a few years before I even knew of him. His one good idea had spiraled out of control into a cottage industry that made most of the city cringe—especially the goths that found themselves turned into Exhibit A in the quest for "real New Orleans vampires."

Suddenly, overweight men costumed in black and matronly goth women led groups of naïve, giggling tourists through the streets of the Garden District and the French Quarter. There, they swore that spirits and vampires lurked around every corner—or did a long time ago, and certainly could once more, if you knew where to look.

The rumors surrounding John were a fucking blessing for those guys. For fifteen bucks a person, some asshole could tell a bunch of warmed-over campfire stories and then stop at John's place. Living near the Crypt didn't help matters. If he was coming, going, or smoking at his window, that made it all seem real. John always denied it when asked, but that didn't stop people from believing.

Unlike his many competitors, Chaz had actually asked John if he could stop outside of his house, and, if the occasion arose, introduce him to the groups. For some reason, John said yes—likely knowing he couldn't stop him. Chaz thought he would get better results if John knew to expect the tours. But, he always played it coy and cool. "Some said" that a real vampire lived at Decatur and Barracks. "Rumor had it" that the tall man with reddish hair might merely work as his daytime aide, but no one knew for sure. And, Chaz never called out John by name or in person. My friend would simply pass by the group, wordlessly, and let Chaz handle the questions.

The night Raven saw him, he did stop. He'd seen her and stopped, and allowed the group to take pictures. I couldn't believe it.

Chaz started the tours. I blamed him. But, I had to admit that he did it well, and certainly better than everyone that followed. There was the "Lord" thing—and his claims that he offered his flock a combination of original research and "street theater." Whatever the man had left in his wake, he prized some level of authenticity in a business that ran on an ever-burning furnace of bullshit. John trusted him. I knew I could, too.

If he knew something about Raven or Jenny, he'd tell me.

***

Monday, September 22, 1997

Jenny Dark's parents had her body shipped home to Alabama. They wanted the funeral there for her family and friends—her old friends, of course. They knew Jenny Anderson. They had ridden the school bus with her, and had worked at the mall with her every summer. They knew her long before she came to New Orleans to play in the streets. Maureen had closed the store and rented a car to make the trip to Birmingham. No one else from New Orleans would drive that far, of course. I doubted anyone actually cared that much. Even if they did, her parents hadn't invited anyone else from the city that killed their little girl.

But, someone decided to hold a memorial the same night at the Crypt—an Alabama funeral in a church in the morning, and a New Orleans send-off in a bar in the evening. I went alone. A few cogs in the rumor machine already blamed John for what happened. A couple of the mouthpieces had already confronted me and demanded to know what happened to him. A few guys said they were going to kick his ass. The self-proclaimed "head DJ" said he was "out of the scene." I knew the truth, but it didn't matter to them. Some people believed me. Most were too busy cultivating their ass-print on a barstool to care one way or another. They were all just so much trouble in black. And when I left my apartment Uptown, I told myself I'd stay away from the Crypt after that night. I'd tell John and anyone else involved to do the same.

***

I walked to the back of the line forming outside of the bar, which would open early and only for regulars. Everyone had dressed in their club finery—knee-high black boots, feather boas, leather corsets, torn fishnets, poets' blouses, and long coats of velvet and leather. The September sky faded to orange as the sun set over the Mississippi River, cooling the French Quarter's evening air as we filed into the bar past the doorman. The tall, bald, pierced brute held a box with small black candles. We each took one and gathered around the dance floor. Someone passed the flame, turning one into many. A single microphone stood in the center. The house lights pointed there, darkening the edges where we all stood. The shadowy ring of friends, dotted with tiny flames, would cradle Jenny Dark's memory. The DJ played This Mortal Coil's "It'll End in Tears." It was loud enough to hear, but quiet enough so that everyone could talk. Melodic, ethereal, and sad, the music filled the room, and a few had already begun to cry.

I stood in the back with a drink in one hand and my candle in the other. I wouldn't speak. I wouldn't stand any closer. Anything else would make the night about me and about John—not about a young woman taken far too soon.

One by one, they took the microphone and spoke. Jake helped her move out of her first apartment after she figured out her roommate was crazy. Misty let her sleep on her couch the first time she got drunk. Nightshade cried with her after Jenny broke up with the boy she lost her virginity to, only a few weeks before she met John. They talked for an hour-and-a-half. The stories drifted from voices to microphone to speakers. One remembered and spoke, and then we all knew. We knew Jenny better than we did before we'd arrived.

The reminiscences slowed to a trickle. The stories, stuttered with tears, shortened. The weeping chorus rose softly, then louder. Two minutes after the last story, the whole club was crying. I wasn't. I wanted to, but I couldn't. All I could see was her body, surrounded by candles, with her throat torn away. The three of us—John, Maureen, and I—had circled her and spoken that night, beholding the killer's handiwork. But no one knew we'd found her. We'd kept that much quiet.

At the end, we drank. In unison, we raised a shot in her memory. We would consume many more with abandon over the hours to follow. Though her body would lay in the soil of Birmingham, five hours away, her memory would ripple in whispers through the Crypt and out to Lower Decatur, echoing through the streets for years to come. Those that knew her might grow up and depart that Land of Do As You Please to become adults. But, whether they remained in New Orleans or moved way, they would carry Jenny Dark's memory with them. Her story would drift through the French Quarter and eventually, she would become another murder ballad to sing among so many others.

Then, it hit me. It was a message.

He didn't want to frame John. He wanted my friend to find him, or he would continue killing. I could imagine him there, hunched over Jenny Dark's body, lighting candles and settling them into the blood that pooled around her. Pale and unkempt with blood running down his face, he would hiss John's name and say, "I did it once. I did it twice. And, I'll do it again." Rick Fremont's wet and tattered face flashed there, along with a hundred others my mind invented. I asked myself how we would find him, or what might happen if we did. And right that second, I needed a drink very badly.

I saw Lord Chaz from the dance floor and decided to ask him what he knew. A pale, corseted girl stopped me in my tracks with her hands on her hips. I looked from the top of her black hair to past the corset, the silver ankh, the ruffled skirt, the fishnet stockings, and the high-heeled boots. She looked like she knew me, but I drew a blank.

I searched a hundred drunken nights for a name, before she finally said, "It's Sarah." I vaguely remembered her, but I couldn't have recalled her name if you'd paid me. The conversation was not beginning well.

"What's up?" I asked, looking over her shoulder at Chaz, as he accepted a tall red drink from across the bar.

"Did he do it?" Sarah asked.

"Did who do what?"

"Jenny," she said. "Did John kill her and that other girl?" At least I knew Raven's name, I thought. The rumor machine had already started spinning.

"No, Christ, of course not," I said. I glanced down, and then resented her for the drink I didn't have in my hand. "Why would you even ask that?"

"Then, why isn't he here?" she asked. "He fucked both of them and now he's hiding?" They were all questions I couldn't and wouldn't answer.

"He's got a lot going on. He's broken up about what happened, but he's not going to come out just to prove it to everybody. Besides," I said, waving my hand to the room around us.

"Besides what?" she asked, crossing her arms.

"Do you think anyone here hasn't already made up their mind? He didn't want to be a distraction," I said.

"So, he sent you instead," she replied. It wasn't a question.

I walked around her without looking back, and said, "Thanks for proving my point," loudly enough for her to hear. I heard her scoff, but I focused on the bar, pushing my glasses back up my nose.

Lord Chaz stood there, leaning on one elbow between the candles that ran from one end to the other. He held a Bloody Mary—naturally—in his free hand. Long, sharp plastic nails adorned each fingertip. His black hair trailed down the back of his coat, which drifted inches from the floor. An ankh necklace rested against his chest. It looked like all the darkness in the world flowed down from his top hat, baptizing the tall, round man in the New Orleans night.

"Chaz," I said, just loud enough for him to hear me over the music. He squinted his eyes. "Jason?" he asked. "You're the writer? John's friend?"

"Yeah, that's me," I said.

"I like your stuff," he said, "Nice to finally meet you. I wish it was a different night, though." He put his drink down, and rubbed his cheeks and goatee hastily with his knuckles. He'd been crying.

"No shit. You know what happened, right?" I asked. I hated to be so forward, but I wanted to know if he'd fallen in with those blaming my friend. He didn't strike me as the nattering high-school type, but I could almost see him playing up the story for his tour—friend or not.

"Yeah," he said, sipping his drink. He put the Bloody Mary back on the bar and rested his hands across his midsection. "Her boss found her, right? That must've been pretty terrible." Someone had talked. I knew I hadn't. That left Brad and Maureen, but at least John and I hadn't made it into the story yet.

I looked at the dance floor again, as the club-goers raised their hands, weaving spells, and drawing angels in the smoke around them. I saw Jenny laying there again, surrounded by candles, her throat gone and a pool of red growing outward.

I nodded, and said, "Chaz, can I ask you something? I mean, can I ask you to do something for me?"

"Yeah, of course," he said, nodding as if we'd known each other for far longer.

"You're not telling the story on your tour, are you?"

"Wouldn't dream of it," he said.

"Telling it or not telling it?"

"I'm not going to tell it. I knew that girl. I'm not here because it's a party. Besides, I couldn't really stop by John's house if there was even a chance he did something like that," he said, taking his drink from the bar for another sip. I sighed, relieved and a bit embarrassed that I'd even thought to ask.

"You knew Jenny?" I asked.

"I know everyone. Every goth girl in New Orleans has to find out for herself if Lord Chaz is really a vampire!" he said, with a low laugh and waving his hands in front of him in mock terror, with his nails dancing back and forth. Nothing could amuse me that night, but he'd piqued my interest. I shot him a quick, cold look, with my brow lowered. He hissed an apology through sheepish, gritted teeth. I waved away the offense with one hand and motioned for the bartender to bring us two shots of whiskey. We raised the cups and touched their edges together.

"To Jenny," he said, firmly, his composure resumed, "May she rest in peace." We drank again. That was the third time I'd toasted her memory, starting with the night she died.

"So, is John still in town?" Chaz asked, setting the drink down and flipping his long black hair over his shoulder. "I mean, I gathered that he's gone. I've been by with the tour and his car hasn't been there. Did he just grab a hotel room or did he hit the road?"

"He's out of town. That's all I know. We talked, and the less I know, the less I have to lie about."

He nodded and mouthed a "yeah."

Chaz and I talked long into the evening. I liked him, as it turned out. I knew John found him agreeable enough, but I'd always kept my distance. His job as a tour guide and the myriad of rumors surrounding him made me less-than-eager to strike up a friendship. The gossipmongers in the goth scene said he was an unlicensed tour guide, a deviant of some unspecified predilection, and probably a Nazi or a Satanist or a cannibal—whatever might be the worst thing you could call someone. I hadn't actually heard the last few, but if I had, it wouldn't have surprised me. He dismissed them all in great detail when my Irish courage got the better of me and I asked about them.

"Smear campaigns by rival tour companies," he explained. I didn't doubt his word. I knew what the New Orleans rumor mill could make of a man.

I cleared my throat and lit a cigarette. "Want one?" I asked.

"Nah," he replied, drawing a cigar out of his long coat. "You want one of these?"

I shook my head. John and I certainly smoked cigars once in a while, but it seemed wrong—almost like a small celebration on the wrong night. I kept it to myself. Chaz clipped the end of his cigar. He sparked three butane flames from his lighter and put them to the tip of the stogie, gently rolling it as he drew back the smoke. He released the grey plume into the air and then rested the cigar in a nearby ashtray. I placed my cigarette there next to it.

"We think this guy might be sort of stalking John," I said. "Like trying to send him a message or something. There are two girls dead, and he dated both of them." The club gradually filled. It had opened for the rest of the world while we talked.

Chaz nodded quickly, and puffed the cigar.

"You know what I mean, though. John was with both of them. And, I think whoever did this might've found out about him and Raven on your tour—or at least saw the pictures on her website."

He shifted his weight on to his other arm, leaning against the bar. He blew a great ring of smoke above us, and then looked away for a moment before speaking.

"You know Raven worked for me, right?"

***

Tuesday, September 23, 1997

Lord Chaz and I agreed to meet with me a few days later. I told him I wouldn't be back at the Crypt anytime soon, and he understood. After my conversation with Sarah, I knew that drinking there would just make the situation worse.

Chaz knew more about Raven. I could tell that much. He wouldn't hold anything back once we had a minute to talk alone. But the night before, we were too many drinks in to discuss a murder and remember the pertinent details. It was already Tuesday afternoon, and Maureen would be back from the funeral. She called before I could.

I shot one hand from under the covers when the phone rang, dragging the receiver underneath into the warm hangover nest I'd gathered around me.

"Hello," I mumbled.

"Good morning, sunshine." I remembered that I'd called John the same thing when I loaded him into my car, right before we found Jenny.

"Are you back yet?" Waking up, I moved the blankets aside and sat up in bed. The black curtains kept the sunlight out, and I'd rarely felt so grateful.

"Almost. I'm in Mobile. I'm on a payphone. I stopped to get gas."

"Make sure you fill up the rental before you take it back. They'll charge you," I said, wiping the morning's green crust from my eyes.

"I know. Just because I don't own a car doesn't mean I haven't driven before."

"All right, all right. Are you opening the store today?" I rolled on to my stomach and pressed my cheek against the pillow, with the receiver resting on my other ear.

"Nah. I might go in later to get caught up on inventory, though. How was the thing at the Crypt?"

"It was fine. They had a microphone set up for people to talk. I didn't really say anything. A few of the drama queens are blaming John. I didn't want to distract from the whole thing. I don't think I'm going back, in any case. How was the real funeral?"

"Pretty normal. It was in a church. She probably would've been pissed. I met her parents."

"They doing okay?"

"Would you be?"

"No, I guess not. Listen, I might've found something about that girl Raven—the first one. You know Lord Chaz, the tour guide?" I knew what was coming.

She nearly spat the words: "Jesus, that guy? What does he have to do with it?"

"Yeah, that guy." I spoke quickly, my tone begging for patience more than anything else. "I think whoever knew about John and Raven might've been on the tour that night."

"Which night?"

The operator's robotic message interrupted us: "Please deposit thirty-five cents for an additional five minutes."

"Fuck. Hold on," she said. "More change, here, I think." I heard the coins rattle into the phone. "What were you saying? Which night?"

"They took some pictures together. It was the first night they met. He's always had this deal worked out with Chaz where he could bring the tour by. Raven had the shots on her website—her with John, I mean. There were some after that, too."

"Anybody could've seen those, then. The Net has thousands of sites," she said.

"Yeah, but to know who they were and to find them there—that's either some guy looking for it or blind luck. Most people don't just pick someone off the web to kill in a bar bathroom. Anyway, she worked for Chaz at some point. So, I don't know. It's just a hunch." I coughed hard. Every smoker does in the morning. "I'm going to talk to him in a couple of days. If anything jumps out at me, I'll call Brad."

"What's his take on all this?" she asked. I thought back to our meeting at the Tower, and how he'd looked sick or worse.

"Not good, honestly. I met him for drinks last week. He knew John had left town somehow. He was pretty pissed that we didn't tell him. But, it was really weird."

"What do you mean?" I heard a few more coins click through the payphone. "I'm almost out of change."

"He looked sick," I said. "Or, at least like he hadn't showered or slept in a while. He was pale, and sweating—and the way he was dressed, it was just..." I didn't finish the sentence.

"Just what?"

"He was wearing all of his old goth clothes like he was nineteen or something. It's like he regressed. I don't know."

Maureen agreed to meet up for drinks later in the week, after she reopened Second Chance and finished her inventory. Halloween was in five weeks, and she had to catch up for the influx of tourists and costume-shoppers.

I finally stood up. I wanted coffee. I put on my glasses and dragged on a pair of black jeans I'd laid over my desk chair. A Siouxsie and the Banshees shirt from the laundry hamper completed my mid-morning ensemble. I lit a cigarette and walked to the kitchen. Without thinking, I looked to the couch, expecting to see John there, still asleep.

***

Wednesday, September 24, 1997

I was supposed to meet Chaz, so I woke up early and cranked out two quick editorials—one on smoking bans in restaurants, and the other on the straight edge movement that had overtaken the New Orleans punk scene. A handful of garage bands had dedicated themselves to clean living—forgoing booze, cigarettes, and drugs in favor of beating each other up in the mosh pit. Within a year, they'd gained a following and brought an old idea from Washington D.C.'s punk glory days down to New Orleans. I would never give up any of the vices they loudly declined, but I found the whole thing interesting enough.

I called Chaz to confirm, and to ask what time he wanted to meet. Rather than meeting out at a bar, he suggested getting together that afternoon at his office. He rented a space in the back of a cigar shop off of Jackson Square, adjacent to Pirate's Alley. Pirate's Alley was, in actuality, both a street and an alley—and the name of a corner bar at its edge. It sat behind St. Louis Cathedral in the Square. There was the bar, the cigar store, and an ice cream parlor that shared the same area. Sometimes the tour groups ended there. Tarot readers and self-appointed psychics of all types held their private magic wars up and down the alley, darting to their tables in the Square with bits of gossip and spite.

A deceptively small door led to the cigar shop, in a small alley off of the main walk. I stepped inside, past a bored looking goth girl seated at a table near the front door. She rested her elbow next to a cash register left over from the mid-eighties. Her head down in a book, I saw the skull barrettes in her hair before I saw her face. She looked up. I pointed to the doorway in the back, where beaded curtains hung and blocked my view of the small room.

"Chaz?" I asked.

"In the back," she said, lowering her head again.

"In the back!" I heard him say, his voice booming through the beaded curtains hanging over the doorway. I walked past the humidors lined with boxes of brown cigars. Fluorescent lights illuminated the cases behind sliding glass doors. To my left, a larger walk-in room showcased the shop's premium selections.

I pushed through the beads of multicolored plastic to see Chaz sitting at his desk, gripping a newspaper in both hands. A pair of reading glasses sat at the end of his nose. The short remains of a cigar sat in an ashtray at his elbow, the smoke rising in a thin ribbon. Chaz lifted the brown stub and took a short puff. He'd retired his tour guide outfit in favor of black jeans and a t-shirt, with a leather vest. He looked over and put the paper down, before standing up with his hand out.

"Jason, thanks for coming," he said, as I shook his hand. "This is Maven." He nodded to a guy sitting in the back corner at his right.

The olive skinned young man wore glasses and held up a small, white acrylic vampire fang in his left hand. In his right, he held a thin electric drill topped with a cylindrical sanding bit. His straight black hair hung over his shoulders and down his back. In front of him, a blue tray of white dots sat on a small table to his left. It looked like an ice cube tray, but it was filled with molds for tiny vampire fangs. I walked up with my hand extended.

"I'm Jason. You're a—" I said, pausing and thinking. "A fangsmith, right? Is that what it's called?"

"That's what they tell me," he said. He stood up, setting down the fang and the drill. He wiped his hands on his apron before returning the handshake. The smell of enamel and acetone burned my nostrils. I looked at the tray again as he explained. The white drops congealed in the fang molds, after which he removed them and would, in time, fit them to a customer's teeth. Once they dried, he removed them again and sanded them to a fine point.

"Dark Awakenings," he called his service, handing me a brochure. On the front, there was a picture of him extending a cryptic hand, inviting you join the fanged fold. I folded it up and put it in my coat pocket. A quick scowl crossed his face.

"I'll give this to someone," I said.

"Yeah," he replied, sitting down to continue working on the canine.

Chaz turned his chair to me and said, "So, what did you want to know? Ask me anything."

"I'm not sure I want to share all this," I said, nodding back at Maven. He ignored the comment and continued his work.

Chaz waved his hand, and said, "There's nothing you haven't told me that everybody doesn't already know—at least the important parts of it. And, there's nothing I can really tell you that Maven hasn't already heard. Don't worry about it."

"Fine," I said, sitting down across from him. I began with Rick Fremont. Chaz knew most of the story, but I repeated it anyway. I told him about the night he came to New Orleans and begged John for help—and then fled to Baton Rouge before the police arrived. We knew he was in jail, in Florida. We hadn't heard from him. We only knew that someone had killed two of John's ex-girlfriends, or whatever he wanted to call them. It might've been a poor shot at a frame-up. But more likely, someone wanted to call my friend out. For what, we didn't know. Maybe it was just revenge for betraying Rick and for failing to protect them that night. Maybe it would happen again. I didn't know of anyone else John had fucked.

Chaz folded his hands across on the table for a minute and stared at the ceiling. He spoke to himself, mumbling, "If I were trying to get to a real vampire, why would I kill his friends? Why would I kill them like a vampire?"

"Even though we're pretty sure this guy isn't," I said.

"Right, right," Chaz said, still looking up at the ceiling. "So, I'm mad at a real vampire. I kill two of his friends, and why?" He looked directly at me, with his eyes wide. "What if he's trying to lure John out to turn him?"

"Doesn't work," I said. "John can't transfer it like that. And if he wanted that, he could just ask John at the Crypt and hear it for himself."

"Do you know he can't for sure?"

"He told me it doesn't work like that," I said. "That's all I know. I believe him."

"Does this guy know that?" asked Chaz.

"I'm sorry," I said, laughing as he sat back in his chair. "It's just a little confused now. Do I know what this guy knows about John that I don't know?"

"It's just an idea," he said. "Maybe he already thinks he's a vampire or something."

Leaning forward, I asked, "What about Raven?"

"Raven, yeah," he said. "Nice girl. Good storyteller, too. Not a lot of female tour guides last for very long. The drunks get to them after a while, but she was good. She quit, though."

"Not because of the drunks?" I asked.

"Nah, there was this other guy."

"Radu," Maven said, looking up at us.

Chaz repeated, "Radu."

Maven grumbled, "Asshole," before looking back at his fangs.

"Well, she started pretty late in the spring as just a side gig while she was going to school. She left to go home for the summer," he said. Chaz took his glasses off and rubbed his eyes. I noticed that he'd removed the talon-length fake nails.

I read all that. Her website's still up. But, Radu?" When I mentioned the website, Chaz frowned.

"Yeah, he was bothering her. Bottom line is she wouldn't fuck him and he got mad. She said he was kind of stalking her. They had an argument in here one day and I finally fired him. She was on her way out anyway, but Radu just sent her out even faster."

"What happened to him?" I asked, sitting up in the chair and resting my elbows on the desk.

Chaz laughed a loud, sharp note. "I don't know. I'm pretty sure he left town. I don't work with crazy fucks like that." I cocked my eyebrow at him and half-smiled.

"Crazy how?" I asked.

"I'm not sure he quite got the line between fiction and reality. Some of the younger guides don't. They're a little too into vampires, if you know what I mean." He leaned forward and said, "Listen. I let people believe what they want. I put a lot of work into this tour, but in the end I let people decide if they really believe in everything. That's up to them. I know John's the real deal, but he's one of a kind. We both know that." Maven scoffed from the corner, without looking at us.

Chaz glanced back at him. "Maven doesn't think he's for real."

I looked over Chaz's shoulder and said, "He's real. Believe me."

"Whatever you say," he replied, turning on the drill.

Chaz rolled his eyes and continued, "Anyway." He leaned in, beckoning for me to do the same. "Where is he? I figured NOPD might want to talk to him. I know you said you didn't know, but it's okay."

I lowered my head at the thought of police intervention, and said, "I really don't know, and I don't really want to know. He's already talked to the cops." He'd talked to one cop, and we had no idea what the rest of the department knew.

"He knows a guy," I said. "He believes him, but not everyone else will. When he comes back, we can all go for a drink or something. Hopefully, this'll be over."

"Fair enough. Well, that's all I got," he said, putting his hands behind his head and leaning back in his chair. He drew a postcard from a stack on his desk. "Here."

I looked at the card and saw an advertisement for a vampire-themed party on Halloween night called the Dark Cotillion, to be held at the Masonic Temple at 333 St. Charles Avenue.

"You should come," he said. "All the freaks will be out."

Chapter 8

Thursday, September 25, 1997

Vampire murders still made the news once in a while. Killers have been opening the veins of their victims and drinking their blood since the beginning of time. Any true crime junkie could tell you that the twentieth century alone had seen its share. Fritz Haarmaan—"the Vampire of Hanover"— had bitten out the throats of at least twenty-four young men before he was executed in 1925. Richard Chase killed six people in Sacramento in the late 1970s, before cannibalizing them and violating their corpses. During the last stretch of his spree, he drank the blood of an infant boy. He committed suicide in prison in 1980, a few years after I was born. There were more.

During the tours, the guides said they happened all the time in New Orleans—or they did at one point. The police always covered them up. The press wouldn't report them. The Catholic Church didn't want the world to know they existed. I knew the routine. Rick Fremont was only the most recent of a long list of guys that couldn't just read a book or watch a movie. They had to live it. They wouldn't even stoop to finding someone who wanted to bleed for them. They needed a victim.

The day after I met Chaz and Maven, I sat at the small, round dinner table in my living room to think. Brad couldn't help me, or probably wouldn't. He'd given me the photos of Raven and directed me to her website, but he'd ignored my phone calls and voicemails since then.

Rick Fremont was my only lead. And, my would-be vampire lived in the Columbia Correctional Institution in Lake City, Florida, west of Jacksonville. Other than the occasional interviewer, he had little contact with the outside world.

I grabbed a yellow legal pad and a marker, and wrote John's name at the center of a page. I circled it and stared. I drew one line and ended it with Rick Fremont's name. Another ended with Raven. Yet another ended with Jenny Dark. I prayed that I wouldn't have to add more names, and that someone else wouldn't have to add mine.

I didn't even know what the diagram would accomplish. I walked to the kitchen and poured myself a cup of cold leftover coffee. Sipping the putrid black liquid, I hoped the bitter shock and the caffeine would bring an answer. Leaning against the counter, I sipped it again before staring at the dirty white linoleum of the kitchen floor. It needed mopping.

I slapped the counter, and mumbled, "Fuck it." I grabbed a bottle of bourbon out of the liquor cabinet and poured a dash of bourbon into my coffee. With the mug in the microwave, I set it for one minute, and waited. The cup spun inside until the appliance beeped. I carried the mug back to the table and sat down. Under Fremont's name, I wrote everything that came to mind—"in prison, probably hates John, might want to orchestrate something." Rick couldn't kill John. But, he could've dispatched someone—maybe Radu—to stalk him. That didn't feel right. Maybe he'd decided to have everyone John knew offed instead. That would make me a target.

I imagined myself in Jenny Dark's place, surrounded by black candles, with my throat torn and a pool of blood expanding around me.

I wondered when he might find me. Maybe he'd pull me into an alley when I was walking home from a bar. People would say that I had left and seemed fine. No one would know that I hadn't made it home. Or, he would just break down my door like he had Jenny's, and hew and rip at the meat of my neck with his teeth. At the edge of my bed, that faceless figure in black would drink deeply of me. I saw him there—everyone and no one—a killer without a name. In my mind, I died knowing nothing.

Looking back at the diagram I'd started, I expected to see my own name. But, I only saw what I had written before my imagination had taken over. Underneath Jenny's name, I wrote more notes—"from Alabama, no contact with Fremont, slept with John, killed on Sept. 13th." By Raven's name, I scrawled half-sentences about meeting John on the tour, working for Lord Chaz, and leaving after that guy Radu had bothered her.

I thought back to the night we met Rick and his band of misfits. He knelt before John, as his four followers stood in the doorway, all of them too young to come inside, and watching hopefully in the rain. I remembered running to the police station and then to John's house, only to find they'd left. Then the police arrived, and we met Brad. After that, a bunch of Louisiana State Police caught up with Fremont at a hotel in Baton Rouge. We never saw any of them again. They all went to jail, and they'd been rotting there ever since.

I pounded the table with both fists, splashing my coffee. I realized it, and when I did, it hit me like a kick in the stomach: Rick didn't know that we'd talked to the police. I didn't know what John told them that sent them back into the wet New Orleans night. He'd always said they just got spooked or heard sirens or something. But if John wanted the police to find them there, he wouldn't have told them they were on the way. As far as Rick knew, John and I had nothing to do with any of it. We never testified. Our names were not in the news. Brad had twisted everything we gave him as coming from other sources.

I tore off a new sheet of paper and asked myself what you write to a killer. Rick Fremont had murdered three people to prove his loyalty to my friend. Now, within two years someone had done it again. But, the crimes were too personal. They were aimed at John. The guy—and I knew it had to be a guy—he didn't want to impress John, or even imitate him. He wanted to send him a message. And if I had my cards in order, Rick wouldn't necessarily have it out for him. If he were to orchestrate a bunch of vampire murders to get our attention, he probably wouldn't go after our friends. It was a leap, but I could only find out by asking.

I wrote. I began—

Dear Rick,

You probably don't remember me, but we met during your brief stay in New Orleans. John Devereux is my best friend, and I saw you at the Crypt that night. I was at the bar when you presented yourself to him. He told me he was going to take you back to his house. I think you all left before I got there. Some things have happened since then. John and I need your help. I'd like to talk to you more. Write back or call me.

Sincerely,
Jason Castaing
504-555-4356

I stared at the letter for a few minutes. I never thought I would see or speak to Rick Fremont again. Shrugging, I drank the last of the coffee and bourbon. By then, it was cold again and tasted like dirt. But, I didn't give a damn. I found an envelope in my bedroom desk and sealed it, but realized that I didn't have his address. I could've found it online, but I decided to call Brad one more time. I stopped and stared at my phone for a minute, unsure if he'd even want to hear from me. Before I could reconsider, I grabbed the handset and made myself dial the number. In one breath, I explained what I was doing and asked if he could give me the number for the Florida Department of Corrections.

"Why?" He still sounded dead, drunk, and tired. I was too stupid and too tired to lie. I told him everything I'd learned.

"Jesus, what the hell makes you think this is a good idea?" he asked. Thankfully, I could only hear him through the phone. I didn't have to see the look on his face.

"It's just a hunch. Do you want me to find out where John went? This is part of it."

"Based on what?" he asked. He sounded irritated, but I knew him well enough to stand my ground.

"Because Rick might be involved. Most vampire-wannabes don't kill people. He did, and now someone else did and they're both tied to John."

"The guy's in prison in another state," he said, coughing. "I mean, that kind of thing happens sometimes. But, this guy—he's a stupid, scared kid, not some gangbanger ordering a hit on the outside. Guys like him write letters and manifestos in their cell and count the days until they die." I heard traffic behind him.

"Are you outside?" I asked.

"Yeah, this is my cell phone. Remember?"

"Brad, have you been okay? You looked like shit when we met at the Tower. Are you sick?"

He coughed again, and said, "Yeah, I've been fighting something off. It's seasonal. It happens every time the temperature changes. I already took a couple of sick days to sleep it off."

"Sorry to wake you," I said.

"I said I was outside. Just listen—we really need to find out what happened to John. It's important. He's tied to this case and I'm going to catch a lot of heat from my chain of command if they find out how well I know him. So…" He paused, trailing off. "Yeah, I'll be fine." I leaned my head on my shoulder, clinching the receiver between my ear and shoulder. I reached for my cigarettes. I'd known Brad for a long time, but he was making me nervous.

Leaning on the table, I said, "I'm not suggesting Rick ordered it. I don't think he did. He respects John too much. He didn't turn him in that night. They just ran for some reason."

"Yeah, I'm not so sure about that, but whatever," he said. I could tell my theories meant something between jack and shit to him. "Why else would they take off? But, look; I can't stop you from visiting the guy. It's a free country. If you find out anything, let me know."

"Are you going to get the number for me?" I asked.

"Just get it off the Internet. I have to run," he said. Before I could answer, he hung up.

I found the address fifteen minutes later, and regretted that I'd bothered to call him. I mailed the letter and waited a couple of weeks. I saw Maureen again. We drank, we smoked, and we fucked. Then, we met again the next night and did it all over again. I felt a word that sounded like "girlfriend" creeping at the edge of my throat whenever I saw her. That toxic label had ended more decent relationships in New Orleans than I could count. But, I liked her in a way that I hadn't liked anyone in a while.

***

Thursday, October 9, 1997

We met for drinks at the bar in Pirate's Alley. Lafitte's Blacksmith Shop already sat at the corner of Bourbon and St. Philip, and Lafitte in Exile poured drinks for the gays hanging out on Bourbon and Dumaine. I wondered if other cities had that many bars with pirate names. I asked Maureen after our first drink, and she rattled off the name of others she knew of, counting them on her thin, reddish fingers—Treasure Isle, Treasure Chests, Pirates'-This-and-That.

We'd walked through Jackson Square towards St. Louis Cathedral—the monolith of God and stone that sat between our table, the Square, the street, and the river beyond it. Beyond the cathedral, the sun began to set. Soon the orange October evening would pass to night.

I lit my cigarette and then hers. We touched glasses after a refill, sipped, and then rested them on the iron tables. The early ghost tours drifted by, starting and stopping and storytelling.

"Chaz come by here?" she asked.

"Don't think so. He doesn't want people to know where his office is. He gets some of the vampire crazies after him once in a while."

"Wonder why that is," she said, blowing the smoke sharply from the corner of her mouth, past her bangs, and into the air above her.

"He knows it comes with the territory," I said. "He's fine. I know what people say about him. I know what you've heard. I'm pretty sure he'd be in jail if half of those things were true." She shrugged. I could tell she hadn't truly committed to hating him. That seemed like enough for me.

"Anyway," I continued, "I've been thinking." I'd been thinking since she'd come back from Birmingham.

"What is it?" she asked, squinting for half of a second.

"I've, uh, been thinking—like I said. We need to talk about a couple of things."

"Shit," I could tell she hadn't anticipated anything serious. "What?"

"Couple of things. One deals with you and me." I sipped, swallowed, and pointed back and forth in the space between us.

"Yeah?" she asked, nodding. "What else?"

"It's about John, and Rick." She took another drag and released it. The smoke billowed over the table.

"The vampire guy?" she asked.

"Jesus Christ. Which one?" I rolled my eyes, and pushed my glasses back up my nose. I reached across the table to put out the butt in the ashtray.

"I know, right? But, really—which one?" she asked, smiling for the first time that evening.

"Jesus." I raised my eyes skyward, briefly. "Not Jesus, I mean. Rick, but obviously it has to do with John."

"Explain the first part—me and you, I mean."

I sat up, touching my fist against my chest as I cleared my throat. I had prepared my speech earlier over a double at my place.

"We've been hanging out for a couple of weeks now. A few of those times have led to us hanging out without our clothes on."

"Complaining?" she asked, with one eyebrow raised.

"Not at all," I said, pointing at her. "But yeah, we've hooked up more than once and continued to see each other elsewhere, and even talked on the phone a couple of times. This is starting to look like more than just a physical thing."

"I suppose. I mean it's only been a couple of weeks. You haven't even taken me to dinner," she replied.

"We've had drinks."

"Everyone has drinks. If that makes us 'dating,' or whatever, then I'm going out with half the city. What are you getting at? Just say it. I don't do games."

"I think we should actually, you know, call it a relationship and stuff," I said. "We should go out." I felt like a seventeen-year-old kid trying to ask a girl to prom.

"Do people even do that anymore? Or, do they do it around here?" she asked. She pulled one knee up to her chin with her foot, wrapped in a red Converse, resting on the edge of her seat. "I haven't had an actual boyfriend in fucking forever." I could hear it in her voice. She thought it was cute, but she didn't mean it.

I played along, and said, "It's been known to happen. But, if you don't—" She smiled and released her leg, leaning forward. She grabbed my left hand with her right.

"Jason?"

"Yes?"

"I would love to be your girlfriend. But, I'm not moving in with you. And, if you make me meet your mom earlier than three months in, I'm calling it. If you cheat on me, I'm going to tell everyone you have a micro-dick. And," she said, pausing to sip her drink, with her eyes peering over the cup's edge, "finally: if you ever hit me, I'll kill you. I mean, with a gun—for real."

I leaned back a little, and said, "I wouldn't even think of—"

"I know," she said, exhaling her cigarette smoke as she put the finished stub into the tray. She held up one hand. "I know you wouldn't. But, I didn't think the last guy would either. I just have to say it."

"Okay," I said, as she leaned forward.

"I haven't had a boyfriend in a long time," she said. "The ones I've had were mostly assholes. It's one of the reasons I got the shop—to get away from that crowd and have something of my own."

I drew another cigarette from the pack. I offered her one. She drew it out as I lit mine, clenched between my lips. Before I could offer her the flame, she pressed the tip of her unlit smoke against the burning cherry at the end of mine and sucked. Her orange ember flared and faded as she released it from her lips and exhaled.

"Can I just kiss you?" I asked.

She laughed, and said, "Like you haven't?"

"I mean for real—in public, with our clothes on."

"Yeah," she said, standing up and leaning across the table. I moved to meet her there, and our lips met over the table, with smoke rising around us. The sun's last glow faded into the autumn sky.

Maureen sat back down and smiled. She bounced her head from side to side for a moment, and then hummed a happy tune. Without trying to, I looked at her eyes. She didn't look away, but held the gaze all the same.

"Seems like we're on to something," I said.

"Maybe," she said, pursing her lips playfully and looking away for an instant. She looked back. "Yeah." We stood and kissed again. "Okay," she said, sitting. "What was the second thing?"

"Fremont."

"What about him?"

"You remember everything I told you? You remember what happened with Brad and John that night?" I asked.

"Yeah, vaguely. They ran off or something."

"Right," I replied. "Rick and his fucking cult took off for Baton Rouge before Brad showed up. I always thought they figured the cops were coming or, I don't know, John slipped up and said something to scare them off. I thought a lot about it." I stopped for a puff.

"And?"

"John just told me they ran away. He didn't really say why," I said.

"Seems obvious, though. The cops were coming. Can't you ask him?"

"They didn't know the police were coming. I've brought it up, but he usually just says they heard sirens or something. It's the Quarter, though. That doesn't mean anything. And, I can't ask him again, because he hasn't called in days. I don't have a number." I said.

"But," I continued, "it means that Rick doesn't know that John and I talked to the police. Brad fixed all that. We were never at the trial or in the press. Rick doesn't know a damn thing. He still thinks John and I are his friends."

"How can that possibly help?" she asked.

"Whoever killed Jenny and Raven is trying to send John a message. They're not trying to kill people he knows for the hell of it. What if I'm next?"

She rolled her eyes, threw back her head, and said, "Oh, Christ. I think you're probably safe, unless you and John are secretly dating."

I ignored the joke. "People talk about John, but Rick's the only one that ever went that far. Now, this guy has too. They might be connected. I can't get to John right now. But, I can get to Rick."

"What?" she asked. She all but jumped, and then slapped the table. The ice in our cups clattered, and the remaining water sloshed out on to the iron grid between us. "Are you seriously going to talk to him?"

"It's not quite that easy, but it's not really that hard to get either," I said. I'd done my research after writing to Rick. I knew what to do. "I wrote him a letter already."

"Fuck," she said, putting her head down. "Maybe, can we space out these conversations next time?"

"I already wrote the letter. If he's okay with it, I have to call and request to be put on his list of visitors. I'll have an easier time of it because I've done some press work, but I don't really have credentials as a freelancer."

Maureen leaned back and waved her hand for another drink and said, "I'm going to need this."

I explained all I knew and all I could. After that, from the look in her eyes to the way she listened and rarely spoke, the second story had come to bear on the first. She wanted to see me again, but our relationship would continue where it had begun—with death, and with vampires both real and imagined. She wasn't just going to date me. I came with baggage—I smoked and drank too much, my best friend was a vampire, and two women were already dead. I only hoped that she was prepared.

Maureen and I had stumbled into each other in a dark room. I just hoped, in the end, we would walk out of it together.

Chapter 9

Thursday, October 9, 1997 – Evening

That evening, Maureen left to finish some inventory work at Second Chance. She declined my offer of a ride home. She wanted to take a taxi, she said, and to not put me out of my way. She grabbed my arm and promised to call. Then, she kissed me and walked down the alley, past the ice cream shop, with her shoes red and bright against the slate pavement. She drew her wallet from her back pocket to check for cash.

Almost on cue, a cab pulled in front of the alley, blocking my view of the shops and tourists across the street. Without so much as a wave, she opened the car's back door. She climbed in and closed it. Then, the taxi drove away from Pirate's Alley.

She'd accepted my offer, I reminded myself—to call us "together." But, hearing about Rick had brought the situation's full and terrible force to bear in her mind. This wouldn't end soon or quickly. I hoped she would decide I was still worth the trouble.

I drove back to my apartment and crawled into bed. It was early—not too early for some people to sleep. But for me, it was unthinkable. I wouldn't and couldn't cry or show a damn thing, not even to an empty room. Laying there in the dark, I wondered what I'd been thinking, and how I'd probably chased her away already. If

I'd kept my mouth shut about one or the other—us, or Rick—I probably could've worked through both with her, after a while. After a couple of years of showing John around, I'd finally found something of my own. And, a situation he'd inadvertently created would undo it—or so I thought that night, as I tried to sleep. The thoughts raced, my heart sped, and I could only stare at the ceiling.

***

Friday, October 10, 1997

My phone rang the next morning. I jumped out of bed, hoping I would hear Maureen's voice and something that would clear the dark air between us. She wanted me. She didn't. She did, but only after the ordeal was over. I could've accepted any answer better than the uncertainty. I'd only slept for a few hours, but I felt instantly awake.

"Hello?"

A robotic voice spoke through the receiver, cold and rhythmic, saying, "You have a collect call from," and another voice broke the recording to finish the sentence with "Rick." He'd hissed his name into the receiver, dragging out its single syllable and snapping the "ick" like a whip.

I felt sharp, salty spikes in the pit of my stomach, and the warmth of fear in my mouth. I shook. I couldn't stop myself, as the recording continued. Would I accept the charges? Of course I would. My mouth went dry. I sat down and waited. The phone clicked. For twenty seconds, the phone breathed into my ear. I eyed my glasses, my cigarettes, and the door of my room, in case the voice told me to run—to leave New Orleans, to disappear, and never come back.

"Jason," he said.

"Um, yeah? I mean, this is he."

"This is," he said, pausing, "Rick Fremont. I received your letter. Are you well?" Prison hadn't stifled the manners he'd faked so hard at the Crypt.

"I'm fine," I said. I cleared my throat. "It's been a while. You remember me, right?"

"I do. You're John's friend. How is he?" Faint eagerness crept in at the edges of his voice. It wasn't the sound of revenge in the making. My gamble had paid off. He still wanted John. The phone slipped, moist against my ear, as I stared at my feet.

"He's okay. Um, that's actually what I wanted to talk to you about. He kind of needs your help with something."

"Does he now? How very flattering. I would be glad to assist him—or you, for that matter." He wouldn't joke. He didn't know how to make a joke. Why he'd fled

John's house that night, I couldn't say. But, at that point, I finally knew he didn't blame my friend.

"Yeah, he does," I said.

"Of course," he said. My heart slowed, finally. I breathed out, and gathered my thoughts. The next words came easily enough.

"I need to meet with you in person. I'm going to drive to Florida tomorrow, and we're going to sit down and talk. If you need anything in return from me, that's fine. But," I said, dropping my voice, "above all, I need your help."

He laughed with a low, guttural sound and said, "Somehow, I knew."

"Knew what, exactly?"

"I always thought that our story—that our time together—wasn't over yet. Somehow, I knew you'd call."

***

I put the phone down and ran to the bathroom to throw water on my face. The cold splash hit my glasses, my forehead, my cheeks, and my bald head. It felt cleansing—like I'd washed away some of the fear and the revulsion. You don't have a friendly conversation with a murderer every day. I took off my glasses and rubbed my eyes, realizing that I'd have to do it again and in person. Still clenching my wet glasses, I looked down. I hadn't put pants on yet. The water spots from the sink spread across the plaid (not black, shockingly) pattern. It looked like I'd pissed myself.

I walked back to the bedroom and pulled on a pair of black jeans from the laundry pile. I didn't know what to do next. I wanted a drink, but even I couldn't bring myself to pour one that early. Coffee wouldn't calm my nerves, but it might make me focus on what I had to do next. In the kitchen, I stared at the coffee pot as it filled with the bubbling black liquid.

A few minutes later, I poured a cup in a novelty mug shaped like Dracula's head. I stared at it for five minutes on the counter, waiting for it to cool. When it seemed safe, I raised it to my lips. I could smell the chicory before I drank. It was still hot—far more than I'd realized, and I spit it across the room as the phone rang. I put Dracula down with a dark slosh on the white tiles of the counter.

My fingers wet with coffee, I grabbed the phone and raised it to my ear with a "Hello?"

"Hey, it's Maureen."

I felt more spikes, and more heat. I swallowed, and said "Hello" a second time.

"What's up?" she asked.

"Well," I began, "a convicted murderer just collect-called me and invited me to stop by for a chat, maybe a coffee—that kind of thing."

"Oh, fuck," she said. "Fremont? He actually called you? I mean, are you okay?"

"Yeah, it was a hell of a thing. He scared the shit out of me, even over the phone."

She laughed and said, "I'll bet. I'm surprised you picked up the phone again." I didn't feel like dragging the conversation out any longer. If anything, I wanted to go back to sleep and hide from the world.

"Listen," I said, after clearing my throat, "I don't like to drag things out, so—"

"Yes."

"Yes, what?" I asked.

"Yes, Jason, I will still go out with you, be your girlfriend, or…" she trailed off and said nothing for a moment. I imagined her arms waving above her head in search of a better word. "I'll be your whatever," she said.

"My whatever? That's sweet of you."

"Don't push it. I'm taking my life in my hands doing this. Now, I'm coming over. You better have a drink ready, because I'm going to need it."

***

After one drink and a round of makeup sex, we discussed Florida. Despite the short notice, she wanted to drive there with me. She couldn't meet with Rick, as he hadn't added her to his visitors list. She didn't even want to, and I didn't argue. We would leave New Orleans the next morning and drive straight through to Lake City, near Jacksonville. She'd hired new help since Jenny Dark died. I questioned her decision to leave the store with a new guy. She explained that he'd worked there the summer before and quit for school. He knew the run of the place.

Smiling, I lit a cigarette in bed. The black sheet covered our naked bodies and she slept gently against my shoulder. I'd started the morning in horror and uncertainty with coffee, and ended it with a drink and Maureen in my arms. The cold whiskey gathered sweat and dripped on the folded paper towel next to my ashtray. On either side of me lay my sin, my soul, and my blessed vices.

By the time we looked at the clock, it was well after noon—too late for breakfast but early enough for brunch. Usually, you could only find that kind of thing on Saturday or Sunday. But, I knew a place in the Marigny that served breakfast late into the afternoon. It's a funny thing to sit down with a bunch of eggs, seafood, and alcohol in the middle of the day, but brunch had become a sacred thing in the city. If you drank before four o'clock, you might have a problem. If you drank bottomless mimosas with overpriced gourmet vittles at around one, it meant you had money and friends. No one ate brunch alone.

That afternoon, I had more than company in Maureen. We ate cheese biscuits and drank the aforementioned orange juice and champagne cocktails. By the time our food arrived (eggs benedict for her, chorizo and crawfish hash for me), the mood had taken on the warm amber hue of the afternoon. She grabbed my hand and laughed at nothing in particular. In the corner, three heavyset New Orleans women crowded around a microphone singing local tunes, alongside a lone piano man in a fedora. Everything all around us fell into a rhythm and a blur of a world all our own. The clutter of dishes, and diners, and passing cars, and the bar blended sweetly with the too-early-for-cocktail-hour songs warbled by the singers

The room spun—for a moment blissfully, before there, breaking the spell, I saw Rick Fremont's face, expressionless and unblinking, staring at me from across the table. I looked down at my hand, to see if his held it. I blinked for a moment, and saw that it did, with dirty hands and long, yellow nails—until I shook my head, returning Maureen to my sight.

My buzz was dead, and the afternoon's spell with it. I pushed my food aside.

"What is it?" she asked, frowning.

"Rick," I said, knowing the name alone would say more than I could. She raised her eyes towards the ceiling once, briefly, and her lips pressed together as she tightened her grip on my hand. I looked again, to see only her.

"Yeah," she replied.

We finished our meal in silence. I thought only of the drive to Florida, and what waited for me there.

Chapter 10

Saturday, October 11, 2997

The next morning, I dropped our black duffle bags into the trunk of my car, and packed the remaining suitcases in the backseat. I slammed the trunk shut, and briefly rested my forehead on it, whispering a prayer to no one. The clear air and the dew of morning lingered around me. Briefly, I envied every dog, cat, blade of grass, and person that didn't have to drive seven hours to talk to a killer. Maureen walked up, holding a thermos of coffee. She wore her usual ensemble—red Converse, blue jeans, a tank top, tattoos, sunglasses, and crimson hair she'd dyed the night before.

She stopped as I rested on the trunk, and asked, "What's wrong?" I lifted my forehead and placed my hands on either side of the car.

"It's okay. It's this—the whole thing—talking to Fremont. It seemed like a good idea."

"Always does at the time," she said, opening the passenger door and lowering herself in. The streetcar jangled by in the distance, as the sun rose over the horizon. I glanced at the door to my apartment, and realized that I could turn back whenever I wanted. Through the back window of the Volvo, I saw Maureen sipping coffee from the open thermos. For nearly a minute, I watched her. Every reason to abandon our trip cycled through my mind. I didn't feel well, the car needed an oil change, I had a deadline, and I wanted to buy a dog and it had to happen today.

Maureen placed the thermos in a drink holder before she leaned out. Under her bright red bangs, she smiled and said, "Get in the fucking car. This was your idea, Sherlock."

"Yeah. It was," I said. I got in and closed the door, adding only, "Coffee, please." She handed me the thermos and I took a long drink. In moments, the caffeine elevated my mood. It opened my eyes just enough to see the road in front of me. The morning's courage had me, if only for long enough to turn the key in the ignition. I pushed the gas pedal, and started us towards I-10 East.

For the first hour, we listened to NPR, sipped coffee, and barely spoke. The restrained tones of the news had a way of silencing chatter in the car, as if no one wanted to interrupt the radio. Maybe it just kept me from talking. As the news faded to classical music, I thought of the CDs in the nylon envelope clipped to the passenger-side sun guard.

Tapping it with my free hand, I said, "Pick something."

"No more news? You seemed engaged," she said.

"Nah, not anymore."

"You going to talk to me now?" she asked, removing the CD holder from above her head.

"Yeah, of course," I said. "Sorry. I just got wrapped up. It's better than what's on the other end of this trip."

She slid the CDs out one by one and withdrew what turned out to be The Cult's *Sonic Temple.* She slid the disc in, and skipped to "Fire Woman." The opening guitars shimmered and hammered, giving way to Ian Astbury's voice—"Shake-shake-shake it!" I sipped the coffee again and stared at the long road ahead, pushing on the accelerator. The end didn't seem quite as bad. I looked at her, and then at the car radio's digital clock. We had at least two hours until I could justify stopping for an early lunch. Maureen bobbed her head to the music, as she withdrew a pack of peanut butter crackers from the backpack at her feet.

"You have food? You brought food and you didn't tell me?" I said, in no way seriously.

"Jesus Christ. They're crackers," she said, pointing the half-open pack at me like a gun. "Do you want one?" she asked, dragging out the "want."

"Yes, I would like some. I mean, more than one," I said, holding out my right hand, free from the shift stick. "Think of it like a tip."

"For what? I'm doing you the favor here."

"What? By not driving because you don't know how to use a stick, and getting a mini-vacation with your new boyfriend?"

"Oh lord." She rolled her eyes and crossed her arms. "You can teach me how to drive stick when we get back. Is that hard for you? With your hand, I mean."

"Jesus, it's not like I've got a hook," I said, laughing. "I'm just left-handed. It's okay. It took some getting used to when I first started driving. But, the stick gets better gas mileage. It's not something I think about much."

"That's good," she said. "But, as for this 'vacation'—"

"Yeah?"

"We're going to visit a murderer in prison. That's not exactly vacation," she said.

"Yeah, but you forgot something. We get to fuck in a hotel room in sunny Florida. It'll be great. We can eat room service and watch cable in our underwear," I replied.

"I heard you on the phone when you booked us," she said. "I don't think the Econo-Dump has room service."

"The meeting with Rick is only going to take an hour or so," I said, rolling down the window and reaching for a pack of cigarettes. I found them in the door's compartment. I lit one and inhaled. Driving a stick while smoking was tricky, but in fifth gear on the highway, I figured we'd be safe—at least in that sense.

"It's not going to take only an hour," she said. "The meeting might, but we're going to be talking about it the whole time after. We're talking about it now. That's not vacation."

"Then, why'd you come? You knew it would be like this."

She raised her hands for a moment, and said, "Look, Jason, I knew—I know—what this was—is, or whatever. It's fine. You're doing this for John."

"Yeah. That's it, isn't it?"

"How far are you planning to take this?" she asked. "This isn't for work. You're not getting paid. Your cop friend doesn't want you to do it." She stared straight ahead and rested her chin in her hands.

"He may say he doesn't, but he knows I can do what he can't."

"Which is?"

"I can talk to Rick without, say, having to get permission from the courts or the FBI or anybody else. I'm just a regular guy, going to talk to a friend who's in jail. I'm doing it for John. If it helps Brad, then so be it."

"Great, but I don't know why you do so much for him. He's a fucking vampire. He should be able to do things for himself." Her tone had shifted in a direction I didn't like. "You're acting like his Renfield or something."

"You went below the belt on that one," I said.

"It's true, Jason. He might think he needs you, but he's a—"

"He's a what?" I asked. "A vampire? You said that already."

She counted off on her fingers, "First, he's an adult. Second, I'm pretty sure he's rich. Third, he's not even in town. And fourth, yes, he's a goddamned vampire. He can't be killed, he—"

"We don't actually know that. Like I told you, we've never really tested it."

"He's been alive for decades and he never fought in any wars or anything? What else do you know about him?"

"He told me he was too sick to go to boot camp or get drafted before Korea. I know he had a wife a long time ago, but she died of cancer," I said.

She furrowed her eyebrows, and replied, "Really? What happened? That seems like something you'd mention."

I slapped the steering wheel and said, "Because you barely know him, and it's not your business. He doesn't really talk about her much. Her name was Maria. All he's ever told me is that it was cancer. There's one picture of them he keeps out, but I don't really know anything else, okay?"

"Jesus," she said quietly, looking forward at the road. "That almost explains some things."

"Well, yeah," I said, nodding. "But, I don't really know all the details. It's not like he refuses to talk about anything, but he just doesn't bring it up. Or, he makes it sound like there's just not much to tell. I don't interrogate him every time I see him."

She turned to face me, bracing herself on the dashboard with her right hand.

"Jason, that doesn't make it okay. I think there's something going on with him that he's not telling you."

"Like what?" I asked.

"Well, what about his parents? Did they just leave him that house and a bunch of money, or what?" she asked. "And where does he get his blood?"

"He has deals worked out with a couple of blood banks, I think. The rest of it, I'm not totally sure about," I said. "I know he's from Texas. The house is owned by a friend. I checked into that. He lives there so he doesn't have to pay taxes or collect Social Security or any of that. It keeps him under the radar." I thought back to my visit to City Hall and the name I had seen on the property's file—Adrian Reynolds.

I didn't want to think about it, but I knew she was right. I'd promised myself time and again that I'd ask John more about his life. I wanted more proof to fill in the gaps between his stories, but he'd always given me just enough to make me stop asking questions.

"When we get back, I'll ask him more," I said. "In fact, if you have any others, please just write them down and give me a list. Are you done now?" I asked.

She crossed her arms and stared at the road ahead, saying nothing more.

We spent the rest of the trip in near-silence, watching the trees and the traffic. I knew this might happen. When she agreed to stay with me, I knew she would take the first opportunity to pull me away from the situation.

It wasn't going to happen. We both knew it.

A few hours later, we checked into the motel in Lake City I'd booked the night before. As soon as we'd carried our bags into the room, I fell on the bed and stared at the ceiling. The light poured in from the open door, broken only by her dark shape leaning in the open doorway as she lit a cigarette. The orange dot moved from her face to her side, as the smoke escaped from her silhouette into the air outside.

"You know, you can light up in here," I said, raising my head from the bed.

"I know. Just give me a second." She turned her back to me as I stood. I moved to put my hands on her shoulders. She moved away, and turned to face me.

"Thing is," she began. "I like you. I'm probably different from the other girls you've been with. I don't like or want John. I'm not using you to get close to him. You're not playing wingman here. I don't want you to try to be him, and I'm not hoping you'll get there someday. You're you." I looked down before I could stop myself.

She put her hands on my face, and said, "That's all I want." I turned and walked towards the bathroom and turned on the water, not knowing what else to do. I unwrapped the plastic from a cup nearby and filled it, drinking the north Florida tap water in one gulp with my eyes closed. When I opened them, I saw her next to me in the mirror.

"Just think about that, okay?" she asked.

I said that I would, but I didn't want to in the least.

***

The ultraviolet lights in the prison's common area shined across his face. It rendered him even paler than I remembered. He was bald and thin, and sat limply on the metal stool across from my own. Steel bolts held both our seats and the table to the floor. He had the faintest shadow of a beard. It betrayed the color of his auburn hair. I remembered the stringy curls of wet, drugstore black when I last saw him.

The Florida penal system had scrubbed away most of the vampire, leaving a slight, lean young man in a blue prison jumpsuit. But, they couldn't take away his eyes—piercing and nearly unblinking. I couldn't read him. Maybe he was happy to see me. Maybe he wanted to kill me. Celebrity murderers like him had no shortage of fans, marriage proposals, and petitions to release them. I might have been his first visitor in months, or his hundredth.

Around us, inmates visited with their families. The white noise of all the conversations around us worried me. Everyone and no one might hear anything we said. Guards patrolled the perimeter of the room, and occasionally crossed through the rows of plastic tables. A few of the prisoners played cards or chess. I had never seen the inside of an actual penitentiary, and I hoped I'd only have to do it once.

"You need anything from the commissary?" I asked Rick. "Want a soft drink or something to eat?"

"Peace offering. Nice," he said.

"Were we at war?"

"No, but I haven't heard from you or John. Why did you wait so long?" He barely moved, his hands still on the table in front of him. A lone guard passed behind him, looking down before moving past the next table. Rick didn't seem angry. He'd sounded happier on the phone. I stole a moment between words to meet his stare.

"I imagine you probably have no shortage of visitors," I said.

"Not really." He tapped the table. "I added you to my list. It's a short list. You could've come," he said, pausing. "You could've come anytime you liked. You knew that." I didn't know that, but I didn't say so.

"We'll get to that," I said. "So, do you want anything?"

"Cigarette," he said, pointing at my pack on the table. I'd already lit one for myself, and it rested in the orange plastic ashtray nearby. I tapped the pack and held it out for him. He took it wordlessly, and then placed it between his lips. I flicked my lighter and held it up to him. He leaned forward and touched the tip to the flame, and then inhaled.

"Thank you, Jason," he said. The look in his eyes when he said my name frightened me. It was cold, direct, and aware—like he'd been thinking about me for a long time. "Now, pleasantries aside, what does John need my help with?" He said "with," not "for." His voice rose ever so slightly. It was as subtle as a dying heartbeat in the middle of a flat-line, but I heard it and he knew. He sat up on the stool and tilted his head slightly, as if to regain his composure.

"I can't talk about this in much detail, but there have been some, let's say, similar incidents in New Orleans recently," I said, and I cleared my throat. "If you know what I'm getting at."

"I do. I've heard. I read the newspaper."

"I'll leave it at that, then," I said. He blinked once, and held his eyes closed for a couple of seconds.

"Shouldn't the police be handling that? Isn't that what they do?" he asked.

"Yeah, they are. But, John might be getting the blame. We don't know yet, but he's an obvious suspect. That's why I'm here." I thought back to Sarah, who had confronted me at Jenny Dark's memorial. I wondered what Brad had told NOPD, and what the rest of the department knew.

He shrugged and said, "John is a vampire in a way that I am not. A person—a man—killed those women. That should be evident to anyone involved."

I leaned forward, gathering my courage. "Not everyone believes him, Rick. Someone is trying to bait him, or frame him, or—I don't know—something. They're not just out for blood. They were both women he knew."

Rick laughed quietly, and said, "Of course they were." He paused again. "I'm sure that the truth will come out and his name will be cleared shortly thereafter. Are you sure you need my help?" He coughed. And then, he coughed again and didn't stop until he was slumped over the table. I almost stood to get him a cup of water when he began laughing—low and short noises that continued for a minute while I watched. I didn't know what else to say. His pale, thin arms rested on the table with his head lying there between them. He twisted his arms to show their pale undersides. On his right, I saw a tattoo—a "V" in a circle, with curved fangs that extended out of the ring from the letter's top two points.

"V for Vampire," I thought, settling on the obvious—the symbol of, I could only imagine, a vendetta against everyone who wasn't like him.

I didn't know what kind of fit he was having—or if he'd just decided to stage one for my benefit. I stood to look for a guard, but he sat up quickly as if nothing had happened. He looked at me with his eyes slightly wide. I pointed at his forearm—at the "V" tattoo that adorned it.

"Nice ink," I said. He half-smiled and rolled his arm flat against the table.

"I'm so glad that you like it."

"Did you get it here?" I cocked my head backward. "As in, here."

"No," he replied. "Before we arrived in Baton Rouge. Those of us that were left did."

I imagined Rick and his friends taking the time to find a tattoo parlor in the rural wasteland between New Orleans and the state's capital. V for vampire, of course, but I knew it meant more. I briefly closed my eyes to see it fade there in red and yellow flashes, committing its simple design to memory.

"Those who were left?" I asked. "Was there someone else?"

He ignored my last question and continued, "We knew we would be apprehended in due time. We wanted something to symbolize our commitment to each other." He laughed again—that low, rhythmic pulse of beats that he interjected at odd intervals, set against the low rumble of inmate chatter around us.

I couldn't take the sound anymore. It was a subtle, knowing mockery that stood in front of an indistinguishable brew of lies and truth. He wanted to confuse me. He wanted to amuse himself. He had nothing better to do. I faked tough.

"You're playing games, Rick. What do you want? Cup of coffee? Another cigarette? Do I need to sneak you a girly magazine or something? Quit with the games and just tell me what it is you want. I have questions, and you may be the only one that can answer them."

His smile dropped.

"I want John," he said, leaning forward. "I want him to visit me. I have questions for him, you see—so many questions, and ideas, and—"

"Not going to happen," I said, holding up my hand to wave away the request. "I told you—I don't know where he is. But, he needs your help." Then, without meaning to, I dropped my guard. "If you really care so much—you know what, though? Why do you care so much? What's he done for you?"

Rick still leaned forward. His demeanor had shifted. He needed something from me—from us—besides a cigarette and some time to talk about vampires. He had wanted me to visit all along, and not just to manipulate me.

"He made us a promise that night," he said.

"You mean the night we all met? You mean when you left the club and went to John's house?"

He nodded, and looked at me with wide, eager eyes, and said, "And, I've written him so many times since then. All I've ever asked was for him to keep that promise."

"Wait," I said, leaning across the table. "What did you write him? What did he promise you?"

Rick sat back on the stool and closed his eyes. He sat there, but unmoving for a few seconds, before he finally spoke.

"He made a promise to five of our six. And, we needed a sixth once more."

"The six of you?" I asked. But, Rick would not answer.

***

I sat in my car, unsure of whether to listen to the news or another CD during the twenty minute drive from the prison to the motel. Rick had just made me question everything I knew or remembered about the night we met. Something had happened while I was at the police station. According to my incarcerated friend, John had promised them something before they left his home—just in time to dodge the police. And, Rick had been writing him ever since. John had never mentioned that to me. And there were, from what he said, six of them at some point. I knew damn well that

I had counted five—Rick in the club, and the four kids outside the door. John had lied to me about at least two things. The hot mixture of suspicion and anxiety swelled from my stomach to my head, drying out my mouth. I rested my head on the steering wheel and closed my eyes. After only a minute, I looked up and twisted the rearview mirror so that I could see my eyes.

"Get a fucking grip," I whispered.

With no music playing, I drove to the motel. I would pick up Maureen and take her to dinner. There, we would drink a little too much, and the story would tumble out into the space between us. I didn't know if explaining it to her would help, but it felt like a start.

I used the brass key to enter the room. The tan door opened with a hard push and a low suck. The shower ran in the small bathroom next to the sink, with only the light above it to faintly illuminate one side of the room. At nearly six o'clock, the sun's light had faded. I sat at the table near the window and lit another cigarette there in the dark. Since John's girls had been murdered, I'd smoked enough to give my cancer a case of its own. The silver ashtray waited within arm's reach, and I tapped the gray detritus off the tip. I stared at the light above the sink and puffed. The water stopped. After a minute, Maureen stepped out of the shower wrapped in one of the motel's white towels, with her back to me.

"Why don't you turn on the light?" she asked, in a low throaty tone. I reached the lamp by the bed and switched it on. She laughed and suddenly opened her towel in front of me like a City Park flasher to show her small breasts and the brown clump of hair between her legs. She stuck her tongue out before covering herself. I saw the plastic cup filled with amber liquid next to the coffee maker. She picked up her drink and took a long sip before joining me at the table.

"What was that for?" I asked, smiling.

"Thought you might like it after being in a roomful of cons." She raised the cup and drank from it again. "They have a liquor store down the street. I grabbed a bottle of bourbon and some ice from the machine. You want one?"

With grave emphasis, I said, "Yes." I stood up to take the cup she'd filled. She wrapped her arms around me for a second and squeezed hard, pressing her cheek against my chest.

"You're in a better mood," I said.

"Yeah. Let's not talk about it, please." I sighed, and she looked up at me. "What's wrong?" she asked, looking up at me.

I shook my head with my eyes closed as I sipped the drink. "I don't want to talk about it yet. Something that Rick told me." The relief of the drink flooded through me.

"Tell me over dinner?" she asked.

"Brilliant idea."

***

We settled on a chain steakhouse of the sort that one finds in small Southern towns. With visiting hours over, the families of inmates filled the dining area to fill up on cheap cuts of meat and fried onions. I'd never prided myself on wearing a suit at the wrong time, but I promised myself I'd never wear a tank top to dinner, much less with a baseball cap. Maureen had even changed hers in favor of a black shirt with silver buttons down the front. She and I—punk girl and goth boy—drew a few stares on our way to the booth in the back. The waitress, whose obsequious greeting identified her as Linda, escorted us past the faux wood paneling adorned by autographed pictures of country singers. I watched Linda's curly blonde ponytail bounce against the back of her green polo shirt, as she adjusted her glasses. We were just customers to her, and two more people to serve before her shift ended. Maureen and I had both forgotten how different the world outside of New Orleans could be. But for all the stares, no one said anything. Linda seated us in a booth in the smoking section and asked for our drink order.

"Bourbon," I said. Maureen held up two fingers, wordlessly.

Linda nodded, and said "Two bourbons coming right up." She walked away with her notepad in hand.

"So, what happened?" asked Maureen.

"Not yet," I said, holding up a finger. "I want my drink first. I want a couple of drinks first." She leaned back a little, and eyed me. "It's going to take a bit to organize everything in my head. It's about John."

"Yeah?"

"I think he might've lied to me about some things—like, they could be big things."

"Go figure," she said, slapping the table with one hand and resting her chin in another.

"Wait," I said, holding my hands up. "Keep in mind, this all came from Rick."

Before Maureen could respond, Linda set a tray at the end of our table and placed the glasses of bourbon in front of us, one at a time. I thanked her, and she asked, "Y'all know what you'd like for dinner? Want to start with an appetizer?" We hadn't even looked at the menus yet.

"Just give us a second," I replied. As she nodded and walked away, I opened the menu and looked up at Maureen. "Let's just order first and then we'll get into it." We ordered more bourbon from Linda—"planning ahead," I called it—and a plate of spinach and artichoke dip. By the time the steaks came, we were three drinks in and laughing about nothing. Maureen cut into her meat and put a small piece in her mouth.

Still chewing, she said, "Now, tell me about John and Mr. Murder."

"Rick? Yeah, okay. I told you the story about the club and how we met him, right?"

"Yeah," she replied with a no-shit nod, still cutting her meat.

"At the club, as far as I knew, there were five of them—Rick, and four others waiting outside. John and I didn't want them to run off before the police got there, so he told them he'd take them in or something. It was just a lie to get them back to his house while I got the police. With me?"

"I remember," she said, before she sipped one of the glasses of ice water that Linda had brought with our third drink.

"I went to the station. When I finally got to John's place, the kids had left."

"And, you're not sure why. You told me all that at Pirate's Alley," she said.

"Right. John never really got into it. He just said they got scared and took off. I assumed they figured out what was going on." I looked down at my food, because I knew what she'd say.

"And, you never asked him why. I remember that, too."

"I did," I said, shrugging a bit. "When we talked about it more, he said the same thing—like maybe they were in too deep, or heard the police coming or something. God only knows. That's not all, though."

"What else?" she asked, flicking her eyes towards the ceiling.

"Rick has been writing to John."

"What? Like writing letters?" she asked.

"Yes—lots of them. But, he says John hasn't answered him." She picked up her knife and cut another piece of meat, before putting it in her mouth.

"That's not weird," she said. "I mean, you know, that happens. Prisoners write people. Charles Manson wrote letters to the attorney that put him away."

"Vincent Bugliosi," I said. "You're right. He did. But," I continued, "John never said a word about it—not one." I looked down at the bleeding ribeye on my plate, the red juice overtaking the potato I hadn't yet touched. "I should probably eat this," I said.

"Makes sense," she said, glancing at her plate. She'd been cutting away at the sirloin and eating the entire time, listening to me.

"Well, my buzz is gone," I said.

Maureen waved to Linda with two fingers in the air. I saw the waitress nod and turn towards the bar. I didn't want to think about John's lies—real or imagined—without a drink in my hand.

I swallowed my food and continued. "There's a little bit more to it, though."

"Like what? She asked. I turned my forearm towards her.

Pointing to it with the knife, I said, "He had this tattoo right there. It was sort of a 'V' in a circle with a couple of points on it. He said they got it on the way to Baton Rouge to, like, symbolize their commitment to each other."

"V for vampire, I assume?" she asked, sipping her drink.

"Yeah. Pretty obvious," I said.

"So, maybe you need to tell your cop friend to look for the missing guy with the same tattoo," she said.

"Wouldn't work," I said, shaking my head. "Rick said something about this sixth person being gone by the time they got inked. I think they wanted John to replace him, or something."

"And, you think the sixth guy is the one who killed Raven and Jenny Dark," she said. "Maybe he got away or something. You should probably tell Brad that."

"I know," I said. "I will. But, I have no idea if Brad's still a friend or just a cop." I said. "But, I get that you'd rather I just drop the whole thing and leave it to him."

She looked down at her food and then back at me. "I also said that I'd stick with you. Remember when I called you in the morning a few days ago?"

"What about in the car today?"

"I'm sorry about that," she said, looking at the wall. "I was in a mood. It was early. Maybe I'm getting my period or something. I don't fucking know. This is just all a lot to take in."

"I'm sorry, too," I said. "I didn't mean to lose it for a second. Being around John has just been kind of overwhelming for the past couple of years. I know there's a lot I still need to ask him, but he really just sweeps you up. He's got a kind of thing about him that makes you just want to go along with it."

"Charisma," she said, sipping her drink. "He's definitely got that." I firmly grabbed her wrist and looked at her in the eye, cold and straight, as if I might admonish her again about the morning drive.

She scowled defensively for a second before I laughed and said, "Let's talk about anything else!"

The conversation drifted freely elsewhere, as the bourbon regained its hold and we floated away to restaurants we'd eaten at, people we knew in the Quarter, and anything else but vampires. In time, we paid our bill and drove across the street to the motel.

There, we climbed into bed and had the drunken out-of-town sex we'd promised each other. We whispered sweetly there in the dark, and even laughed a little more. In time, she fell asleep across my chest.

***

Sunday, October 12, 1997

We drove back the next morning. Maureen didn't try to make me discuss John at all. Still, I didn't like recalling the things she'd said. I'd never seen myself as John's lackey—only his friend and his saner half, although "partner in crime" had been thrown around the Crypt a time or two.

I didn't speak much to Maureen during the drive, though. She asked me if I was okay a couple of times, and I said that I was. More than anything, I felt like the situation had reached a point where I couldn't walk away if I wanted to. If Rick had told me the truth, then someone from his group had escaped along the way. Maybe I hadn't seen all of them at the door that night, with their huddled group blurred by the rain and the darkness. But, the image hit me hard again—Rick inside and four dirty kids, gathered in the rain. And in the news, the State Police had removed five of them from the motel room—one a corpse, bled out in the bathtub by her hungry friends.

I knew what I had seen. No amount of second-guessing could change that. And, John knew more than he'd let on. That part hurt the most. I would confront him, I knew, but I couldn't until he called me. I'd always hated waiting, and the bottomless uncertainty made it worse.

When I finally entered my apartment at about half past seven, I saw a message on my answering machine, with the red "1" blinking from across the room. I set my keys on the table. I'd dropped Maureen off, and she'd promised to call the next day. I hadn't written in a while, and I swore that I would hole up for a couple of nights and churn out enough pieces to pay the rent. But, all of my plans faded away as soon as I saw that "1" and heard John's voice on the tape.

"Jason, it's me. You know who. Looks like you're not home. I'm still gone, but I will call you back again tomorrow around seven. It's Sunday right now. If I miss you again, I will try again the next night at the same time. I hope you are well."

I looked at the clock. I had just missed his call, and he'd left no second message.

"Damn it!" I yelled to no one but the walls of my apartment.

I wanted to sleep. I didn't want to endure the time waiting for his call. But, I had to write. I took my shirt off and laid down on my bed. Rather than sit at the computer with a cup of coffee and an ashtray, I picked up a notebook and a pen off the nightstand, and just began a free-flow scribble of ideas. I wrote and crossed out topics for columns. Would it be, I asked my notebook, the rise of cover charges for dive bars masquerading as nightclubs? Could I actually write a thousand words about the state of safe sex among twenty-somethings in New Orleans? Or, would I compile a top-ten list of drunken chicanery I'd witnessed on Decatur? Would I weave those tales to make a grand point about responsibility in a city with enough booze to power a train? I drew a thick, black line through every one of those and at the bottom of the page, wrote only "JOHN" in large block letters. I would write about John.

After an hour-and-a-half of rambling free association, the pages looked like something between a journal entry and a scattered prose poem of notes, boxes, stars, and words underlined and circled. It wasn't a story or even anything I'd show to another person. And, it was nothing that I could sell. But, I felt better after I set the pen down on the nightstand. I'd written words like "impatient" and "dishonest" and "loss" over and over again. The notes and scattered bits of text made it almost as much a visual thing as a written one. I turned the notebook in my hands and, out of boredom, tore out the five pages.

In the other room, I laid them flat on my round dinner table. They overlapped each other to form an amorphous, jagged shape. I traced around the edges of jumbled nonsense with a red pen, drawing a formless blob. It wasn't anything recognizable. It could've been an amoeba or a wad of gum on the pavement.

I still didn't want to wait for John's call any more than I had before, but the absurdity of it all made me smile. I reached for the half-empty bottle of bourbon on the ledge between my kitchen and the dining area. I stared at the bottle and wondered if I should just take it straight from the source. I shook my head and went to the kitchen for a glass of ice.

Pouring the drink, I considered the situation. Two girls were dead. Someone killed them to send a message to John—or possibly frame him, but I no longer believed that. My only lead was rotting in a Florida prison. I knew he wanted to see my friend, and it forced me to believe that he might have nothing to do with the murders. He hadn't threatened me or led me to believe anything else might happen. He was not the angry convict I'd imagined, but a lean and lonely young man—desperate, addled, and sad.

"And, he's the only fucking clue I have," I said to no one, raising my glass—me, not a detective but a drunk writer in a town full of drunks. There just weren't enough decent writers to overshadow my efforts. Right at that minute, I didn't hate myself for drinking as much as I did. I sure as hell deserved it, I thought, right at that moment. I took a firm sip and set the glass back on the table.

I held my head in my hands for a minute. I looked at the bottle and the glass again through the spaces between my fingers. I had to call Brad tomorrow and tell him what

I'd learned. I owed him that much. There were six kids in Rick's group. They all probably had the same tattoo. Rick had written letters to John. And knowing Brad, I couldn't sit on evidence so that I could play detective. He stood as my only link to NOPD's own investigation. I wondered if they'd even found anything. I'd checked the papers a few times and seen nothing

I laughed again and looked down at the collage of notebook paper in front of me. I thought about taping it together, getting it framed, and calling it art. I wondered who would buy it. I raised my glass again, toasting no one, before I downed the remaining bourbon in a gulp. I stumbled into my bedroom and turned off the lamp. I fell asleep across my bed with my glasses on.

***

Monday, October 13, 1997

When I woke up, morning had passed to early afternoon. I wished I could sleep until John's call woke me at seven. But, I forced myself out of bed to write something that might actually make money. I took all of my rejected article ideas from the notebook pages on the table and typed them. I made myself write, knowing full well that I would likely create the same piece on each subject and not particularly care. Two hours in, at around three, the phone did not ring, but my doorbell did. I stood and glanced down at my bare feet and briefly considered putting on shoes. The bell sounded again, and I stopped.

Visions of vampire assassins flashed across my imagination and I wondered if Rick Fremont might have sent someone to kill me. I was, apparently, his best hope for reaching John again—his unanswered letters aside—so it seemed doubtful. The knock sounded again.

"Jason? You home?" the voice asked. I unlocked the deadbolt and opened the door. Maureen stood there, and then extended her arms for a hug.

"Hey," I said, nodding.

"Hey. Feeling better?" she asked, wrapping her arms around me and looking up with a smile. She stood on her toes and kissed me.

"A bit," I said. "John tried to call while we were gone. He's supposed to call back tonight around seven."

"What have you been doing all day, besides waiting for the phone to ring?" she asked, walking past me toward the living room.

"Sitting in the kitchen sink," I replied, as I closed the door and turned to follow.

It took her a moment to remember the song. "Aren't you only supposed to do that at ten-fifteen on a Saturday night?" she asked.

"Anytime is a good time for The Cure," I said. "I was writing. I need to get some pieces churned out to make the rent. Playing private detective doesn't pay much." She sat down on my couch with a great flop, and landed on her side.

With her eyes closed, she asked, "You need me to go then?"

"Nah. I could use the company," I said. "You can keep me from crawling the walls. I have to get this stuff done, though. If you want to watch a movie or something, go for it." She stood and walked to the kitchen.

"Got anything to drink?" she asked from the kitchen.

"Yeah, there's some gin in one of the cabinets, and a bottle of bourbon on the table," I said loudly, looking over my shoulder. I paused for a moment and saw the bottle there. It sat there quietly, and nearly empty. I didn't remember drinking that much. Before I could think about it any further, Maureen walked out with the bottle and a glass with some ice in it. She looked at the single tumbler in her hand.

"Shit. Do you want one? I should've asked back there," she said. I rolled my eyes. Maureen smiled again with a wide mouth and shook the glass of ice, as if to say, "You know you want to."

Instead, she said, "Don't make me drink alone."

"In the middle of the day while I'm halfway through the job that sort-of pays my bills? No, I'm going to pass," I said, walking to the kitchen for another cup of coffee.

Hurrying past her and her drink with my mug, I said, "Watch a movie or something." For about twenty more minutes, I wrote another quick editorial about strip club etiquette. Don't stand too close to the stage with less than a five. Don't talk for too long if you aren't buying a lap dance. Be careful about buying drinks. I recounted what I could and made up the rest. And, I hated every word of it. It was all the same shit. I wrote fluff, dreck, useless editorials, and worse. It was all observational quips, stories from bars, and life lessons obvious to anyone over twenty-one, meant to be read quickly by bums too cheap to buy a real newspaper.

"Fuck this," I said out loud.

Ten minutes later, Maureen and I were on the sofa with the bottle and another two glasses on the cherry wood coffee table in front of us, laughing about nothing in particular.

***

I woke up a few minutes after seven to the phone ringing, still leaning on Maureen across the futon.

"It's John!" I yelled, jumping up to find the phone. I picked it up with a short "Hello" as Maureen looked around, confused. She looked unsure of where she'd awoken.

"Jason, it's me," he said. A million little accusations crowded my mind. But, my questions would come first. I sat down at the table and lit a cigarette.

"How's it going?" I asked.

"Well enough, with all things considered," he answered. "It has been quiet. I can't tell you where I am, but can I assure you that I am safe."

"Never thought you weren't," I said, taking a drag off of the freshly lit cigarette. "Is that all?"

"This time, I'm afraid so."

"Any plans to join us here in Wonderland again?"

"Eventually," he replied. "I have to know if it is safe first. I assume you or Brad will tell me when that's the case. Is it?"

I rolled my eyes. "Not right now, I don't think." I knew I wouldn't get anything more out of him if I didn't say something. "Listen, I need to ask you about some things."

"All right," he replied.

"I, uh, visited Rick. I mean, I went to see him in prison."

He didn't say anything for a minute, and then he asked, "How did that go?"

"He told me some things that were kind of interesting," I said. "For instance, he told me there were six of them—not five. Did you know about that?"

"No, I did not," he replied. "There were only five at the house that night. Did he tell you anything about this sixth person?"

I shifted a bit and looked at Maureen. She had laid down again and closed her eyes. Her pale stomach peered out in the space between her t-shirt and jeans. The bottle hadn't moved. I thought for a moment about what else to say.

"No, nothing," I said. "They all got this tattoo of a 'V' in a circle before they hit Baton Rouge, but this guy wasn't with them. Maybe it's all bullshit. I don't know. But, there was more."

"Go on."

"Rick told me that you made some kind of promise to them before they left that night. He also said that he's been writing to you about whatever that was. What did you tell him?" I asked. "And why didn't you tell me he tried to contact you?"

He was silent for another moment. "My god," he started. "Jason, listen—I panicked that night. I realized that if the authorities found their group at my house, they might have discovered what I am and probably arrested me as well—maybe even you. I told them that I could sense that the police were coming. I said that if they departed I would meet them in Baton Rouge and turn them."

"Turn them? Into what? Like you?" I asked.

"Like me."

I stood up, and said, "So, you just changed your mind at the last minute? You sent those kids back on the run, hoping they would just believe you? You remember that they bled out one of the girls when they got there, right? What would've happened if they hadn't listened?"

I stopped for a moment, thinking about what else to say. I wanted to hurt him. "They could've stayed in New Orleans or escaped to Christ knows where," I said. "They could've killed even more people. And, Brad found out about you anyway. Does that even mean anything to you?"

"It does. It does. And, I do regret what happened to that little girl. But, I knew they would be caught. I told Brad soon after what I knew, and he agreed to send the information on to the State Police."

"Did you tell him that you sent them away?" I asked.

"I did not," he said. "I only said that they had departed of their own volition. And, they were caught."

"All's well that ends well, right?" I asked, still standing. Maureen opened her eyes and looked at me. I'd awoken her.

She sat up straight and mouthed the word "What?" at me. I ignored her question to continue telling off John. "You covered your own ass and it doesn't matter because the rest of us will be dead one day, right? Let me ask—have you always lied to me like this to me? Did you lie to me about Maria too, or is this a new thing you've taken up?" I wanted to hurt him so much.

"Jason, I…" He trailed off. He knew I'd caught him. I sat down again, knowing that I had more to ask him before he hung up on me. "And the letters? What has Rick been writing to you about? Can you be honest about that, at least?"

"Yes, absolutely" he said. "They were nonsense Jason—just random letters strung together in paragraphs."

"What? Like a code?" I asked.

He spoke quickly, as if trying to compensate for his earlier admission. "I thought that at first. For a while, I tried looking them over. I didn't see anything in them, and I never answered."

He breathed again with a muffled rush into my ear.

"Where are they?"

"The desk at my house," he replied. "Why?"

"You know why," I said. Then, I hung up the phone.

Chapter 11

Monday, October 13, 1997 – Night

The courtyard outside of John's house sat empty, save for his black iron chairs and table. Cigarette butts soaked in rainwater filled the ashtray there, surrounded by wet leaves and fat drops from an afternoon shower. Maureen and I had missed most of the day, asleep on the couch before John called. My friend would never allow me to visit his house alone, but I couldn't have cared less. Outside of my first evening there, and the first night we met Brad, I had never been any closer than the gate. John always insisted on meeting outside or somewhere else.

He had also given me a set of keys after our first few meetings, though, with the understanding that I only use them if and when he told me. He knew I could get inside whenever I wanted, but he trusted me. We entered and I quickly locked the gate. We walked straight to the iron door that protected the side entrance. I unlocked both and shoved the keys into my pocket.

Maureen followed me into the dark hallway, closing the door behind us. She tried to turn on the first light switch, but I grabbed her hand.

"Not right now," I said. "The police might be watching his house." I reminded myself that, outside of Brad, I had no idea if the police even knew John's name.

"How the fuck are we supposed to see?" she hissed. "They would've seen us just come in."

"You can talk normally. If they can't hear us walking through here and looking around, they aren't going to hear us talking. I still don't want to attract any more attention."

"Okay, then how are we going to see what we're doing?" she asked, rolling her eyes.

I picked up a bronze candelabra on a side table in the hallway. The candles appeared relatively new and not like the antiques I'd expected. I reached into my coat pocket for a cigarette lighter. One by one, I lit the white tapers, and saw Maureen's face flicker with shadows. With the space around us illuminated, I saw the picture of John and Maria in Cancun.

"Who's that?" Maureen asked. "She looks happy."

"That's Maria," I said. "She was his wife. I think I told you about her."

"Jesus, he looks so normal," she said, as the flames reflected on the glass covering their portrait. "It even looks like they took it during the day."

"Yeah, that's what I was thinking. I'm pretty sure he hadn't changed over then." I looked down the hallway, but I couldn't see more than a few yards ahead of us. "Let's get moving. We don't want to be here for too long."

The wooden floor creaked beneath our feet. We passed a few more pictures I hadn't seen—one or two others of Maria, and an older couple that I presumed were his parents.

"He's been decorating," I said. "These weren't here before."

Turning the corner into the den, we passed more candles. The distinct, aged smell of John's house struck me again as we walked. I had dined there before, true, but I'd never seen his house in darkness. It reminded me so much of a grandparent's home, replete with lace, bronze oddities, and shelves of yellowing, musty books.

"Where's the desk?" Maureen asked.

"That way," I said, pointing to a hallway at the room's right. We turned another corner there into a small office. A streetlight near the window illuminated the room, enough that I blew out the candles and set the bronze holder on the floor. I didn't want to accidentally burn down John's house.

I stopped for a moment and looked around the space before me. A large desk sat at the far end of the room, opposite the doorway. More bookshelves lined the walls. At the center of his desk, I saw only a mechanical typewriter. I walked towards it, step by step, across a red oriental rug.

"Now, where would the letters be?" I asked aloud.

"He didn't tell you?" Maureen asked. She'd joined me at the room's center.

"No," I replied. "He doesn't even want us here. He already lied to me once. I want to see if he did again." I sat in the chair and started opening drawers.

"He said they were just bullshit," she said. I had told her everything on the drive over.

"Yeah, he did," I said, opening each drawer and holding the papers up to the streetlight's beams. "But if they were really just gibberish, why would he keep them?" She shrugged and made a don't-know noise as she paced back and forth. I continued searching through the yellowed pages—old bills, deeds, other letters, and the usual fragments of a life you'd find in a desk. But, I found nothing from Rick.

"Maybe he lied about where they were," she said.

"Nah," I said. "If he was going to lie he would've just told me he didn't have them," I said. "They're hidden."

"How do you mean?" she asked, leaning over my shoulder.

"He hid them on purpose, because he didn't want anyone to associate him with Rick—but, they're here. They're in the desk. But, they're not with the other papers. There has to be a catch or a latch or something."

She leaned back, looking down at me with a half-smile. "You think it's a puzzle or something? Like if we slide two knobs apart, it'll open?" I slid the chair back, and felt its wheels dig through the soft carpet. Just as quickly, I got down on my knees in front of the desk.

"Maybe," I said, peering at the desk's center face. There was no knob or handle to pull. A carved cherub peered back at me. I ran my hands over it, pushing its wings with my thumbs. Nothing happened. I opened all of the side drawers again. The same papers waited there. It all seemed plain enough. I pushed on the carved flowers that dotted the front of the desk, turned knobs, and shook it by its edges. I tried everything short of yelling out passwords.

I stood back and saw only the mahogany desk, no more than four feet wide. There were only so many places to hide something.

"I don't fucking know," I said, feeling stupid. "They're here." I turned to look at Maureen, but saw that she had left the study. Leaning out of the door, I called her name. The living room appeared as it had before, with its silence and its high, white walls. I clenched my fists—unafraid, but with no interest in exploring John's house alone. Turning to the dark hallway behind me, I called out to her again as I fumbled for my lighter.

Before I could speak or walk another step, Maureen emerged from another doorway at the end of the hall. A door to a bathroom sat open at the end, and I could hear the faint trickle of the toilet refilling. She'd slipped away to piss, and nothing more. Before I could say a word, she thrust one pale finger against her lips to silence me. She beckoned with her free hand. I put the lighter back in my pocket as I covered the space between us. There at the end, she pointed to, not a hallway, but a small flight of steps leading up to an attic door.

"What?" I asked, in a whisper

Speaking faintly and spacing her words, she said, "I just heard something."

I put my lips to her ear and replied, as quietly as I could, "What was it?"

"I don't know. But, it's coming from behind that door. There's something in there."

I raised the lighter again, and ascended the steps on my toes. I reached the door and pressed my ear to it. I heard nothing.

I turned to face her, and said, "There's nothing." Maureen jumped.

We'd both heard the hissing, feral noise on the other side of the door—and a knocking sound from deep inside the room.

"Does he have cats?" she asked. "It sounds like some kind of animal trapped in there."

I shook my head. Another knock sounded, and I reared back a bit. I gripped the dull brass knob and turned it in both directions. The door was locked, and I felt sure my own key wouldn't open it. John would have hidden the key as carefully as Rick's letters. For all I knew, they were in the same place. I carefully walked down the steps past Maureen.

"Where the hell are you going?" she asked.

"The desk," I said. I entered the room again and stood in its center. Right at that moment, I hated the desk more than another piece of furniture in the world. Maureen joined me there. Without a word, she walked up to the mahogany monolith and grabbed the typewriter. She lifted the heavy machine and set it on the rug. Then, she grabbed the surface of the desk by its edges. She lifted it up, and revealed a compartment beneath.

"It's like a school desk," she said, looking over her shoulder. "The top opens. They weren't exactly hidden."

"Hell of a puzzle," I said, rolling my eyes. I was surprised that it wasn't locked, but John rarely allowed anyone inside of his house—except for Raven, Jenny, me, Brad, and maybe some other women, I realized. Within the desk's four dusty corners, I saw everything I'd wanted and more. Rick's letters sat in a bundled stack, weighed down by a long and imposing revolver. It looked like a warning. I picked up the gun and held it in the light.

"What the fuck?" she asked. "That thing's a cannon."

".44 Magnum," I read from the barrel. The gun was heavy, and I switched open the cylinder to see all six rounds ready to go. "Jesus, John," I said, turning to her. "This thing's a Dirty Harry gun."

I placed the gun back in the desk drawer to look through the papers. Among the yellowing documents scattered in the drawer, the envelopes shone new and white. John had carefully opened each one, and they bore the familiar return address of Rick Fremont's penitentiary. Multiple passports and what looked like birth certificates sat neatly stacked in the space next to them, alongside a small green book bound in cloth. I picked it up and opened it. Even in the dark, I saw pages of handwriting. But, I couldn't read them.

In the opposite corner of the desk's center compartment, I saw a set of keys—an older one with a long stem and an oval head, and a few smaller modern ones. Maureen grabbed them, and held them in front of my face. She shook them and smiled.

"What the hell?" I asked, staring at the objects in front of me. I held the book up.

"What do you mean?"

"This seems wrong," I said as I picked up the passports and filed through them. Most had expired years before, but a couple bore current dates. They had different names on them, but most had John's picture. In each one, he looked different—bald in one, wearing a beard in another, and a third with the man as I knew him. The names followed no pattern—John Anzalone, Mike Trudeau, Randolph Todd, and others equally unremarkable.

"He never told me about any of this. I didn't get the impression he'd even left New Orleans much. And not all of these are him."

"What do you mean?" I opened one, and revealed a dark haired woman with yet another new name—Susan Wright.

"I think this is still Maria," I said. Maureen took the small booklet from my hand and opened it.

"It's expired," she said. "So, she had a passport before she died."

"When did it expire?" I asked. She turned to hold the passport in the moonlight.

"Shit. It expired in 1954. When did you say she died?"

"In the 1950s, but I'm not totally sure."

"He probably lied about that, too," Maureen replied. "Are the letters there?"

"Yeah," I said, picking up the stack. I pulled the first one out of the envelope and turned to the moonlight that fell across the room behind me. But, what I saw made even less sense to me. I muttered, undoubtedly, my forty-third "Fuck" of the evening as I clutched the sheet of paper in both hands.

"What is it?" she asked, as I held up one of the papers to the window.

"It's just what he said. It's gibberish. It's just a block of random letters."

"Is it a code or something?" She held her hand out for the sheet, and I gave it to her. She looked it over and shook her head. "I'd need more light and more time," she said.

"John didn't think it was when we talked on the phone. Knowing Rick, I don't know if it's anything useful, but it's got to be something more than gibberish." I looked back at the desk, and saw the other letters, still stacked with the revolver next to them.

Another knock echoed through the house, and one more animal shriek sounded from the attic. We both looked back at the door leading to the hallway.

"What do we do?" she asked.

I paced the room for a minute, thinking. We couldn't call Brad. If I told him that I'd snuck into John's house without telling him, we might be outside with our hands on top of a squad car. We either had to leave, or open the attic door. I already realized how much John hadn't told me about himself. All of it was bad, but I had to make sure he wasn't keeping something worse up there. I looked at the .44 and the keys, and then grabbed both of them. I set the stack of envelopes and the green book back in the open desk.

"You're going up there?" she whispered.

"Yeah," I said, double-checking the revolver to make sure it was really loaded. It was heavier than I'd expected. And, I hadn't fired a gun in my entire life. "I want to know what's up there."

"You're going to get us killed!" Maureen hissed.

With the revolver in my left hand and the keys in my right, I said, "No, I'm not. Whatever's in there, it's chained up or trapped. If it wasn't, it would be banging on the fucking door. It's coming from inside."

Guided by the moon's pale light from the living room, we exited the study into the hall. The knocking had stopped, I noticed, as I ascended the steps to the attic. Maureen stood behind me. At the door, I sighed and gripped the keys in my fist. I closed my eyes for a second before driving the largest one into the keyhole and turning it.

With a click, the lock gave way. I opened the door, holding the gun up, and its aged hinges creaked as it swung wide and away from us. Without stepping in, I looked across the space. Darkness veiled the entire room, but gave way faintly to the light behind us. I held up my free hand behind me to signal for Maureen to wait. I took one step when the bang sounded again, this time directly in front of me across the black expanse of the attic. As my eyes adjusted, I saw what looked like a bed—and at its end, the doorway's light flashed gold across a pair of eyes.

I looked back at Maureen and whispered, "There's someone on a bed."

She climbed the five or six steps between us and joined me in the doorway. The growling and hissing grew louder and louder from the bed, as the eyes flashed once more. I reminded myself that whatever it was clearly couldn't leave—and couldn't harm us where we were. I felt like an idiot for not grabbing one of the candelabras from downstairs.

I thought to turn back for one, when Maureen said, "Attics usually have lights, right?"

"Yeah," I said. I ignored her tone. "And there are no windows up here." I felt along the doorframe and found nothing.

Directly ahead, the faint outline of a bulb and chain dangled a few feet from the bed. I stepped forward before I could convince myself to do otherwise. I yanked the chain, and the attic flooded with light.

The woman—the creature—on the bed before me, screamed again and louder. Jaundiced and yellow, her dry, thin frame fought a tangle of sheets. Black, frizzy hair crowned her pointed face. Her lips peeled back to reveal long teeth in receded gums, with even longer canine fangs.

A blood bag was on the floor nearby, with its contents dribbling out of a needle attached to a long plastic tube. A rolling IV stand was toppled on the ground next to it. She had worked one hand free from the restraints that held her to the old bed. Her left wrist bled from where she had tried to bite through it, like an animal in a hunter's trap. But somehow, she had unfastened the strap that secured the cuff. I imagined her working it free with her teeth. At least she had the awareness not to bite off her own hand.

She had ripped the needle out of her right arm. With her free hand, she had already begun to remove the cuff on her other wrist. As I approached, she stopped pulling on the strap, and reached for me with long, brown nails. She hissed as I walked the few steps between us, but she could only reach for a few precious inches. A second set of straps bound her ankles to the rail at the foot of the bed.

"Jesus, she's a fucking vampire," Maureen said. She was right. Our newest discovery wanted blood. The blood bag had sustained her, but without the needle she had quickly begun to wither. Maureen walked in and stood next to me. "Who the fuck is this?" she asked.

"I think this is Maria."

"You mean, like, John's wife?" she asked, turning to look at me. "You mean the dead one?" She all but spat the word "dead" like it was a curse.

"I think so," I replied.

Maureen looked at the bed, and then back at me. Tears gathered in her eyes, and for a moment she struggled to speak.

"Why the fuck is he keeping her like this?" she yelled.

"I don't know," I said. I repeated those three words a couple of more times as I turned to face the door. "Keep your voice down. Watch her. I'll be right back," I said, as I ran downstairs. I quickly walked to the front hall and retrieved the picture of John and his wife. After lifting it off the hook, I returned to the attic. I held up the picture for comparison.

Maureen looked back and forth between the picture and the woman bound to the bed. "That's her," she said. "That's her." She wiped her eyes and her nose with the back of her hand. She sniffed hard and took a deep breath. "Okay—now, why do you think John's keeping her like that?" she asked, with her hands on my shoulders. "Is he some kind of serial killer or something? Look at her!" she said, pointing.

"Stop," I said. "Calm down."

"I am calm. I am absolutely fucking calm," she said. "Jason, this is not okay."

"Yes, I know," I said. "Look, she's obviously a vampire. She's not human at least. He hooked up the IV and left her here. Maybe he has someone else looking in on her."

"I thought you were supposed to do that kind of thing," she said, gesturing at the bed. "Don't you get it? She's not like him. He can't just keep someone up here like this." She grabbed the top of her head and breathed again. "You know what? It doesn't matter. She needs help. She needs a doctor or something."

"I don't think most doctors know how to treat this kind of thing. They don't teach vampirism at medical school."

"I guess he's not the only one, then," she said. "He lied to you—again."

"Yeah, apparently," I replied, turning my back to both of them. John had only let me come to the house twice. At that moment, I finally knew why. Maria hadn't died. She'd somehow contracted his disease, but it affected her in a way I couldn't begin to understand. She looked like a vampire out of the oldest stories—a hungry night creature that lived in a grave and consumed and transformed those around it. I wondered if John had bitten her, or if she'd caught it the same way he had.

I reminded myself of his words. He told me hadn't caught anything. He'd simply developed it.

"The bullshit just keeps stacking up," she said. I could hear the vampire woman groaning behind me. I told myself that she was no worse than a starving animal—frightened, hungry, and alone.

"We have to find a way to feed her," I said.

"Um, okay. How do you suggest we do that? Do you think she's going to let us near her?" Maureen asked.

"No, but the IV is out of her arm. I guess if we can get her other hand back in the cuff, we can put the lock back on. Do you think we can get the needle back in?" Maureen stood next to the bed and picked up the IV stand. She examined the needle. Blood dribbled on her hands and landed in small dots on her shoes.

"Uh, do you have a belt?" she asked. "If we can find a vein, I should be able to get it back in. But, Jason—we can't just stick it back in. We need gloves, and gauze, and tape, and like—"

"A first aid kit?" I asked.

"Yeah," she said.

With no other furniture in the room besides an empty chair, I blindly swept my foot under the bed a few times before kicking a tackle box. Bending down, I pulled it out and opened the lid. The whole time, I kept one eye on Maria. She just looked at me and made the same low growl.

The small shelves lining the box included all the items she'd mentioned, including a couple of pairs of gloves crammed into a small plastic bag. It even had a couple of spare needles with the butterfly-shaped plastic head on the end.

"You know how to do this?" I asked, setting the .44 down on the ground.

"My half-sister's a nurse, and I spent time on the streets."

"I'm not even going to ask," I said.

"You shouldn't," she replied, snapping on a glove.

***

I held Maria's bloody wrist back with a towel I'd managed to loop around it. I had to sit on the floor to keep enough weight on it. For a starving vampire, she was unusually strong. Her nails almost swiped my glasses off twice in the process. I watched Maureen struggle to fasten the cuff with a few utterances of "Hold fucking still" littered throughout. She managed to secure it, and I adjusted the length to keep her arm far away from her teeth. We bandaged the wound on her wrist where she'd tried to gnaw through. With the thick cuff in place, we effected a shoddy packing of gauze underneath it and secured the edge with tape. I would have failed nursing school, but it worked well enough.

We switched sides, and Maureen attached the needle to the line leading to the half-full blood bag.

"Take your belt off," she said. "Wrap it round her forearm and tighten it. I need a vein." I did as she asked, and sat on the ground to pull down on Maria's arm. With all my weight, I held her arm flat against the brass bed frame as she snapped and growled. Maureen quickly slapped the crook of her arm and waited a second.

"Anything?" I asked.

"Yeah," she said. "Actually, it's right there." She slid the needle in and motioned for me to move away. I relaxed my grip, and the blood streamed into Maria's arm. She seemed to calm down a bit—but not much. Maureen and I stepped back and looked at her. Her noises had lowered to a rhythmic, guttural moan. She knew enough to realize that she was being fed again. In a way, I felt good about myself.

"Something's not right," Maureen said.

"That's the understatement of the century."

"No, that's not what I mean," she said. She rolled the gloves off and walked to a trashcan near the door. "If she hadn't been fed in a long time, the blood bag would probably have had enough time to leak all over the floor. And her vein showed up pretty quickly. If you're dehydrated and low on blood, your veins shrink. She hasn't been like this for very long."

"You think someone was just here?" I asked, looking around the room.

"Yep," she said, from the corner. "Come see this."

"What?" I asked, crossing the room. We looked down in the trashcan to see a collection of discarded medical supplies in a red bag—gloves, needles, and bloody bits of gauze. "He probably has someone checking on her," I said.

"No, you don't get it," she said. She walked back to Maria's bedside and pointed at the wrist we'd just cuffed. "Anyone that knew what they were doing wouldn't leave her with her hand out like that. Someone undid the strap, and then left in a hurry."

"You don't think she pulled it out herself?" I asked.

"Look at her," she said. "She's like an animal. She was trying to bite through her fucking wrist. I don't think she would even know how to open the cuff."

"But why free her arm, then? Was he trying to set her loose or something?"

"I don't know." She pointed to the trashcan and the red bag inside of it. "If John has someone checking on her, he's not going to undo the strap and then leave her like that. Even if we caught him, it would be worse if she got out."

"That's a lot to presume," I said.

"Shit," she said. "Do you think he heard us and left?"

"If he did, he might still be here," I said. I scooped the .44 from off of the ground and headed down the steps. Maureen ran down after me as I turned the corner into the den.

"It's got to be the same guy!" she said.

"From Jenny's place—I know," I said. I held up the gun like I knew what I was doing. I didn't, but if he was still in the house I planned to figure it out. Someone had gone after two of John's ex-girlfriends, and now his wife.

But in the living room, there was nothing and no one to be seen. At the far right side, I saw the door near the bookcases. I'd always assumed it was a closet. I tried the knob and found it unlocked. A glass door to the outside hung open, revealing another set of iron bars, with a brick wall and an alley beyond. Sticking my head outside, I saw only trashcans and nothing else.

I turned to Maureen to say all that I'd realized. She held up a set of house keys.

"These yours?" she asked. "They were on the dining room table. You've got the ones from the desk, right?" I checked my pockets and found them, along with my own set.

"Yeah," I said. "I think those belong to our visitor. Can you check them?"

Without saying a word, she bounded to the front door. From the hall, I heard the rattling and fumbling of keys. She came back to the den. "House keys," she said. "Someone else has a set. He left them here when he ran out."

"How the fuck would someone get those?" I asked. "Can I see?"

She dropped them in my open hand, and I held up the two brass keys on a simple silver ring. A plastic tag hung on them with a wrinkled paper sticker. I found my lighter again and held it up to the label.

"What do you see?" Maureen asked.

"Jesus Christ, John," I said. When I read the word, I nearly threw them across the room.

"What? What does it say?"

"Spare!" I said, raising my hands in disbelief. "It says it's a spare key. Look at the sticker." I handed it to her and she held it up to the light.

"Yeah, this has seen some abuse," she said. "He must've kept this outside in a flower pot or under a mat or something. I guess the guy found it and used it after John left town."

I sat on the long ornate couch and rested my head in my hands.

"This is not good," I said. "Why the fuck would he keep a key outside like that? Listen, we have to take those and wait for John to call. We also need to get the letters and some of the paperwork out of the desk. I want to take a look at that book I found." I thought back to the small green volume I'd discovered.

"What do you want to do about Maria?" she asked. She knelt in front of me. She could see I was losing it.

"Leave her here," I said. Maureen started to speak, but I held up my hand. "I know how that sounds, but it's the best thing. It's the best thing for now, I mean. She's getting fed, and the guy can't get back in. We're coming back soon, anyway."

"What if he breaks in?" she said. "Like what if he just kicks in the door? If this is the same guy that killed Jenny, a lock isn't going to stop him."

"He can't," I said. "There are bars on all of the doors and windows. He'd be at it all night. He had to look for that key for a reason. I think she's going to be safe if we lock up and take this with us." I held up the keys and jingled them.

"Okay," Maureen said. "Shit. Okay. You sit here. I'll get everything." She departed, and I heard her steps up—and then down—the attic stairwell. I eyed the teak liquor cabinet against the wall. Maureen returned holding the letters and the green book.

"What are you doing?" she asked.

"I'm taking something," I said.

She smirked, and said, "Only you would think of booze at a time like this."

"He owes me," I said, kneeling in front of the open door. I withdrew a fifty-year-old bottle of Scotch. I didn't recognize the name. At that point, it might as well have been MacHooligan's or something. I closed the cabinet door and moved to leave. Maureen was already in the hallway, putting the picture of John and Maria back on the wall.

I drove us back to my apartment, saying little but to ask her in for a drink. In my apartment, I opened the Scotch and found two rocks glasses. I dropped a few ice cubes into each, before filling them with John's liquor. He had already brought me enough trouble for one evening. I would gladly confess to stealing the bottle after what we'd seen.

Maureen took the glass from my hand, with one leg folded up on the futon. We both sipped our drinks for a few minutes before looking at each other, with neither sure whom would speak first.

"Now, what did we just see?" she asked. I leaned forward and rested the glass on a coaster. My eyes darted to the two books resting on the coffee table—*Dracula* and *The Big Sleep*. It seemed like a fitting combination.

"John is a vampire," I said. "As far as I knew, he was the only one on Earth. He was married to a woman named Maria, who died of cancer in the 1950s. It is safe to say that Maria is not dead, and she is also a vampire."

"Yeah, but she's not like him."

"No, she isn't," I said. "He's been lying to me for two years and hiding her." I sipped my drink, and silently begged it for clarity. "He's keeping her alive with either his blood or someone else's—Christ knows. So, it's not some kind of—I don't know—he's not doing it to hurt her. She's sick or something."

Maureen stood up and put her hands on her hips, her eyes alternating between me and the floor. The hardwood at my feet shined as I looked down, too. We simply didn't know what to do. Too much was missing. I rested my face against my hands, clasped together as if praying to someone.

"We need John back," I said.

She turned her back to me for a moment. I knew what she would say next. I didn't know the words. But I knew the tenor, the tone, and the spirit of all she wanted to say. She turned to face me again.

"You think he's going to be honest with you this time?" she asked.

I knew she was thinking it, so I just said, "Well, he hasn't been so far. But, I've got enough to talk to him about." I pointed at the couch, hoping she would sit, and said, "Please?" She sighed and sat next to me. I felt worse than trapped. A couple of years ago, John had shown me that there was more to the world than I had ever known. But, I had taken what he said at face value. I believed that he was some oddity of nature and nothing more. I wondered how I could have been so blind. John's swagger, his wit, his money, and the thrill of his company—they'd drawn my eyes away from the obvious.

I looked back at Maureen and continued, "There are some really extraordinary people out there. Through genetics or whatever, they have super-strength, or they can hold their breath underwater for a long time, or even—"

"But, they aren't vampires," she said. "I'm not a biology student, but it seems like it would take more than a birth defect to make you need blood. There is a psychological condition where you want to drink blood, isn't there?"

"Yeah, but he doesn't have it," I said. "You've seen the fangs. He's not human—at least not like us." I almost wanted to grab a paper and pen and start making notes. It all seemed like too much to sort through. Hell, I needed a chart that covered an entire wall of my apartment. I imagined the windows papered in white as the growing dawn—and it was very, very late—shone through. But instead, I sat down again.

The Scotch began to creep to my head, and my thoughts floated outwards. Then, I asked a question—of both Maureen and myself—that I had never asked before that moment.

Chapter 12

Tuesday, October 14, 1997 – Early Morning

"Where does John get his blood from?" I asked, standing and raising my glass to Maureen.

She looked up at me with a raised eyebrow, and said, "I thought he used blood banks or something." She grabbed the bottle of Scotch and took a sip straight from the mouth. I didn't blame her.

"That's just it."

"What's it? He doesn't?" She stood and moved next to me.

"No—I mean, yes, he told me that he just buys it under the table from blood banks. But, think about it. How long could someone get away with that? It might work for a little while, but eventually people are going to ask questions."

"Couldn't he have, like, a network of people that know?"

"That's possible, but think about the numbers. How many people actually believe in vampires?" I asked.

"Not many," she replied. "I sure as hell didn't."

"Right—eventually, someone's going to start asking questions or just call the cops. He can't risk being exposed like that. If he has ten guys that all sell him blood, one or two of them are almost guaranteed to turn him in." I was on to something. "No ring of doctors or clinic workers is going to hold it together for that long." I took a quick sip of the drink. "So, if he probably doesn't have a network of people helping him, then that means he has—"

"Just one," she said. "He has someone who knows what he is, and believes him enough not to tell anyone. Fuck." She sat down again. "He has a guy." I sat next to her, almost falling into the cushion and nearly spilling my drink.

"That's what it looks like," I said. "But who?"

"It would have to be someone that could, you know, get at the blood bags without getting caught, and then keep doing it. So, it's probably not some clinic worker. A guy like that would just get fired after a while."

"That means it's a doctor or someone higher up," she said, refilling her glass. "It's someone who understands his condition enough and who isn't likely to get caught."

"Again, yeah, someone who knows and understands blood—and believed John so much that he'd risk his own career to help him."

"But who?"

Unable to sit still, I got up again, pacing in a circle, thinking out loud, "Maybe it's the same guy he has checking on Maria. Remember all the stuff in the trashcan? You can't just leave a patient with no attendant like that for days on end."

She stood next to me again, and said, "Okay, let's think about this. Someone comes during the day, so it doesn't look weird."

I imagined Someone—a man whose face I could not see—entering the house.

She continued, "And, he takes care of Maria. He feeds her and cleans her, and then he leaves." I saw Someone enter that house and retrieve the same keys from the same desk. This man would turn to the attic stairwell and enter the darkened room. He would pull the chain by the light bulb and wish Maria a good morning.

From underneath the bed, he would remove the first aid kit we had found. He would open it, and put on a pair of gloves. Then with a bucket of water retrieved from the bathroom downstairs, he would clean her body. She would allow this, because she knew that Someone fed her. Then, he would change her needle and the attached blood bag. He would pat her on the head, turn out the light, and leave the house.

She would allow this, because she knew him. John would have taught her not to fear Someone who would visit her every day. But, she would fear the man who came that night—the one who did not know how to care for her. And, he wanted not to give—but to hurt her, to unbind her, and to do what else? We did not know.

"We're sure this caregiver is not going to be the same one we interrupted, right?" I asked.

"It's not the same guy," she said. "Anyone trained to take care of her wouldn't leave her like that. If we'd caught John's guy, then he would've either lied or shot us or anything else."

"There have been two people visiting that house," I said. "And the one that John doesn't know about forgot the keys when he heard us tonight."

She turned to me, and said nothing for a few seconds. Then, she stood up and faced me. "He killed Raven, and then Jenny, and now he's after Maria," she said.

***

We drank and debated for another hour. So many questions remained. If John couldn't transmit his condition, then we had no idea how Maria contracted hers. We'd almost seen the man who had troubled us so thoroughly. The questions formed and faded and swam with the Scotch.

I excused myself to use the bathroom. After a long and glorious release, I stared at myself in the mirror. Stubble covered my head and face. I needed to shave both. Bags had formed underneath my eyes. I opened the bathroom door, and saw John's bottle resting on the table in the next room. My empty glass sat next to it.

When I crossed into the living room, I saw Maureen asleep on the futon. Stepping lightly, I took the bottle, my glass, and the green book we'd found. One more clue with more questions of its own. It had rested atop the pile of letters Rick had sent to John.

I needed to read all of them, but I thought, "One thing at a time." I sat on the edge of my bed and poured another splash into the glass. Lying back, I opened the green book. I'd expected a list of financial data, or travel expenses, or more puzzles—anything else than what I found.

It was a journal.

It bore no title page and only a name written on the inside: "Nicholas Marston, USMC." Most of the entries were no more than a few sentences long. The handwriting varied in size, much of it overly large, and looked more like scratch and scrawl in places.

And so, I read.

***

26 Nov. 1950

Fucking cold here. Couple of pens froze & burst already. Been in country since June when we flew out from Pendleton. Made Sgt. right before we left, so makes things a little easier here. Less shit work, but still just as cold. 2/5 Easy Co. and all of 1MarDiv operating under the Army's X Corps. Sounds like something out of a goddamn comic book. Keeping this so the wife can have something to read when I get back. Not exactly easy to get mail out from here!

27 Nov. 1950

Got some excitement today. Easy Co. (2/5 "Retreat Hell!") was in on the attack on the Chinese PVA here at Yudam-Ni. Word is that 2/5 might join up with the rest of 1MarDiv in the next few. The warming tents help, but you can only go in for about 20 mikes and we have to take turns in groups of six. Sometimes they have a pot of slum cooking—just leftover C-RATs and canteen water, kind of like stew. Really just looks like shit. Sometimes tastes that way.

29 Nov. 1950

Took an extra C-RAT in exchange for my time in the warming tent. Cold doesn't bother me as much as some of the DDs. They think I'm crazy. Some of the guys are losing it. A few stopped shitting. Can't imagine how that feels. Guys using packing tubes from mortar shells to piss in. It freezes as soon as it comes out, though. Most of Easy Co. taking it all okay though.

30 Nov. 1950

They're calling the path through Chosin a "strategic retreat." I never thought you'd have to fight just to run away! Word around the camp about moving out to 1MarDiv spreading like wildfire. The sooner we move, the sooner we get the hell home. But moving means shooting. Without much to do, Marines always start bitching. You think more about chow, rack time, and freezing. Makes it worse to think about it.

2 Dec. 1950

News finally. 2/5 has been ORDERED to meet up with 1MarDiv, just like we thought. They keep saying "home by Christmas" but I have my doubts. We can finally grow beards now. Hard to shave in the ice & snow, so why not? Good-bye, Yudam-Ni and FUCK YOU. Finally getting used to writing with gloves on and when I can't feel the damn pen.

***

On December 2nd, the ink changed to blue. The handwriting became more legible and assured. Closing the book for a moment, I turned it over in my hands. The book measured about six inches across and nine inches long—narrow enough to shove into a deep pocket. The pages Marston had written looked dog-eared and wrinkled, compared to their blank counterparts. About half of the book had been used. The green cloth cover frayed at its edges, and blotchy water stains covered the back. It looked as if someone had set it in a pool of water—or more likely, I thought, melting snow.

I knew the names well enough. With a father in the Navy, I'd heard of the campaign to depart the Chosin Reservoir during the Korean War. The Marines and the Army had to fight their way back through thousands of Chinese in below-freezing temperatures. They eventually made it, and killed thousands along the way. My dad called the veterans "the frozen Chosin." I don't think he made up the term, but I'd never asked.

If John and Nicholas Marston were the same man, he'd lied about his service in the war. I'd asked him about the draft and the wars when we first met, and he said a burst appendix kept him out of boot camp. None of the details matched his story. And, the young man sounded nothing like John. My friend had a kind of composure about him, and Sgt. Marston sounded like any other Marine in the field—cold, tired, and pissed off.

"Who the fuck are you?" I asked, as I turned the page.

"Who's that?" a voice asked from across the room. Peering over the book, I saw Maureen leaning against the doorway, swaying a bit. Her hair hung in front of her face like red lace.

"Just reading this book I found," I said. "I'll tell you about it tomorrow."

She mumbled in agreement and staggered to the bed. I moved my legs to the side, and she climbed in the space next to me. She rolled on her side and faced the window. Within a minute, she had fallen back asleep.

I opened the book again and continued to read.

***

3 Dec. 1950

Heavy fighting with PVA. M1 keeps getting frozen. Have to move the bolt back and forth to be able to shoot. Sgt. Ski started calling his rifle "Pecker" because he can't stop pulling on it. I allowed myself about 30 seconds to laugh at that before taking cover again. Didn't really get a kill count, but I know I hit a few. Caught one in the chest twice from my position behind the vehicle. Looked like he was going to pull a grenade, but I dropped him. From what I saw when I ran up, the blood started freezing almost as soon as the round went through. Docs say that can keep the wounded alive longer. He wasn't going anywhere though. Not sure how I feel about that, but it's what we're here for.

5 Dec. 1950

Entered Hagaru-ri finally and met with rest of 1MarDiv. Lots of new faces. Thought I saw a couple of guys from San Diego, but hard to tell through the snow—and more and more have beards! Fighting has been brutal. PVA were pouring in like waves on en route. They came at us unarmed, and they picked up the weapons from their dead on the way. Dropped a couple of more, but still haven't kept a kill count like some of the Devil Dogs. I don't blame them, but I can't say I wouldn't rather be elsewhere. One of my machine gunners broke down in the warming tent for a minute. Too cold. Too much fighting. Not enough chow. Not enough sleep. The other guys and I helped him get it together before others saw. Saying "Run Hell" usually gets the blood going.

***

I imagined the young man whom I did not know, bundled in a Marine's winter coat, standing over a dying Chinese soldier. Steam would escape from the wound and the man's dying lips. Then he would step over the soldier to kill another, and think about his wife back home, of course. I swallowed the last of the drink.

The writing changed from blue ink to pencil. I flipped ahead. The entries ended only a few pages later.

***

6 Dec. 1950

Still at Hagaru-Ri. Had a little downtime, if you can call it that. Started writing a letter to Angelica. Pen froze again. Decided to switch to pencil. Scrapped the letter. I don't know what to say to her—it's cold, and I hope I get home. The docs are keeping the morphine syringes in their mouths to keep them from freezing. Might have to try that if I use a pen again.

7 Dec. 1950

Headed towards Koto-ri now. Scuttlebutt is that we might be out of this frozen shithole by next week. Someone reminded me it's the 9th anniversary of Pearl Harbor. We traded one oriental country for another. Dad told me about Guadalcanal. If I'd been 10 years younger I might have been right there with him having to call him SgtMaj. Marston. I'd say I'm glad I missed that one but I'm not sure if this is any better. My guys are still holding it together though. SSgt. Paul makes me lead them in the "Run Hell" chant after formation. Seems kind of stupid but the guys are doing as okay as they can. We're on the move…

9 Dec. 1950

The fucking bridge is out. Met up with some more Army dogs from X Corps (under Gen. McArthur). Sighted a bridge from from Koto-ri and Chinhung-ni over a gorge. Engineers say it's about 1,500 feet. The PVA blew it up to keep us from crossing. Vehicle batteries freezing anyway so might not have done us much good.

9 Dec. 1950 (later)

The Air Force to the rescue. Flyboys actually dropped bridge parts in so we could cross. A bit more complicated than that but don't ask me how the fuck it works.

10 Dec. 1950

Across the bridge and headed towards Hungnam. Don't know if we'll be home after but definitely out of the Chosin. I can't wait to feel the sun again. They tell me it's pronounced "Shang-Jin." I can't

***

The words ended, and across the page I saw a brown splatter of human blood. Sgt. Marston had fallen while writing his last few words and dreaming of a warmer place.

"Who are you?" I asked, again. John could've known him, and picked up the journal. I told myself he could've found it at a garage sale, or retrieved it from a dead relative's house. My friend never struck me as the military type.

I imagined John Devereux as I knew him, dressed as he did now in a black suit, with snow beating against his coat, his face, and his hair. I saw him standing over Sgt. Marston's body. Steam would escape from the wound and the man's dying lips. Then he would lean over him, and Nicholas would tell him about his wife, Angelica. John would nod, and promise to give her the journal and tell her all that occurred. In the distance, the corpsman would yell for John to stand aside as they knelt there in the snow. In the warming tent, they would work to remove the bullets. They would remark how the cold might preserve him. And John would watch. I imagined him again, there, dressed as he always had in the time I had known him.

I could not see him as a Marine fighting his way through a frozen war.

I set the book down and leaned back against my pillow. I stared at the ceiling and allowed the room to spin.

***

Tuesday, October 14, 1997 – Morning

We'd woken up early enough for Maureen to get to Second Chance on time, but just barely. We ran to my car, and I floored it to travel the six blocks or so to her store. She said she didn't have time to shower or change, and "the other guy" was off work that day.

When I reached the space on Magazine Street, she leaned in and kissed me before saying, "Bring me coffee!"

I told her I would, and parked near the Rue Café. Without paying the meter, I walked inside and ordered two cappuccinos with extra espresso shots. When I returned to the store with her coffee, I saw her resting her head in her hands, with her elbows on the counter.

"Jesus, don't ever do that to me again," she said. She took the coffee from my hand and sipped it through the white plastic lid. "I'm going to hate you all day. I don't know how you drink that much."

"Lots of practice," I said. I sipped from my own cup. "Listen, I hope you're done hating me by the end of the day. We have to go back to John's house."

She looked up at me with a mixture of disbelief and contempt, and said, "And, why do we have to do that?"

"We have to find out who his doctor is," I said. "If we can't talk to John because he's Christ-knows-where, then we have to talk to his guy."

Maureen sighed, and allowed her head to land hard on the glass counter.

***

Even I couldn't believe we were sneaking back into John's house for the second night in a row. But that night, again, we stood outside of its gate. I dug in my jeans to find the set of keys John had given me.

"Still got the keys?" she asked.

"Yeah. Believe me, I wouldn't forget them. I left the other set we found back at my place."

We entered the darkened house again, and returned to the desk. I opened it and searched the papers, reminding myself that Rick Fremont's letters were still on my coffee table.

"What are we looking for?" Maureen asked.

"An address book or something that might have his doctor's name and number—of whoever gets him his blood and takes care of this place during the day. I don't know. It might not even be here—in the desk, I mean. Can you go look in the den?"

"Yeah," she replied, turning towards the door. "Are we going to check on Maria?" I looked up. I didn't want to, but it seemed like the only humane thing to do.

"Fuck. Yes, we will—but, after we find this thing." She quickly assented and left the room. I shuffled through the papers, but found nothing—no phone numbers in any case. The passports, handgun, and other papers remained. I stopped for a moment when a faint noise came from the other side of the house. I heard a drawer open and shut.

"Found something!" Maureen called from the other room. "Wait, Jason, there's—"

She had stopped in the middle of speaking, and I looked up towards the door. She walked in at a clip, almost running, holding up a small leather address book.

"Thanks," I said, taking it from her. I flipped through the pages and saw the lists of names and addresses we'd expected to find. There were lines and lines of handwritten entries. I knew we'd have a hell of a time looking through them all.

I looked back her and said, "This is probably—" She clapped her free hand over my mouth and nodded towards the desk. Confused, I allowed her to lead me across the room by the cuff of my coat. She grabbed a scrap of paper and a pen, and wrote a few words with one hand. She held her finger to her lips with the other.

She held up the note to me, and I read. Not in her normal quick scrawl, but in heavy capitals she had printed "THERE IS SOMEONE OUTSIDE."

I looked at her and then at the door. I didn't know if we should hide or if I should grab the gun. I still couldn't imagine myself shooting anyone. I glanced at the window to my left and thought, for only a moment, that we might open it and escape. But my curiosity beat out my fear. We stepped lightly into the living room. I beckoned her to follow me to one of the tall windows that faced Barracks Street. We looked through the curtain—thin, white, and translucent—that hung limply in front of it. We knelt and looked towards the gate. There was no one there.

A second later someone banged on the main door and screamed.

I knew a man's shriek when I heard it. The cries came in long, angry howls as he rattled the iron bars and beat on the glass behind them.

We looked at each other before glancing at the front hallway. The pounding continued with a rattling bang-bang-bang, and I could understand all too well the words that he growled over and over again: "No keys."

"Get the gun!" Maureen hissed. Before I could answer, the noise ceased.

I whispered, "Let's just wait a minute." She rolled her eyes and stared through the window, looking at nothing. The minutes dragged through the silence. Maureen and I locked eyes.

"What if he breaks in?" she asked.

"He won't," I said. "If he doesn't want anyone to know he's been here, then he's not going to make it obvious. And, there are bars everywhere, remember? The place is locked down."

We heard the faint scrape of a boot heel on the gravel that filled the driveway. Our visitor was leaving, finally. We looked through the white haze of the curtain to see a dark form crossed the window's view to the outside. It stopped in front of the gate before looking back at the house. I thought he might see us through the window, but he held his gaze for only a moment.

It was a man all in black, with his face covered by a black ski mask. His head turned as he surveyed John's home one last time, and then he jumped to grab the top of the heavy black gate. After a brief struggle, he planted a boot flat against it, finally pulling himself over the top. His dark form tumbled over the gate to the pavement below. He walked to the right, past the edge of the brick wall that surrounded the property. Maureen and I looked at each other.

"Yeah," she said. "That's not the caregiver. That's the other guy. We took his keys last night. He forgot them when we showed up, and then tried to come back anyway. Who the fuck?" She wasn't whispering anymore.

"Don't know," I replied. "I don't fucking know."

"Wait. Should we chase him or something?" she asked.

"No," I said. "But I'm going to call Brad soon. We're getting in over our head. Whatever John's got going on, somebody can't just break into his house and try to kidnap his wife." I thought back to the unfastened cuff.

"Maria," she said. "Shit. Let's go back to the attic." Maureen slapped her sides and walked that way before I could. I knew what I was looking for there, and I could explain it to her in a matter of minutes. It just depended on what we saw. We climbed the steps, her behind me, and I opened the door. I walked to the center of the room and pulled the chain attached to the light bulb. The room lit up around us, and I saw Maria there, still chained to the bed. She seemed to be sleeping. A new blood bag was connected to her arm.

Maureen stopped next to me, and said, "Looks like the caregiver was here."

"Yeah, I see that," I said, pointing at the IV stand.

"You want to check that address book?" she asked.

I remembered the small leather book she had discovered. I'd dropped it in on the desk. I looked at the attic door, and then back at Maria, who only slept.

"We will, back at my place," I said. "Get the book. We have to dig through it."

***

It was too late to call anywhere. We planned to read the names in order, to see if anything made sense. Anyone called "doctor" would make the first cut, as would anyone with John's last name of Devereux, or the name Marston. Numbers with a hospital prefix or any kind of medical building would be next. But on the way back, Maureen changed her mind and said she wanted to head home. I didn't argue with her.

After dropping her off, I went back to my apartment. I hadn't edited or submitted any of the pieces I'd written. My answering machine blinked with a bright red "8." I listened to at least (by my hasty count) three editors demanding "something-anything" from me before a deadline. I poured a drink and turned on my computer. I found the few pieces I'd written the day before and made a quick round of edits. Mostly looking for grammar and spelling, I flew through them to make the deadline.

About fifteen minutes after I sent the pieces, I felt the buzz of John's expensive Scotch. I sauntered back to my living room, feeling like a kind of maverick gumshoe journalist. I looked at my small dinner table and saw my friend's black address book next to the stack of Rick Fremont's letters. John would be furious at me once we had time to talk—if he called, and if he ever came back to the city. Right that minute, I didn't particularly care. I wanted to stay drunk and stupid and never again speak to anyone about vampires. Upon picking up the letters, I set the drink down on my coffee table and collapsed on my futon. I didn't want to make sense of them. But, promising myself another drink if I at least looked at them, I removed them from their envelopes one by one and laid them out flat.

John was right. They hadn't exactly changed since I'd looked at them in his house. I saw only gibberish in dark and faded letters, blocky and black.

I read them—if you could call it reading—over and over. I looked for words hidden up and down. On a piece of scratch paper, I tried to rearrange the lines into something sensible but I had no idea where to begin. Though I scribbled line after line of possibilities, I knew that even if I created something remotely meaningful, it might have no bearing on the truth—Rick's intentions, and his message to John.

I stood up to make another drink. I looked at my glass and the bottle nearby. I'd already drained the bottle.

Minutes later, the coffee pot rumbled. I paced my den, then I walked into my bedroom, to keep the blood and the inspiration flowing. I started to sit on my bed, when I saw several scraps of paper on the nightstand. They were the result of the drunken word-dump I'd performed the other night. I'd thought about John and just let the pen do what it wanted.

"What did I say?" I asked, aloud. I remembered that night. *I laughed a bit at the thought of taping it together, getting it framed, and calling it art.* Together, the scraps formed nothing. I'd only thought they might if I wanted them to.

"Anyone can see what they want anywhere, if they stare long enough," I thought.

I ran back to the letters on my coffee table. Standing over them, I looked at the pages—there were nine—laid flat next to one another. The words were gibberish. I was still absolutely sure of that. But, I saw again the pattern of light and dark, grouped in great swaths that, for a few of them, cut across the lines in wavy downward slopes. Some appeared darker altogether than the others. I put the three darkest in the center of the table, in a line of three that crossed from edge to edge. I placed the others in equal rows of three on either side. They formed a square of nine pieces of notebook paper—making the entire space twenty-two-and-a-half inches across and thirty-three inches high, as I later measured. I lifted, shifted, and replaced the pieces of the puzzle until I saw something.

The darkness and light of the letters created a mosaic image of a face. His hair flowed long and dark to his shoulders. He had a moustache and wore dark sunglasses. I did not recognize the man, but I knew who might.

***

Wednesday, October 15, 1997

A scratch sounded from the door of my apartment at half-past midnight. I called as soon as I saw the face in the pages, and I knew he would be awake. I opened the door, and Lord Chaz stood there holding up the sharpened claws he wore during his tours.

"Can't knock?" I asked, swaying a little.

He moved past me, laughing, and said, "If you call me to come over at this hour, I can come in however I want." He removed his top hat and set it on the table before moving over to the couch. "So, it's been a while. You coming to the Dark Cotillion?"

I fought to remember, and then the day we met in his office filled the slot. He and Maven had a party on Halloween at the Masonic Temple, where a bunch of fake vampires would dance and drink too much.

But, I held my tongue and replied, "Should be. Depends on a lot."

"Show me what you got," he said. I'd explained some on the phone, but not enough to give away the story. I joined Chaz at the table, looking down.

"See that?" I asked. Chaz didn't look at them closely or pick them up. He lowered himself on to the futon, with the edges his floor-length vest settling on the ground at his feet.

"What am I looking for?" he asked, leaning over the pages.

"Do you see it?" I asked. He looked back at me, and then drew his reading glasses out of a pocket inside his vest. After placing them on the end of his nose, he picked up one and looked it over.

"Is this a code?" he asked. "It doesn't look like anything to me."

"Look at all of them," I said. "Put the letter back for a second and look at all of them." I could hear my own tone darkening, and he looked at me with his brow furrowed.

"All right," he said. "You called me, remember?"

"Sorry," I said. "I didn't mean to snap. But, look—do you see the face?"

He looked over them for a minute more, before whispering, "Holy shit."

"You know him?"

"That's Radu," he said, running his long claws through his straight black hair.

"The guy you fired?" I asked. "The one that was after Raven when she was with John?"

With his face inches from the pages, he mumbled, "That would be him."

"Christ, I knew it. Simplest solution is usually the right one," I said. I ran to the kitchen to top off my drink from one of my own bottles. I didn't bother adding ice. "You want one?" I asked, holding up the bottle. He waved it away, still peering at the collage.

"Yeah, that's him. Whoever did this did a good job. I mean, I know it's kind of strange to say, but it's a great likeness."

"You said you fired Radu in the spring, right? And you haven't heard from him since then?"

"Right, right—I guess he went back to Florida, but you know guys like that. They don't always stay in one place. Where did you get these?" he asked. I sat down again and rested my head in my hands.

"If I tell you, will you promise not to tell anyone?" I asked. "This is important. It can't end up in one of your tour stories."

Chaz flipped his straight black hair back over his shoulder, and said, "I went to law school, you know."

"You're a lawyer?"

"I never took the Ohio State Bar, but I graduated. My bloodstained lips are sealed," he said, smiling.

Picking up my drink again, I took a sip and continued, "They're from Rick Fremont. He sent them to John." Chaz practically jumped as he turned to face me on the futon.

"The guy from Florida? I thought you guys almost got him arrested. Why would he be sending him pictures of one of his friends?"

"That's what I'm trying to figure out," I said. "I went to visit Rick in prison, and it was weird. He wasn't mad at John or me at all. He didn't even know we'd talked to the police. He acted like we were his friends or something."

"How so?" he asked. "You know, maybe I will take that drink." I grabbed a glass from the kitchen and added two cubes of ice. I poured the bourbon, and made myself another one. Chaz gestured with one claw for me to hand it to him.

"In any case, he really wanted to see John. That was the only thing he was kind of annoyed about—that we hadn't actually visited him. He seemed to be expecting us. That night—and get this—John told them he would contact them about turning them."

"That he'd make them all vampires? Why the hell would he tell them that?" When anything excited Chaz, he talked to the edge of yelling. Years of giving tours had trained him to emote so that a whole crowd could see and hear him. I was glad someone else was just as confused.

"I only talked to him for a few minutes on the phone. He admitted it all. He told them so they'd leave," I said.

"Weren't the cops on the way?" he asked.

"Yeah," I said. "He was worried that they might just arrest him with the others by association, and then everyone would find out about him. He did it to save his own ass. He also copped to the letters Rick sent."

"How did you get ahold of these?" Chaz asked.

"From John's desk," I said. "He knows I was going to get them, but I doubt he's real happy about it."

I skipped the part about finding Maria in the attic, the masked man who tried to break in, or the doctor's name we wanted to find. And, I said nothing at all about the journal or Nicholas Marston.

"But, there's a thing I've got to lay on you about your buddy Radu," I said.

"Sure," he said. "Like I said—between us." I stood up and swallowed the rest of my drink.

"I think Radu was with Rick Fremont's crew that night. We definitely counted five, and Rick told me there were six. He sent John these letters for a reason. I'm not sure why, though."

He stood up next to me, and said, "You know, if he's got such a thing for John—and I'm not saying this makes him a good guy or anything—he might be trying to warn him."

"Why? Why not just put it in a letter or tell me while I was there?" Chaz picked up his hat from the table and dusted it with the back of his hand.

He shrugged, and said, "You got me. Maybe he doesn't trust the mail system in prison. Or, maybe he's trying to play games from inside. Not like he's got much else to do."

"Whatever," I said. "He's crazy. Maybe there's a reason. Maybe not. But, Radu's still out there, and I think he might have killed those girls." I recalled the masked man who screamed and banged on John's door. "Maybe he's looking for revenge because John never fulfilled his promise."

"Jesus," Chaz said. "And, John was with her when he wanted her. If I'd known he was that far gone I would've called the cops." He looked grave, and tilted his head towards me. "Brother, believe me."

Part of me wanted to leap in the air with a "Yes!" because so much of it made sense. I didn't know about Maria. I didn't know for sure that it was Radu that tried to break in the house. But, it felt like the puzzle had grown outward from one corner towards the center.

"What's next, then?" asked Chaz.

"I need to drive back to Florida."

***

Thursday, October 16, 1997

I'd already made arrangements with the penitentiary to visit Rick Fremont at some point in the future, and he hadn't objected. I woke up early on Thursday and called the prison about coming the next day. Somehow, my meager press credentials allowed me to both get in, and have a short private visit. Ordinarily, they didn't allow that kind of thing. But, I got lucky.

That morning, I stood at Second Chance watching Maureen tap her nails rapidly on the counter. Beneath her hand lay the glass, and beneath the glass, watches, necklaces, and baubles in hues of brass and silver (none gold, to be certain) lined the shelves. I looked back at her. She wasn't happy. We were alone in the store. She'd locked up for lunch and pulled curtains over the glass door and picture window that faced Magazine Street.

"You're not angry with me, are you?"

"No," she said, turning to the register. She pushed a button, and the drawer clattered open. She removed a handful of cash and began counting. "You know what it is. I was hoping we wouldn't be involved in this bullshit with John to begin with. I thought you were going to just turn it over to Brad after what happened the other night."

"I am," I said. "But I didn't know that Rick still had a friend hanging around town. Whatever I find out here, I can tell him and it'll be even easier."

Her face relaxed a bit, and she said, "Well, it's not really what I signed up for. But, I don't have much of a choice at this point. Go to Florida. If whoever this is running around kills me while you're gone, spread my ashes in the Mississippi."

I leaned my elbows on the counter and looked up. She still had the old fire that made me care in the first place. I couldn't fault her in the least.

"I know. I know," I said. "Neither of us wants to be here. But, I keep finding out stuff that makes me think there might be more to this. I feel like this guy's still trying to send a message that we're not getting." I explained further—about the mosaic of Radu and all that Chaz and I had discussed. She withdrew two bottles of the generic soft drinks she stocked from a cooler behind the counter. I remembered the day that we met, as she sniffled and took long drinks from one of them.

"So, this guy is still around. Does John have any other ex-girlfriends he could go after?"

"I don't know," I said. "He's pretty private about that stuff."

"Part of that old school gentlemen shtick of his?" she asked. I took the soft drink she offered, and twisted off the white cap before setting it on the counter.

"Not a shtick," I said. "That's just from when he grew up."

"Don't you think it's a little strange that he just became a vampire all of sudden?" she asked. I thought back to the passports and birth certificates we'd found. "You saw all of those papers we found. Maybe he's a spy or a war criminal or something." She sipped her own drink and cocked her eyebrow at me, with the bottle still at her lips.

"No, no," I said, holding my hands up. "We've seen his fangs come in and out. He never gets sick. He doesn't age. He heals pretty quickly."

"You've only seen him for two years. Ever seen him drink blood?" she asked.

"No," I said. "I've never watched you pee, either."

"You haven't?" she asked. "Damn. I guess I can start leaving the door open now."

We both stopped to laugh for a second. I picked up my soft drink and took a gulp.

"I'm just saying," she said. "You guys clearly have a lot to talk about."

"If and when he calls," I replied.

We agreed to meet later to watch a video. I still planned to leave for Florida the next day. I needed to pack and look through the address book. Driving home, I mulled over everything I had to do. The list just kept getting longer.

***

I woke up three hours later to a banging on my door. I'd had a couple of drinks and then fallen asleep without looking at the address book. Peeling my face off of the pillow, I saw the empty glass next to my bed. Standing, stumbling, I made my way towards the door.

Passing the coffee table, I yelled, "Hold on. I'm coming!" to the banger. Reaching the door, I turned the deadbolt and then the knob.

It was Maureen.

Through the haze, I managed to say, "You doing here?"

"We were supposed to watch a movie, remember?" she asked, walking past me. She saw the half-full bottle on the dinner table and looked back at me. "How much have you had to drink?"

"Only a couple," I replied. That was true. I'd had more from the same bottle with Chaz, but I'd poured one as soon as I got home.

"Jesus," she said. "Kind of early. You still look like shit. Have you ever thought about cutting back a little?"

"You're one to talk. We always drink when we hang out."

"Yeah, well, we don't have to," she said. "It's only eight and you're already passed out?"

"Not passed out—asleep. I wasn't drunk. I was just tired. And, it was only two. I'm sorry," I said. I felt the fog clearing. I sat on the futon and pointed at Rick's letters, still laid out in order. "Look at this. Remember the letters we grabbed? I told you how they made, like, a drawing?"

"Right," she said.

"This," I said, pointing, "this is fucking Radu. He was stalking one of John's ex's—Raven, I mean."

"The other one?"

"Right—not Jenny. He used to work for Chaz, just like she did. He fired him and he just disappeared. But, he probably got the job because he saw Raven and John together on the internet."

"You told me most of that at the shop," she said. We sat in silence for a few minutes before she asked if we could still watch a movie. I told her we could, and I knelt before the video shelf in search of something without vampires.

I found a hand-labeled copy of *Star Wars* and asked if she would like to see it. She said that she would. Moving to the VCR and television, I slid in the tape and returned to her side. The film's rolling score and opening crawl played, and I knew both of us wanted to escape to its world for as long as we could. It felt childish, but I knew that we both—right at that moment—wanted to run away. For two hours of laser fights and thunder, we forgot about John. We ignored the world around us—one that had become at once labyrinthine in its order and detail, and utterly chaotic.

When it ended, she took my hand and led me to the bedroom, saying nothing after a single whisper of "Come here." Removing the same white tank top and blue jeans she so often wore, she turned and looked at me. There was a question in her eyes, and I answered only by moving closer and kissing. We had been together for a little over a month, one way or another. But we had already been through more than most.

As she climbed on top of me and took me inside, I wondered if we would survive the ordeal. We might live, but I wasn't sure if we might find ourselves together on the other side. I held on to the sight of her, and promised I would never forget that quiet, perfect moment. She moved—we moved together—and I felt her gasp in my ear as she wrapped her arms tightly around my neck. And when it ended, she laid next to me. The sweat on us and between us cooled in time, and I pulled up a blanket. I still had to drive to Florida in a few hours, but for a while, I could pretend otherwise.

Chapter 13

Friday, October 17, 1997

Driving to Lake City the next morning, I reminded myself that no matter what happened, 500 miles stood between me and New Orleans. Any problems that came up could bother someone else, if only for a couple of days. I left Maureen sleeping in my apartment around nine. I'd found an extra key and placed them in the open hand she reached out from under the covers.

Second Chance opened at noon, and my thin, drowsy girl saw no reason to wake up earlier than absolutely necessary (or so she mumbled, wishing me a safe trip and taking the keys back under the blankets).

Something felt different as I threw a black duffle bag into the Volvo's passenger side. I didn't feel that lingering fog and hangover I experienced most mornings (at least by then). The quiet moment spent watching *Star Wars* seemed too perfect to disrupt, and I'd stayed there as she rested in my arms, never bothering to find another drink.

I hadn't felt that way in a long time, and I wondered if I should think about easing off the bottle. As I continued on I-10 East towards Florida, I decided to stay dry for my one night in the motel room. With no one to share a drink, I felt more than capable of watching a sober movie on HBO. The trees and the small towns along the interstate passed as the sun moved across the sky, from morning to afternoon. I gathered my thoughts as I drove, unsure how to present the pieces of the puzzle to Rick.

I saw the stack of letters in my open bag. I'd checked for them again at the halfway point, after a brief and terrifying moment in which I couldn't remember packing them. I wanted to ask Rick about Radu, and if I didn't have the pages he might just lie to me.

Stopping for gas and a cup of coffee, I decided to think about something else for a few minutes. The pieces all but floated in front of my eyes. Then, I remembered the address book. I'd fallen asleep after a drink a couple of nights before, and never looked through it. I parked my car at the pump closest to the entrance. Spotting a payphone at the grassy edge of the parking lot, I ran to it while fishing change from my pocket. I had to call Maureen and beg for her help.

She picked up the phone at Second Chance within a couple of rings, and asked, "What's going on? You're not there yet, are you?"

"No," I said, leaning my arm against the side of the phone booth. Cars continued to pull in and out of the lot behind me. A black Honda Civic pulled up at the pump closest to the main road. "I need a favor," I said, closing my eyes.

"Sure, what's up?" she asked.

"I need you to go back to my house and get that address book."

"Is that all?" she asked.

I counted to five before speaking, and said, "Can you look through it for me?"

She sighed and grumbled, "Jesus, I was just there." After another few seconds, she said, "Okay, what am I looking for? You know I have to walk back there after work now, right?"

"Yes, I know. I'm sorry. This just really needs to get done. Look for anyone called doctor, obviously. Or, anyone with the last name Devereux or Marston. And, look for any numbers with prefixes of medical places—hospitals, blood banks, that kind of thing." I glanced back at my car. It sat parked where I'd left it. No one had exited the Civic yet.

"Marston?" she asked. "Who's that?"

"Um, you remember the green book we found?" I asked. I hadn't told her. I hadn't fucking told her. I stared at the sky to see the grey clouds overhead and cursed.

"Yeah, you never told me you read it."

"I read it the night we found it," I said. "You were half-asleep. It's a journal from some guy in the Korean War named Nicholas Marston. He might be a relative of John's or something."

"Or, he could be John," she said. "Did you ever think of that?" I hadn't admitted it to myself or anyone else, but the thought had crossed my mind.

"John didn't serve," I said. "He was sick, remember? I've never seen anything that would lead me to believe that. But, somehow he got the guy's book. So, the name was Marston."

"If you say so," she said. I didn't want to argue with her. "What about the medical numbers? How do I know what I'm looking for?"

"The Internet," I said. "Look up hospital numbers and see if anything matches the first three digits."

"I don't have a computer, Jason!" she said. My mind went back to our night at her house. She'd only ever come to my place since then. I couldn't recall seeing a computer in the half-shotgun where she lived.

"Please deposit thirty-five cents," the recorded operator said.

"Listen," I said, "I'll pick up looking when I get back, I promise. Just please do whatever you can. Go to the library if you have to."

"Which means I have to take streetcar down there on my day off tomorrow," she said. "This is why I didn't want to start out like this."

"I think we're a little past that point," I said, throwing a hand out. The operator's voice interrupted us again. "I'm almost out of time."

"You know what? Fine. Fuck it. I'll do it," she said. Without saying good-bye, she hung up. I slammed the phone down and leaned my head against the edge of the booth. Remembering my coffee, I turned towards the gas station.

When I got inside the Stop-N-Go, I looked around the room for a magazine rack. Passing rows of candy, boxes of Coke stacked waist-high, automotive fluids, and roadside "souvenirs" (if you needed a collectible bald eagle plate in the middle of a road trip), I found the rows of paperback books and magazines. Removing an issue of *Rolling Stone* with Chris Rock on the cover, I moved towards the coffee pot. After selecting a very tall Styrofoam cup, I filled it and locked on a plastic top. At the register, I withdrew my wallet and looked up at the girl behind the counter. Not much older than twenty, her brunette hair sat atop a pretty face and a form inflated too young by years of Southern cooking. She smiled, and I smiled right back at her.

"Fifteen on pump five," I said.

She tapped the register keys until the drawer popped open, and said, "That'll be fifteen dollars, then."

I looked down at my hands. "Damn it. Sorry. The magazine and the coffee too, please."

"That's all right!" she said. She grabbed the edge of the magazine to look at the price and punched it in, along with the price of the coffee. The new total popped up, and I withdrew a twenty and three ones. "Y'all in from New Orleans?" she asked.

"Yeah," I said. "Does it show?"

"Little bit," she said, smiling again and taking the money. I glanced down to see my usual ensemble—black jeans, t-shirt, and a sports coat over it. The shirt had the angular Bauhaus face in white and I saw her trying to read it through the opening in my jacket. Briefly, I opened it so she could see.

"What's Bauhaus?" she asked.

"It's a band," I said. "They were from Northampton in England. It's like eighties stuff, but kind of darker."

"Oh, that's cool," she said. "Well, y'all have a safe trip!"

I walked towards the door holding my coffee and my magazine, before I stopped. I looked back at her, and then returned to the counter.

"Forget something?" she asked.

"No," I said. I extended my hand to her, which she took with a firm clutch. "Hi, I'm Jason. What's your name?"

"Caroline," she said, emphasizing the high "ine" sound at the end.

"Caroline, you asked if we were in from New Orleans. What did you mean when you said 'y'all'"

For a second, she lowered her gaze and raised an eyebrow at me.

I realized what she thought, and stammered, "No, I'm not making fun of you. I know what you meant. 'You all.' I mean, I'm by myself. It's just me and the car out there," I said, cocking my head towards the door.

She leaned across the counter, and said, "Right, the Volvo. I thought it was you and the other guy all in black. Y'all aren't together?"

***

I'd begged her to explain what she'd meant. While I was pouring my coffee and staring into the distance, someone—a man she described as "tall, with long hair and a moustache, all in black"—had walked around my car twice. We were both in black and near a black car. She'd assumed we were together. I couldn't blame her.

After thanking her, I walked outside so fast that coffee splashed through the slot on top of the cup. Glancing at the car, I decided to walk around the building first. Like so many one-horse Southern towns, forestlands surrounded the interstate and its restaurants, motels, and gas stations. At around three, the sun remained high and bright. I looked at the woods on all sides, and again at the minimart behind me.

Looking down, the coffee was drying on my hand. With no one to see, I sucked up the brown liquid.

The Volvo peaked around the corner of the building as I returned. It sat there, apparently undisturbed. The Civic I'd seen earlier was gone. Moving past the pump, I walked around the car myself. The tires were intact. I realized I hadn't pumped my gas yet. As I did, I glanced through the passenger window. Rick's letters stuck out of my bag. I thought back to the mosaic drawing. In my mind, Radu's face stared back at me—long-haired and mustachioed. It was a common enough look, I reminded myself. But, that didn't make me feel much better. Glancing at my watch, I saw that I only had a few hours to make my appointment with Rick Fremont. I could make it, but just barely. I cursed loudly to no one and drove away, hoping that I wouldn't hit commuter traffic.

When I got back to the interstate, I pushed it at about fifteen miles above the speed limit. With nothing written down, I counted off a mental list of everything I needed to ask Rick. He might toy with me, as he had last time. But, I had the one thing he wanted. I could talk to John. Maybe I couldn't right at that moment, but I knew I would again. I'd promise him whatever I had to. And if I had to lie, then to hell with it.

***

Rick Fremont sat across from me again, this time in a small private room. The stack of letters laid on the silver table between us. He was still bald, and looked no worse for the wear. The guards had cuffed his hands and chained them to the table. He raised a cigarette to his lips with the shackles dangling and rattling. He stared at me and seemed unsure of what to say. I'd caught him trying to move pieces on the outside.

"Try being honest with me this time," I said.

"About what?"

"These aren't letters. It's a picture of someone, and I know who." Through the mirrored glass, the guards were, I felt sure, watching and listening. But, he was in jail for life. Nothing he told me could affect a thing. But still, I wanted to be careful.

Rick's eyes met mine, and I glanced down at the notepad in front of me. I wrote a small "R-A" before looking back at him. He moved his eyes up and down, and I stopped before reaching the "D."

"In New Orleans?" I asked.

His eyes flicked up and down again.

"What for? Old business? To follow me?" I thought back to the gas station, but thought better of mentioning it. More than anything, I wanted to grab him and demand to know if Radu had killed Raven and Jenny—and if he'd stolen John's spare key and hurt his wife. I couldn't do much with the guards watching, and he knew it.

"For no reason," he said, pausing, "that you are very likely thinking. His hands are pure."

"What do you mean?" I asked.

"Why do you think he stayed?"

"His hands are pure," I repeated.

"We all have our lines. He wouldn't cross mine, and we parted ways."

My mouth hung open for a second, and I concocted a scenario in my mind. I knew that Radu hadn't gone to Baton Rouge with them, or even to John's house. He had to have left the group before they even arrived at the Crypt that night. That was why I hadn't seen him at the door. But, Radu still wouldn't betray the group.

After a moment, I said, "He didn't want to hurt anyone. He never did. He was just with you until you got to New Orleans? And no one said anything. Am I right?"

Rick didn't answer, but his eyes flicked up and down.

"Okay," I said, "Then why send John the drawings? Is it so that he would find Radu?"

He flicked his eyes up and down again.

"Was it so that John could help him? Turn him? Something like that?"

He twitched his eyes left to right. It didn't mean that.

"You wanted John to find him. Why?" I asked.

"It's happening all around you. It's bigger than any of you. It's bigger than any of us. We came to New Orleans that night for a reason. We were starting something."

"But you were arrested, so you had to stop," I said.

"Who says I've stopped?"

I leaned forward, and said, "What do you mean? Are you starting a cult or something?"

"You have the next set of pieces. Now, make your moves," he said.

"Is this a fucking game to you?" I asked. "Two girls are dead. Doesn't that mean anything to you?" The absurdity of it struck me as soon as I said it. It didn't mean a damned thing to him. He wanted to be a vampire, and human beings sat a step lower on the food chain.

"You asked to see John," I said. "Is that what you want? Do you want me to try to get him here?"

"I'm going to stand up," he said. "There is something on my chair."

"What is it?"

"A gift," he said. "Read it. Learn from it." He stood, never breaking eye contact with me. I walked around the table and looked down. A small red book sat there—rough, and clearly handmade. I picked it up, and began to open it.

"Not here," he said.

"Okay," I replied. I moved back to the other side of the table, and he sat down. I took my seat again and looked at the crude pamphlet. "How did you get this in here?"

"I made it, with my own hands," he said, fixing his gaze back at mine. The fluorescent lights above us reflected in his eyes. "Think of it as religious material. They have their Bible, and I have mine."

I turned the book over in my hands. The red cover was blank, and crafted from layers of paper glued together. He'd hand-stitched the spine with tightly wound black thread. It must have taken him weeks of work, but I couldn't imagine that he had much else to do.

"Where did you get the materials to do this? Do you guys have art class or something?" I asked. He stifled a laugh and then licked his lips.

"You'd be amazed at how persuasive I can be," he said. "How do you think we got this room? You're not my attorney."

It took me only a second before I cringed at the thought of Rick trading his mouth for the thick red paper, the glue, the thread, and the room in which we sat. I shook my head and looked back at Rick, saying nothing for a few seconds but "Jesus."

His eyes broke the gaze and stared straight ahead at the door behind me.

"Guards!" he called. The door clicked and opened behind me. Before closing his eyes, he spoke one last time. "Now, don't promise me things you can't deliver. We both know you don't know where John is. Take the book, and run along."

***

Back in my car, I cursed and pounded the steering wheel. Rick knew more than he'd let on—or he'd learned more since we last spoke. But, he was feeding me clues on his own terms. I asked myself why, but I knew the answer. It was all he had in there. And while I could return to New Orleans almost certain that Radu hadn't killed anyone, I had to look for someone else entirely. There was a new man in black.

The sun had set while I was inside the prison. It began to rain as I drove away. The neon sign of the steakhouse shined from the other side of the Interstate. A couple of other chain restaurants, a porn shop, and gas stations surrounded the road near my motel. I stopped at one of the stations. Inside, saying nothing to the sandy, pimpled young man working behind the counter, I paid for the overpriced bottle of bourbon and walked back to my car. The mixture of relief and shame hung over me like a personal rain cloud darker than the real ones overhead.

Finding my motel room—on the first floor, facing the outside—I parked and pulled the key from deep within my pocket. Inside, the bed looked inviting, and I jumped on it with all my weight in an exhausted flop. I cursed Rick Fremont for only giving me more work to do. Now, I had to read his prison diary or whatever the hell he'd given me. Back in New Orleans, I couldn't call the police directly without possibly implicating John and blowing the whole thing open.

I would call Brad soon, I promised myself. But, the details kept stacking up and I didn't even know where to begin. Because he hadn't phoned me himself, I assumed he was still angry.

With one eye open, I saw the bottle of bourbon waiting for me on the nightstand next to the phone. A cardboard standup advertising Jimmy's Pizza down the road stood next to it. I hadn't eaten since before the coffee I drank on the way. Forcing myself to sit up, I reached for the phone and the menu.

I ordered a large pepperoni pizza, lacking the energy to ask for anything else. And, to my great relief, my room sat next to the ice machine. I poured a measure of bourbon into one of the hotel's plastic cups with three cubes of ice. Sitting on my bed with the drink in my hand, I examined the book further. The cover's rough edges looked as if he had torn them to size. Thick and red, the binding was sewn around the spine, with a line of glue further connecting the pages to the cover. He had torn and assembled the entire volume by hand with the crudest of tools—a needle, thread, and either a butter knife or blunted scissors.

I set it down, and took a sip.

The bourbon's cool, pleasant sting filled my mouth, and I looked up in gratitude for a moment. I didn't exactly believe in God, but Rick Fremont could have driven me to it.

Resting my drink on the nightstand, I picked up the book again and opened it. I nearly dropped it upon seeing the first page—a familiar "V" in a circle, with points like fangs at its edges. Rick Fremont had rendered his tattoo meticulously in black ink. The pages that followed were, as he'd said, a bible of sorts—but not any that I recognized. With a tedious series of "begats," it described the lineage of vampires from an ancient tribe in Eastern Europe called the Bogomils, alongside arcane rites of pagan sorcery. It proscribed rituals perfected long before Christianity, and practiced in secret through the present day. What I found at the end, having skipped several pages, disturbed me the most.

I remembered my coffee table, where I'd laid the letters Rick had sent John—the mosaic that formed the image of Radu.

The last pages of the book featured drawings of each of Rick, Radu, and the rest of their Clan (as they called themselves, apparently). I remembered the four children outside the Crypt, gathered in the rain. Their eyes looked at me for succor, and inward to Rick—to John—for an invitation. In those last pages, Rick had drawn himself with fangs bared and a beckoning, clawed hand extended towards me. The image of Radu was identical to the one he had copied to John in a mosaic of block letters. Lastly, with an almost sainted quality—hands clasped and eyes downward—there was John. The image was eerie in its accuracy, and stunning its Satanic grandeur. I almost expected to see one of myself, but was relieved to find nothing of the sort.

I laughed a little and thought, "Always a Renfield, but never a Dracula."

Someone knocked on the door, and I blinked and jumped. For a moment, I felt unsure what to do. I remembered, in quick succession, all that had happened. Radu probably wasn't the killer, but he had followed me. Rick was still in prison. Had the man from outside John's house tracked me all the way to Florida?

"Pizza!" the voice said, and the knock sounded again.

Ten minutes later, I sat on the bed eating slice after slice of pepperoni pie. With it, I drank great, cold slugs of bourbon and sank deeper into the bed. Spotting the remote on the other nightstand, I forgot about the book and turned on the television. I promised myself I wouldn't think about any of it—any of them—for the rest of the night. After flipping through the channels for a few minutes, I stopped on a black and white movie. Bela Lugosi skulked across the screen. It was October. Of course the networks would show their back catalogue of old horror movies.

Wordlessly, I threw the remote across the room. It hit the wall and shattered into pieces

***

Saturday, October 18, 1997

Driving back on I-10 West to New Orleans the next morning, I made yet another mental list of all that I had to do. I had to find Radu, if he hadn't stayed in Florida. I had to talk to Maureen about John's doctor, or whoever he had checking on Maria. Then I might be able to fucking find John, or at least talk to him on the phone. I knew that barely covered it, but it felt like a start. Looking back on the morning, it seemed like an inauspicious beginning to the second part of my ordeal.

The motel clerk believed my story—that I'd stepped on the remote. Or, he didn't give a shit one way or another. Per their written (and quite visible) policy in the lobby, he should've charged me for an extra day for not leaving until after two o'clock. The bourbon had knocked me on my ass.

Waking up every few hours, I saw the movie channel transition from black and white monster flicks to infomercials. I remember my dad telling me that the old stations would play the National Anthem at the end of the broadcast. Now, it was just ads for stain removers and blend-o-matics.

At around one in the afternoon, I peeled myself out of the bed and staggered into the shower. The bourbon stood next to the bathroom sink. Seeing that I hadn't finished it, I silently congratulated myself.

Just after nine, I arrived in New Orleans. Upon entering my apartment, I saw the answering machine's red number "3" flashing at me from across the room. After sitting on the couch, I reached for the triangular play button and pushed it.

The first was Maureen blurting out, "Hi, just checking in. Call me when you get this. Okay, bye."

The next was from Brad. "Hey, it's me. Can you give me a ring when you get this? Got a couple of things to run by you." He rattled off his phone number and said good-bye.

He sounded fine, I thought. Maybe he was feeling better. Deciding to worry about it the next day, I played the final message. It was from John. I couldn't catch one of his phone calls to save my life.

"Jason, I'm just checking in," he said. "I'm all right. I hope you have not gone to my home for those letters. But if you have, I suppose we'll need to talk about some things." He paused, and said, "I know all of this has been very hard for you. I will call you again soon." Click. Beep. End of message.

I reached for the phone and dialed Chaz's phone number. I thought I might catch him at his office. I needed someone to talk to. Unsurprisingly, he didn't answer. I checked my watch, and realized that he would finish his tour within the hour. If I timed it right, I could catch him on the street.

Driving to the French Quarter, I knew that everything I had to tell him would all come out in a stream of stories and speculation. Maybe he could help. Maybe he couldn't. Right then, the thought of sitting alone in my apartment for another minute scared me more than anything. Along South Claiborne Avenue, the sight of other cars en route to the French Quarter made me feel better. The world continued on its way around me.

I pulled up near the corner of Royal and Governor Nichols at the mansion of Delphine LaLaurie. The gray and black monolith was the capper to any ghost tour worth its salt, and the reason half of the tourists bought a ticket. In 1834, LaLaurie and her husband were chased out of New Orleans by an angry mob. Firefighters had uncovered a den of tortured slaves in the attic, where she and her dentist husband kept their household staff in close quarters. The house had been rebuilt, repurposed, and reoccupied more times than anyone could count. And always, the stories of ghosts remained.

I'd looked into it during my wanderings through city archives and a couple of university libraries. As best as I could tell, most of it was bullshit. Something probably happened there, though. Most people could agree on that. And, it sold tour tickets. I wasn't going to tell the guides how to do their jobs.

As I looked up at the house from my car window, I saw Chaz strolling down the street with a tour of about twenty at his back. The group stopped and he positioned himself on the Governor Nicholls side of the mansion, on the other side of the street. The group settled into a small crowd across from him, and he raised his arms to tell the tale of "Mad Madame LaLaurie" for the millionth time. I had my window rolled up, but I could still hear bits and pieces of the story, as he described the mutilated slaves discovered "only a few yards from where we now stand." I wasn't going to step out until he finished.

About ten minutes later, the story ended and the crowd stepped off in groups of two and three. A few teenage girls clung to their mothers. That story had a tendency to undo at least a couple of tourists in every crowd. And no matter how many timed I'd heard and doubted the worst parts of the story, Chaz had a way of making it all seem real.

With the last of his audience on their way down the block, Chaz turned to walk back towards the corner. I opened my car door and called out his name.

"Jason!" he said, turning towards me. I closed the door and walked towards him with my right hand out. He grabbed it and gave a firm shake. I could feel the tips of his claws against my wrist.

"How you doing, man?" he asked, with a smile. The tour had gone well. I'd seen that myself, and his mood just proved it.

"Good," I said. "I need to run a couple of things by you. You want to get a drink?"

***

We walked over to The Morgue—a twenty-four-hour dive on St. Philip that served an odd mix of goths, tourists, tour guides, and bartenders just off work. Pint glasses clinked behind the bar. The sound of chairs scooting across wooden floors mingled with the music from the jukebox. Someone had played Iron Maiden, and a few of the scruffy kids at the bar raised their fists with the chorus of "Number of the Beast." The smoke from their cigarettes cut through the cool fall air that rushed into the bar every time the door opened. You could feel Halloween coming like a quiet storm. And, Chaz reminded me as much when he handed me another flyer for his party shortly after we arrived.

He slid the advertisement to me, and said, "You doing okay?"

"I'm all right," I replied. I raised two lazy fingers for the bartender to bring a couple of whiskey-and-sodas. The skinny young man with a bandana on his head put the drinks in front of me. I withdrew a few dollars from my wallet and paid him. Handing Chaz his, I continued, "I've got a lot to tell you, and I'm not sure where to begin."

"Go on," he said, sipping the drink.

"I need to talk to Radu," I said.

Chaz sat up in his seat and looked down at the sunglasses he'd rested on the bar. I thought he wanted to put them on again to disguise his reaction.

"For what?" he asked. "You know what kind of guy he is, right?"

"I do," I said. "Or, I thought I did. I know what you told me, but I just met with Rick Fremont and I'm hearing something else. You ready?"

"Yeah. Yeah, tell me," he said, sipping his drink.

"Radu was with Rick's group in New Orleans that night." That got his attention.

He lowered the cup to the bar, and said, "He wasn't arrested with the others?"

"No, that's the thing. He was with them when they got here, but I don't think he killed anyone—I mean, ever. Best I can tell, he might have helped them get to the city after Rick offed that girl's parents. I don't know what happened to him after. He wasn't at John's house or with the others that night, either."

"That's when the cops came, and—right, right. I remember," he said. Chaz gestured with his free hand—the other holding the now-empty cup of ice. He motioned for the bartender to bring two more. I couldn't have been more thankful.

"I got to meet with Rick in private this time," I said. "He opened up a little bit."

"That's where you got all this?" Chaz asked.

"Yeah. Thing is, something strange happened on the way there. Someone was checking out my car while I was in a gas station. I think it might've been Radu."

"Did you actually see him?"

"No," I said. "The cashier did, and she described the same guy I saw in the letters."

"Why would he follow you, though? Obviously, he doesn't want to kill you."

Chaz was right. The nimble slasher had left Jenny Dark's corpse minutes before we arrived. He'd cut Raven Cartwright's throat in a bar bathroom and departed without notice. And, he'd found John's spare keys and snuck in to his house at least once. He would've found a way to kill me. My body and my car would have rested at the bottom of a swamp, or in a Jacksonville junkyard.

Finishing my drink, I said, "There's a lot more, but I don't want to tell you here. Can we go to your office?"

"Sure," he said, grabbing his hat and sunglasses. With only a couple of blocks to cover, we departed on foot and arrived at the shop behind St. Louis Cathedral. Chaz searched the keys he'd drawn out of his the pocket of his floor-length vest. We entered the shop, and I turned the lights on. We passed the rows of cigars behind glass along the wall, and the counter case filled with lighters and cutters. Over Chaz's shoulder, I saw the bead curtains leading to the same office in the back where I'd met him with Maven.

As soon as we entered, I unshouldered the tote bag I'd brought from my car. Placing it on his desk, I withdrew the small red volume Rick Fremont had created in prison. Chaz had maneuvered behind his desk.

Holding up the book, I asked, "Have you ever seen this? Please be honest."

Without hesitating, he shook his head and said, "No. Can I?" He held his hand out, and I gave him the book. Chaz examined the outside of the book, nimbly maneuvering his long costume nails around it. "This looks handmade," he said.

"It is," I said, sitting across from him.

"Who made it?"

"Rick-fucking-Fremont"

For a moment, he looked impressed and turned the book over in his hands. He finally opened it to the page with the great encircled "V." He frowned and said nothing for a few seconds.

"What's wrong?" I asked.

Holding the book open to me, he asked, "Have you seen this before?" He emphasized the "you," turning my earlier question back at me. He looked almost angry—as if I'd broken a rule by bringing it to him.

"Yeah," I said, flicking my hand towards the book. "Rick had it on his arm—I mean a tattoo. Said he got it before they arrested them."

"This could be bad news," Chaz said. "I wish you'd mentioned this earlier."

"What is it, then?"

He stood up and walked to the back corner of the cramped office. Shifting aside the stool where Maven crafted his fangs, he scanned the ramshackle bookcase that sat in the corner. From where I sat, volumes of different sizes and pedigree lined the shelves. Scrapbooks and leather-bound tomes shared the company of cheap vampire novels, true crime paperbacks, and yellowing pulp magazines. Before he could find whatever he was looking for, the beaded curtains parted behind me. Nearly jumping out of my chair, I turned to see Maven. He toted a backpack, and wore blue jeans and a printed white t-shirt. He looked less like a vampire and more like a bartender off work.

"Hey, what brings you here?" he asked.

"Research, apparently," I replied, still turned in my chair.

"Brother Maven!" Chaz called. "Do me a favor."

"I'm not putting on the thong for you. Stop asking me," he deadpanned, as he moved past me and towards the corner.

Chaz lowered his gaze, and said, "Seriously. Look at that book on the desk." Maven shrugged and sat across from me, picking up Rick's creation. He opened it, and glared.

"Aw, Jesus. This again?" he asked.

"Looks like it," said Chaz, grabbing a brown, clothbound book from one of the lower shelves. He placed the volume between us so that we could all see it. Before he opened it, a familiar dryness crept into my mouth.

"Hey, do you guys have anything to drink?" I asked.

Maven looked across at me, and asked, "Been thirty minutes?"

"No, but if we're just going to be sitting here—"

Chaz cut me off with, "Listen, Jason, this is important." He opened the book. I ignored the feeling and tried to focus. In the center of the book, lain flat across the desk, I saw the same "V" that adorned Rick's arm and his book. Chaz pointed at it with one of his black claws. "Same thing, right?" he said.

"Obviously," I replied. "So, this isn't new?"

"I think it's mostly bullshit," Maven said.

"Some strange stuff out there, brother," Chaz replied.

"Will someone please tell me what the hell you're talking about?" I asked, dropping my elbow on the desk with a sharp thud. I ignored the pain.

Maven scowled at me and said, "Somebody needs a nap. They're people that think they're real vampires—or are trying to be, anyway. Like I said, mostly bullshit."

"What do you mean?" I asked. "People like that are all over the place around here. John's the only real one. We all know that. How are these guys any different?" Chaz stood again, shaking his head.

"No, no, no," he said, and repeated it a few more times.

"So, they drink blood," I said. "I know some of the ones around here do that, too."

"It's worse than that," Chaz said.

Maven leaned forward and lowered his voice, saying, "Think of it like an underground church. It's like a cult within the vampire scene. So, there are people in the vampire scene that just like to dress up. And, there are a bunch who treat it like a spiritual thing, right?" I'd heard of the idea.

"Energy vampires or something like that? Isn't that what they're called? Sounds like kind of a copout," I said, smiling.

Maven rolled his eyes, and continued, "Yeah, so there are those. And then there are people who drink blood—like sanguinarians."

Parsing the differences between subcultures and their many subgroups had become easy for me. The goth scene constantly divided itself into smaller sets based on music (traditional versus electronic), fashion (overdressed versus t-shirts), and commitment (full-timers versus weekenders). If you weren't knee-deep in it, the particulars would make your head spin.

"So, yeah, sanguinarians," I said. "They drink blood. How are these guys any different? Do they even have a name?"

"Not really," said Chaz. "They're not that organized. It's more like a certain type of person. What's different is that they're committed to living like real vampires. They say they don't go out during the day. Obviously, they drink blood," he said, rolling his hand.

"Obviously," I replied.

Maven chimed in, "Some of them say they're willing to kill people."

"Where the hell would they say something like that?" I asked. "That's usually a good way to get arrested."

"Online," said Maven. "Usenet discussion forums, IRC chat channels—that kind of thing. It's all anonymous. Where did you even get this?" he asked.

"Rick Fremont made it," I said. Maven slapped the desk with both hands. I looked over at Chaz. "Do you still have Radu's contact information?" I asked. "I need to talk to him."

"Yeah, you asked about that at the Morgue," he said. "What for?"

I picked up the book from where it lay on the desk, and asked, "Did you look all the way at the end?" Flipping to the back, I held up the image of Radu to both of them. "Recognize him?"

Chaz's mouth fell open, and even Maven look surprised.

"Jesus," Chaz said. "That's the same picture."

"That's definitely Radu," Maven said. "Same picture from where?" He didn't know about the letters. I'd only spoken to Chaz.

"Rick sent John a few letters. We thought they were just random bullshit, but if you put them in order they form this word mosaic—like, this big picture—of Radu. I just talked to Rick, and I think he wants John to find Radu for some reason."

"What for?" Maven asked.

"We don't know," I said. "But it's looking like Radu might have been with the rest of the group that night. He just walked out on them before they got to the bar. And, I think he may have tried to get Rick to turn himself in. So, he's also probably off the table for killing Raven and Jenny." I felt myself rambling. I stopped before I mentioned Maria or the break-ins.

"Jesus, this is getting complicated," Maven said, staring at the ceiling.

"Yeah," I said. "It is, and there's more in the book. Look at these." I flipped the pages in succession, showing them Rick, his accomplices, and John himself.

Maven took the book from my hand, and asked, "What the fuck is this thing, anyway?"

"Vampire bible," I said. "I think Rick's trying to start some kind of movement from prison." I stood up and leaned on the desk. "If Radu's even in town, he's here for a reason. Rick wanted John to talk to him, but he wouldn't tell me why. He's the next step. Do you still have his number?"

Chaz nodded, and said, "Do you really think that's a good idea, though? Or even safe?"

"If he didn't kill those girls and he didn't kill me when he had the chance, there's something else going on."

Looking over at his grey file cabinet, Chaz said, "I think I had a number for him, but it's in an old file. Can you give me a few hours?"

I told him I could, and I took the book with me as I left. I still wanted that drink.

***

I stopped at the Tower for the whiskey I'd so desperately craved—three of them, before I finally left. When I got home, another message waited on my answering machine. Chaz enunciated a phone number, digit by digit. It was, he said, very likely Radu's cell phone. Disregarding the late hour—Radu wanted to be a vampire, didn't he?—I called the number, only to hear a robotic "Please leave your message after the tone."

I explained myself with the best thing I could offer him: "I'm a friend of John's. I know you've been trying to get in touch with him. Call me back as soon as you can."

If he called me back, I would wake up and answer. But, it was almost one in the morning. I hadn't had a good night's sleep in a while. Sleeping drunk hardly counted. Listening for just a moment, the silence and relative peace unnerved me. I'd grown so used to talking—constantly talking—and the sounds of cars and bars, and of the noisy streets and sidewalks between exiting one bar and entering another. I wondered if I should bother with another drink before bed.

Maven's retort when I'd asked for one at the cigar shop played in my head.

"Everyone in New Orleans drinks too much," I answered silently, to him, myself, and everyone else.

I almost asked myself a question I'd dreaded—one that came to mind more often since John's departure. As it circled my thoughts, it took shape and gained a name—a simple, if obvious one—"The Question." But that night, I would not ask it of myself.

I realized I didn't have a drop of liquor left in the apartment. And knowing that, I fell across my bed, fully clothed again, and went to sleep.

***

Sunday, October 19, 1997

I awoke a few minute after nine to my phone ringing. Fighting through the morning haze, I found the phone and mumbled "'ello."

"Jason?" a young man's voice asked. My eyes popped open, and I sat up and stared at the wall.

"Yes," I replied. "Who's this?"

"You know who it is," the voice said.

"Radu," I said. Silence followed. "Listen, I'm just going to talk. I need to see you. I need to meet with you. John and I both need your help. Are you available later today?"

"The Daily Brew on Magazine Street. Noon," the voice said, hanging up.

Knowing what to do next gave me the kick in the ass I needed. Showering, shaving, and chugging half a pot of coffee in rapid succession, I all but ran to my car. I would meet him, and I would arrive before him. I'd brought a notebook to write something while I waited. Regardless of what, I needed to work. My output had slowed to a trickle, and the thought of asking my parents for money turned my stomach.

At the coffee shop, I moved through the rows of square wooden tables to one in the back corner. A few college students sat around me, with books and notepaper spread everywhere. The baristas worked behind a line of clear jars holding bagels, cookies, and other baked goods. The occasional slam of an espresso machine's portafilter echoed through the coffee shop. Faintly, classical music played through an unseen stereo. I sat down, and glanced at a corkboard covered in flyers for upcoming concerts and club nights. Most were on colored paper of yellow, orange, and green. A few were professionally printed on slick, glossy cardboard, and interrupted the rows of handwritten lo-fi ads.

Looking around the room, I didn't see Radu yet. But, I was an hour early. Stopping for a moment, I realized how odd it seemed by comparison. I expected to meet him in a goth club or a dive bar—or, before I learned all that I had, some back alley where he might kill me. Uncertain, I opened my notebook and prepared to write.

I had absolutely no idea what, though.

For lack of anything better, I started recounting what had happened thus far. Outside of another coffee shop, I showed John photographs of Raven—dead on the floor of a bar bathroom. I told him to look at them and then destroy them before meeting me at my apartment. We talked about Rick, and then I left him there to sleep. While I was out, I met Maureen for the first time at Second Chance.

The words came quickly, and the story of those first two days formed on the paper in front of me. It was good stuff, and I decided to continue with the rest of the story when I had more time. So many details had spiraled together into a fog punctuated by blood and whiskey. Coffee shops remained one of the few places where I wrote without a drink in my hand. I asked myself if I planned it that way, time and again, or if I still possessed the self-control to not drink myself to death.

I put the pen down and stared ahead.

The roomful of students and coffee drinkers sipped, and studied, and chatted across the wide expanse of my view. I forced myself to watch them, as if seeing a movie screen without edges. I didn't want to look to my right or my left.

The Question all but sat on my shoulder, like a crow clutching a slip of paper in its claws, with the words scrawled upon it in my own hand.

I wondered if that would be the moment I finally did ask myself, there, in the sober light of day, with no one to talk to but my own voice and a sheet of paper. For just a moment, I put my head down and stared at the sheet. I'd only just begun.

But, I looked up and saw him walking towards me. I'd seen Rick's word mosaic and the same illustration within the pages of his red book. The thin, pointed chin ended the slightly pockmarked face, below a thin mouth with a mustache above it. His face was framed by curly brown tresses that ran past his shoulders. Wearing a white dress shirt and black slacks and a jacket, he appeared less like a vampire and more like a respectable rock star traversing a red carpet—probably fresh out of rehab and on his second trophy wife. He removed his round sunglasses and raised his eyes slightly to meet my gaze. I nodded, and with a single finger raised he quickened his pace. I stood to meet him, and he shook my hand firmly.

"Jason?" he asked.

"Yeah. You must be Radu."

He smiled for a second as he sat across from me, and said, "Just call me Michael. You want to stay here or go somewhere else?"

"Here's fine," I replied, sitting again. "Michael what?"

"Fremont."

***

We talked for two hours there. The sun moved across the afternoon sky outside as we sipped coffee and poured over the details of all that had transpired.

After he sat down, with my usual tact, I immediately lowered my head to whisper, "So, you didn't kill those girls?"

Without flinching, he answered, "No." I think he'd expected me to ask.

The night that Rick had approached John at the Crypt, they'd had a disagreement—"as half-brothers do, sometimes," he said. The disagreement had traveled with them from their battered white van to a corner two blocks from the club, where it graduated to an argument and then to screaming. Michael wanted to call off their entire adventure. Rick was seventeen, and he was eighteen. They'd get off lightly if they just stopped and gave themselves up at the nearest police station. Rick had already killed two people and crossed state lines. Michael had only helped him run. And before Rick had even killed anyone, he'd been all for leaving town.

Run away from Florida to New Orleans? Certainly. Tell everyone they were vampires? Of course. Find this "true vampire" they'd heard about? Sounded fun. He would even drive, being the eldest of the group and the only one with a license.

But, Rick Fremont wanted blood and he wanted to take it from the couple that had tried to stand in his way. He'd dated—and fucked—Hillary, and her parents would have none of it. At a wisp of fifteen, she'd never leave Florida on their watch. Her thin, brown hair had turned to black, along with her clothes. Her young adult novels had been (literally, Michael later learned) burned in a hole in the backyard. An afternoon sojourn to the used bookstore left her shelf filled with Poe, Lovecraft, and all manner of vampire pulp.

She'd purchased enough black tulle to turn her bedroom into a layered forest of hanging darkness. Rick Fremont had stolen their daughter—now "Carmilla"—and returned something they wouldn't allow in their house. The razor lines she'd tried to hide on her thighs and upper arms finished it. She wouldn't lay eyes on him again if they had anything to do with it. They might even just move to escape the haunted young man who'd seduced their little girl.

Rick spent the night before telling "Radu" what would follow. He had, a year prior, cajoled his brother into picking a vampire alias. Michael had acquiesced and selected the name of a Wallachian prince and brother to the historical Dracula. Rick had refused to call him by his real name since then.

That evening, their mother had left their manufactured home for her bartending job. Rick used her absence as an excuse to play Cradle of Filth as loudly as he could and then tear all of the posters off of his wall. He'd moved on to his bookshelf and brandished a grill lighter at it before his half-brother stopped him. For fear that Rick might otherwise burn down the house, Michael agreed to listen to a plot he felt sure was long in the making.

They would gather the vampires (all of them in their neighborhood, anyway) and journey to New Orleans. Rick had heard stories and seen pictures on the Internet of an "elder vampire." And, he knew the bar on Decatur Street where the vampires met to drink and dance their immortal lives away. When Michael asked him to make a distinction, Rick assured him that they—he and his friends—were all real vampires, too. It was question of degrees, really. To ascend to something greater, they needed the counsel and the blood of one older than themselves.

I thought back to the cable specials on late at night, and the rumors circulating along the dark pockets of the Gulf Coast. To people like Rick, I realized, logic dictated that all of those vampire stories about New Orleans came from something real. The tree of folklore sprung from an undying seed still waiting for someone to discover it.

After Rick had killed Hillary's parents with a tire iron, Michael did what any Southern brother would. He gathered their friends in his van and fled. No matter what, he wanted to keep Rick from going to prison or worse.

My hand began to cramp, and I stopped writing for a minute. My eyes met Michael's again before I spoke. "You didn't think that taking a van full of teenagers and a fugitive across state lines was a bad idea?" I asked. "I realize that you're younger than me, but—"

He cut me off with a wave of his hand, and said, "I know. I know. It was stupid. The cops had bothered both of us for years in that hellhole. I didn't exactly think of them as friends."

"What did you think you were going to do when you got here?" I asked. "Did you think John was going to keep the police from finding you?" I realized the irony of that question as soon as I finished asking it. That was exactly what John had done, at least initially.

"Not necessarily," he said. "I just knew we had to get out of town. I was going to figure it out once we got here. I thought it would be easier to, you know, let Rick have his way at first. But, this is a big city, right? We could've gotten jobs or fake IDs or just hidden out, you know what I mean?"

"So, you got here. You were gone by the time Rick found us. What happened before?"

"Like I said, I told Rick I'd had enough. I told him it was over. We were on that corner yelling at each other and he wouldn't budge. He wanted to find your friend at the Crypt. I finally just threw the keys down, grabbed my bag, and walked off. The others didn't follow me. They wanted to stay with him. They really believed."

"What did you do after?" I asked. "I heard you were working for Chaz as a tour guide."

He nodded, and said, "I just crashed on couches for a while until I got with Chaz and Maven. They hooked me up with the tour guide gig, but I quit after a while."

"They told me you went to Florida after Raven accused you of harassing her."

He smiled, and said, "Aw, Jesus. That story? Do you believe all of the drama you hear? I liked her, and we hung out a couple of times. But, she really wanted John. I got her the tour job she wanted. I knew Chaz, and Chaz knew John. She used that to get closer to your friend."

My mind flashed to the pictures of them together. I couldn't deny that she'd sought him out. Her journal entries online and the images of them together made that clear.

"And?"

"And, I was pissed off at her. She led me on and then kicked me to the curb. We had an argument in Chaz's office one day. It got a little heated, and Chaz came in and told me to leave. I think he was just trying to break up the situation. But, I just never went back. I bummed around. I was literally begging for a while. I mean holding the sign and everything. But, our mom wired me some cash to visit Rick in prison. After that, I ended up back at home for a while."

"What are you doing back in New Orleans?" I asked.

"Same thing everyone else is," he said. "I'm not moving back to Florida. My friends are here. I just started school again, finally. I visited there just recently—"

"You followed me," I said, remembering y'all-Caroline at the gas station.

"Not exactly," he said. "I was on my way to visit Rick. I was supposed to go the next day, though, and I was going to crash with my mom the night before. I saw your car and got out to look. I know what you drive. I've passed by when you were getting out at the Crypt a couple of times. After what happened to Raven, I thought you or someone else might come looking for me."

"Just coincidence, then? Sorry, but that's a little hard to believe."

"World's a strange place," he said, sipping his coffee again. "But, I visited Rick the next day and he filled me in. I knew you might be getting in touch."

I looked down at my bag. The corner of the red bible poked up towards me, as it often did.

"None of the group ever turned you in?" I asked. "None of the others pegged you as the driver?"

"No," he said. "We always agreed that if we got separated, no one would turn the others in. Rick is Rick. I'm not saying he's okay, but he took the fall on that one. He just said that he stole my van and that I came to get it back. I was kind of a 'person of interest' for a while, but I had enough cover to say I was on the road with a friend's band before they took off. Once they got Rick and the others, they dropped it."

With no warning, I reached into my bag and removed the vampire bible. Dropping it on the table, I looked up at Michael. "Is this why you visited Rick?" I asked.

He laughed when he saw it, and said, "Jesus, one of those things. Where did you get it?"

"One of them? There are more? Rick gave it to me."

"Yeah, there are a few more," he said. "That's what he fucking does all day. He's in there for life. Making those things and writing about all of his vampire bullshit—it makes him feel better."

I realized that our conversation—however anonymous to most—would be better served someplace louder.

"Can we go somewhere else?" I asked.

***

Michael and I walked further down Magazine Street to a bar-and-grill. Sitting on barstools at a high table across from one another, we ate hamburgers and drank pints of amber beer amidst the happy hour milieu. Led Zeppelin played from the juke box, as attorneys and businessmen off of work mingled with the regular neighborhood barflies. All brown, wooden, and warm, the place buzzed with a hundred indistinguishable conversations. The burger I ate was a wet mass of seasoning, cheese, and grease sitting atop a pile of fries. I had no regrets.

Anyone can write to a prisoner, Michael reminded me. And, his half-brother received volumes of mail from people from all over the world. Some men threatened to kill him "if you ever get out." A passel of women wanted to marry him. And of course, teenagers and vampire freaks everywhere wanted Rick's immortal bite. Some swore they would follow him to the gates of Heaven in his campaign to destroy all that had harmed them—the churches, the schools, the bullies, and of course, their parents.

Rick answered the letters selectively. The threats and marriage proposals, he ignored. The requests from journalists he sometimes indulged. I remembered our two meetings. But, the missives begging for spiritual guidance, bites, and immortality, he liked to answer. Rick had a following—though of what size, Michael could not say. And those whom he trusted the most were sent one of the books and told to share it with others. Rick wanted all of the vampires in the outside world to read his words.

I looked up from my hamburger and took a bitter, cold swallow of my beer. The drink softened the sharp edges of the ordeal, and that felt like more than enough reason to ignore The Question.

"Fly away, crow," I thought to myself.

Refocusing on the young man seated across from me, I said, "The 'V' on the book and Rick's arm—do you know anything about them?"

He cleared his throat and looked at his own food for a minute, saying, "'V' for vampire."

"That's all it is? Nothing else?" I asked. "Chaz and Maven told me about this group. They said they don't really have a name—that they're like this group of wannabe vampires that are more extreme than the rest. They said that's their symbol." He nodded, and looked at me. For a moment, he didn't blink.

"It might be from some older occult group that he's calling back to. Historically, they haven't had any kind of organization," he said.

"What do you mean?" I asked. I glanced on either side of us. To the right, the wall and a boxed set of condiments faced back at us. To the left, customers passed without stopping. No one seemed to notice us. I was grateful for that small favor.

"You can call yourself a witch, or a vampire, or whatever you want," Michael replied. "It doesn't mean you belong to a church. Plenty of people think they practice witchcraft, but that doesn't mean they're the heir to some ancient group. I can declare myself King of New Orleans if I fucking want. That doesn't make it true." I smiled at the image of Michael with a crown and scepter, presiding over the city—all of it.

"In the case of vampirism," he said, "there are a couple of organized groups outside of New York and L.A., but nobody owns the 'scene,' if you can call it that. There's no national organization that controls everything."

"But, they'd like to," I said.

"Everyone would—all of the different groups online and in the clubs. But, it's not like the Catholic Church. Nothing stops anyone from saying they're a vampire." He paused for a moment, and looked as if he was unsure how to proceed.

"This group, though—they're an old rumor. That's why Chaz knows about them. He showed you that book in his office, right?"

I said that he had, and Michael continued, "They think they're descended from the earliest folk stories about vampires. I'm talking about village shit from Bulgaria. Vampires in the old stories aren't romantic. They're dead things that come out at night and spread disease. This tribe from Eastern Europe—the Bogomils—some people think the legend may have started there."

"So," I said, "they think they're descendants of that group?"

"They'd like to believe so," he said. "Word has always been that they would do anything to become more real—closer to John, you know? Some of them already think they are. And, that's the thing—they fucking love Rick. To them, he took it all the way."

I asked, "Do they think they're for real or not?" I sat back against the barstool. I remembered what he said at the coffee shop. It sounded like people who thought they were already vampires still trying to be vampires.

He nodded, swallowing a mouthful of his hamburger, and said, "They do. But like I said, it's a question of degrees. A lot of religions have some kind of ranking system or spiritual ascension." He said pointed up at the ceiling with his free hand. "Angels above saints, the enlightened above the unenlightened—that kind of thing."

Something occurred to me. We'd been discussing the group in the present tense for a minute or two. "Do you think there are any of these guys out there? Maybe in New Orleans? Do they meet somewhere?" I asked.

"There weren't any of them when I first showed up. Most people don't announce that they're willing to kill someone. Maybe they never even existed before Rick started sending out those books. But, I think he kind of made them real. A few of them organized around him. He calls them 'The Fellowship.' If they're in New Orleans, someone might be telling them to come here."

"Rick, obviously," I said, clearing my throat.

He shook his head, and said, "Nah. I'm sure he'd like you to think that, but no. Most people aren't going to leave home just because a felon writes them from prison. Someone else could be convincing these kids to pack their bags."

"Have you seen anything like that? Like them, I mean?"

"Maybe," he said, shrugging. "There seem to be a few more young kids in black running around town. But, it's October for Christ's sake."

"If you're even right, how would someone just call a bunch of runaways to the city?" I asked. I realized we were speculating by then, but I had already seen Maria in the attic and the man at the door. I was prepared to believe a lot.

"It's probably online, but I'm not sure who it would be," he said. "Rick doesn't have access to a computer. But, he's probably happy to take credit for it. Think of it this way—if they're gathering here, then it's not him doing it. It's more like the president of his fucking fan club."

"But, he would know they were coming," I replied. I remembered Maven's words. "A friend of mine said there's been some weird traffic on Usenet and IRC about this kind of thing."

He nodded and took a swallow of his beer, then said, "I guess. Rick said something kind of like that when I visited him, but you know how he is."

"You mean he hints at things and plays head games? He does that to you, too?"

"Oh, yeah. I think he's still mad that I left him that night. And obviously, we can't talk about everything that happened with the guards around. God knows what would happen if that got out."

I remembered Rick Fremont licking his lips.

"I'm not so sure about that, but fair enough. You know he wants John to find you, right? He sent this really weird drawing of you—"

"The letters," he said. "Yeah, he's been trying to connect us since he landed in there. He still thinks John is, like, the key or something. The vampires will never be really-real without him."

"Why haven't you talked to him?" I asked. "To John, I mean." He didn't speak for a moment and then looked around. I did the same. There were no cops or anyone listening that I could see.

"I dodged a rap for accessory to murder. Do you think I'm going to approach a guy who—if he even is a vampire—"

"He is," I said.

"—and confess to helping Rick like that?" Michael looked visibly agitated. "For one thing, I know John doesn't want to talk to him. For another, I don't want to end up in jail myself. I talk to Rick because he's my brother. Doesn't mean I'm going to help him start a cult."

I spent the rest of my dinner with Michael writing notes of everything he said. After a while, I excused myself. In the bathroom, I took off my glasses and splashed water on my face and head. Faint stubble had started to appear on both, and I told myself to shave soon. But right at that moment, I needed another drink. On my way back to the table, I ordered a shot of bourbon to calm my nerves. There might, apparently, be a killer vampire cult in New Orleans and virtually no one knew about it. Or there might be one of them trying to get John's attention. I'd pinned it on Michael for the longest time. I'd sworn I'd already seen him trying to break into John's house wearing a ski mask. But, he was no killer. I sat down again, and began asking him to repeat parts of his story. I wrote as he spoke.

Michael reiterated that he didn't know who killed Raven and Jenny, and he was not involved with the Fellowship. And unlike Rick, he would always answer a direct question. The rest he repeated and laid out carefully. When I asked him again if he knew where the Fellowship met, he laughed behind one hand and asked if I wanted to attend—but, he still didn't know if or where. Part of me expected him to slip up and reveal more. I imagined myself grabbing him by the collar and whispering fiercely—demanding more. The words I heard inside were the bourbon talking—the drink's own music—and not my own. I was not a violent man, and I never would be.

"You okay, man?" Michael asked. The room hadn't begun to spin yet, but I knew I needed to hold it together.

Focusing, I replied, "Yes." I looked down at my notebook. He'd answered nearly everything I wanted to ask, except one thing. "I have another question."

"Ask it," he said, wiping his hands on a wad of paper napkins.

"If they're here, and if they're at all organized—and hypothetically—how would I get in touch with the members of the Fellowship?"

"Like I said, I don't know. I'm done with all that. My name's not fucking 'Radu.' It's Michael. I just started school over at the community college, and I'm trying to get my life together."

"I don't blame you," I said. I started to get up. I could tell we were done.

"Just remember one thing," he said, standing. "Rick loves John. He worships him. We drove to New Orleans to find him. John's in that book, and anyone that follows that group has been taught that he's a god. If your guy is from this group, then they want something from him so badly that they've started killing people close to him."

***

Unannounced, I drove to Second Chance to catch Maureen locking the door. I hadn't seen her in the two days since I'd returned from Florida. She looked over her shoulder and saw my car parked at the curb. After pushing the keys down into her jeans pocket, she scampered across the sidewalk to my car. She'd tied a blue bandana over her hair.

"You look like Rosie the Riveter," I said. She laughed and flexed her muscles.

"I was cleaning all day," she said. She leaned forward and kissed me. "What have you been up to?"

"A lot," I said. "Let's grab a drink near your place." My buzz had started to wear off, and we still had plenty to discuss.

Near her home sat an Irish pub that broadcast soccer games and, so the rumors said, boasted old ties to the IRA. True or not, it wasn't the kind of thing you asked the bartender. Sitting there in front of the beer taps, I told Maureen everything I'd learned. I explained the letters, the book, and all I'd learned from Michael Fremont.

She slid something across the bar. Looking down, I saw John's leather phonebook with a piece of green construction paper sticking out of the middle.

"You're welcome," she said.

"For what?" I asked. Then, I remembered. I'd asked her to dig through the phone book and find John's doctor—or supplier, or someone who might still reach him.

"Oh, I only spent four fucking hours yesterday compiling numbers of hospitals, blood banks, and doctors' offices. Remember what you asked me?"

"Thanks," I said, picking up the book.

"Do you know the name Adrian Reynolds?" she asked.

My mind returned to that afternoon at City Hall two years before, when I'd tried to research John. I'd found nothing but the name of the home's real owner. And, I'd never told him that I knew.

"Yes. Yes, I do," I replied. "I'm sorry for not asking about it." She raised a fresh tumbler of whiskey to her lips.

"Who is he?" she asked.

"Uh, I think he's the friend that owns the house," I said. "I did some digging when I first met John, and that name was associated with the property."

I picked up my drink and took a sip. Raucous Irish punk erupted from the stereo. I glanced up to see soccer highlights on the television screen near the ceiling in front of me. The dizziness suddenly hit me, and I focused on the tube. If Maureen would have me, I'd sleep in her bed that night instead of driving to my own.

She laid her hand on my shoulder and asked, "Hey, are you okay?"

"I think so," I said, not entirely lying. Wiping my nose with a bar napkin, I looked outside the open door. Night had settled over New Orleans. "Couple things. One—can I crash at your place? I probably shouldn't drive."

"Sure. I mean, I thought you said you were okay," she said.

"I'm fine," I replied, "Don't worry about me. Two—what did you ask me?"

She cocked her head at me, and said, "I asked you who Adrian Reynolds is. You just told me. He owns John's house."

"Oh, right. I'm thinking about Lord Chaz. We need to meet again."

"That was kind of random," she said. "I'm not sure you're okay."

***

Maureen didn't speak much as we walked back to her house. Stumbling up the three steps to her door, I tried to find my keys. She reminded me that we were at her place.

After opening the door, she pulled my jacket off and said in a low tone, "Come on. Let's get you to bed."

I turned to explain the plan I'd spun. She told me to tell her in the morning. Through the front living area, I stepped over a few scattered books and past half-burned candles on the scarred coffee table. After the kitchen, I found her bedroom. I'd forgotten she only slept on a mattress, and that I hadn't even seen her apartment since we started dating. After nearly falling, I closed my eyes before feeling her hand remove my glasses and then my shoes.

"You comin' to bed?" I asked.

"In a little while," she said. I heard what sounded like a book being removed from the shelf past my feet, and then the soft steps of her own across the hardwood floor. Cracking my eyes, I saw the kitchen light on through the door to my left. Near me, a digital clock showed the time. It was only a quarter after eight.

***

Monday, October 20, 1997

I woke up at about half past noon to sunlight that pouring through her window. Licking the inside of my mouth, I sat upright against something hard. My glasses fell into my lap from the milk crates she kept stacked next to the mattress. The sun stung just enough to make me blink, and I asked myself if I'd become a vampire as well. Smiling at my own joke, I slipped my glasses on and staggered into the kitchen. Maureen had left for work, I realized, when a folded white piece of paper caught my eye on her small kitchen table.

"At work. We need to talk. Lock doorknob before you leave. –M," the note read. The memories of the night before replayed in quick flashes, and I realized I'd gotten very drunk early in the evening. My conversation with Michael Fremont remained clear enough. But, by the time I reached the Irish bar with Maureen, the world had fallen into a haze. I remembered that she'd found the name of Adrian Reynolds in John's book. Searching, I found the book on an end table next to the tan sofa in the front of the house.

As I walked back to the kitchen, the rest of the evening returned in slips and slivers. She'd led me to her bed and left me there. Sitting at the chair behind the note, I scratched "OK" in big letters. I knew what she wanted. But, I refused to think about the particulars—and the questions and accusations she would undoubtedly prepare throughout the afternoon. Instead, I thought about the rest of the day.

I had to find out if any of Rick Fremont's Fellowship had made its way to New Orleans—and who had called them. Because I knew John so well, I couldn't do it myself. If they so much as caught my scent, the killer might follow me or worse. If John wasn't responding to his message, someone else might be next—perhaps me, or even Maureen. Remembering my conversation with her the night before, I scrambled to find her phone and dial Chaz's office. Tourists and fans called there during the day to make reservations, and I imagined he would have stationed himself there for the afternoon. Finding the yellowed phone on the kitchen wall, I dialed his number and waited.

Two rings sounded before he answered with an unusually chipper "Lord Chaz Tours!"

"Chaz, it's Jason."

"What's going on brother?" he asked.

"I found out something about that group—the cult thing, with the 'V.' It's not good. I need help from you and Maven."

"It's good you called," he said. "I've got something you'll want to see. Come by the office?" he asked. I said that I would, and then left Maureen's house.

Rounding the corner two blocks away, I saw my black Volvo with a bright orange ticket pinned to its windshield. I'd parked the car in a residential zone for too long, and the meter maid had left me a love note demanding fifteen bucks within thirty days. Shoving the ticket in my pocket, I walked around the car to make sure they hadn't left a boot on one of the tires.

Through an open door, the bartender called out, "Looks like they got you!" He was a large man, and bald with a white t-shirt. After withdrawing the ticket from my pocket, I waved it in his direction. He smiled and drew a pint of Guinness. Placing it on the bar, he slid it a few inches and yelled, "On me!"

Glancing back at my car, I nearly left. But, ignoring a drink bought for you in New Orleans was tantamount to two middle fingers. Chaz could wait for a few minutes.

Sitting at the bar, I glanced around the brown wooden interior. Flooded with daylight, it looked more like a comfortable neighborhood spot and less like an alcoholic hellhole. The bartender slid the pint glass a bit further, and I took a sip.

"Beer for breakfast," I said.

"It happens," he replied, smiling. "You know, your girl was in here this morning. Was on her way to work. Stopped for a coffee, like she does."

"Irish or regular?"

"Just regular. She didn't look too pleased."

I nodded, taking another sip, and said, "I think I got into it a bit too early. She had to let me crash at her place."

"Said as much. I'd go talk to her, mate. I see her here often enough, but never seen her look quite like that."

"Angry?"

"A bit. More worried," he said. "You know, the drink's been the undoing of men harder than you. I read your stuff, by the way. Be a shame if you were end up like one of the sad old fucks that practically lives here—telling everyone how you used to be a writer, and such."

A thousand retorts played in my head: "You run a bar. You'd thank me if I spent that much time here. You just bought me a beer."

Instead, I went with a classic: "All writers drink. It's part of the job."

"So they tell me," he said. "Someone also said a writer can die like anyone else. Your words might be around, but you have to ask yourself how many of them you'll leave behind. A crashed car, a fight with a drunk goes wrong, or you just drink yourself to death—it's all the same. I quit myself, years ago." I looked at the beer he'd bought me. It seemed rude to argue with him after that.

"I've been thinking about it, to be honest," I said. And, I had. The Question remained, where it fluttered just outside of my thoughts. If I finally asked it of myself, I wouldn't do it there. "I'm still going to finish this, though."

"Moderation, my friend," he said. "Moderation in all things."

After thanking him, I finished the beer silently. Sliding the glass to him, I left a dollar tip and walked back to my car.

On the way to the Quarter, I began thinking about the bartender's words. Cars passed on either side of me along Claiborne Avenue, and I wondered if any of the drivers were drunk.

"Lucky them," I whispered to no one.

Upon reaching Jackson Square via Royal Street, I parked and then walked to Chaz's office inside of the cigar shop. He sat behind his desk reading a newspaper, smoking a robusto he'd retrieved from one of the glass cases in the front. An appointment book sat open next to the phone. Maven sat behind him in the corner, setting out his materials to make a fresh batch of fangs. Chaz put the newspaper down and tipped his cigar into an ashtray at the desk's corner.

He waved the smoke away and said, "Sorry about that."

"No problem," I said. "John smokes them, so it's not a huge deal. Besides, I smoke unfiltered. They'll kill me before secondhand cigar smoke does."

"Light one," he said. I drew the pack from my coat pocket and tapped out a cigarette. Chaz watched me light up, and left the cigar resting in the ashtray. He folded his hands.

Looking almost happy, he said, "You first."

"They're real," I said. "Or at least, I think they might be." Maven looked up at me, his eyebrows raised.

Chaz leaned forward, and said, "Tell me everything."

I recounted all that I'd learned from Radu—Michael—and the two nodded silently through most of it. Chaz shouted a loud "Son of a bitch!" when I explained his connection to Rick—half-brothers the whole time. Rick had built a small group by writing letters from prison. And, someone had called them to New Orleans just in time for Halloween. No, I didn't know who had killed Raven and Jenny yet, but Michael seemed unlikely. Chaz confirmed the rest of Michael's story, though the two disagreed on the details about his firing the young tour guide.

Tales of breakups and job loss in New Orleans inevitably had multiple takes running through the French Quarter. The goth scene had a penchant for adding bits of sex, violence, and humiliation to any story involving one of its own. You learned to see the truth in the gaps and spaces between particulars. We agreed that his old guide's story seemed legitimate enough, all told.

"That's it?" asked Chaz. "Some of Rick's fan-boys might be in town? But, we don't know who told them to meet up?"

"It's possible," I said. "I don't know how organized they are, or how many of them there might be." He laughed. I leaned back and frowned. "How is this in any way funny?"

Standing, he replied, "Have I got something for you." Chaz scooted around the desk to the filing cabinet. He pulled open the top drawer and withdrew a manila envelope. "I found this," he said, "in the office this morning with my name on it. Someone dropped it off in the middle of the night." Thinking back to the night before, I remembered the incident at the pub and sleeping at Maureen's. The story had continued, even while I laid there unconscious.

Chaz opened the clasp on the envelope and dropped a familiar red book into his free hand. He held it up.

"Look familiar?" he asked, holding it out to me. Leaning forward quickly, I took the book. Though different in its minute details, it was undoubtedly Rick's work. Flipping to the back, I saw the same images of himself, his friends, and, of course, one of John—or Nicholas, or whomever he was.

"Yeah, it's the same," I said. "Any idea who dropped it off?"

"No," he said. "It was just on the ground like someone pushed it through the mail slot. This was in there," he said, handing me a folded up piece of paper. The small half-sheet was the sort of fake parchment you could buy at an office store. I opened it to see florid black script that formed a letter.

"Dear Lord Chaz," I read, "We, the members of the New Orleans chapter of The Fellowship, cordially invite both you and Maven to attend a meeting at…" I trailed off and stopped for a moment. "This is too perfect. But they're seriously meeting there?"

Maven finally said, "Monday at Kaldi's? Then it's a bunch of kids."

"It's also tonight," I said.

Kaldi's mock Greco-Roman interior housed two floors of wooden tables, pay-by-the-minute computers, and a passel of sassy punk rock girls behind the counter. My usual crowd liked to hang out there before the Crypt opened on Fridays and Saturdays.

"They meet at a coffee shop out in the open," I said.

Chaz nodded, and said, "They probably can't all get into bars, I guess."

I planted one elbow on the desk, and said, "These are Rick's followers we're talking about. They must be a bunch of runaways."

Maven stood, and said, "They're probably just talk."

"Rick's first group wasn't," I said. "That's them. Rick's got a cult and they've been gathering in New Orleans. All we know now is that neither Michael nor Rick actually brought them here."

"You talked to your cop buddy?" Chaz asked.

"He tried to call me, but I was out," I said. "I'm going to, though."

"And John?" Chaz asked.

"Where John is? No," I said, shaking my head. "He tried to call me last time I was in Florida. I should probably just get a fucking cell phone."

"Hate those things."

"You wouldn't have to sit here all day waiting for the phone to ring," I said.

Pointing his thumb behind him at the gray and black device, he replied, "I have an answering machine. It gets the job done."

"What do you need from us?" Maven asked, as he dragged the wooden stool from the corner and sat at the desk.

"Somebody has to go to that meeting. I need one of y'all to do it for me and find out what's up."

Maven looked at me for a moment like he might refuse. Then, he said, "I might be able to sell fangs there."

Chaz shrugged, and said, "They know who we are, and they know where my office is. I doubt they're going to jump out and kill us or anything."

"Right you are," I said, pointing at him. "I didn't get a letter from them. That's a good thing. If they knew that I'm close to John, whoever killed those girls might try to use me to get to him. I don't mean to throw you guys to the wolves, but they obviously respect you. And yeah, they might buy fangs," I said laughing and looking over at Maven, who cracked a half-smile.

Chaz leaned forward and asked, "What are we trying to find out?"

I moved to meet him across the center of the desk. When his mood grew dark, Chaz rarely blinked. I never learned how he managed it, but when his dark eyes met mine I knew he was listening. I spoke, after a moment.

"I need to know who called them to New Orleans. And, I need to know why. These guys are obsessed with John, and Rick gave me that book for a reason. The guy that called them—I think he's the one that killed the girls."

Chapter 14

Monday, October 20, 1997 – Evening

Chaz and Maven said they would attend the meeting and find out as much as they could. The latter volunteered to search for the group online and hype their arrival. For this growing chapter of runaways and misfits, their attendance might increase the turnout. Knowing Chaz, he would guide the conversation and find out as much as anyone might share. I'd look like nothing more than reporter trying to dig up a story in time for Halloween. I didn't dress or act like a vampire. And, if they knew about my friendship with John, my guy wouldn't tip his hand. Or, he might follow me home and kill me. With that task safely handed off to my friends, I drove to Second Chance to meet Maureen.

"We need to talk" remains, undoubtedly, the worst thing you can hear from a lover or a friend. No one ever wants to remind you that they love you and, by the way, made you dinner. Without calling, I drove to Second Chance.

When I entered the store, she looked up from the register. Counting out a stack of cash, she freed one hand to slide the store keys across the glass counter to me.

"Lock up for me, will you?" she asked.

She offered me no smile, and no further greeting. I turned the key in the lock, and flipped the sign. She had cut it to read "Sorry, We're Open" on the side facing me. I could tell she'd been considering "The Talk" all day. I knew the subject. The Question made a quick lap around the room and settled on my shoulder.

"Want to go somewhere?" I asked.

"No," she replied. "Let's just talk in here." I didn't argue with her. She walked towards the back of the store, past the hanging racks of dresses and jackets. With the cool weather finally settling over the city, she'd bought more warm clothes than usual. Through an open door next to the curtained dressing room, she walked to a folding table with two grey metal chairs on either side of it. She sat in one and pointed at the other.

"Sit here and talk with me for a minute," she said.

"Okay." I sat down and looked around at the worn metal shelves and stacked blue plastic bins all around us. The room—dull and grey—appeared larger than I'd guessed from the front of the store. I'd never seen it until then.

"Listen, we've been together for five weeks. But, a lot's happened. And, I've gone along with most of it. I didn't know fucking vampires were real, and now I know they are. I haven't even had time to wrap my head around that." She let one arm fall and hit the table, as the other one supported her chin. "And, I really like you. I wouldn't have helped you if I didn't."

"All that's good to hear," I said. I knew what was coming. I didn't particularly care to listen, but I knew I had no choice if I wanted to keep her.

"But," she said, "I think you drink too much. I think you might have a problem." Lowering both arms flat on the table, she slid one leg forward and visibly shifted in her chair. Crossing my arms and looking around, The Question crawled through my ear and in the space behind my eyes before turning, twisting, and screwing its way into my thoughts. I had avoided it for weeks, but I could tell she was someplace different. I knew then that if I wanted to save whatever we had, I would have to ask it out loud.

"Do you think I'm an alcoholic?"

She looked down, avoiding my eyes, and said, "I haven't known you for that long, but I'm worried you might be."

"How?"

"How am I worried or how might you be an alcoholic?"

"Second one," I answered.

"For starters, you drink every chance you get. You're either at a bar or on your way to one. Whenever we hang out, we get drunk."

I started to return the accusation, but she saw it and spoke first: "I know that I drink with you a lot of the time. I'm sorry if sometimes it's my idea. We both drink a lot. The difference is that I don't need to. I go days without it. I just usually drink with you. That was one of the reasons I got away from the street kids and crusties. All of them live in the bottom of a bottle or at the end of a needle. That wasn't me."

"We don't have to drink every time we hang out," I said.

"That's the problem. You say that, but I think we do—because you want to. I see the empty bottles in your garbage can. Whenever things get, like, whatever—whenever they get stressful or we finish any kind of work, you want to get a drink. Maybe it's that things are crazier. I mean, I know they fucking are. You've taken on a lot trying to help John, and he's not even in town. Did you drink like this before we met?"

Barely considering the question, I replied, "Some." Beginning with Raven's murder, in a matter of weeks, it had escalated. No one ever woke up with a drinking problem. Even I could admit that. "So, what do you want me to do?"

She took my hands in hers and looked me in the eye, and said, "Just stop, or at least cut back some. We don't have to drink a bottle of bourbon every time we hang out. I like you sober, too. You weren't drunk when I met you, remember?"

"I was caffeinated, and then we went to meet Jenny. Then, we got drunk," I reminded her.

"Fine. Whatever. I won't offer you drinks if that's part of the problem," she said, raising her hands up from the table.

Defenses and excuses filed through my mind. I wanted to blame New Orleans, her, John, and anyone else. As far as I knew, I wasn't addicted to anything. But, denying alcoholism was practically an admission in situations like that. I could admit it or call her wrong, but I just opted to delay.

"Let me think about it."

"Okay," she said, almost whispering as I stood. She released my hands.

With that, I opened the lock with the keys she'd left on the counter and departed the store. I had shit to do, and giving up drinking sat somewhere near the bottom of my list. I knew I drank a lot. But, I liked it and I'd never denied that. The most transcendent nights of my life—often with John—involved enough booze to turn an AA meeting into a frat party. I wanted to rage at Maureen for making me ask myself The Question, but I—sober, at that moment—refused to hate her.

As I drove home, I thought about opening my front door. I imagined myself yelling "Fuck her!" and making a drink. I could also imagine the half-empty bottles from my liquor cabinet in the trashcan outside. I could make a pot of coffee and just decide I'd already quit drinking.

Pulling up in front of my apartment complex, I took a minute to think. Staring ahead at the trees, trashcans, and houses that lined the Uptown street, I decided to wait. If I dove in as soon as I walked in the door, Maureen would've been absolutely right. The creeping dryness had returned to my mouth, but hardly in its worst form. I could survive for a little longer.

I reached the door and took my keys. But when I opened it, I saw a single brown shoe—a man's—through the crack. Someone was sitting in my living room.

***

I didn't know if the man had heard me open the door. Surely he must have, I thought. I closed it quietly and turned the lock back into place with equal restraint, withdrawing the key. I didn't own a gun, and I had nothing like a weapon on me. I reached for the light switch nearby and flicked it down to darken the entire hallway. Listening for steps, I flattened myself against the wall next to the door and waited. I could have run, I knew, but I refused. He had to have heard me. Even if he thought I'd taken off down the street, he would wait or he would just come back some other time.

I waited. I breathed. For a second, Maureen's words replayed through my mind. I wanted a drink worse than I ever had in my life. But at that moment, even she wouldn't have blamed me. But, I banished the thought just as quickly. With my body flat and tight against the wall, I pushed my toes in my shoes and into the hardwood floor beneath them. I wanted to close the sliver of space between myself and the sea of white behind me, and stand ready to spring like a cat. I was never a violent man. But, I replayed scenarios in my head, and wondered what might drive me to finally act. If someone hit a woman—any woman—I would. If someone hit a friend, I probably would. If someone entered my apartment and sat on my couch waiting to kill me, I wouldn't have a choice. But, I desperately searched for an alternative.

I looked at the doorknob and remembered that I had used the key to enter. The man in my home had not kicked in the door. The splintered frame outside of Jenny Dark's apartment blazed through my memory. And, unlike John, I didn't keep an extra key under a mat or in a flower pot. The guy sitting in my living room on my ancient futon—I knew him. He'd entered with a key. Or, maybe I'd forgotten to lock the door. I couldn't remember.

A man sat in my home and I knew him and he might be the one who killed Raven and Jenny, and in moments I would see his face.

Sweat gathered on my pale, stubbled head and curls of heat gathered in my mouth. My heart's rhythm played like a drummer trapped in a cave. I felt—no, heard it—and wondered if the man did, too. Looking down the dark hall, I prayed for a neighbor to find me. I could finally call Brad. Chaz and Maven and I could storm the apartment together and tackle my intruder. I could just dial 911 and explain the situation.

The steps sounded from the other side of the door, and a faint thud followed. I recognized the sound and raised an eyebrow. Another bump followed. The man had not come to the door. He was in my kitchen.

I peeled my hands and arms from the wall, and relaxed for just a moment. Briefly, I glanced at the ceiling and wondered what would happen next. The man knew my apartment, or he had searched it while he waited.

Bumps and faint noises sounded from the corner, and cabinets opened and shut. Steps crossed the apartment again, and then grew louder. A few more sounded, and then stopped.

"Jason, I can hear you out there," the voice said from the other side of the door.

"Who's there?" I called out.

"I'm coming out," it replied.

I stared at the doorknob as it began to turn. Every millimeter tore through my eyes and I waited, ready. Breathing hard, I raised my fist to throw a punch. A thin light opened at the door's edge, as my intruder prepared to exit. I blinked the sweat out of my eyes and, in that second, the door opened and a foot fell. I launched myself across the space between us.

In a couple of seconds, a tangle of limbs fell to the hardwood floor. A glass of liquor and ice flew from his grip and hit the ground with a burst of clear, jagged shards. For that moment, I had the better of him and I wondered what to do next. He grabbed at the edges of my jacket and tried to push me up, but I pressed all my weight against him. Unsure of what sort of punch I could throw, and looking past his shoulder to the wood beneath us, I wrapped my hands around his throat and squeezed.

"You can try that, but it won't work," the voice said, calmly, straining through my grip. I recognized it and relaxed my grip. Sitting up, I looked down at the man underneath me.

It was John.

***

After composing ourselves and apologizing, we sat in the living room. He had a key I'd given him when he offered me one to his own house. He had let himself in when I didn't answer the phone. I told him I'd just visited Maureen, but I kept the particulars to myself. John drank more than any man I knew, because he could. He was the last person to ask for advice on cutting back.

"I'm sorry I tackled you," I said.

"It's fine. I should have waited until you were home."

"I really thought you were here to kill me," I replied, looking over at him. "Things have gotten strange since you've been gone."

He smiled, and laughed for a breath, and said, "I thought I should come see you as soon as I arrived back in town."

"Where have you been?"

"Mobile, Alabama," he said. "It's close enough. I knew that I could return quickly if it were necessary. I found a hotel room in the downtown area and stayed there. I hardly left"

"What about your supply?" I asked.

"I have my ways. With enough twenty dollar bills, you can pay someone at a hotel to take care of almost anything." I didn't know if he meant that they left his stash of blood bags alone, or that he'd paid them to find willing donors. I didn't ask, either.

Sitting forward, I leaned my face into my folded hands and breathed. We had, I realized, hours of conversation ahead of us. The night would pass slowly, each word between us a step uphill until we reached I-knew-not-what. I glanced at the pass-through to the kitchen and wondered if I might succumb to the call of my cabinet before the night ended.

In the hours that followed, I told my friend the story of all that had passed in his absence. The grit and darkness I'd felt before faded and gave way in the face of his easy charm. We could always talk for hours. The personal shit could wait, I realized. There was too much to do.

"I know," I said, "that you didn't want me going in your house to look for those letters. But, Maureen and I did."

"I suppose, by then, you thought you had no choice," he said, sighing and frowning.

"That's basically it, John. And, I got the letters and I know what they mean. I also found a lot of other stuff—passports, birth certificates, and a fucking gun. I also found the attic." He stood, placing his hands on his hips. Wearing a gray suit and a pale linen shirt, he looked like a 1960s corporate executive on vacation.

"Do you have anything to drink?" he asked. "I think my last one ended up in several pieces on the ground."

I stood and said that I did, without asking what he wanted. At my kitchen counter, I held the bottle of bourbon over a glass filled with ice. It looked wrong, the glass, to see it there alone. For a second, I thought about adding my own. But, I recalled Maureen's words. Even John's return wouldn't stand as an excuse to her. I walked back to the living room and handed him the drink. Taking it, he finally spoke: "Tell me everything."

"I need to know something," I said.

He sipped his drink, and said, "Yes?"

"I found a journal," I said. "Who is Sgt. Nicholas Marston?"

He turned his back to me and looked up at the ceiling for a second. He sighed again, and finally turned to face me. He moved to speak, but stopped himself.

"Well?"

"I am," he said.

***

I excused myself under the guise of finding Rick Fremont's letters and the book he had created. I went to my bedroom and found the green journal and opened it. The images came pouring back—Korea, the Chosin Reservoir, and the page where his blood had landed beneath his last words.

John had lied to me about everything.

For two years, he had lied to me about his life, Maria, the night we met Rick, and Christ knows what else. I wanted to scream and yell—and to drink, damn it—and throw it all back at him. But, knowing his real name just left me with even more questions. I found the letters on the corner desk in my bedroom, and took them in a stack with the journal.

When I returned to the living room, I said, "Well, what should I call you? John, or Nicholas, or Nick?"

"John is still fine," he said, looking up at me.

"First, look at these," I said, holding up the folded pieces of paper. We sat down, and I laid them out on the glass coffee table. He sipped his drink and waited as the image of Michael Fremont—"Radu," I said—came together. Settling back into the space next to my friend, I said that he was, undeniably, a relation of Rick—our old millstone, with whom I had spoken twice. But, he had no stake in the vampire game. His brother wanted more of him than just the occasional visit or a call. He wanted John to find him. He wanted Michael to see that the promise my friend had made in haste might be fulfilled. But, the young man had kept his distance.

"Wise of him," John said.

A cult called the Fellowship might be gathering in New Orleans, I explained, summoned by one we did not know and guided by Rick's cryptic writings. And, it was a cult that saw John as the key to some kind of vampiric revelation.

Raven and Jenny remained quite dead, and others connected to him might follow. I hadn't spoken to Brad yet, but now we had no choice. We were in too deep.

And, Halloween was coming.

I finished all that I had to say, and sat upright. I'd slid deeper into the couch as I spoke. John had only nodded during the course of my story. His drink was nearly empty, and I felt the dryness in my mouth and wanted one of my own. He cleared his throat and stared straight ahead at the window across the room. The dawn's light had yet to appear. We had time. Finally, he spoke.

"I assume you met Maria."

"Is her real name Angelica? Like in the journal?" I asked, holding up the book.

"Yes, that was her old name. I changed it for her when we had to go on the run."

"So, let me tell you what I saw," I said, standing up. "You seem to have your wife chained up in your attic. You told me she died of cancer," I said, wagging a finger and walking in a small circle. Without speaking, I removed my cigarettes from my jacket pocket. I took a one out of the pack and placed it between my lips. Then, I lit it and inhaled. The smoke billowed in a cloud in front of me, as I stood with my back to John.

"But apparently," I continued, "she is also a vampire?"

"That story requires another drink," he said, standing.

He poured it himself in the kitchen, and called, "Do you want one?"

"Not right now. I'm cutting back."

He walked back with the glass of bourbon and looked at me, saying, "Let me assure you that I always meant to tell you. You are my only real friend here, and I have always wanted to protect you." He sat on the coffee table across from me, and held out his hand. I took it, and he held it there and stared into my eyes as I stood in front of him.

"I need your trust," he said, "and your confidence, and above all, your silence. Parts of it don't make sense, even to me. But, I will take you to visit my doctor in the morning. He can confirm all that I am about to tell you."

"Adrian Reynolds," I said.

"How do you know that name?" he asked, frowning.

"When we first met, I looked up your address over at City Hall. I saw who owns the house. It's not that hard to find," I said. "And, I have your address book. Maureen and I realized that someone had to be taking care of Maria. We took it from your house to figure out who it was. We went back the next night to get it." The man at the door erupted into my memory. John laid his face in his hands for a few seconds. He sniffed loudly, and then looked up at me.

"Dr. Reynolds is my supplier," he said. "And, he was caring for Maria while I was gone." He was the Someone I had imagined who visited during the day.

"Yeah, I figured as much," I said. "But, there's something else."

"My God, what?" he asked, looking down.

"Do you keep a spare key outside somewhere?" I asked.

He slapped his leg, and took a sip of his drink, and said, "Yes, I do. It's in one of the plants. What does that have to do with anything?"

"Give me a second," I said. I returned to my bedroom and found the dirty keys on my desk. Back in the den, I held them up and shook them. "Are these them?"

John snatched the keys out of my hand, and said, "Yes. Where did you get them?"

"You're not going to like this, but I'm just going to say it. Have you been home yet?" I asked. I sat down on the futon and took a drag from my cigarette.

"No, I have not," he said, with his eyes lowered.

I said, "Someone was breaking into your house. We found Maria with her IV needle out and one of her wrists unstrapped. This guy found your key, came in, and then undid one of them. He might have been trying to kidnap her or something, but I think Maureen and I scared him off the first night. We found Maria and bandaged her up."

"Bandaged what up?" he asked.

"I think she tried to bite through her wrist before he got there," I said. "But, I think when the guy heard us he took off and forgot the keys. The second night, he tried to get back in when we were there. Obviously, he couldn't."

"She's never tried to do that before," he said, looking off to the side. "What did this man look like?" He stood up and swallowed the last of his drink.

"All black," I said. "I mean completely—gloves, boots, the whole nine. He even had a ski mask on. It could've been anyone. Until yesterday, I thought it was Rick's brother. Now, I have no fucking idea."

John moved towards the door, and straightened the edges of his jacket. "What are you doing?" I asked.

"Leaving," he said. "I have to see her."

"Wait," I said. "There's a lot we have to talk about."

"Yes, we do," he said. For a second, he closed his eyes and tried to calm himself. "But, all of that can wait. Meet me tomorrow at my house, and we'll go see Dr. Reynolds. He can fill you in on the rest. I'm sorry that I kept so much from you, but I have to see my wife."

We had so much more to discuss. I had to tell him about the talk I'd had with Maureen, and how Chaz and Maven were meeting with the Fellowship.

The stories nearly fought their way out, but I only replied, "Okay."

"Come pick me up at ten o'clock," he said.

"Early for you," I said.

He nodded, and said, "Some things can't wait."

***

As I laid on my bed that night, I imagined John and Maria as two elderly people—seeing matinee movies at the Prytania, driving an oversized Cadillac, and clogging the buffet line at some casino in Biloxi. Just like any older couple, they would have settled into their retirement and their quirks. And like so many, though they might fade from those around them, they would fade into each other until she held his hand on his deathbed. A funeral would follow at whatever Protestant church they belonged to, and a preacher would give Maria a folded flag "for your husband's service to our country in Korea." He would return to the earth and she would move into a retirement community—for they would have no children—and excel at crafts and senior aerobics, and outshine so many around her. I stopped myself before my reverie led to Maria's death as well.

John had always confused me. I'd never doubted that he kept parts of his life from me. But the shadow that crossed his face when he spoke of Maria—one I had seen for but brief moments before—showed me all I needed to know. Something terrible had happened to her. I wondered if he might stop at another bar or do anything to avoid his own home. I reminded myself that he probably kept her more comfortably when he wasn't on the run.

For the first night in years, I fell asleep sober. Any other time, I might have had trouble sleeping as such—but not then. The night sky called to me, and I answered dreamlessly.

Chapter 15

Tuesday, October 21, 1997

The phone rang a bunch of times before I woke up enough to stumble over to the cordless. The hangover and the lingering malaise I'd come to know so well were notably absent. I'd had nothing to drink, I recalled. The phone rang again, and the haze around my eyes retreated to the edges as I grasped it and pressed the green answer button.

It was John, and he asked me to pick him up in an hour for a trip to the hospital. I looked to the digital clock on the nightstand, and saw the time was 9:07 a.m. I'd wondered why John was driving a borrowed car when I first met him. After last night, I understood. A car meant registration. It meant taxes and a mailing address. Living in Dr. Reynold's house and using mostly cash afforded him a degree of anonymity. To the military, he had died in Korea—one more frozen Marine airlifted away to a funeral in the United States. To others, he had always lived in New Orleans. None of the younger barflies, artists, and would-be vampires particularly cared where he was from. And, though he had not visibly aged in the time that I knew him, only two years had passed since our initial meeting. Prior to knowing me, my friend had kept his own company. I had, without meaning to, helped to create the man-about-town I called my friend.

I drove down Esplanade and then on to Decatur, before turning on to Barracks Street and stopping at the black gate that surrounded his courtyard. I tapped the Volvo's horn and waited. He wouldn't stay outside any longer than absolutely necessary. The side door opened and John emerged. The air felt warmer that day, yet he still wore a suit jacket—khaki this time, to match the pants—along with a fedora and sunglasses. He walked quickly from the door and through the gate before entering the car. I could smell the faint coconut of his sunscreen as he greeted me with a nod.

"Good morning," he said.

"Late morning, now."

"Daylight all feels the same to me."

"You could be on fire, like in the movies," I replied. "So, are you going to talk to me now?"

Without looking at me, he said, "What is it that you would like to know?" The aroma of coconut lotion permeated my car. The sun's rays poured through the windshield. He would not lie to me there. I knew that the heat, the light, and the strain of the morning would hold him in place. John had always wanted to tell me more. At that point, he couldn't wait any longer

"Okay, I'm just going to ask this as concisely as I fucking can," I said.

"Please do," he said, ignoring my tone.

"All right. First, what the hell is wrong with Maria, and why are you keeping her in your attic? I thought you couldn't, you know, pass your thing on to anyone."

"I can't," he said. "You saw her."

Maria flashed in my mind, wild, hungry, and cuffed to the bed, as I had seen her there. She cried out for help, alone and desperate. For instincts she could not control, she would have killed me or Maureen. Most of all, she wanted someone to free her. But, no one would in the dark moments between visits from Dr. Reynolds and the man who came at night.

For good or ill, John had reduced a woman to an animal, and I only wanted to plead, "What have you done?"

Instead, I just said, "Yeah, I saw her."

"That is what happens when I drink from someone," he said. "They don't become like me. They become like that."

We rounded the turn onto Rampart Street. The houses, the churches, and the gas stations crawled by us en route to the hospital. The grey blur of the French Quarter passed on either side of us. People waited to on the green neutral ground that divided the street. On the other side, they ambled down the craggy sidewalks, parked their cars at gas stations, and sat on bus stop benches, clutching newspapers and puffing cigarettes.

"What if people drink your blood?" I asked. "What happens then?"

"I honestly do not know," he said. "I haven't had occasion to find out. But, I believe that whatever I have is simply a fluid transfer. It doesn't matter if it's saliva, or blood, or anything else. It is highly contagious once it reaches the bloodstream. As far as I know, if someone catches it, they become like my wife."

"So, you can still kiss then? Just like AIDS?" I asked, remembering the girls.

"Yes, that seems to be the case." He looked down at his lap, almost as if he was ashamed.

With all the will I could summon, I held myself from stopping the car. The next question fought The Question and any other thought I had out of my skull and to my mouth. I wanted to yell, but instead I inhaled deeply and stared at the black road ahead of us.

Reaching a stoplight on North Rampart, I asked, "How did she get it?"

"From me," he said. "When I couldn't drink from anyone else, she offered herself to me."

"Jesus," I said. "Jesus Christ. You drank your wife's blood?"

John said nothing for a block.

Finally, as we turned on to Poydras Street, he said, "I think there are a lot of things you need to ask my doctor."

We drove the rest of the way in silence. I had more to tell him. Chaz and Maven had already met with the Fellowship the night before. I still wanted to cut back on my drinking. I had to make sure things were okay with Maureen. Quietly, I hated John for leaving town. So much had happened, and we were fucking around playing catchup.

Reaching the hospital, we parked on the street. I dug in my pocket for change for the meter.

"Shit," I mumbled, realizing that I had none. John reached deep into his pocket and pulled out a handful of quarters. He dropped them into my hand, and I thanked him. Regardless of what else I could say about him, my friend always had cash on him. I plunked the quarters into the meter's slot, and remembered the parking ticket I'd earned in front of the Irish bar. I remembered the beer the bartender had slid me, and what followed. It was only the day after I'd decided to hold off drinking for Maureen. But, I had only told her I would consider it.

The question of whether I would last or not loomed over me. It wasn't The Question. But it scared me all the same as we entered the hospital's corridor. With so much of the walls and ceilings made from plate glass, John looked no better than he had outside. Still wearing his hat and sunglasses, he removed his coat and folded it over his arm. His loafers tapped across the green marble floor, and I ran to catch him. We passed a security guard at the stone half-circle of a front desk. The graying black man peered over his glasses at us for a moment, and then returned his attention to the paperback mystery novel in his hands. The elevator met us, alone, almost instantly. Inside, John removed the hat and glasses.

I asked, "Do we need to check in or anything? Is this like an appointment?"

"No," he said, shaking his head. He fished in his jacket, and withdrew two ID badges that bore the hospital's green logo. They were for staff members, though not doctors. He handed me one, and clipped the other on to his shirt.

"Put that on," he said.

"Do these belong to anyone?" I asked, looking at mine—a card that belonged to one Bill Hunt. His image—unmistakably not my own—seemed banal enough: a white man in his thirties with dark blonde hair. I touched my own bald head, and reminded myself that if anyone asked, I would say that I shaved my head and had to get glasses.

"I'm Bill," I said, limply extending my hand to John. "It's nice to meet you."

He smiled, and then stifled a laugh. He shook my hand and said, "Rick," as I read the name on his own badge. I covered my eyes with my hand for a moment and groaned.

"Really?" I asked.

"Just a coincidence," he said, as the doors opened. We walked past the brown marble walls that bore the name of the Hematology Department—and the list of doctors on the floor. John knew where to find his contact, and I remained two steps behind him. Though staff members, patients, and the occasional doctor passed us, no one gave us more than a glance. It occurred to me that wearing all black and a staff badge made me look out of place, but I quickly invented a story about stopping in on my day off. And of course, I worked on a different floor—in a different building, even. I felt like a spy.

John passed through the green double doors, and nodded to the nurse working the desk just inside. Without stopping, we passed more nurses on their way to lunch. I understood, then, why John had chosen the hour. No one would notice or care who we were. Charts, colorful educational posters, and other detritus filled the walls. White patches of reflected fluorescent light obscured some of them. I looked over my shoulder for a moment to see how far we had walked. If we had to run, I wanted to remember where to turn. As I looked behind me, I bumped into John. He had stopped at a closed door that bore a room number on a grey plaque.

"Here we are," he said. He tapped on the door with two knuckles. It opened after a moment, and a balding older man in a white lab coat rolled his chair a couple of feet back to his desk.

"Who's this?" he asked, chewing on a withered red pen cap and barely looking over. "Come in, and close the door."

We entered and shut the heavy wooden door behind us. It clicked, and for a second John remained silent.

"This is Jason," he said. "He's the friend I called you about." The office seemed small for a doctor. He'd fit a small filing cabinet and a desk that took up much of the narrow space between the two walls. Family photos were taped to the desk and the walls around it, and office clutter filled much of the space in front of him. It looked like a storage closet with a desk in it.

The doctor looked to me, and asked, "Were you the one that patched up Angelica while I was out?"

"Yeah," I said. "I think she tried to bite through her wrist, but someone undid the strap."

Before I could say anything else, he held up his hand and said, "I know. I figured. Thank you for doing that. She's never tried to free herself like that, but she pulled out the needle, too. She might have starved. You did pretty well, all things considered."

"My girlfriend was with me. Her sister's a nurse," I said. "I guess she picked up a few things." I thought back to the life Maureen had led long before I met her, but said nothing more. The doctor put the pen down and turned to me, still seated.

"Anyway, I'm Adrian Reynolds," he said, extending his hand. I shook it, and told him my name. "So, you know Nicholas then? I guess you call him John."

"Yes, I do," I replied.

"What do you know?"

"Well, I read his journal," I said. He nodded, as if I'd described symptoms of an illness.

"Then you understand he's not dangerous, right? Other than that—" he paused and glanced at John, "—the one incident. But, that was a long time ago and we're now able to keep that under control." He turned his chair to the other side of his desk, revealing a blue-and-white ice chest no bigger than a twelve-pack of beer. It sat against another door to the left of his desk. Dr. Reynolds tapped the cooler with his foot. His brown penny loafer thumped it, and I nearly jumped.

"That's you," he said, looking at John.

John nodded. He rarely appeared that docile. Whether the daylight subdued him or he was cowed by his dependence on Dr. Reynolds, he appeared nothing like the man I knew.

"Thank you, sir," he said.

Reynolds smiled slightly, and said, "You don't have to call me that, you know."

"Old habits," John replied. I'd never heard him talk to anyone like that in the time that I had known him. He dropped an occasional ma'am here and there, but rarely allowed anyone else to feel in charge. He pointed at the doctor as he leaned past him for the cooler. "Officer," he said.

"Army?" I asked.

"No. Navy," Dr. Reynolds replied. "That's how I met Nicholas. I was stationed Santa Margarita, the Naval hospital, when they bought him back from Korea."

"My father's Navy," I said. "You've been practicing for a while then?"

"Got out in the '70s as a Commander. I've stayed on the civilian side since then. I try to stay near Nicholas so I can keep working with him. I tracked him down after he got away from those bastards. That's my house he's living in—I mean, I own it. I don't live there."

I said nothing, but I remembered my trip to City Hall, and when I had first seen his name. It was funny how he talked about John—as if he were a different man, and not standing in the same room.

John held the cooler up for a moment, and asked, "Do you all mind if I do this right now?"

"No," the doctor said. "You can use my office. Jason, would you mind coming with me to get a cup of coffee? I don't think you want to see this."

"That's fine," I said. John looked down at the cooler, waiting.

"This could take a few minutes," he said. "It doesn't always go quickly."

The doctor stood and moved to open the door. As he grabbed the knob, he looked back and said, "You know where the sink and towels are in the next room. We'll be back in, what, twenty minutes?"

John didn't look when he answered, "That should be fine." He held the small chest with both hands, staring at the wall. He only wanted us to leave.

***

Reynolds sat across from me at a table in the hospital's dining area. A couple of fast food restaurants and a cafeteria lined the walls. The illuminated yellow and red signs caught the corners of my eyes wherever I looked. The bright lights advertising burgers, pizza, and wings (and a salad, in small print) reminded me that I hadn't eaten all morning. Doctors, nurses, and patients lined up for lunch, and dined at the small rectangular tables all around us. Reynolds bought us two cups of coffee, and a bagel for himself. He'd offered to buy me lunch. As hungry as I was, I'd declined and just asked for coffee.

"How do you get the blood out of here?" I asked.

"I have someone offsite put in an order for it. It's pretty easy if you create a paperwork trail. If anyone asks, then Nicholas is just a courier."

"I probably shouldn't ask much more, I take it," I said.

He considered that for a moment, and said, "Might be a good place to stop. There's a lot of risk involved here, and it'd be a hell of a thing to explain to someone in charge. No one would believe most of it, anyway."

"'My patient is a vampire,'" I said, imagining him saying the words.

"I don't even really like calling him that," he said. "He has a blood-borne virus, but he's resistant to it. His body has some kind of natural immunity. There's a lot I still don't know. I'm still not sure how the teeth came in."

"So, if he transmits it to someone, they have a reaction that he doesn't. Lucky him," I said.

"I'm not sure he sees it that way," Reynolds said, overlooking my joke. "He might hide it well, but you've never seen him break down the way I have. He hates himself for what happened to Angelica. I guess you only know her as Maria. He'd cure her first, if he had the choice." He picked up half of his bagel and took a bite.

"I read the journal," I said. "He called her that a few times. I know he had to change it."

I thought of John in all the time I'd known him. He took shit from no one. He behaved like a gentleman, until he was drunk and sometimes he didn't. He'd found solace in liquor and women and all that the New Orleans night had to offer. And, I couldn't stop thinking about him crying in Dr. Reynolds's office.

"Now," I said. "I need to know what the hell happened to him. Who did this?"

Reynolds looked down at his bagel, and said, "I'm going to tell you what I know. There are some things I'm not clear on. And, there are other things I can't talk about. If I told you and certain parties knew that you knew, you'd be in danger. I can't be responsible for that." The doctors, nurses, and patients milled around the food court, passing us on either side. I looked around for men in dark sunglasses, peeking over newspapers and talking through earpieces. As far as I could tell, "They" hadn't found us.

"Do we need to go somewhere else?" I asked.

"No," he said. "Hiding out in the open is best. No one can hear us with all the noise. They won't see me walk somewhere else with you. I'll keep my voice down, but this is safest."

Sipping my coffee, I nodded and said, "All right. So, what happened?"

"Nicholas Marston officially died in the Chosin Reservoir during the Korean War. And medically, that is accurate. But the cold and something unique to his physiology preserved him in such a way that he was the subject of an experiment that brought him back to life."

"By who?"

"I really don't know," he said. "And, I was instructed not to ask. Could've been the CIA or the Army. It might've been an outside contractor working through them. I was given my orders."

"What did they want with him?" I asked.

"To turn him into a renewable biological weapon," he said. "I don't know for sure, but I suspect that because no one else has his resistance, you could drop him into a foreign locale. His bite would infect someone, and they'd become—"

"Like Maria," I said.

"Yes, exactly. Once one person is infected, it's only a matter of time before everyone else is, too. One man could throw a country into chaos and then slip out undetected. After that, the Department of Defense would have all of the justification it needed to carpet bomb a place back into the Stone Age, or even detonate a nuclear warhead. And, no one would fault them for it."

"Jesus Christ. How did they make him like this?"

He shook his head, and said, "I don't know, and what I do know I can't really share. I was given very simple instructions to administer certain agents to him, without being told what they were. I was always told what to do, but not how or why it worked. Nicholas was sedated most of the time and unaware of what we'd done to him. Then, he woke up."

I saw Sgt. Nicholas Marston open his eyes and gasp, with his face covered by an oxygen mask. Chained to the bed and surrounded by tubes, he would awake as a medical horror who had already died.

"What happened to him?" I asked.

"He escaped. He thought he'd just been in surgery, and that he'd survived the Chosin. But, it became clear that there was more to it. I still had to administer his treatments. He asked me and asked me over and over again what was going on, but I couldn't even tell him."

"You didn't know," I said.

"I didn't—not really. After a couple of days he broke through the restraints, knocked down the door, and killed two guards with his bare hands. And, he went straight home to Angelica in a stolen jeep. Remember, she thought he was dead and he had no idea what had happened. He thought he'd just been kept prisoner for some reason. They left California that night and headed east. But, a few things became apparent—first off, when the sun came up."

I saw Sgt. Nicholas Marston throw his hands up and cry out as the rising sun shined through the windshield, as his wife stopped the car and tried to help.

"Then, what?"

"He noticed his body had changed. You know what happens when he eats, right?"

"You mean regular food? Yeah, he just shits it out. His body doesn't really use it," I said.

"Right, that's correct. There are no nutrients in it. Imagine those first few days—eating and eating and still feeling hungry. After a while, though, the real hunger came."

"Did he attack Maria? I mean, Angelica."

You can just call her Maria," he said. "It's fine. That's what he does. And no, I think once it became clear what was going on, she let him do it."

I saw Maria holding her wrist out with tears in her eyes, as John drank from a wound he'd made on her wrist. They'd seen Dracula bite a girl at the Saturday matinee. His instincts guided him, and they understood what he had become.

Reynolds took another bite of his bagel and set it down on the plate. After chewing for a moment, he said, "She gradually succumbed to the virus. It doesn't take immediately, and I know Nicholas fed on her more than once. Maybe if he had stopped, she would've survived. But, over the next few days, she ran a fever that should've killed her. She started sweating and shaking, and she begged him to keep the lights off. Within a week, she'd degenerated into what you saw in the attic."

As Dr. Reynolds explained, the story played out in my mind. Maria thrashed and cried out on a motel bed in a dimly lit room, as John struggled to lift her. In the bathroom, he laid her down in a tub filled with ice to lower her temperature.

"Remember," he said, "Nicholas is a Marine. He knew to keep them moving. He was able to sedate her before they moved on. She still had her initial payout from his death in Korea, so they had money. And, they drove across the South. They lived in cheap motels or rented apartments for a few weeks, or even months. He would just tell people that she was sick. And, they always paid for everything in cash." Two years before, I had noticed that my new friend never used a credit card at the bar. Then, I knew why. I felt like I should have written all my questions down on a piece of paper, but I remembered them all.

"How did they find blood?" I asked.

"However he could. He bribed doctors or he lured vagrants. I think he even killed a couple of dogs and cats. He tried to avoid hurting anyone, but I'm not sure how successful he was."

"How did you find him?" I asked, sipping my coffee. For a moment, a small and fiery thought emerged from the corner of my mind. It needed the kick I could so easily add at home. I wanted a drink. I rapped the table with my fist.

"Are you okay?" the doctor asked.

"Yeah," I said. "I'm dealing with something else right now."

Reynolds cocked an eyebrow and tilted his head. I think he knew, but wouldn't presume to ask more. I wondered if I'd been shaking, or showing any of the other telltale signs of man who needed a drink.

"Is it obvious?" I asked.

"I've certainly seen enough of it in this town. If you need to talk to someone, I might be able to point you in the right direction." I clenched my jaw and then relaxed.

"I'll keep that in mind," I said. "How did you find him?"

"When I learned he had left the facility, I knew I had to look for him. When he was awake for those couple of days, we talked some. I had the nightshift at the lab. If I wanted to waste some time, I'd visit him in his room. And as his doctor, I was one of the only people who had access to him. They kept him pretty isolated otherwise. Besides getting out of Korea, he had a lot to say. He was sharper than most of the enlisted grunts I'd met."

"So, why chase after him?" I asked.

"Because, he said. He stopped for a moment and glanced down. I leaned in, struggling to hear him over the din of chatter, glasses, and silverware. The fluorescent lights whitened his face and reflected in his eyes for a moment as he looked back at me. "I was following orders, but I'm partially responsible for what Nicholas became. I've never forgiven myself for that."

"How did you find him?"

***

In the years following the escape of Sgt. Nicholas Marston, Dr. Reynolds searched for newspaper articles and listened to rumors about anything that might lead back to his patient. He asked every bartender, biker, and whore he could find about an ex-Marine with a taste for blood. He even employed a couple of private detectives, and paid out bribes whenever he had to. For the first couple of decades, he didn't find a damn thing.

But, it's hard to hide a trail of dead animals and wide-eyed hookers with cuts on their wrists. Nicholas had traveled east for the first few years, but doubled back—anything to shake the trail of anyone who might follow them. He described the scene—the squalor—in which he'd finally discovered my friend.

A prostitute had passed out on one of two double beds in a by-the-hour joint near Houston. She had blood running from her upper arms. His wife Maria, as unconscious as ever, occupied the second bed.

Nicholas hadn't answered at first, but finally agreed to when Reynolds yelled "It's me! It's Adrian!" through the closed door. He—Nicholas, I mean—would later note that the likelihood of a doctor dropping in at that hour of the night seemed beyond coincidence.

Closing the door behind him, he noticed the curtains taped around the edges. The young woman passed out on one of the beds looked every bit her calling—fishnet stockings, high-heels, too much makeup, and a gaudy getup of black and pink. Syringes, gauze, rubbing alcohol, and a bunch of over-the-counter medical supplies littered the table near the window. Maria slept in the other twin bed, closest to the bathroom.

Nicholas stood at the sink at the end of the room and stared into the mirror. Blood covered his hands and the white porcelain in front of him. He caught his breath and spoke to Reynolds, with his back still turned. The young lady, as it turned out, feared needles worse than a having her upper arm sliced open. As long as she got her money, she said she didn't really give a fuck. But, the sight of blood did it anyway. Nicholas thought he had cut too deeply, and wondered whether he would have to kill her or leave her in the parking lot and call an ambulance.

Dr. Reynolds examined the cuts, and no, they weren't actually that deep. He bandaged her and promised a quick trip to a woman's shelter with a story—one for her if she woke up ("I found you in an alley.") and one for the staff ("I found the poor, poor girl in an alley.").

Upon returning, he used the spare key my friend had provided. He found Nicholas sprawled on the free bed with a trickle of blood running from his lips. An empty plastic cup with a red bottom sat on the nightstand next to him. Maria was still sedated in the other bed. The television played the "Star Spangled Banner." The last program of the evening had just concluded. Nicholas was not watching.

The two men talked until dawn. Nicholas—and he told Dr. Reynolds to stop calling him Sgt. Marston—asked him the same question that I did that morning. He wanted to know how, nearly two decades later, Reynolds had tracked him down. The doctor explained as he had to me, and begged Nicholas to let him help them.

Nicholas agreed to move to New Orleans. The doctor owned a second family home there, and he would ensure that both he and Angelica (now "John and Maria") were provided for while he treated them. He promised to work on their case privately, for free, and for as long as it took. That was about twenty-four years ago, and they had only devised a plan to keep them fed and hidden. Not much else had come of his private research.

***

"So, the CIA or whoever wasn't looking for him?" I asked

"They might have been," he said. "They probably still are, for all I know."

"John told you about the girls, right?" I asked. Dr. Reynolds nodded, and his eyes fell.

"Yes, he did. That's about the worst thing that could have possibly happened. Used to be, he would leave town with his wife if something like this happened. Things are different, now."

"How's that?" I asked.

"Well, I'm treating him here and he's living in my house. He has a life again. And, he has you," he said.

"Me?"

"Oh yeah," Reynolds replied. "He's very fond of you. I think you're the first person he's trusted in a long time. He and I have to keep our distance in case any of our old contacts come calling, if you know what I mean."

"You don't think they're behind those two girls, do you?"

He sipped his coffee and said, "No. No, I don't. That's not their style. And, even if it was, they would've found both of us by now. I'd be either dead or in solitary confinement at Ft. Leavenworth. John and Maria would be in a lab somewhere."

"What if they find you?"

"Anything's possible. That's one of the reasons I've advised Nicholas to keep a lower profile. I know about what happened with those kids in Florida. If the wrong person gets word about him, then someone might find him."

"You know he told a cop, right?" I asked. I still had to call Brad, I reminded myself.

"I'm aware, and I don't agree with it," he said, waving his finger at me. "If you haven't spoken to him recently, I'd contact him and make sure he's still on your side. If what he knows gets passed up the chain of command, there's no telling who might hear."

I thought about Brad. I would call him. He had tried to call me, and I'd been too drunk or busy to contact him. I thought about John's own nights with the bottle. He wanted to bury the worst kind of pain. He regretted not only what he had become, but the cruel fate he'd inflicted on the one person that would shelter him. Some people had to care for sick family members for years or even decades. John had to watch over his wife forever. And when he awoke each evening, he had to remember who made her that way.

I felt a hand on my shoulder. Looking up, I saw John standing behind me holding the cooler.

"Catching up?" he asked.

Dr. Reynolds stood, and said, "Just filling him in on things, mostly." He extended his hand to John. My friend took it and shook. He looked down at me, and then glanced back up at the doctor.

Reynolds said, "I suspect that you two have a lot to talk about." Without another word, he walked out of the food court and towards the elevator.

***

We returned to John's house, and I pulled curbside to let him out of the Volvo. He turned to look at me. "You can come in, if you like," he said.

"Don't you need to sleep?" I asked.

"I'll make some coffee," he said, getting out of the car.

I parked a few cars up and followed him inside. We entered the long hallway that led to his living room. Glancing at the photograph of him with Maria, I could no longer think of her as the creature that lived in his attic. At my apartment, he'd explained that she usually stayed quiet as long as he fed her. As we crossed into the living room, I listened and heard nothing. He'd been back in New Orleans long enough to check on her. The cavernous living room stood open and quiet and dark, lit only by the sun's rays that poured through the edges of the curtains.

"Want me to make that coffee?" I asked. He only nodded.

I crossed back towards the kitchen, not knowing where to find anything. John heard me opening and shutting cabinets. He rapidly called out the locations of the filters, the mugs, the milk, the sugar, and the yellow bag of coffee he kept in his freezer. I found everything, and poured the black grounds into the filter I'd dropped into the top of the pot. I still hadn't had a drink since my chat with Maureen. Some of the AA crowd said coffee helped.

But, I also remembered that I hadn't even decided if I would quit drinking. The coffee maker bubbled and rumbled, and the black liquid filled the pot with a thin trickle. I joined my friend in the living room to wait.

"So, what did you think about all that?" John asked, sitting on the couch.

"Uh," I said, slapping my sides, "it's pretty unbelievable, but at this point I've seen pictures, your journal, and Maria; and, I've talked to your doctor. Unless this is the most elaborate hoax ever cooked up, I don't see what I can argue with."

"The Department of Defense considered all manner of unconventional methods during the Cold War," he said. "You have likely heard the stories about mind control and psychic combat."

"Alien weaponry and ex-Nazi scientists?" I asked. "Yeah, I've seen the stupid cable shows."

"I can't speak to all of those rumors. But, here I sit. I am the end result. They wanted to drop me into a hot zone so that I could infect the local populace. Once the virus spread, any country could be made to tear itself apart."

"What about containment?" I asked. "If something like that spread, it wouldn't stop at the border."

"At that point, the military would have every reason to use extraordinary measures," he replied. "No one would argue with using chemical or nuclear weapons on a country overrun by, well, you know."

"Vampires—or zompires, I guess?" I said, stifling a laugh. "That seems like an awfully complicated way to nuke someone. But, I guess it makes sense. No world power would stop the United States from squashing that kind of an outbreak. Doesn't seem like they could use you very often, though."

I listened for the trickling of the coffee pot, and heard only silence. It had finished brewing.

John looked up at me, and said, "They were researching many different ideas in those days. Not all of them were practical. But, if I were dropped in and succeeded in spreading what I have, no one would survive. People would tear themselves apart. It was considered a final solution of sorts."

"If we ever went to war with the Russians," I said. "Nice choice of words, by the way." I stood up and walked back to the kitchen, and returned bearing two cups of coffee with nothing added to either of them.

"I've been drinking this stuff like a fiend lately," I said.

"Do you have trouble staying awake?" John asked. He took the mug and sipped from it.

"No," I said, sitting next to him on the couch. It was as good a time to tell him as any. "It's another thing."

"What do you mean?"

"Maureen thinks I might have a drinking problem," I said.

"Well, do you?" he asked.

"I don't know," I said. "We drink a lot, but so does everyone around here. I don't know if it's a case of just liking to drink or if I really need to do it. I told her I'd think about it. I've been trying to cut back. I haven't had one since I talked to her. But, Jesus, that was only yesterday."

"I suppose you should see how long you can go. I may not be the best man to ask for advice, but we certainly don't have to drink every time we meet." I could tell he wanted to move on to the rest of the matters at hand. "What do you propose we do next?" he asked.

"About what?" I asked.

"This entire ordeal," he said, rolling his hand.

"Uh, you remember the group I told you about that worships you? The Fellowship?" I asked.

"I do."

"They meet upstairs at Kaldi's on Mondays. Remember that coffee shop I took you to on Decatur and St. Philip?"

"That seems like a very public place to gather," he said.

"Some of them are kids. They're runaways. God knows where they're all living—probably on the streets or something. Besides, that place has drug deals in the bathrooms. Hacker collectives meet upstairs," I said.

"What collectives?"

"Groups of people that like to break into security systems over the Internet," I said. "A bunch of pretend vampires would fit in with the rest of the crowd there. Anyway, Chaz and Maven just went to their meeting last night. They were going to try to figure out who called them here." Tasting my coffee, I felt that it was cool enough to drink. I took a long sip.

"And that would be our killer?" he asked. He raised his mug as if we'd reached the answer. I touched it with my own.

"I think so," I said. "But, I was convinced it was 'Radu,' for a while. Now, we know it wasn't Rick or Michael. So, it's someone trying to pick up on what they started."

"To have me turn them into vampires? They really don't know what they're asking for, do they?"

I shifted towards him on the couch and said, "Right, but how could they? And, they aren't going to believe anyone that tells them differently. We just need to wait until we talk to Chaz. We have to find out who called them to New Orleans."

"When were you planning to do that?" John asked.

"Right now," I said. "That's my next stop."

Chapter 16

Tuesday, October 21, 1997 – Afternoon

I sat in Chaz's office across from him. Maven stood in the background with his arms crossed, as he usually did. I'd noticed that he often rested that way, as if waiting for someone to challenge him.

"Do you have any coffee?" I asked, nodding at the pot on a side table nearby. Light poured over it in flat beams through the blinds, and I could see the green leaves of the courtyard outside. It felt like God himself had unveiled the pot.

"Sure," Chaz replied. "Should be a couple of extra mugs over there."

"I've been guzzling the stuff lately," I said, standing up. I grabbed a black cup with a pair of vampire fangs on it and the words "Bite Me" printed in script below it.

As I poured the black coffee into the cup, Maven asked, "You quitting drinking or something?"

"Taking a break," I said. "I haven't decided past that." I looked at my watch. It was a little after two. I normally didn't start that early, but it had happened before.

"Good luck with that," Chaz said. "Not easy in this town."

"No, it isn't," I said, sitting down across from him. "The fucking town reminds me constantly." The dead girls flashed in my mind there, again—Raven dead in the bar bathroom and Jenny bled out in her apartment. I wanted a drink. I closed my eyes and shook my head.

"Coffee too strong?" asked Chaz.

"No, it's perfect," I said. "What did you find out?

"You're going to love these guys," Maven said, laughing and shaking his head.

"Am I?"

Chaz looked serious for a moment, and said, "Those are some seriously fucked up kids." He recounted how, the afternoon before, Maven had tracked down a member of the group online and introduced himself. They had been invited, after all. To the misguided children in black outside of New Orleans, the two stood as nothing less than vampire royalty.

They'd arrived a few minutes late so that Chaz could make a proper and pronounced entrance. He'd donned his full costume and the persona to go with it—loud and confident, with enough force of character to make you believe even his most questionable stories. Ascending the stairs with his long vest trailing, his sunglasses on, and his top hat high as high as the heavens, the youths had stood for him and parted to reveal a large chair at the end of the space—not quite a throne, but a place of honor.

Chaz described a cluster of white teenage faces marked with grease-black raccoon eyes. They wore hoodies, and band shirts, and striped socks on their arms with holes for the fingers. Some of them already had prosthetic fangs, and others bore healing cuts on their arms. A young blonde girl kept a stash of razors, neatly set in a small coffin case she kept at the edge of her table. Another wore an ankh necklace that concealed a sheathed blade. They hailed from different states. They claimed that Rick had "appointed" a few as the head of their local clans.

But, he hadn't called them or even written to all of them personally. Of that, they were quite clear. No one expected Rick to lead the Fellowship from prison.

"Did they have copies of the book?" I asked.

Chaz shook his head, and said, "I don't think there are as many as you think. One of them had one. It was this girl who just got in town."

"No others?" I asked.

"I got the one here at the shop. You've got yours. Somebody said there was one missing from somewhere else," Chaz said. "A few of them were looking at the one the girl had." I realized that Rick had only been in prison for a year, and he was never out on bail. He couldn't have made many in that time.

"How many were there?" I asked.

"Books or kids?"

"Kids," I said.

"Maven guessed maybe twenty of them," Chaz said. Apparently, he hadn't sold any fangs, either. Most had little money to spare, and a few couldn't even afford to buy a coffee. A couple claimed not to need any, because they, of course, lived on blood. Regardless, he and Chaz were greeted warmly. They pretended to represent "the New Orleans vampires" and welcomed the Fellowship to the city. I laughed, but he told me the group took the pronouncement very seriously. And, they said that the head New Orleans vampire was not in attendance that evening.

"I thought that was you," I said to Chaz.

Maven laughed hard, and said, almost yelling, "So did he!" Chaz rolled his eyes and flashed a will-you-stop look at his friend in the corner.

"I'm getting to that," he said.

Chaz told them he knew why they had come, and his foreknowledge made him seem all the more important. He might be in regular contact with Rick Fremont even, but for legal reasons he could say no more. They all understood that. And, Radu was "very, very busy," what with All Hallows' Eve on the way.

Michael was busy, in fact. He was busy avoiding all of them. But, Chaz's wording made the young man sound like Santa Claus. He couldn't be at every mall, but always sent one of his helpers. But, Chaz intoned, there had been a minor breach of protocol. With one great, sharp nail extended, he explained that this insignificant infraction bore no consequences. Maven explained hastily that the matter only needed clarification, and that he had a minute to make fangs if anyone would like them. No one stood, and Chaz continued. He explained that they were unsure of who had declared himself the head vampire of the city. Not one of the city's vampires had come forward. It seemed like, at worst, a miscommunication—a missed phone call or e-mail, or perhaps an erased message or forgotten conversation.

"Verdilak," they called him. And he was not in attendance.

"Verdi-what?" I asked, interrupting Chaz.

"Hang on," he said, one hand raised.

Verdilak was not at the meeting, nor had he ever attended one. They had met four times since September—three times at the public library, and now once at Kaldi's. He communicated only through e-mail. Before they'd arrived, he had left a bouquet of roses and a letter of thanks for their attendance. He asked for their patience, and assured them that he was in contact with the vampire John.

They would have "The Blood" soon, the note assured them.

He charged them to continue meeting, and to find others that might join their cause. One day soon, all of them—Rick, Radu, John, and the Fellowship—would unite. Everything would begin in New Orleans.

In the meantime, the youths met and read aloud from Rick's red book. They did not feed from each other in public. Per the slim volume's instructions, vampires should only feed in private.

"So, a bunch of kids are holding vampire bible study at Kaldi's," I said. "Did they have a guitar, too?"

"Guitar?" Chaz asked.

"Like 'Kumbaya'," I said, strumming the air in front of me.

Chaz laughed loudly for a second and clapped, before dropping his eyes and assuming his gravest look. "No, they didn't," he said, almost growling. I knew the tone, and he usually reserved it for the end of his darkest stories—when someone died.

"Do you think they've killed anyone?" I asked. As with Dr. Reynolds, I had a list of questions I'd failed to write down.

Chaz glanced upward, and said, "No, I don't think so. But, keep in mind," he said, quickening his words, "they might not come out and talk about something like that. We were in public." I leaned forward on the desk and folded my hands.

"We should keep an eye in the paper for any more vampire murders," I said. I stopped for a second. "I can't fucking believe I just said that out loud." Maven laughed again, and let his arms fall. The joke seemed to have relaxed him for a moment.

"What's with the name, though—Verdilak?" I asked.

"It's a kind of Russian vampire," Chaz said. "It's sort of an Old World myth. They feed on family members only, but I doubt this guy even knows that."

The word rang familiar, and then I remembered all the books I'd read in college. "Oh, right. Tolstoy wrote a short story about it, I think. I've heard of it. God, that guy's digging deep."

Maven looked up, and finally said, "Whoever he is, it's going to be trouble for all of us. He's trying to build a cult of underage kids in New Orleans. People have tried to 'unite' the vampire scene before. They're completely full of shit. It's a social scene and a lifestyle. It'd be like trying to be the head gay guy or the top goth DJ or whatever."

"And," Chaz said, "if they're really planning to go after civilians then we've all got a problem. I don't need cops coming in here and trashing the office and associating us—or John, either."

"He's back, you know," I said.

"No shit?" Chaz asked.

"Came in last night. He scared the shit out of me at my apartment."

"What did he do?"

"Let himself in and waited on my futon. I just saw that someone was in there, and I tackled him when he came out." Both of them laughed. For a second, I held back. Then I remembered the sight of John's drink flying everywhere and I couldn't stop myself. It felt good to relax for a minute.

"Anyway," I said. "He's really grateful you're helping with this. Speaking of cops, have either of you seen Brad?"

"Your friend?" Maven asked.

"Yeah," I said.

"Weren't you going to call him?" he asked.

"I will. I've just been busy. That's next on my list. So, are y'all going to find this guy?"

Chaz pointed his thumb back at Maven, and said, "He's already asking around town and online. We want to meet him. If he really wants John, he'll be easy enough to find."

***

The three of us talked for a while longer before I left. I was more than grateful that they wanted to help, but I reminded them that Verdilak was probably out of his mind. I couldn't say with certainty that he was the man in black; or, that he had murdered Raven and Jenny Dark. But, it seemed most likely at that point. I also hadn't told either of them what I'd learned about John. The more they knew, the more liable they'd become. I saw one version of the future where we all ended up dead or in jail—John for murdering those girls (because we couldn't prove otherwise), me for not calling the police about Maria, and Maureen for helping me. Chaz and Maven would go down as accessories and plea for suspended sentences.

Knowing what I did, I thought about contacting Rick again. I had enough pieces of the puzzle to get the next round of clues from the psychotic fuck. I finally decided to call Brad to let him know I'd be back in Florida—and to see if he knew that John had returned. I could arrange the meeting through the usual means and with the usual excuse (journalist, follow-up interview), but I figured I should at least let him know. I called his cell phone and waited through a couple of rings.

"This is Captain Williams," the voice replied. I caught myself before I began pouring out my story. It wasn't Brad.

"Is Detective Simoneaux available?" I asked.

"No, he's not," the voice replied. "This isn't his number anymore."

"Um, okay. What happened to him?"

"I'm not really able to say. Who is this, please?"

I rattled off a few press credentials, and said, "But, I'm a friend." I didn't know if that would help or hurt my situation.

"Uh, I can't really say what happened. I know he was ill for a while, and then he was placed on leave pending some administrative stuff. Does that answer your question?"

"Not really," I said. "But, thanks." Without another word, the phone clicked. I noticed my answering machine still flashing. I hadn't erased Brad's last message. I listened again and wrote down the number he recited at the end. It was a different one than I'd just used. I dialed the new number only to hear his voicemail message.

"Brad, it's me," I said. "I just tried to call your old number. Give me a ring when you can and I'll catch you up on everything."

***

I hadn't seen Maureen since we'd spoken in the back of Second Chance. I'd decided to visit Rick Fremont one more time, and I needed to let her know. I could've called, but I decided to tell her in person. The shops on Magazine Street passed my side windows in a multicolor blur of antique stores, used clothing exchanges, and record shops. Tourists with shopping bags blended together in streaks on either side of me. Through the windshield, I glanced at the clear sky and wondered when the autumn gray of New Orleans would finally arrive. At a stoplight, I glanced at my watch. It was 2:48 p.m. on the twenty-first of October. Halloween would be here soon, and I remembered Chaz and Maven's party. The light changed, and I pulled my car into an unoccupied space outside of Maureen's store. I remembered the first time I saw her there, picking through a box of clothes and sick enough to have stayed in bed. As soon as I entered, she looked up and smiled.

"Hey," she said.

"Hi," I said, recalling all we'd discussed. I hadn't decided how to approach her. Part of me wanted to stay angry at her. She'd pointed out something I'd already suspected. She made me ask myself The Question. But, I told myself she'd done it out of concern. "Love" hadn't crossed my mind yet. Everyone in New Orleans "loved" their new boy or girl two weeks into fucking them regularly. I didn't want to fall into that trap, but I accepted that she merely cared as much as anybody possibly could, by that point. The quiet and easy tone she greeted me with said as much.

The afternoon sun shined full through the picture window, casting bright spots and leaving shadows on the racks of colorful clothing. I leaned on the counter and looked at her there in the light.

She took both of my hands from the other side, and asked, "How are you feeling?"

"Uh, not bad," I said. "Drinking a lot of coffee. I think I'm kind of hooked on the stuff." I knew what she meant, and she understood my answer. No, I hadn't taken a drink since our last meeting. I wouldn't bother announcing that I'd turned into a bean addict otherwise.

"They say that helps," she said, still holding my hands.

"Wait, let me get clear on this for a second," I said. I looked around the shop to see no one else around us. She eyed me for a moment, and I knew she didn't like my tone.

"Clear on what?"

"I didn't say I was an alcoholic. I just said I'd try to cut back and I have."

"Have you?" she asked. "It's only been, like, a day."

"Yes," I said. "I haven't had anything since we talked."

"And, how's that going?"

"Like I said—not bad. I don't know. I might try to moderate it. I might not try again at all. I'm just waiting to see what happens. I've got to go out of town again," I said.

"To Florida?"

"Yeah," I said. I turned my back to her. "A lot's happened since we talked. I've found out some more stuff, and it's getting complicated. Do you want to come by my place for dinner tonight?"

"Sure. Going to make me dinner?" she asked.

***

I'd planned to order out for Chinese, and I had nothing to prepare at my place. I stopped at the Save-A-Center on Tchoupitoulas to buy groceries. If I had to drive to Florida again, I at least wanted to spend some time with her. The tension might cloud the evening, but I decided to overlook it for the moment. And, I hadn't cooked a proper meal in ages. I usually just made a sandwich or dragged out restaurant leftovers for days. I didn't even know what to buy. But, I parked in the great black lot among the rows of cars and trucks, and walked up to the store anyway.

At the front of the store, I pushed a shopping cart through the entrance under the large green awning with the store's name. For a second, I felt like my mother. No matter how many times I'd shopped for myself, I could never shake that feeling.

I headed past the florist and the deli to the meat in the back. Chicken seemed easiest. It was cheap enough and no one ever complained. I could find a recipe to roast one online or call my parents. Thinking of a list of seasonings and anything else I might need, I pushed the cart past the bins of meat before I arrived at the whole birds. Picking one up, I felt its cold weight and looked at the sticker to check the price.

Then, someone tapped me on the shoulder.

I nearly jumped at the sight of Brad Simoneaux, standing behind me with a broad grin on his face. He looked better than he had at the Tower, to say the least.

"Brad," I said. "What are you doing here?"

"Shopping!" he said, with another wide smile. "What else would I be doing? I got your call, by the way." He wore a shiny black shirt with a collar, and dark blue jeans. He seemed almost overdressed for the occasion. His red-brown hair had grown out a bit, and the telltale stubble on his face confirmed what I already knew—that he no longer worked for the NOPD.

"How have you been?" I asked. "I heard that you weren't with NOPD at the moment."

"Yeah, that's pending some things. I might be back on. I was sick for a while," he said. "I had this flu I couldn't shake, and I ended up burning through my sick days. It's a pain in the ass. There's all this stuff that has to get ironed out with the union, and I have to submit some paperwork. Who told you?" It took me a second, but I realized that he probably knew the answer.

"The cop that got your phone—Williams," I said.

"Jesus, that fucking guy?" he asked, lowering his voice. "What did he tell you?"

I explained the story as quickly as I could. He nodded at the end of every sentence. They hadn't, he explained, played well together. His assignment of Brad's old phone only made his suspension all the more insulting.

He listened to my story for a few minutes, before asking, "How's John? I heard he's back in town."

I could have lied, but I didn't.

"Yeah, he just got back. He's trying to lay low." I looked around for a minute, worried that someone might hear. Women and children passed and dutifully ignored us on their way to the cereal aisle. We were as alone as two people could be in a grocery store in the middle of the afternoon.

"He may not be a suspect then," he said. "I never told anyone up the chain about him. But, you know I've still got my own piece. If you need my help, let me know."

I said nothing about Verdilak, and I laughed and waved away the remark. But part of it, I couldn't let go. When I saw Brad at the Tower and talked to him on the phone, he told me that the NOPD might want to talk to John. I was thinking about it, but I decided to forget about it for a minute because of the last thing he said. Brad didn't know about Verdilak, and the last thing I wanted was him finding and killing our mystery man on John's behalf.

But, he insisted on giving me his new phone number again. He quickly scrawled it on the back of his old "Detective Brad Simoneaux" business card. I took the card and shook his hand. He patted me on the shoulder and told me good-bye. Before I could say anything else, he turned walked down the aisle, past the coffee and tea.

At the checkout, I swallowed as the cashier swiped each of the items for my budget dinner date—chicken, potatoes, French bread, asparagus, and all the necessary seasonings. I'd grabbed a small cheesecake for dessert on the way there. The entire milieu rang to about forty bucks—more than I'd wanted to spend, but less than I'd feared. I decided to skip the wine, in light of all that had happened. It was easier than I expected, and part of me wondered if we'd overestimated the problem. I shelved that question after seeing the time printed on the receipt—4:07 p.m. Maureen would close Second Chance in less than an hour, and presumably show up at my door after that. Though I gave her rides often enough, she always swore she could take the bus and the streetcar without complaint.

In the parking lot, I loaded up the Volvo's trunk with groceries. An enthusiastic "See you 'round!" came from a car passing behind me. I quickly turned to see Brad again, waving from the driver's side window. No longer in his NOPD unit, he now drove a blue Nissan Sentra I had never seen. He smiled as the vehicle slowed, and he waited for me to respond. I waved, and forced a smile back at him. He seemed better than he had before, certainly, but also not like the acerbic and cynical man I'd known. Reaching into my pocket, I felt the business card he'd given me. I drew it out and read over the new phone number he'd written in black marker. I decided I might check in with him again in a few days. He might be able to direct us to someone trustworthy at NOPD, or tell us what else they'd done on the case.

***

Maureen knocked shortly after I'd loaded the chicken into the oven. Dressed with onions, peppers, and olive oil—and guided by a simple recipe printed from the Internet—I figured it would impress her enough. Or, it would convince her that I could cook without burning down my apartment. I answered the door wearing a black apron, and she laughed at the sight of me.

"You even wear black in the kitchen," she said.

"Hides the dirt better," I said. "Come on in." She followed me into the kitchen. Looking back, I said, "Should be an hour or so. The chicken just went in. The potatoes au gratin are just a package thing I'm going to dress up with some extra cheese, so that shouldn't take long. The asparagus just need a few minutes in the oven."

"Packaged potatoes," she said, laughing. She held up the red box and shook it like a maraca. "You fucking went all out, didn't you?"

"Jesus," I said, hugging her. "You didn't give me any notice. I hit the grocery right after I saw you. Just be grateful I didn't order pizza and act like I made it myself."

"I think I'd know," she said. She opened the refrigerator and took out a can of Coke. After cracking it open, she took a sip and turned towards the living room. "What do you want to do until the bird's done?" For the moment, I thought about finding the last half-bottle of bourbon in my liquor cabinet. We could pass the time quickly, but I knew we had more important things to discuss.

"I, uh, I should probably show you a couple of things," I said, walking past her to my room. Emerging from the hallway, I held up Rick's letters in one hand and his handmade book in the other.

"What are those?" she asked, resting her soft drink on the table.

"Sit for a second," I said. She did, and I joined her there. Laying out the letters on the coffee table, I formed the word mosaic just as I had the first time and for Lord Chaz afterward. "I know I told you about this already, but here it is."

She leaned over the image of Michael Fremont, constructed in letters both dark and light, and said, "You mentioned it when we were at the…" She trailed off. She meant the pub where I'd gotten so drunk I couldn't drive.

"Yeah, at the Irish bar," I said. "I remember. I don't know how clear I was about it."

"Not very," she said. "You kind of unloaded a lot all at once."

"This is Radu," I said. "His real name is Michael Fremont. He's Rick's half-brother. I don't think he killed anyone. And this," I said, holding up the red book, "is by Rick. He makes them in prison and sends them to people."

"Why?" she asked. After opening the book to its center, I handed it to her. She looked through the pages of archaic calligraphy, punctuated by drawings that looked like Gustave Dore's nightmares.

"Have you read this?" she asked.

"Parts of it," I said. "I've met him twice now. That was enough. I probably should read through it again, though. Go to the last few pages." She flipped to the end of the book, and saw the sainted images of Rick and his Clan—and of course, my friend.

"That's John," she said.

"I think Rick has some followers, and they've kind of turned into a cult. They think John is practically a god."

She laughed, and said, "Christ, if only he knew him better."

"Yeah," I said. "That's the thing. I know what John is now."

Maureen turned, almost hopping a bit. "What do you mean?" she asked.

"He's an experiment."

Patiently and slowly, I explained all that I had learned of the Fellowship, John's past, and his association with Dr. Adrian Reynolds. She recalled the name from the leather book we'd found. I'd already shared what I read in the journal, not knowing it was by John himself.

"What, the Marston guy? I told you that was probably him," she said.

"You were right," I said. "Nicholas Marston is John. I didn't want to see it, but you were right. Feel better?"

"Yeah Shit. Anything else?" she asked, resting her head in her hands.

***

The story continued through dinner. I withdrew the crispy brown chicken from the oven, and then finished the potatoes and asparagus, talking about vampires the entire time. The story flowed freely, and I mentioned that I had been, bit by bit, writing the whole thing down.

"Going to publish it or something?" she asked.

"No," I said, shaking my head. Then, I shook it again. "It's more like a testament. It's for if anything happens to me or John or something. If we all die or disappear, someone needs to know."

"My dad will love that," said Maureen.

"Remember when I told you at the shop that I might need to go back to Florida?"

"Yeah. Why?" she asked. I took a sip from my own glass of Coke. I looked down at my plate. My chicken sat only half-eaten. I picked up a piece and bit into it.

Swallowing, I looked back at her, and said, "I know what's going on now. I know what he's not telling me. If he knows who 'Verdilak' is, that might put us on the right path."

***

Wednesday, October 22, 1997

Maureen departed for work the next day, and I allowed myself to sleep for a couple of extra hours. Running around town every day had taken its toll on my schedule. I felt like I couldn't sleep enough. We'd watched *Frankenstein* ("Anything that doesn't have vampires," she'd said.) and fucked on the couch before reaching the bed. After she left, I settled back in to the black pillow and congratulated myself for another evening of not drinking.

I had more than enough work to do. I needed to churn out a few editorials and organize the documents I'd assembled. I planned to write a calendar starting on the day when I'd first shown John the pictures of Raven. As best as I could tell, I had a day to myself. I had to drive to Florida again in the morning.

But first, I had to call John. I had an idea.

***

Thursday, October 23, 1997

Rick Fremont stared at me with unblinking eyes. In front of him, I'd laid a single sheet of paper with the name "Verdilak" written in black marker. He'd barely glanced at it before returning his gaze to me.

"Back again, I see," he said.

I leaned forward, never breaking my gaze, and said, "You know him, don't you?"

"Even if I did, why would I tell you?"

I finally blinked, and then I spoke: "Because he very likely killed two women to get to John. And if you care about John at all, you'll help me stop him from doing it again. Unless you're the one with your hand on all of this." He swallowed, and closed his eyes for a moment. The accusation took him aback, and I saw my chance. Even I didn't believe it, but I knew I could find a way in from there.

"How do I know you're not telling this guy what to do from in here?" I asked. "You were already sending messages to John. What's your end game? Killing people he knows isn't going to get him here any faster."

"I want to see him," he said. "Bring him here and I will tell you everything I know."

I waited a few seconds to speak.

"I want, from you, plain answers in fucking English," I said. "No more puzzles, or riddles, or poems, or drawings, or any of this bullshit." I held up my copy of the red book that I'd brought with me. "If I bring John to you for a visit, will you tell us what happened?"

He nodded, but his eyes betrayed his desperation

I waved towards the two-way mirror behind Rick. The lock in the door clicked behind me. It opened. John stepped through past a guard. He wore a black suit with a red shirt, and had put on a few silver rings. He looked more like the legendary vampire our friend wanted him to be. Rick stood, his mouth hanging open. He reached out, with his hands still cuffed. John moved towards him and took his hands in his. Rick sank to his knees and lowered his head. Still holding his grip, John looked down wordlessly.

After a moment, we heard sniffling and low, miserable groans from Rick. On the tiled floor beneath him, I could see tear drops land in splatters and splashes. John released one hand to touch him on the head. If Rick saw John as some sort of vampire demigod, he certainly had even more reason to do so. Neither of us had much pity for the man, but my friend played his part well.

The two of us sat across from Rick as he sobbed for a few more minutes. At first, he only wanted to know why John hadn't come earlier. On the way to Florida, I'd explained to my friend what Rick believed in savage detail—that John still owed it to him to change him, but that he'd only left him to rot in prison.

In the car, we discussed how much to tell our incarcerated subject. John wanted to just tell Rick the truth. He wouldn't turn him, knowing the consequences. The idea of Rick as a creature like Maria scared the shit out of both of us. John adjusted his sunglasses for the hundredth time, and continued to apply sunscreen while I talked. I told him that if Rick didn't believe him, he might hold out on whatever he knew. A delayed promise might play better than a broken one. John only nodded, and moved the visor in front of him to shield his face.

"How does he expect to live as a vampire in prison?" he asked. "That does not make a great deal of sense."

"I think he thinks they won't be able to keep him in there," I replied.

And we both knew the truth of it. Rick wanted to be out in the world again, to gather his followers and finish what he'd started. Nothing else would satisfy the miserable bastard.

Sitting in that room with him, we both knew what John would do: promise to return, if only he might help him. Nodding, his face still wet with tears, Rick explained all that he knew. Verdilak had contacted him in prison. The letters had come gradually at first—one or two a month—but then more arrived. Verdilak didn't want to fuck him or fight him.

He wanted to learn.

And, Rick offered all that he knew—of the origins of an ancient vampire tribe he'd adopted as his own. It was nameless, old, and devoted to finding the true secret of the Turn, as they called it.

To Turn meant to ascend to the highest plain of vampirism, as if climbing the ladder to a sanguine heaven. At the top, there was John, who drank blood and needed it to live. He wasn't faking. He hadn't redefined the word "vampire." He was the real thing. The ancient Bogomils of Bulgaria had searched for the truth. Occultists, writers, the Catholic Church, and God knows who else had tried to make sense of it all. And,

Rick would carry out their work. And, he knew that at the end of it all, John proved everything that they believed. After centuries of looking, vampires were real.

But, Rick hadn't told Verdilak to do anything.

The young man who wrote him so often had taken it upon himself to suggest a gathering of the Fellowship in New Orleans. With enough faces there, young and wanting, they might draw out John and begin the Turn. Verdilak never said how or why this might work—only that he knew where to find the key to it all.

Rick couldn't stop the gathering of the Fellowship. Verdilak had organized them online. He contacted anyone who had written to Rick, and especially the few that had the red book. By the time he wrote Rick and explained all that he had done, the meetings had been planned.

Under the banner of "Free Rick Fremont," they had joined together and organized. For a few months, Verdilak courted their favor and assured them that he acted with Rick's blessing. Rick wouldn't argue with anyone that asked.

When I asked him the first time we met, he told me that something was coming.

"Did you want them to stop?" I asked. "Did you want them to stay out of New Orleans and stop using your name?"

"I didn't..." he said, wiping away tears. "I didn't like that he was acting on my behalf. But, we all wanted the same thing. We wanted to find John." He looked up at my friend. "If he could get you to come out, then I wasn't going to tell him to stop." He lowered his head again, and cried some more.

John stroked Rick's hair, and asked, "What is his name? And, I do mean his real name."

Rick shook his head, and whispered, "I don't know." He said that he didn't a couple of more times. Then he swore it, and we believed him.

John and I looked at each other. Rick didn't know much more than we did. His movement had spiraled out of control, and one of his followers had killed two people. He could only watch and wait for scraps of news—"whispers scrawled across paper," he called their letters—to find their way to the penitentiary, past the guards who would inspect them, and to the small cell in which he lived.

That moment hit after just over an hour, when I realized we'd stayed for too long. He didn't know anything else. If we kept asking questions, he'd start making shit up just to keep us there. John took the young man's hands from across the table and held him there. Rick cried louder and begged him to stay. John shook his head, but said that he would return in time. They could discuss the Turn more then. But, before we left, he wondered if Rick remembered anything else about Verdilak that he might share.

Rick said only that Verdilak studied the red book at the New Orleans Public Library on Loyola Avenue.

***

Saturday, October 25, 1997

"In over your head," I kept repeating to myself as I ascended the steps of the City's Main Library on Loyola Avenue. Homeless people congregated near the steps and at the corner bus stop across from the Walgreen's. A few older men clutching half-pints in shabby clothes sat amongst hippies and punks, with their dingy brown backpacks and dogs taking up space on the steps.

I ignored a few requests for change as I walked through the doors and past the guard. Seated on a stool, he glanced up from his newspaper and promptly looked back at it. I walked on to the main floor and beheld the array of desks, card catalogues, and a handful of boxy computers. The polished green tiles beneath my feet reflected the fluorescent lights overhead, and shelf after gray metal shelf filled the back half of the room.

I'd been to the library my fair share of times. When I was writing bullshit for the weeklies, sometimes I had to look up old records or newspaper articles. I always knew why I was there. That day, I had no idea where to start. I didn't know what to look for. Rick said that Verdilak used the library, but that didn't mean anyone there would know a damned thing. Chaz and Maven told me that the kids from the Fellowship had met at the library at some point. But, they didn't say which one. I had to pull the string, one way or another.

I all but hit myself on the side of the head when it occurred to me. Most librarians knew their regulars, and they all had horror stories. The bums used the facilities as shelter space during the summer and the coldest days of winter. That meant unspeakable bathroom nightmares and napping bodies all over the place. If Verdilak had come in and gone to the same spot a few times, someone might know him.

I looked around the room before my eyes stopped at a librarian. She was a black girl, and younger than I'd expected. She wore thick glasses beneath a pile of curly hair. She was cute, and she looked like a bookworm because she wanted to. The sleeveless black and white top she wore said as much. I thought she might have an eye for someone out of the ordinary who, I assumed, mostly read about vampires. I approached the desk, and she looked up from an open book in front of her.

"Hi, um, I have kind of an odd question for you," I said.

"Yuh-huh?" she asked. I could tell I hadn't piqued her interest yet.

"A guy I'm looking for used to come here a lot, and I haven't seen him in a while."

"What does he look like?" she asked. She rested her chin in her hand, one elbow planted in the pages of the open book.

"I actually don't know," I said.

She stood up, no longer leaning on the desk, and said, "And, this is your friend? You don't know what he looks like? Have you talked to him at all recently?"

"No, that's what I'm saying. I haven't seen him before. He's caught up in some other business with a friend of mine, and I really need to talk with him."

"Anything you can give me to work with? Any kind of details? What's his name?"

"He uses a fake name. I'm sorry, but this is kind of dumb—saying it out loud, I mean," I said, holding my hands open as if begging for forgiveness.

"Well, what is it?" she asked.

I took a deep breath, and said, "He calls himself Verdilak online. He was probably reading about vampires—like, a lot."

Without saying a word, she beckoned me to follow her as she rounded the desk and crossed the main floor. I ran a few steps to catch up as she looked over her shoulder.

"Someone tried to steal a few books about vampires after we asked him to leave. This guy would sit there at the desk kind of talking to himself. He'd be normal at first, and get, like, a couple of books open like he was doing research." We crossed into the shelves, and rows of volumes passed us as she quickened her pace.

"He'd start making these weird noises, like he was whispering to someone. He'd do it for a couple of days, and then he'd leave. But, the last couple of times, he didn't go anywhere. The guard told him to get out. The last time, he tried to shove a couple of books into his bag and just take them."

"Jesus, why not just get a library card?" I asked. She stopped at the end of a shelf and dropped into a squat, looking over the books.

"Uh, I don't know. Maybe he didn't want anyone to know what he was reading. Some people think the government keeps track of what you check out. Here we go," she said, drawing a couple of books from the rows in front of her. She stood and handed them to me.

I read the titles out loud: "*Vampires, Burial, and Death* and *Vampire Lore*. These are just regular books. You can get them anywhere."

"I know," she said, looking up at me through the thick glasses. "That's not the weird part. I've got one more thing to show you. Do you have a minute?"

"Sure," I replied, doing all I could not to roll my eyes. Every turn I made led to a new hallway with endless doors. And, John stood at the end. "Hey, wait a second. What's your name?" I asked as she turned to lead me further.

Looking over her shoulder, she flashed her brilliant white smile, and said, "Anne!" with a tiny dip of her head. Clearly, the mystery surrounding Verdilak hadn't dented her mood. Maybe she was just glad he was gone.

"This way!" she said. I followed her to the back, watching the sleeveless top and the red skirt. She led me to the edge of the library, to a locked door. Imposing and gray as the rest of the walls around it, she made no move to open it. Instead she produced a ring of keys from her skirt pocket, and thrust one of them into the knob. I followed her into the plain office. Venetian blinds covered a window to another room. Fluorescent lights brightened the already white space and shined across the top of the long silver table in its center. The green tiles of the floor matched the ones in the rest of the library outside.

Anne walked to a file cabinet. It was the last of four lined up in a corner. Using another key from the same ring, she opened the small silver lock and pulled the long, gray drawer out. After reaching over its edge, she withdrew a book in a plastic bag.

I had almost expected it. But, I held back for a moment before we walked to the table and sat down on either side. She spun the book so that it faced me. Through the plastic, I could see the cover I knew so well. Rough, blank, and red, it was the same as all the others.

"What is this?" I asked, feigning ignorance. "Can I take it out of the bag?"

"You can take it out of the library."

"What do you mean?" I asked.

"I mean get rid of it. Take it. Don't bring it back."

"Why? It's just a book," I said, playing dumb. I peeled back the tape that closed the plastic bag, and withdrew the book. I put it on the table between us.

"Remember how your friend tried to steal some books?" she asked. I nodded. "That was one of them. But, it's not one of ours. I mean, it's not in the system. It doesn't have a barcode or an ISBN or anything. Someone brought it here and left it on the shelf."

"If it doesn't belong to the library, why not just take it?" I asked.

"The guard stopped him on the way out and they kind of had a fight," she said.

"Like an actual fight?" I imagined the faceless man with the false name struggling with the security guard for a stack of books. Why he would take them, I did not know.

"Uh, not really," she said. "They pulled back and forth on them, and then the guard yanked the whole stack out of his hands. Everything kind of went up in the air. Then, our guy just threw him out and told him not to come back. We picked up everything after, and this was with our stuff." She tapped the red book with her fingernail.

I leaned forward, and said, "So, someone put this book here and then this guy tried to steal it. Why would anyone leave it on the shelf in the first place?"

"I don't know," she said, growing more frantic. "So that *they* would find it and read it."

"Who are *they*?"

She lowered her head and leaned close, and whispered, "The vampire people."

The scene she described played out like a trailer for a bad horror movie in a season filled with them. For a couple of weeks earlier in the month, rain or shine, two or three young men and women—teenagers, mostly—wearing hooded sweatshirts and all in black, would enter the library. Usually, they would arrive an hour or two before closing, just as the sun began to set. They would always approach the same shelf that Anne and I had, and remove the same battered red book.

The description Chaz gave me of The Fellowship played through my mind. Verdilak brought the book there so that his followers could use it. And then, for some reason, he tried to remove it. The kids had said one was missing.

Gathered in a far corner of the library—the same each time, and on the second floor—they would huddle over it and whisper. The small cluster of hoods would remain there until closing. Whenever a librarian—or anyone else for that matter—ventured by, one would always peek out and stare. They did not, it was quite clear, wish to be disturbed. The library was a public place, Anne reminded me, and you weren't required to check out anything. "Acting creepy" wasn't enough to have you removed. Otherwise, all of the vagrants and suspicious characters that filled its floors wouldn't be there, camped day after day.

No one knew about the book, and no one asked. They always put it back on the shelf, next to its fellow vampire volumes. And, aside from the menacing stares, they were always more than polite. On the occasion that a librarian passed one of them en route to their table, they would look up with a curt "Good evening" and continue walking. When anyone caught a glimpse beneath their hoods, they saw a similar array of pale makeup, with dark lips and raccoon-black eyes.

And Verdilak, the book thief, was never with them. He always came alone. She remembered him because he didn't dress like the others. He looked "so normal." After he tried to steal back the red volume, the librarians locked it in the very office where we sat. They were prepared to throw it away, until I came around.

"And the whole time, you didn't know that it wasn't the library's book?" I asked.

She gestured towards the door. "How many books do you think are out there?" she asked. "We can remember a lot of them, but we only handle what people check in or out, or anything else we have to put back. They'd take the book, and then just put it back. We never really saw it."

"Until this guy tried to steal it with the others?"

"Right," she answered.

She explained that *they* stopped coming every Monday. I knew that they'd moved to Kaldi's. And then, I knew why. No book meant no meetings. Maybe Verdilak wanted it for himself, or maybe he meant to move the group. I didn't know. Chaz said a new girl had showed up with one. It made sense, though. If a few kids got together at the library, no one would care. If twenty of the brats showed up dressed like vampires, someone was bound to notice. As more and more came in from out of town, Verdilak had to change the meeting place.

Regardless, I kept it all to myself. Their missing book was in my hands. I hadn't even opened it yet, but I knew what was on the inside.

"What did he look like? When did he come in?" I asked.

"No time in particular. During the day sometimes, like around lunch. He just looked normal, though. I mean, he had dark hair. He was a white guy," she said.

"Any kind of clothes in particular?"

She shrugged, and replied, "Pants, shirt, and a tie sometimes. He was pretty nondescript. I mean, I see a lot of people every day. I can't remember every single one of them, and it's been a few weeks since he came in."

I thanked her, and then took the red book. She had helped a lot, and not at all. Verdilak had used the library, but he seemed smart enough to avoid dressing like the prince of darkness. Someone dressed like Chaz would've imprinted himself on everyone in the room. Our guy had managed to look like everyone and no one.

Sitting in my car outside, I turned on the engine and the radio and I tried to think. I flipped through the book again to find the same symbols, the same intricate gothic text, and the same drawings. Opening it from the back, I realized that someone had torn out the image of John. I sighed. It was one more clue about what I already knew—whoever Verdilak was, he wanted John. He would do anything for my friend's disease, and he walked the streets of New Orleans biding his time. He wanted John badly enough to kill two women, but had no idea what would really happen to him.

I wanted a drink, right at that moment. I still hadn't had a drop since Maureen confronted me. I wanted, even more so, to prove to her that I could stop. But, I wanted one almost as much. I hadn't talked to Maureen since before I left for Florida. So, back to Second Chance I went. Part of me wanted permission to drink again. She'd been watching me. Even John had kept it in check while we were out of town. He'd only snuck one drink at the restaurant's bar in between courses, to make it easier on me.

Driving to the shop, I glanced at the book on the passenger seat. She'd seen the first one, so this new one wouldn't be much of a surprise. I'd have to dance around the other issue. Certainly, I could just invite her for drinks after work. Her reaction would tell me everything I needed to know. I rehearsed my pitch as I parked alongside the store. But, I looked over to see that Second Chance's sign was flipped to "Yes We Are Closed."

Expecting to see a note about a lunch break or an errand taped to the glass, I got out of my car and walked to the door. But, the shop was locked and dark, as if she'd never opened it that morning. Through cupped hands, I saw the rows and racks of clothing alone there in the shadows of the early afternoon. I tapped on the glass, hoping to see her emerge from the back, with that smile I knew so well. After five minutes of waiting, I left.

After ten minutes of waiting outside of the door of the one-half of the shotgun double where she lived, I left again. I'd knocked and called her name, all for nothing.

At my house, I called her number, and then Second Chance, and then home again. Telling myself that surely she'd fallen asleep or been held up somewhere, I called John. I wanted to talk to someone. At only a quarter after five, I knew I would wake him up. But, the seeds of panic had begun to grow and the sickening, warm fire of worry filled my stomach and pushed up to my mouth.

"M'ullo?" he answered, through the day's fog.

"That's not even a word," I said.

He cleared his throat, and said, "Jason?"

"Yeah. I need to see you as fast as you can get here."

Chapter 17

Saturday, October 25, 1997 – Evening

After explaining the story for the fifth time, he told me to calm down. I stood with my arms crossed, and then paced another circle across the living room floor. John watched me from the futon, his head following me like a cat's.

"Jason," he said, "she is probably just out by herself in the French Quarter. Or, she's ill and fell asleep. Did she tell you she might be out of town?"

"No," I replied. "None of that. I talked to her before we left for Florida. Everything seemed fine."

"And, I am quite sure everything was," he said. "If she planned to simply leave town she wouldn't have left her store unattended."

Resting my hands on my bald head, I threw them out and said, "That is not what I'm afraid of, John. I don't think she left to start a new life back in fucking Austin. She is literally missing."

"Calm down," he said. "Should we call the police?" He paused, and then said, "Don't answer that."

"No, not for a while," I said. "We haven't heard anything from them, which is good. But, we'd be taking a chance if it turns out they know who we are." I collapsed on the couch next to him. "God knows whether the cops are even trying to find you. I'm surprised they haven't come by your house. Besides, she hasn't even been gone for a day. That doesn't qualify as a missing person, I don't think."

He shrugged, and said, "There are many people in New Orleans who claim to be vampires. You and I haven't exactly spent much time around them."

John was right. Only Brad knew about him, and with him off of the force—however temporarily—there might be no one left to consider John in the first place. Everything else came down to the rumors. We might have been worried for nothing.

Instead of talking, we stayed up watching TV. Rather than putting in a movie, I flipped from channel to channel on an endless loop. John didn't object. Occasionally, just as we had that night with Jenny Dark, I called Maureen's house and Second Chance. But, I just heard the same endless ringing. I decided to spend the next day talking to her neighbors.

A bit after two, John headed home to check on Maria. I tried to sleep, but I couldn't. The evening that I asked Maureen to stay with me replayed itself. I asked her and she said yes, but then she quietly walked away to a taxi. I spent the rest of that night waiting for her to call, certain that she would end "us" when she did. But, she didn't. She called, of course, but she didn't end it. She never liked the way we'd started, though. We got together after finding her friend with her throat torn out on her apartment floor. Part of me wondered if her early concerns had finally blossomed—if she'd just left us all behind, and taken off to her father's house, or another town, or country, or another life.

Like a great hand, the thought of her leaving scooped me out of bed and on to my feet. Wearing only black boxer shorts and a Kommunity FK t-shirt, I stumbled through my den to the kitchen, and to the liquor cabinet. I withdrew the half-full bottle of bourbon and unscrewed the red top. I held it up, and looked through the amber sea to the streetlights outside of my window. I turned my head and moved the bottle with it, and saw my apartment and all that I owned in a hue of gold. I held it there for one more second before I whispered her name and took a long drink.

The sweet fire filled my mouth and trickled down my throat to my stomach, to my loins, and then radiated outwards.

I wondered why I had ever tried to stop.

I would tell her one day, I promised myself. She might lecture me or threaten to leave (if she hadn't already). But, nothing else would put me to sleep—not John's reassurances, and not my resolve to search everywhere I could in the morning. I took another swallow and walked back to my bedroom holding the bottle, confident of all that I might achieve the next day. Maureen would turn up with a perfectly reasonable explanation, and Verdilak would give himself up at a police station. Dr. Reynolds would find a cure for John and Maria.

For all I knew, Christ himself would come back and fix everything else. I drank more lying down there, until sleep finally crept upon me with the first taste of a dream. With what little I had left to give, I stood the bottle upright on the nightstand.

***

Sunday, October 26, 1997

Crying out at the end of a nightmare, I awoke. I saw the nearly-empty bottle of bourbon and remembered what had happened. A dark print of sweat colored my pillow. I saw the time on my alarm clock and cursed aloud. I'd gone to sleep with every intention of asking Maureen's neighbors if they'd seen her. I wanted to call Brad and run a list of other errands. The time showed 2:04 p.m. Shaking my head, I paused to feel a hangover. All told, I hadn't drank as much as I might have in the past. It was an improvement on something, at least.

I dressed while the coffee brewed, and I thought about the order in which I might finish my day—one nagging fucking task after another. To save a trip, I called Second Chance to see if she might have opened the shop. As before, the phone rang for as long as I would let it. Then, I dialed her house. I heard the same mocking ring, and slammed the cordless phone into the base. After grabbing my suit jacket off the corner of the door, I wrestled into it on my way to the kitchen. I opened and shut several cabinets before finding my silver travel mug. I poured the coffee into the cup, screwed on the lid, and walked as fast as I could out the door.

It wasn't too late. I had slept longer than I meant to, but the day wasn't over yet.

The air outside had finally reached that moment of perfection—the kind that only a fall day in New Orleans could. A blue, cloudless sky met air with only the faintest chill—cool enough for a jacket, but warm enough to sit outside the bar. In the Volvo, I turned on the radio. Switching to the news station, I expected to hear a story about all that had happened—vampire murders, Maureen, John, and the coming of Halloween. But, instead the two voices spoke about Saints scores, traffic, the emerging scandals of the Clinton administration, and everything else. I wondered if the murder of the two women stood beyond notice at that point.

I realized I hadn't seen any media coverage about the killings at all.

When I pulled up to my Maureen's apartment, I turned off the car and got out. But, I didn't bother knocking on her door. Standing back from the apartment, I looked at the houses on either side of hers—also shotgun doubles. Cars sat parked in front of the two to the left, yet none on the right. Some of them might have been at church. Her neighbor that shared the double didn't answer. I decided to start two houses to the left and work to the right.

At the first—white, with green trim—no one answered, despite the blue Oldsmobile parked on the curb in front of it. At the second, a sleepy young woman in pink pajama pants and a white tank-top answered. With a streak of purple in her blonde hair, I knew she probably worked nights. I said I was sorry for waking her, and asked if she knew Maureen.

"Yeah, of course," she said, rubbing her right eye.

"Sorry," I said, extending my hand. "Jason." She shook it before looking out past me.

"Micah," she said.

"I'm her boyfriend. Have you seen her?" I asked. "I haven't heard from her in a couple of days."

"No," Micah replied, shaking her head. "She kind of keeps to herself. I mean, she says hello and everything but she doesn't, like, drop by."

"So, you wouldn't see her every day anyway?"

"Yeah, that's what I mean. Do you need to use the phone or something? Have you tried her work?"

"Yeah, I have—a couple of times," I said. "Actually, I could use your phone if you don't mind." I decided to check in with Brad. I wanted to hear his take on the situation. When I'd seen him at the grocery store, he looked like he had it together and even like he wanted to help. He might be able to help me look around before I called the real cops to file a missing person report.

Micah led me through her small living room, over hardwood floors and past a sofa, particleboard bookcases, and an old television. A yellowing Nintendo system sat on the floor in front of it, underneath a tangle of wires and flat gray game cartridges. Next to the thread-worn couch, she stopped and picked up a white phone and handed it to me. The curly cord dangled to the base, with a knot in its middle. I turned it over in my hand and began to dial Brad's number from memory. Then, I remembered that it had changed, and I might accidentally call Capt. Williams. Pulling my wallet out of my back pocket, I looked for the business card with his new number. When I found it, I carefully dialed before putting the phone to my ear. Micah crossed her arms and waited for a few seconds, before mouthing the word "coffee" and pointing at the kitchen. I nodded, and gestured as if I was drinking a cup with my empty hand. I'd left the silver mug in my car.

She turned away as the phone began to ring. And, he didn't answer. Nobody wanted to answer their phone. But, his voicemail message played. I spoke after the beep, on the off chance that he might immediately call back.

"Brad, this is Jason. I'm at a friend of Maureen's. She's been missing since yesterday. I could use your help. Call me back at this number."

Micah returned with a cup of black coffee in a white mug, and said, "I don't have milk or sugar right now. I need to make a grocery run. Is that okay?"

"It's fine," I said. I sipped the hot, bitter liquid. "Do you mind if I wait a minute to see if my friend calls back? He's ex-NOPD. He might have some ideas."

"Yeah, no worries," she said. "I was getting up anyway. I had the coffee on right before you knocked. You want to sit?"

"No, I'll stand," I said. Sitting would feel like a break, and I didn't want or need one. Staring at the phone, I waited. "You work a night shift?" I asked.

She nodded as she swallowed, and said, "Over at the Golden Buddha." I knew the place. Not far from my apartment, the bar was on Magazine Street, and it had the usual New Orleans array—pool tables, a juke box, cheap booze, and a beloved bartender that would learn your name after two visits. That must have been Micah, I realized.

I stared at the door. I looked back at the phone. I wondered which would capture my attention first. Neither Micah nor I said anything for a minute. We had nothing to talk about except Maureen, and they barely knew each other.

She spoke first: "So, what do you do?"

"Writer," I said. "Mostly the weeklies. I'm looking to see if Internet writing might pay." I hadn't seriously considered taking my work online, but it seemed like the right thing to say.

After glancing at my coffee and then the couch, I finally sat. Standing wouldn't make things happen any faster. I asked myself how long I might wait for Brad to call.

Next to me, Micah rested her mug on her knee. I saw the neon pink script across it that read "World's Greatest Sister."

"Got that from your brother?" I asked. She held it up and looked at it.

"Yeah, my mom drops him off here once a week or so." She gestured at the old Nintendo on the ground. "I got that at a garage sale so he'd have something to do. I know it's kind of old, but he likes it."

"How old is he?"

"Ten," she answered. "Kind of a late birth. I'm twenty-two, so I don't think my mom exactly planned for him."

"Yeah, that's one thing you learn," I said. "Life doesn't respect your plans. Sometimes, you have to take care of things you didn't ask for."

As we talked, I decided to wait for Brad's call for as long as it took me to drink my coffee. Then, Micah and I looked towards the front door.

We both heard the noise.

Tires screeched with the fast stop of a vehicle from outside, followed by the slide-and-slam of a van door. Seconds later, it peeled out and sped down the street. We both stood up, and I nearly spilled my coffee as I swallowed the last of it. Tossing the empty mug on the couch, I turned to open the door. Micah had beaten me there by a second and flung it open to reveal the day's light.

She ran outside and yelled, "Holy shit!"

I jumped down the two steps to the sidewalk and the grass that followed. There, in the yard, lay Maureen. With her hands bound and a piece of silver tape across her mouth, she struggled to stand. She thrashed and kicked at nothing. Blood and water soaked the white tank top she so often wore.

"Maureen!" I yelled, running across the short space between us. Micah had reached her and moved her to a sitting position on the grass. As she tried to scream through the tape, I grabbed a loose corner at her cheek.

"Ready?" I asked, hurriedly. She nodded, and I yanked the tape away from her face.

"Fuck!" she yelled. A red rectangle came up around her mouth.

"Jesus, what happened?" Micah asked, as she tried to untie the ropes that bound her hands. I looked down at her arms to see a series of thin red razor cuts. The blood had flowed down her arms in drips and trickles and dried into a sticky film.

"Get me inside!" she said.

"Can you walk?" I asked. She nodded, and Micah and I each grabbed one of her arms and lifted her. She cried out in pain when we grabbed her.

"Be careful!" she yelled. On her feet, she broke free of our grip and stormed inside the house. We followed her there, and I shut the door behind us.

"Jason, get me some water," she said. "One of you get something to cut these goddamned ropes!"

"What happened?" Micah asked. Maureen turned to her with a red rage in her eyes.

"I haven't had anything to drink in almost two days," she said, with a hissed whisper. "Get me some fucking water." Brushing past them, I found the kitchen straight behind us and grabbed a glass from the green dish rack next to the sink. I filled it and turned off the faucet before stepping back to the living room. Micah's hands shook as she tried to untie the ropes, and I saw that she'd started to cry.

"Get a knife or something!" Maureen said. With her hands still bound, she leaned forward and nodded. I held the glass up and tilted it into her mouth. She drank as much and as fast as she could, while the water trickled down her chin, through her bloodied tank top, and on to the ground.

"Oh fuck. Oh fuck," she said, when she finally stopped drinking. "Get me some more."

I opened the refrigerator and looked for a gallon jug or pitcher. Finding a half-full gallon of spring water, I slammed the door and ran back again. Micah had finally found a pair of heavy scissors. She quickly cut the ropes around Maureen's wrists. Shaking off the ropes, Maureen jerked her arms free and stretched them out. She rubbed her wrists, now as red as the space around her mouth. The wounds on her arms weren't deep enough to kill her or anyone else, I realized. But, the sight of her blood stung something deep inside of me.

I handed her the jug of water, and she grabbed it without a word. She leaned back on the couch and turned the bottle upright like a water cooler and drank. When she finished, she released the bottle and looked down at her bloodied shirt.

"That better?" I asked.

She nodded, and said, "Yeah, thank you. I'm going to keep this," she said, holding up the remaining water. I took a chair from the dining room table and placed it in front of her. I sat down and looked at her for a moment. The sweat on my face slid my glasses down my nose.

Pushing them back up with one finger, I said, "All right, what happened? I think we have to call the police now."

"No. No cops," she said.

"Why?" I asked. I wanted to yell it, but I knew that was the last thing she needed.

"Because, he'll fucking kill me," she said. "It was him. It was Verdilak."

***

On Friday afternoon after work, Maureen began the short walk between the bus stop and her house. The evening's orange sky shown above her, and she thought nothing of returning home—and perhaps stopping at the Irish pub on the way for a pint with Jonesy, the bald bartender who always served her. Well after five o'clock, she thought little of the few cars that passed through the residential neighborhood in Mid-City where she lived. At a corner, as she prepared to cross the street, a plain white van with blackened windows stopped in front of her. Its sliding door opened.

Inside, behind the driver, sat a single man dressed all in black and wearing a ski mask. With his arm extended, he pointed a pistol at her. She could not say what kind, because she knew nothing about firearms. For a moment, she thought he wanted her purse. She held it out, and he shook his head.

He continued to point the gun at her as he mouthed two simple words from deep within the van: "Get in."

She only nodded and did as he said. He would certainly kill her if she didn't comply, but he might not if she did. Inside the van, she smelled the spray paint they'd use to blacken all the windows except for the front windshield. It looked like any other utility van—likely rented or stolen. The man held the pistol in one hand and a roll of duct tape in another. He instructed her to put a piece over her mouth. She only nodded and complied.

With the tape affixed, he instructed her to face the side window. She felt the barrel of the gun against the back of her head. She closed her eyes and prayed—yes, prayed—as he whispered how he would need to set the weapon down for a moment to bind her wrists. And if she tried to escape, he would kill her. He told her to nod if she understood, and she did.

Resting the pistol on the seat's back (still pointed at her, she suspected), he reached to the van's floor and uncoiled a length of rope. He instructed her to put her hands behind her back. Again, she complied, and he tied them. He said little, but when he spoke, his voice sounded guttural, alien, and as if he had affected a gruff voice that was not his own. With her eyes locked forward on the black window, she only glimpsed the back of the driver's head (also masked) and the van's movement on to the interstate. It helped little, because her captor promptly tied a black cloth across her eyes. The blindfold would remain there for most of her ordeal, and until moments before they kicked her—yes, literally, she insisted—out of the van on to the grass in front of Micah's house.

After an hour of driving, the van finally stopped. The driver's door opened and shut. She felt the barrel of the gun against her back, and the man whispered for her to exit the van. Someone—the driver, she presumed—opened the sliding door in front of her. She stepped out, nearly falling. Upon regaining her balance, the man behind her took her roughly by the arm. He walked her forward, and up a short flight of steps. She heard nothing around her but the low hum of the world—perhaps traffic, or even the sea. As the man pushed her forward, she felt the air change. The evening's coolness now behind her, she passed into a room filled with suffocating warmth. The smell of dirt and dust greeted her nose, and she supposed that they had brought her to a warehouse. The man pushed her for a few more yards until she felt the edge of a metal folding chair against her shin.

"There," the man hissed, as he directed her around the chair and forced her down. She sat as instructed. She felt his fingers at the corner of her mouth, and he ripped the tape away from her face. She cried out, but otherwise restrained herself. She only asked him what he wanted.

"In time," he said, in the same disguised voice. He told her to remain still and put her arms over the back of the chair. She felt a set of hands binding the ropes already around her wrists to the back of the chair. Again, she asked them what they wanted. The man only cocked and fired the gun once behind her. She jumped in the chair as the weapon went off and echoed throughout the cavernous space. Her ears rang, but she remained calm. He warned her that no one would hear her if she cried out. And, if she called for help, they would reaffix the tape over her mouth. With a single "Okay," she agreed to remain silent.

The man remained behind her the entire time. She knew this, because she could hear his breathing. Thus, she had no time to fight the ropes that bound her wrists, or the ones that bound her to the chair. She waited, and wondered. For how long, she did not know.

In time, the dusty warmth and the silence brought a light sleep. She dreamed of nothing, but woke some time later with her chin resting on her chest. She woke not to noise, but to the feeling along her arms. A razor blade crossed the soft, white flesh between her elbow and her wrist. And then, it crossed it over and over again. She dared not move, for fear that someone—perhaps him, or the other man—still had a pistol trained on her.

The man had made a series of small cuts with the sharpest edge she had ever felt—one so fine that the initial pain faded, leaving only cold shock. Her eyes still covered, she could not see the warm mouth that fastened itself to her arm. Quietly crying, she heard and felt the sound of the man lapping up the blood that ran down her arm. His tongue traced the length of her forearm to claim more. Every few seconds, she heard the faint sound of a swallow. After a few minutes, he stopped. She heard his steps shuffle to the other side of the chair, where he began to cut her left arm. And then, he drank as he did from her right. She hissed and winced, but otherwise remained silent.

And then, he stopped.

Unable to inspect her own flesh, she leaned forward and tried to raise her arms behind her, however little. The warm air of the space around her danced coolly across the wet streams of saliva and blood left there. But, though frightened, she did not feel faint. The cuts were not deep, and she hoped he meant not to kill her.

As she raised her head, she felt a cold splash of water hit her. She remembered she'd had no water to drink since before the men took her. She swallowed what few drops she could. In the heat of the warehouse, the coldness briefly revived her.

"Wake up," the rough voice said.

"I wasn't sleeping, you fuck," she said, gasping. Her heavy breaths continued. Deeply aware of all that had preceded that day, she said only, "Verdilak."

He grunted in the affirmative, and she heard faint steps towards her back. The ropes binding her hands and her arms relaxed and fell away. He had freed her.

Then, the barrel of the gun pressed against the space between her shoulders. The small, metal circle felt cold against the water that ran down her skin. He told her to get up, and she did. She felt his hand clench her arm against the cuts he'd made, and she cried out. He only pulled at her right arm, and she walked where he directed her. No light breached the blindfold, and no sound echoed around her.

For three minutes (she counted the seconds), they walked. Verdilak ordered her to stop. Then, he gave her a sharp push, with the word "In."

A door closed behind her. She called out to him, but he did not answer.

She removed the blindfold, only to see complete darkness. Feeling the space around her, her fingers met the cool, smooth surface of a mirror on one side—and the gritty spaces between tiles on the other. She was in a bathroom. She felt the tug of her bladder and realized she hadn't gone since before leaving work, however long that had been. She called for Verdilak once more, but no answer came. The windowless bathroom revealed nothing more of her location. She walked until she bumped her shin on the porcelain edge of a toilet. Leaning forward, she felt a shower curtain. To her left, she felt the same tiled wall and then pressed her back against it. Sliding away from the shower, she moved right until she felt a corner.

Three knocks sounded on the door next to her, and the voice admonished her to hurry.

Her back was to the wall. The door was to her right. The light switch was, as she suspected, directly across from her. Reaching across the space, she flipped the switch and darkness remained. He'd either cut the power or removed the bulb.

Swearing quietly, she found the toilet again and pulled her wet jeans to her ankles. Sitting down, she relieved herself and rested her head in her hands. As she finished, she reached into the darkness next to the toilet. Touching a sink, she groped for a faucet. Finding a knob, she turned it. No water came. She found a few sheets of toilet paper on a diminished roll, and used those to clean herself. Dropping them in the space below her, she heard no water. She grabbed the handle behind her and moved it up and down. There was nothing in the tank. The entire bathroom had no water, and he'd made her piss in a dry hole. The shower nozzle behind the vinyl curtain yielded the same result.

He wanted her to panic, and dry out, and beg for something to drink. At least, she thought, he might give her water if he planned to bleed her another time.

The knock sounded again, and he yelled for her to put the blindfold back across her eyes. He'd known she would remove it. Pulling her wet jeans up, she fastened her belt. She felt her thin shirt, still soaked. She removed the tank top and stood in the darkness alone. Holding the shirt over her head, she twisted it into a tube. Opening her mouth, she wrung the wet cloth until drops fell down her throat. She swallowed the cold droplets, and they tasted like iron. The water was mixed with her own blood, but she did not care. It wasn't much, but for a moment it felt like more than enough, and better than any light. She wrung it again, until little remained.

She rolled the damp shirt over her bra and down to her jeans. She touched her arm where he had cut her. Sticky and drying, she thanked no one in particular that he had done nothing worse. She knew he would punish her if she emerged without the blindfold, and she moved to return it to her eyes. Searching her pockets and the space around her, she found nothing.

She had dropped it.

On her hands and knees, Maureen felt across the dirty tiles. Behind her and in front of her and in the sink, she searched and found nothing. She contemplated yelling to him that she'd lost it, and then considered what he might do to her. Grabbing the edge of the sink, she stood. She remembered the shower, and wondered if she'd dropped it there somehow. Turning to feel for the curtain, she heard the door behind her open. Faint light flooded the bathroom, and the dark shape of a man filled the threshold—featureless and black, still covered as he had been in the van.

"No blindfold?" he asked.

"Wait, I can't—" she said, as he stepped towards her. Behind him, she saw all that she expected: a dirty warehouse—all tall walls and long windows dimly glowing with the sun's light through a layer of filth. They could have been anywhere. Before she could finish her sentence, a fist connected with her stomach. She cried out and gasped for air. Verdilak and the other man in black each grabbed one of her arms and dragged her back to the chair.

Dehydrated, exhausted, and out of breath, she allowed them to tie her wrists and her arms a second time. When they finished, they fastened another blindfold across her eyes. What little she had seen of the warehouse revealed nothing.

"What do you want?" she asked.

"The blood."

"Fuck you. I think you already got that," she said.

His fist hit her deep in the stomach again. She gasped and tried to breathe. Leaning forward she coughed. He told her that wasn't what he meant. He had the blood, but she and her boyfriend had put an end to that. Maureen recalled the night that someone had fled John's home—and then the next, when the man in black tried to enter again. He had shrieked and rattled the door, but finally departed.

Maria hadn't tried to bite her way through her own wrist. He had freed her arm and opened her veins. The marks were not from her teeth, but his own. Now, he needed more. He tried again, but John had removed the hidden key and changed his locks.

Verdilak couldn't complete the change without it.

"You don't understand," she finally said. "You won't be like John. That's not what it does. He's alone. It makes you like her—like a thing. Do you want to live like that?" He didn't believe her. He didn't care. He left her with instructions on how to give him the blood. If she failed, this would happen another time. He would watch her.

She remained there for another night. He returned to unbind her and drag her to the bathroom one more time. She did not lose the blindfold that time. In the chair, she slept periodically and reminded herself that he would return her soon enough. Refusing to weep, she silently assembled what she knew. She cycled all that had occurred that concluded with her kidnapping.

The next morning, he returned her to the van with one of his nameless partners and taped her mouth shut. Still blindfolded, they threw her into her neighbor's yard and sped down the street.

***

I dialed Brad's number again. Micah kneeled before Maureen on the couch and cleaned the blood from her arms. Maureen held an ice pack to her stomach where he had struck her. After telling her to wait, she took the keys and ran to Maureen's apartment for clean clothes.

She stood from the couch, and said, "Fuck it. I'm taking a shower." I looked over my shoulder and nodded as the phone rang in my ear.

Brad answered with a "'yello?"

"Hey, it's me," I said. "Can you come over?" I explained the situation—kidnapping, no cops—and he all but hung up on me before telling me he would be right there. A few minutes later, Micah returned with a stack of fresh clothes.

Maureen had returned from the bathroom by the time Brad arrived. Wearing a pink bathrobe she'd borrowed from Micah, she walked slowly towards me. I saw Brad there at the glass door, wearing a white t-shirt and a pair of blue jeans. A pair of aviator shades completed the ensemble. He tapped on the glass before moving to open it himself.

Maureen stopped in the middle of the den as he entered, and said, "Brad?"

He took three quick steps to the middle of the room, past Micah and me, and grabbed her in a strong hug. She allowed it, and stood there for a moment before I heard the first of her muffled sobs. I recalled what Brad was, had been, and might be again—a good cop. It occurred to me that he'd comforted a victim or two in his time. As he held her there, he turned enough so that I could see the Beretta hooked to the back of his waistband by a clip. The sight of the gun reminded me how serious things had become. Verdilak had killed two women, drank Maria's blood, and then come after Maureen. If we went to the police, something worse might happen.

I rarely got angry. Up until that moment, I had felt more shock than anything else. But, I saw the gun and thought about finding Verdilak and killing him myself. I stood up next to them, while she sobbed and he held her. Maureen looked over, and moved to wrap her arms around me. Holding her there, I looked Brad in the eye.

"Tell me everything," he said.

Chapter 18

Sunday, October 26, 1997 – Evening

Before everyone arrived at Maureen's house, I laid it all out to Brad. I told him about visiting Rick more than once, about Verdilak, the Fellowship, and everything else I knew. I kept quiet about Maria and John's past. If there were any holes in my story, then Brad didn't ask about them. I told him how sorry I was for keeping him out of it. I thought he would yell at me, and maybe just leave.

Instead, he apologized for drifting away from us. He said he wished he could have helped sooner. He'd been sick. Then, the NOPD counted his sick days and put him on notice. He might rejoin the force in time, but the unions, the lawyers, and the endless rules meant nothing would happen soon.

But, he understood why I had kept so much from him. He still wanted to help. Before we made another move, he wanted to talk to Maureen in private. The two sat in the living room and talked, while I waited in the kitchen. They stayed there for over an hour, while Brad took notes on a few pieces of paper she'd given him.

***

John sat across from me at Maureen's kitchen table. Brad sat to my right, with Chaz and Maven at my left. A half-empty bottle of bourbon and a cluster of used glasses sat between us. Before she laid down in her bed, I told Maureen that I'd started drinking again. By then, she didn't care. She told me that she didn't blame me.

Brad had examined her after their chat. NOPD's cursory first aid training was enough for him to clear her. He said that Verdilak had wanted to scare the shit out of her—and us—more than anything. The punches knocked the wind out of her, but a hospital wouldn't prescribe much more than an aspirin. The cuts just needed ointment and bandages. She didn't frighten easily, though. The tears finally ran out, and shock gave way to anger.

At Brad's urging, I'd called everyone and asked them to come to Maureen's house. Everyone would meet—all who knew the truth about John and the man who wanted him. We left Michael Freemont out, because I knew he didn't want in. Chaz and Maven agreed to come immediately, but John begged me to wait until after sundown. He'd already seen more daylight than he cared to over the last few weeks.

By the time the guys tromped through her living room, Maureen had started drinking and raving. She wanted to find him. She wanted to kill him. The audacity to force a woman into a van at gunpoint. She couldn't believe that it had happened. Brad told her we—all of us, including her—would take care of it.

We weren't going to wait for the police to do anything. In New Orleans, you took care of your own. You did things yourself.

Before the rest of us sat down to talk, I begged her to lay down and rest. I promised that I would sleep next to her when we were finished talking. She wanted to sit at the table, but I knew that any plan she suggested would just end with her stabbing Verdilak with a kitchen knife. We needed to talk and to think, and I would lay out our plans for her the next morning. We wouldn't forget about her. She finally agreed, and laid down on the mattress in her bedroom.

As Maureen slept, Chaz cleared his throat. Our impromptu war council looked at him. Both of his fists were on the table in front of him. His large sunglasses lay between them, with an open can of Coca-Cola nearby.

"Let's keep in mind," he said, "that those kids we met at Kaldi's didn't specifically talk about killing anyone. None of them claim to even know this guy in person."

Brad kept looking at Chaz, and said, "They're the only link we have. Everything else is just what the librarian told Jason, and what happened to Maureen." He flattened a stack of three sheets of notebook paper in front of him. Scrawled in blue ink, he had written down everything Maureen told him—her ordeal, and the instructions Verdilak had given her.

He wanted John. He wanted John's blood. He wanted to be a vampire, no matter what the cost. He'd had it before, from Maria. But, it hadn't done anything. Maybe he hadn't swallowed enough. We didn't know, and he didn't either. He wanted more, and he'd grown tired of waiting. He'd targeted Maureen first, but the rest of us were next.

John touched his chin, and asked, "How exactly does he want me to present myself?"

Maven propped an elbow on the table, and rested his chin in his palm, and said, "What do you mean?"

"If he wants me," John said, "am I supposed to stand in the middle of the street and yell out his name?"

Brad leaned back, and said, "You want to lure him out like that? You're in luck, though." He straightened the white pages again. He tapped a pen on the edge of the table. "Maureen told me what he said. He told her how he wants to do it."

"Where?" Chaz asked.

Pointing the pen at him, Brad said, "Your Halloween party. He wants John to leave with him there. After that, Christ knows."

Chaz laid his palms up on the table, and asked, "Why there?"

Pouring myself another half-glass of bourbon, I said, "It's crowded, and it's a private party filled with people dressed like vampires. Neither John, nor this guy—whatever he looks like—would be noticeable unless they came in dressed in pink. And with all of the people around, he knows John won't pull a gun on him or anything."

"Haven't fired one in years," John replied. I thought back to that cannon I'd found in his desk drawer. But, that didn't mean he had used the thing.

"Plus," Brad said, "it's a threat. He means he'll pull something else in retaliation if you don't show. Some other kid will get taken, or we'll find another girl dead in the bathroom. He's setting you up so that if you don't reply, he'll do it again. It'll be your fault."

John pointed at himself. "My fault?"

"No, no," Brad said, gesturing at him. "Not saying it'll actually be your fault, but that's what he wants you to feel."

"Does he go then?" Chaz asked. "I mean, that's a hell of a thing to do to John." He looked back and forth between the ex-cop and the vampire. "Not to mention doing it at our party," he said under his breath.

John said, "What choice do I have? We can't exactly call and reschedule."

I stood up with my glass and downed the drink. "Wait, hang on—are you just going to give yourself up?" I asked. "And then what?"

And so, through the rest of the evening, we played through every scenario we could think of. We ruled out not sending John in the first place. After Maureen's ordeal, no one wanted to wait for Verdilak to make his next move. In the second, John might simply go with him and take the first opportunity to escape, call the police, or just kick his ass. We all kind of liked that idea, but no one really expected it to go that way. But, John had been to war and faced down worse than one lunatic with a handgun and a razor blade.

Except for Maureen, none of them knew about Nicholas Marston, the Chosin, or Maria. When it was my turn to talk, I stuck to the basics. We could tell the police and hope they would react. On Halloween night in New Orleans, though, the booze and the costumes filled the streets and it would be easy for Verdilak to slip away. They couldn't catch a guy when we didn't even know what he looked like. And, we knew that if he so much as smelled a cop, he would just fade into the crowd. We would only hear from him again later, when another body turned up.

We all agreed that there'd be no cops. If Brad had to pull the trigger, he'd have the most breathing room with the NOPD. In the worst case scenario, we could bury Verdilak's corpse in the swamp. We all laughed, but we also knew that it might come to that.

Brad pointed out that he'd been in and around the black-clad masses for years. If he managed to arrest Verdilak (strictly as a concerned citizen), one of his many remaining contacts with the department could finish it for him.

"Hell," he said, laughing, "they might even reinstate me right then and there."

Chaz slowly looked around the room. "Well, where does he want to meet? At the party, I mean."

Brad picked up the papers and looked over all of them, his lips moving quickly as he reread his notes. "Doesn't say."

"There's a chapel down the hallway past the bar," Chaz said. "We have the keys, and there's only one way in and out."

You met with some of his pals at Kaldi's, right?" asked Brad.

Maven nodded, and said, "Yeah. Want us to tell them?"

"Seems like the easiest way," I said. "Some of them still have to be in contact with this guy."

Chaz stood, sliding his chair across the hardwood floor, and said, "I guess we know what we have to do, then."

Brad stood as well, before asking the group, "Well, does everyone actually want to go through with this?"

Shrugging, Chaz said, "I don't really want the guy at my party, but I have no way of stopping him. We don't know what he looks like. We don't know his real name. He could be anybody. You can't just ask everyone on their way in if they're a serial killer."

We all knew what he meant, and it was all too true. He could have been anywhere. Clearly, he'd had eyes on us at different times. But short of stopping the event, we had no way to prevent him from attending. As our plan came together that evening, flaws and all, we knew that it might work. John could wait for Verdilak with Brad nearby. Brad could bring a gun and a pair of handcuffs and, in good conscience, perform a citizen's arrest.

I stood as well, looking at Brad, and said, "You and John are in the most danger. It's really up to you guys. What if he's armed, or if he brings extra people with him?"

Brad replied, "He won't hurt John. That's who he wants. And, unless he's really stupid he's not going to shoot into the crowd or pull the fire alarm. He wants John to go quietly and," he said, pausing and rolling his hands, "bleed him out somewhere. I don't know. You never know what kind of things guys like this have cooked up."

John continued to sit quietly, nodding each time someone made a point. He poured a glass of bourbon with no ice and drank it in one swallow.

"I'll do it," he said. "Even if he's armed, he'll have a difficult time hurting me. Whatever he wants after, I can deal with. You all can follow, or I can relay a message—or even escape, if I have to."

Maven raised an eyebrow, and asked, "Aren't you invulnerable or something?"

"Not exactly," John said, staring at the empty glass. "I can withstand a great deal, but it's not something I've ever tested to its limits. I could just kill him," he said, shrugging.

"Be careful with that," Brad said, waving away the suggestion. "You never know how that'll turn out. And, having to face a murder charge after those other two—I mean the girls—and you just killed the guy that probably did it. That might not look good."

"What then?" I asked.

"Best of all possible outcomes is you let me worry about the fireworks. If someone's going to shoot him, I'll do it. Hopefully, John and I can just get him down and cuff him. Then we call one of my friends and it's done. He can go drink blood in prison." I thought of Rick Fremont again, and wondered if he might like that idea.

Chaz cleared his throat, and said, "So, we're agreed then?" We all looked around and nodded. He spoke again: "All right, everyone—hands in the center."

I laughed and said, "All for one, and one for all?" But, I extended my hand. Chaz, Maven, Brad, and John all extended theirs and laid them on top of mine. We all knew what kind of trouble lay ahead, but I could still see everyone suppressing a laugh.

"No, come on. This is serious," Chaz continued. "We all pledge to see this through? We pledge to take this guy down for the sake of both man-and-vampire-kind?" John rolled his eyes.

"Yes," we all said in unison. We raised our hands to break the circle. I turned to face Maureen's room. I heard her faintly snoring from the mattress on her floor. Part of me felt like we should have included her in the planning. But, swaying there for a moment as the bourbon washed over me, I recalled all that she had endured. Sleep still seemed like the best idea. Brad had done his best to calm her, but I knew what she'd experienced wouldn't simply fade away after a good talk. She wanted to find him. She wanted to kill him. I did, too. But, I reminded myself that Verdilak could answer for all that he'd done once we captured him. The police couldn't help until then. Right at that moment, we were the only ones who could stop him. Chaz interrupted my reverie with a tap on the shoulder.

"Hey, we're leaving," he said. "We have to get caught up on everything for the party." Halloween was less than a week away, on Friday. Maven stood near the kitchen door, and cocked his head towards the front of the house.

"Oh, yeah," I said, extending my hand. Chaz shook it, and Maven waved from across the small room. They left through the kitchen door, and Brad turned to follow.

He turned back to shake hands with John, and then me, saying, "Don't worry. We'll get this guy." I watched as he followed Chaz and Maven out through the kitchen, into the darkened living room, and out the front door.

John looked over at me with his arms crossed, and said "He wants to use this to return to the NOPD. Seems like a rather complicated way to go about it."

"Yeah, and it's risky. But, he's a friend and he wants to help. You okay with all of this?"

John looked at his empty glass again, and said, "I am not completely thrilled with the idea, but it seems like the easiest way to apprehend this man. I don't intend to wait until he breaks into my home again or kills another woman." He sat down, and pointed at the bottle of bourbon. A third of it remained.

"Want to help me finish this?" he asked. "I know you were trying to cut back."

I sat across from him, and said, "Seems like now might not be the best time to try." He poured more into each of our glasses. There we sat for the rest of the evening. We drank and talked as we always did, as though nothing had happened.

***

Monday, October 27, 1997

Stumbling blithely out the front door just before sunrise, John assured me that he could drive. He wanted to reach home before the sunrise, check on Maria, and then sleep until dark. I couldn't say that I blamed him. Sitting at the kitchen table by myself, I stared at the empty bottle and wondered what might happen to us—me and the drink. I'd quit, briefly, and then relapsed. Maureen had said she understood, but that didn't change the facts.

I didn't feel like I had to drink, but I didn't want to stop, either. The Question had, in its own small way, returned and resumed its place just outside of my thoughts. It almost made drinking again not worth it.

I looked over at Maureen's cat clock that hung against the yellow wallpaper above her sink. She had one of those where the tail and the eyes moved. She'd once told me that a customer traded it in and, even though it wasn't clothing, she took it for herself. After stepping over to the sink, I looked up at the cat again and saw the time—half past six. If Maureen went to work, she would leave around just before eleven to open the shop at noon. I doubted that she felt like working that day, after all that had happened. After turning the tap, I splashed water on my face. I leaned my face under the cold stream and drank.

I moved to turn the light off, but stopped and glanced back to see if I'd turned off the faucet. Everything spun a bit. The faucet was off. I moved into Maureen's room. My fingers still wrapped around the door frame, I reached back to turn off the light. The moonlight showed her small, sleeping form on the mattress under a checkered quilt of green and white. After removing my jacket and laying it on top of a bookshelf, I laid next to her in my clothes. Sleep took me quickly, but time and the sun would wake me just as suddenly.

***

She sat cross-legged at the foot of her bed, illuminated by the morning light. Wearing only her pink t-shirt and panties, she stared at the wall behind me and said nothing. I wondered how long she had sat there. Shielding my eyes from the light, I realized I had slept in my glasses.

"Are you okay?" I asked. She nodded steadily, sucking on her bottom lip.

"All things considered, yeah," she said. She held her arm up, and I could see again the wrap of gauze bandages Brad had applied for her. "Need to change these sometime soon."

"How bad was it?" I asked. I hadn't been there when he dressed her wounds.

"Not as bad as you'd think," she said. "Brad said it looked like he might have used surgical steel razors. The guy seemed to know what he was doing." I sat up, and leaned against the bookcase at the head of the bed.

"Yeah, well he's probably done it before. Sounds like it was just to get his fix—and to, you know, scare the shit out of you."

"Well, he succeeded," she said. For a moment, her face relaxed and I saw her lips quiver as she fought back tears. I moved to put an arm around her, but she put both hands up. "I'm fine," she said, sucking back the tears. "I'm going to work."

Before I could speak, she stood up and grabbed a pair of worn jeans from over a closet door. "Do you always just wear pants?" I asked.

"Pretty much," she said. "I own the store. I wear the pants. So," she said, pausing, "I wear the pants." She'd buried the memory, however briefly, to show me her bravest face. I wanted to tell her it was okay, and that she could stay home and we could talk for as long as she wanted. But, I knew she would refuse.

"Do you want a ride to work?" I asked.

"Uh, yeah," she said. "That might be better, after what happened. That means I can leave a few minutes later. We can—" The phone rang and cut her off. We looked at each other for a minute and said nothing. It rang again, and neither of us moved. "Let the answering machine get it," she said.

After a four more rings, her answering machine's message echoed through the shotgun house. The beep followed, and then a few seconds of silence passed. I stood and walked to the living room.

Chaz's voice sounded through the answering machine, saying, "Hey, Maureen. Sorry to bother you. Brad gave me your number. I'm trying to reach Jason and he's not at—"

I picked up the phone and caught my breath, and said, "Chaz!"

"Jason!" he replied. "Just the man I was looking for."

"What's up?"

"Glad to hear you're up and around. Listen, we're going to do a little walkthrough over at the Masonic temple today to get this thing sorted out. It's me, Maven, and Brad."

"Did you call John?" I asked.

"He's asleep, remember?" I shook my head. Of course he was asleep. I'd seen him only a few hours prior, when he'd left Maureen's house. We could wake him if the situation demanded it, but I recalled how much we'd drank.

"Yeah, yeah—right, he is," I said. "Sorry. You want me to come to this?"

"That was the idea," he replied. "Can you make it? Looking at around noon."

Throwing myself on the couch, I took the cordless phone with me. "Yeah, I think I can," I replied. "I have to get Maureen to work first, but I'll meet you right after."

"Sounds like a plan," he said. "See you then." We said our good-byes, and I placed the phone back on its base. Forcing myself to my feet, I walked back to the kitchen. Maureen had started a pot of coffee.

"Chaz?" she asked, picking two mugs up from a dish rack.

"Yeah," I said. I sat at the table, and she placed a black mug in front of me. Hers was white, and I held mine up and smiled. "You know me so well."

"You're easy to color coordinate," she replied. "Can you please still take me to work?" I knew that she wouldn't want to take the bus again for a while. I didn't blame her in the least.

"Yeah, of course," I said. "As many times as you need me to."

"Thanks," was all she said, as she turned her back to me and watched the coffee brew. I had never met anyone that had survived two nights of torture. I knew Verdilak had restrained himself. He'd only hurt her enough to send a message—that worse things might follow. She ran her hands over her red hair. And I knew that, in the coming days, she would punctuate whatever tasks she undertook—at home, at work—with those brief moments. She would likely close her eyes, clench her teeth, and push the memories down to black before the tears came. My Maureen—but more, her own: possessed of herself and too hard to let two nights ruin all that she'd built. I laid one hand on her left shoulder, and she reached back to touch my fingers for a moment.

"I'm fine," she said, standing up with the coffee pot in hand. She filled both mugs, and we drank together and talked as if nothing had happened.

Chapter 19

Monday, October 27, 1997 – Late Morning

After dropping Maureen off at Second Chance, I continued down Magazine Street towards downtown. Before the Ponchartrain Expressway, I turned left towards St. Charles Avenue. At number 333, there stood an unremarkable building with a more ominous presence on its thirteenth floor. The Masonic Temple waited there for the brothers' rituals—and anyone with the coin to rent it. I parked on a side street to avoid the meter, and walked towards the corner with towering stone walls on either side of me. Chaz's gray SUV sat parked in front of the building, where he had brazenly ignored the loading zone sign. I walked through the glass doors into the marble corridor.

The elevator to my right opened with a loud clang, and I entered. Dutifully, I pushed button number thirteen and waited as the door shut with an equally loud clunk. Checking myself, I felt my back pocket for the small notebook I'd found in my car and the pen in my left pocket. The touch of a hangover I'd awoken to faded with the coffee I'd drank—and the four ibuprofen I'd swallowed dry after Maureen left my car. I leaned against the elevator wall and rested my head against it as I ascended. I knew The Question would return in force, but I whispered aloud, "Not now," and thought of what lay ahead.

At ten, eleven, and twelve, it rose. At thirteen, it stopped.

Giving my jacket a tug and standing up straight, I faced the opening door. Chaz, Maven, and Brad stood waiting for me. My cop friend—or whatever he was—hadn't changed his clothes. Maven and Chaz wore their requisite blacks, and the latter carried his imposing top hat.

"Jason!" Brad said. "Glad you could make it." I searched for a hint of sarcasm in his voice and glanced at my watch to see the hands at noon. He meant nothing more than what he'd said, I realized. Reaching out my right hand, I shook hands with each of them in turn.

"So, what's the plan here?" I asked. Chaz swept his hat with a single swoop towards the main auditorium to our left. The heavy doors, closed, shined at us with painted gold and a great brass lion's face on each—a ring in their mouths, naturally. To their right, a rather plain wooden bar stood unattended with empty troughs that would, in time, hold buckets of ice and bottles of beer. Chaz grabbed one of the rings of the great door with both hands, clenching his hat in his teeth by the rim. With one great heave, the door opened to reveal the auditorium behind it. Rows of red velvet seats descended to a dance floor. A balcony with even more seats circled the room. A vast stage opened at the end of it all. We walked down the sloped aisle towards the floor, passing seat after seat on either side. Upon reaching the dance floor, Chaz turned to face the three of us.

"Well, this is it," he said.

A bronze rail lined the balcony over our heads. Above the stage, a golden tableaux showed the murder of Hiram Abiff, the founder of Freemasonry, by the three intruders in King Solomon's Temple—a story all of the brothers knew by heart. Other than the notorious murder occurring above the stage, the auditorium looked like any other.

"So, this is it," I said, walking to his side. Above us, a booth of low wooden walls held the mixing board where a DJ would play all manner of gothic-industrial mayhem in just a few days. "So, what are we supposed to be walking through?" I asked. Brad and Maven looked around from the aisle, though I knew the latter had already seen the place.

Chaz said, "Let's head back to the lobby," he said, pointing at the door. We walked out the way we came in, with Brad shoving open the door. Gathering near the bar, I glanced there to see if, by chance, someone had left a bottle there. But, it stood empty and The Question came and I reminded myself that it could wait. After what happened to Maureen—and to all of us—I deserved to drink for a little while longer.

Brad hooked his thumbs in the waistband of his jeans, and asked, "Can we see the chapel?" Chaz looked to the left and pointed past the two bathrooms along the wall. There was a staircase to the balcony on the opposite side. The hallway ended with the chapel door on its left, and another narrow corridor on its right.

"Yeah," he said. "It's the only thing that's close to private you're going to get in here. There's an office, but I doubt he'd do it there."

"Are there security cameras here?" I asked.

Maven replied, "Yeah, but they're going to be turned off." He pulled his long hair back and let it down. "If you knew some of the shit that's going to go down here, you'd want them off, too."

Brad turned to him and smiled with that same broad grin he had flashed in the grocery store. "What is this? A fucking key party or something?" he asked.

"More like anything goes," said Maven, leaning on the bar. "It's a private party. Whatever happens, happens."

"Well," Brad said, "just keep in mind that if my guys kick the door down and see some shit there might be more than one guy getting arrested." I took my glasses off and wiped them on the edge of my black t-shirt.

"I think we can take that chance," I said. "Can we see the chapel now?"

Chaz said "Sure" and walked down the hall. We followed him, and I stopped to look down the narrow corridor opposite the chapel's entrance. I saw more doors and, at the end, a gray utility closet. Opening the wooden double doors, Chaz gestured for the four of us to file inside. The space was small, with five pews on either side. Red shag carpet brushed under our feet as we walked to the front. A mahogany altar with a single open book sat at the head of the room on a raised platform. Carved wood paneling lined the walls all around us. I looked at the double doors where we'd entered and saw that they had a deadbolt.

Walking around to stand behind the altar, I looked in the book. Bound in red leather and filled with thin pages, it detailed a history of the Freemasons.

"Weird that they would leave this out," I said.

Chaz glanced back at the book, and said, "They aren't as secretive as they used to be. A lot of the information about their history and rituals are online now." I recalled all that I'd found about Raven Cartwright on the web. What might have once taken days of legwork could be done in a few minutes from my bedroom.

I pointed at the double doors, and said, "There's a lock. It's like Chaz said—this is the only place where he can get any privacy. He'll have to wait until it's just him and John, and then I guess he can show his cards."

Brad looked down at the lock, and said, "Besides the men's room." The rest of us just laughed. "Seems reasonable, though," he said. "No one knows what he looks like. Chaz still has to talk to those kids. But, sounds like he'll probably set a time and meet John in here."

Maven looked over his shoulder at us. "Brad, where are you going to be?" he asked.

Brad looked around the room before he spoke, and said, "Uh, I guess right outside somewhere. Maybe I can hide across in that little hallway we passed. Maybe I can just follow John in. We'll figure it out."

"And then you'll come in and draw on the guy?" he asked, placing his hat on the altar in front of him.

"Right," Brad said. "If he's in here, there's nowhere to run. And, the door will be locked. It'll just be me and John, so no one else is going to get hit if I have to drop him. Once I've got him cuffed or whatever we can just call one of my guys." He turned to Chaz and said, "I'll need to get the keys from you."

"Or once you're in there, we could just call 911," I said. "That would work, too."

"Yeah," Brad said, "Worst case scenario, that would work. Somebody'll show up. They're going to be pretty slammed for Halloween, so one of my direct contacts is probably best."

***

The four of us parted ways, exiting the glass doors into the bright, blue day. We agreed to meet one more time before Friday—before Halloween. Chaz and Maven would contact the kids from the Fellowship. I would speak to John and lay out our plan in more detail. At only one, five hours remained until dusk. With Maureen at work and my friend asleep, I wondered how I might occupy my time.

I still needed to write and check my mail. I imagined a stack of envelopes I would need to sort. The work of clearing my friend's name had consumed me, and all else had fallen to the wayside. With only a few blocks between the building at 333 St. Charles Avenue and my apartment complex, I drove home and resolved to fill the remaining hours with work.

At my apartment, I stepped over the pile of mail that had landed there. Gathering up the many envelopes, I sat at my small supper table to sort them. I set aside a couple of credit card offers and coupons before stopping at one. A familiar and intricate handwriting spelled out my name and address, and the return address of the Columbia Correctional Institute.

Rick Fremont had written me a letter.

Turning the envelope over, I noted how thin and light it felt. He hadn't sent me a red book or a stack of mosaics. I tore open the envelope and unfolded the piece of notebook paper. In large florid script, he had written, "Remember me."

Setting the note down, I stared at it and wondered what he meant. Rick trafficked in riddles and veiled references, but the note seemed pretty direct. I flipped it over and held it up towards the window's light. There was nothing else.

I logged on to the Internet to see if his name had turned up in the news—or if another girl lay dead in another bar bathroom. I walked into my room and saw my unmade bed—a mass of black, rumpled sheets underneath two windows that met at the corner. I reached over and switched the computer on, and sat on the bed. On the nightstand lay an open pack of cigarettes with a cheap lighter shoved inside of it. After lighting one, I puffed away while the computer booted. Once the home screen flashed in front of me, I clicked the Netscape icon and waited for the modem to squeal and grind. The familiar noise sounded, and I relocated to the rolling desk chair. I rested my cigarette in the dirty ashtray on the edge of the desk, and searched for the news. I typed in Rick Fremont's name and waited. The page loaded, and I saw his picture there next to a headline: "Vampire Killer Found Dead in Prison."

Scrolling and scanning, with my heartbeat growing louder, I read not of his suicide, as I'd expected, but a stabbing in the shower. The guards found him facedown, naked, and with his throat cut. But, the killer hadn't slashed his throat clean across. The guards and coroner didn't find that wide, red smile. Instead, there were two deep punctures made with a crude prison blade. The Columbia Correctional Institution did not, I felt sure, have a vampire with nine-inch fangs stalking its halls.

Someone wanted to send a message, and to silence Rick Fremont.

I sat back and stared again at the simple picture the internet news site had posted—a profile image, taken at some point during an earlier interview, where Rick still maintained the cool and murky mystery I'd known. We would, I realized, never speak again. I couldn't decide whether I was relieved, or sad, or something else. I blinked, hoping that I had misread it all, and that the headline would say "Nearly Dead" when I opened my eyes. I clicked the refresh button on the web browser and waited to see if some writer had updated it to reflect the new truth—that, no, Rick Fremont hadn't been killed, but merely wounded, and was recovering in the prison infirmary. But, nothing had changed. He was as dead as ever.

Standing, I wondered who to call. John would still be asleep and I knew it could wait a few more hours. I wanted to tell Maureen in person. I knew I had to tell Brad, and Chaz, and Maven. But, Michael—Radu—sat at the top of my short list.

After rushing to my living room, I played back Chaz's old message with the number and wrote it down on an old receipt from the drugstore. I turned it over, and saw that it showed a purchase of a bottle of bourbon from several days ago—before Maureen and I had talked in the back of Second Chance. I couldn't remember buying it. The Question circled around me, and I shook my head and closed my eyes until it faded. I picked up the phone in one hand, clutching the scrap of paper in the other, and dialed with my thumb. Putting the phone to my cheek, I listened.

It rang three times before he answered, "Hello."

"Michael, it's Jason," I said, sitting down hard on the futon.

"Yeah?" he asked. He knew. I could tell from his voice that he knew.

"I just heard about Rick," I said. "I'm so sorry."

He sighed, and said, "Me too. I think we both know what's going on here."

Playing for the devil, just for a second, I asked, "You don't think this might've just been something personal? Maybe he just crossed the wrong guy over a card game or something?"

His tone deepened, and he said, "Two distinct puncture wounds on the throat? It's a fucking message, Jason"

"Verdilak," I said.

"Yeah. He got to someone on the inside."

I quickly explained that we had a handle on the situation. Out of necessity, I overplayed Brad's status with the NOPD. "Former cop buddy" sounded better than "temporarily suspended and packing a handgun." I omitted the details about where and when. I didn't want Michael to turn into Radu again and vow revenge. But, he asked anyway. He wanted a hand in it.

"I can't really get into that," I said. "I guess it's kind of police business." It wasn't official police business, and I wasn't a cop. I felt like an asshole for saying it.

"You have to get into it," he said. I could hear his patience waning. "This is my brother we're talking about. I need to help you take this guy down." Leaning forward, I rested my head on my knee and rolled my eyes as I clutched the phone.

"Michael, this isn't a movie. Leave it to the police."

"The police and you?" he asked. "Don't worry. I'll be there." Then, he hung up the phone. I laid back on the futon for a minute and stared at the ceiling. I couldn't wait for Brad to arrest or shoot Verdilak or otherwise get him out of our lives. I hated even calling him that. The guy had to have a real name. Moving through a world of fake vampires—thinking on their terms, and even with their terms—left me feeling like a sane man trapped in an asylum. But, even as the walls closed in, I had too much work ahead of me. I thought about the alternative. Maureen and I could pack our bags and move across the country. We could sell her business. I could write from anywhere. We would marry and live as far from New Orleans as possible.

But, the city had a way of trapping you. Home, honor, and proximity drove you to think and act in ways you could never recommend to anyone else. People—white and black—did their business in bars and preferred to leave the authorities out of things. Everyone policed their own. Someone flirting with your girlfriend or stepping on your shoe could mean a solid ass-kicking outside. Or, a bought drink and a swift apology could turn you into best friends. I couldn't leave John, and I couldn't stop what I had set in motion. The city wouldn't let me. The plan to trap and take Verdilak at the Dark Cotillion would occur whether I helped or not.

I swallowed nothing in particular, and glanced over at the phone once more. I knew I had to call Brad, and then Chaz and Maven. At the end of her shift, I would tell Maureen. And at sundown, I would tell John.

Chapter 20

Monday, October 27, 1997 – Afternoon

Speeding down Claiborne Avenue towards the French Quarter, I considered what might wait for me there. I had phoned Brad, and he already knew about Rick Fremont. He'd asked for time to think, and to figure out what to do about Michael.

When I called Chaz, he only said, "You'd better get down here."

"Now?" I asked.

"Yes, now."

Something had occurred in the short time since I'd spoken to him—only two hours prior, at the Masonic Temple—that he insisted on seeing me in person at his office. I maintained a healthy nine miles above the speed limit, weaving around the afternoon traffic moving towards the Superdome and downtown. The Claiborne Avenue overpass provided the fastest backdoor to the French Quarter from Uptown, and I made full use of its four lanes and lax police presence. The green neutral ground passed in a peripheral blur on my left as gas stations, laundromats, and fried chicken joints passed on my right. It wasn't a "good neighborhood," but that described a lot of the city. Ahead, the overpass and the Superdome grew larger.

In short order, I crossed over and passed the edge of the Central Business District, the cemeteries, and then the French Quarter. Rounding Esplanade, I sped past North Rampart to Royal and made another right. After exiting, parking, and paying the meter, I walked—quickly, nearly running—past the art galleries and restaurants that filled the street that ran behind Jackson Square.

At Jackson Square, I turned left—practically spinning on my heel—and continued my fast-walk to Chaz's office in the back of the cigar shop. The young woman with black hair and the skull barrettes looked up from her book, only half-interested.

"Chaz," I said.

"In the back," she replied, pointing a thumb over her shoulder as she had the first time I visited.

Through the beaded curtains, I saw Chaz at his desk. The same familiar folded newspaper and a smoldering cigar sat in front of him. Part of me wanted to check the date and see if he ever bought a new one. He could've been smoking the same half of a cigar for all I knew. I could see Maven a few feet behind, and someone else at the left corner of his desk. The limp, swaying beads parted as the stranger pulled them apart for me.

It was Michael.

"Well, hi," I said. Michael extended his hand, and I shook it. Maven stood with his arms crossed, saying nothing. Chaz picked up his cigar and took a puff. For a moment, none of us spoke.

Michael finally did: "They told me everything."

I turned and put my hand over my eyes, and said, "Oh, Jesus. Really?" I turned to face Chaz. "As if enough people didn't already know about this." Chaz didn't flinch, or blink. He puffed the cigar again, and then rested it in the ashtray. The leathery scent filled the room.

"It's his brother," he said. "He has a right to know."

"So he can do what?" I asked. "Is he going to go with John? Are they going to 'take this guy down' together?"

Michael looked at me. He relaxed his scowl a little, and said, "I just want to be there. If I can help, I will. If I can't, I'll just watch. I was planning on going to the party anyway."

I looked at Chaz and Maven—one, then the other. Maven said, "It's true. He bought a ticket last week."

Leaning against the door, I said, "I thought you were done with vampires. And, I thought you guys were fighting."

Michael shrugged, and said, "We talked a little while ago and cleared things up. It's all fine now."

"Does Brad know?" I asked. Chaz nodded, still smoking. I turned around and threw my hands up.

"Am I the last to know everything around here?" I asked.

"We just talked to him," Chaz said. "It's fine."

Glancing back, I saw the bead curtains and the wall behind me and my friends in front of me. There wasn't much I could say.

"What about the funeral?" I asked. "Don't you have to go to Florida?"

"Isn't going to be one," Michael said. "He was a double-murderer behind bars for life. The only one sorry to see him go is our mom and me—and 'sorry' is stretching it. He belongs to the state. They'll bury him."

I turned to look over everyone in the room, and said, "If he—Michael, I mean—just wants to be there, I guess that's fine. Just, please, for Christ's sake, don't try to step in. Brad's got a gun, and I don't want anyone to get shot. Don't try to take Verdilak by yourself. We don't even know what he looks like. We don't know if he'll have anyone there, or what."

"I just want to be there," he said.

"Can I sit?" I asked Chaz. He gestured towards a chair in the corner behind me, which I spun to face him. Sitting, I rested my elbows on his desk. "Do you mind if I smoke?" I realized how stupid the question was as soon as I asked. I'd asked him before, and he always said yes. He held up the cigar and waved the orange, glowing tip in the air in front of him.

"Be my guest," he said. I pulled the pack from my jacket pocket and picked up Chaz's cigar lighter from his desk. The three sharp, blue flames shot up and met the tip of my cigarette. It lit quickly, and I inhaled just as fast.

Dangling my smoke to the side, I finally asked, "So, do we know anything else about what happened?" I looked over at Michael. "You're family. Did they tell you anything?"

"Not much," he said. "I know what you know. I only heard it a few hours before it hit the press. Seems like most people are pretty happy about it."

"Most people where?" Maven asked.

"Internet, right?" I replied.

Michael nodded, and said, "Yeah, some of the newsgroups are saying he got what he deserved. It's that kind of thing. I expected it."

"This has got to stop," Chaz said. "This is bad for all of us." He had set his cigar down again, and he planted two fists on the desk in front of him.

I inhaled through my cigarette, and said, "Let's look at what we know. Rick sent a few of those books out and answered some letters. Those people he got back to started talking on the Internet. But, Verdilak really brought it together. He took it to the next level. Rick knew that. He tried to convince me he was responsible, but Michael thinks that was just talk, right?"

Michael coughed as the smoke swirled through the room. The light from the blinds cut through the haze around him. He stepped closer to the window, away from the plumes, and blocked the light.

"He knew Verdilak was doing it," he said, "I think it was what he wanted, but he couldn't actually do it from inside. All he could do was send and get mail in there, and use the phone. He didn't get Internet access and he could only see people if they were cleared as visitors."

"So, why kill him? Or have him killed? What could he possibly do from in there?" I asked, crossing my leg over my knee.

Chaz pointed one long claw at me, still clutching his cigar, and said, "He could talk to you. You brought John. He opened up to you. If Rick found out who Verdilak really was, he could tell you. They only ever wrote letters, correct?"

"As far as I know," I said.

Maven waved the thickening smoke away from his face, and said, "That, or he planned to kill him all along. He used Rick's name and his contacts to build this thing. If Rick's dead, then he's a martyr and this asshole can say he's carrying on his work."

"That's it," Chaz said. "This guy has his group here in New Orleans now. If he gets John's blood, then he can use it to control all of them. If Rick's dead, there's no one to get in his way." Planting both feet on the ground, I stood and pointed at Chaz.

"You're right. That's it. That's fucking it. Rick would never hurt John. And, he wouldn't have wanted anyone close to him killed. If he had enough time, he might've shut down the whole thing." I turned around and pointed at Michael. "Your brother was obsessed with John, but I saw them at the prison together. Rick would've told anyone that asked that he was against it."

Michael coughed again, and I put my cigarette out in the ashtray at Chaz's elbow. Michael said, "To the extent that he could have stopped him, that makes sense."

"He had a voice," I said. "He's been interviewed. He had contacts. Those kids wrote to him. He's the only one besides John that could've undercut Verdilak."

Chaz leaned on his elbow, and said, "Then Verdilak told him what was going on, or found out you and John went there, or Christ knows. Then he had someone on the inside kill him."

Maven asked, "Any idea who did it?"

Michael shook his head, and replied, "They just found him like that. It was probably just a hired hit. And, they're not going to find the guy if he had the time to pull something like that."

"Well," Chaz said, raising his cigar, "rest in peace, Rick."

***

Thursday, October 30, 1997

Chaz and Maven went to the Fellowship meeting at Kaldi's the same Monday we learned about Rick. It was the last chance to establish contact with Verdilak. A would-be vampire old enough to attend the event promised to carry a vaguely worded message that we all agreed upon—that John said, "Come to the Dark Cotillion and accept what is rightfully yours." The young acolyte said that he would contact Verdilak online and tell him to meet John in the chapel at midnight. There, the two would talk. The outcomes and possibilities floated free and wild in our imagination.

In the last meeting we held that day, we smoked, drank, and argued through happy hour in the back of Sally's—an old bar on the corner of Decatur and Ursulines. John even joined us. By then, Jenny Dark's murder lay nearly six weeks behind us. Even Brad reasoned that if the NOPD suspected John, they would have contacted him. We all agreed that my friend might return to lingering in the bars on Decatur and otherwise living his life. We'd long ago sworn off returning to the Crypt to keep the gossip mill out of the equation. I hadn't set foot in my favorite bar in weeks, and I wondered if I'd wear blue jeans next. With the trap set for the Dark Cotillion the next night, I thought about the future, and wondered if we'd ever leave it all behind us.

While we drank at Sally's, Maureen stayed close to me and nursed a lone beer. The entire time we were there, she kept looking around the small courtyard—at its corners, its entrance, and the bar behind us. The bricks were wet beneath our feet, and a patchwork roof of green fiberglass and sheet metal stood between us and the occasional dusting of rain. With no one there but us (and the occasional bathroom-goer), I knew she could feel safe. But, she wouldn't—not for a long time. And, I told myself to only hold her closer.

"Are they all going to be there?" I asked Chaz, as I leaned against the space between the bathrooms. Ivy grew up the space and over the crack between the wall and the roof.

"They might," he said. He pointed back and forth between himself and Maven. "We can't stop anyone from buying a ticket over the phone. If they can show an ID and they're eighteen, they can come in." I remembered Rick and his fake ID that started all of it.

Maven sipped the lone drink he'd held the entire evening. He never drank much. I wondered how he managed to stand in a bar all evening and only have one. He spoke then, saying, "We can't exactly identify people by the way they look. Everyone there's going to be dressed like that."

"The look," I said. We all knew it. The Masonic Temple would flow black with velvet, leather, fishnet, lace, and dyed hair. Verdilak's followers would look no different.

John shouldn't kill Verdilak. We agreed on that. He could hurt him, knock him out, or incapacitate him, but an actual murder charge would do us no favors.

All along, we'd assumed John might be a suspect. Brad had urged him to lay low. But, no call had come. No officers came knocking with a search warrant. In a city full of self-proclaimed vampires, we realized that John may have simply blended in with the rest. The denizens of French Quarter bars often spoke of who they could, would, or should kill (or pay someone to do it), but even when faced with the man who had killed Raven Cartwright and Jenny Dark, we knew better than to let John pull a trigger.

Brad would follow him a minute, and open it with the key Chaz had given him. Trapped in the chapel, Verdilak wouldn't hurt John. He wanted him alive. He wanted to bleed him. With a quick step, Brad could enter with his gun drawn and assume control of the situation.

As Chaz rested his tiny plastic cup on the edge of the bar, the female bartender wiped the counter and looked down at his half-full drink. He outlined an elaborate series of questions. What would happen if Verdilak escaped, if Brad was injured, or if he somehow took down John? All of us had, through a self-important liquor haze, pronounced our own version of events. One would speak, and the entire group would clamor to yell over one another. It would happen over and over again, until the volume would aggravate even the bartender. More than once, she begged us to keep the volume down. And we did, if only for a few minutes at a time.

Michael said that if Verdilak ran out of the chapel, he'd grab him outside. If Brad couldn't stop him, he wanted the guy who had his brother killed. Maven said we could wear two-way radios and keep track of each other. We actually agreed on that. Maureen wanted to stay far away, and only came at my insistence. She could tell the arresting officer what he'd done to her, as if trying to kidnap John wasn't enough.

Maven said he'd pick up the radios. Brad told everyone to meet him at eight in the Temple's office to walk through the plan one more time. Before we could talk any louder, the bartender asked us to pay up so she could count out from her shift. Chaz volunteered that we should all leave then. We had too much work the next day to continue drinking through it.

We filed out through the main bar, past the assortment of punks, goths, service industry personnel, and Irish patriots that frequented Sally's. A few already wore Halloween costumes. Masked killers and a few superheroes sipped drinks and laughed among the usual collection of werewolves, mutants, and post-apocalyptic bikers. I overheard a fairy explain that Halloween began at midnight, and she was, in fact, right on time. They blended well with the motley assortment of pictures and souvenirs that dotted the brick walls of the place—cheaply framed newspaper articles about the bar, pictures of visiting celebrities, and anything else that the owner deemed worthy. They hung all around the bar's patrons, and over an ATM, a video poker machines, and a couple of long tables across from the bar. The whole place looked like someone had decorated it from a garage sale.

When we exited, John turned left down Decatur towards his house. Holding Maureen's hand, I walked faster until we reached him.

"Can we invite ourselves over for a nightcap?" I asked.

"Sure, I guess," he said.

Maureen didn't speak, but I saw the slightest frown across her lips. We were already drunk by the standards of anyone outside of New Orleans. But that's why we lived there—lax liquor laws and an extended adolescence. I knew she might still worry about me. I'd decided to ignore The Question until after Halloween.

John let us in through the gate, and we walked in a single line to his front door. After opening it, he pointed with a quick noise to the living room. I switched on the antique brass lamp near his sofa, and we sat down. From the kitchen, I heard ice hitting the bottom of glasses. He hadn't asked us what we wanted, and I didn't inquire. He appeared a second later clenching three tumblers.

"Maureen," he said, "I hope you drink Scotch. I should have asked. If you like something else, I'm happy to open the cabinet for you."

"No, this is fine," she said, taking one of the glasses from him. She sipped from it and rested it on her knee, looking bored. I drank from my own, and felt glad that the relief would continue. We had to confront a murderer tomorrow night. From there, the plan looked simple enough. But, we all knew the risks. Verdilak might arrive armed. He might not arrive at all. If no one believed our story, he might walk free. I stared at the tall windows across John's living room and focused.

"Jason?" John asked. "Are you all right?" I shook my head and looked at him and Maureen. Both stared at me. He'd asked me something, I reminded myself.

"Shit," I said. "Yeah, I'm fine. What did you ask?"

"Maureen asked if we could visit Maria," he said.

Maria. Maria. Maria. My mind raced and I almost asked "Who?" until I recalled his wife—the feral woman in the attic for whom he cared. I nodded and stood, mustering a little enthusiasm.

"Let's head up there," I said, as if I'd planned to all along.

We ascended the attic steps. John shoved his hand in his pocket and pulled out his keys. He unlocked the door and walked through. The light flickered on as I crossed the threshold. She was sleeping. He stood at her bedside with his hands folded in front of him, as if he wanted to pray. Maybe that's what he was doing.

"Do you need a minute?" I asked.

He shook his head and waved for us to join him there. She looked clean and strangely content, sleeping deeply. I smelled the freshly-washed sheets, and saw that John had brushed her hair. The presence of the needle in her arm broke that momentary calm. She wasn't at peace, and she never would be.

Maureen stepped forward, and asked, "Can I touch her?" John looked up at her as if he might say no, but then nodded wordlessly. Maureen knelt and ran the back of her hand down her cheek. "This could've been me," she said.

"What do you mean?" I asked.

"Verdilak drank some of Maria's blood. He hadn't, I guess, 'turned,' but Christ knows what could have happened. I was so thirsty if he forced me to drink some I might've done it." I pictured the scene with her there, blindfolded, and the bastard's wrist forced against her mouth.

John rested his hand on Maria's shoulder, and said, "What happened to my wife was an accident. She tried to save me the only way she knew how. In the end, I might as well have killed her."

Maureen looked up, and then stood. "Do you think your friend can ever cure her?" she asked.

"No," he said. "I do not. But, I owe it to her to at least keep her," he said, pausing, "as best as I am able to." His faint Texas accent showed itself there, and for a minute I pictured Sgt. Nicholas Marston—a Marine, dirty and freezing in Korea. From what my father told me, I knew they never left anyone behind. The way he kept Maria made the only kind of sense he knew. The room swam a bit, and I shifted to sit at the edge of her bed. Her foot touched my leg.

Maureen stood between us, and said, "Do you guys want to go back down and finish our drinks?" We hadn't brought the glasses of Scotch with us. I knew I didn't need anymore, but I wanted it anyway. We left the attic, but I saw John stop and look back to the darkened room for a moment.

"Good night," he said, though she couldn't hear him. I remembered all they'd endured. She'd lost her husband once in the Korean War, only to see him alive—but changed. They'd fled, unsure of who even chased them. On the road, she had offered herself to her husband. He drank from her, unaware of what might happen. And then she herself changed, but in a way they could not control. John had spent decades caring for a woman he loved, but had made desperately ill. And, I knew he would never forgive himself.

We returned to the sofa and remained silent for a minute. Maureen finally said, "John, can I ask you something?"

"Certainly," he said, shifting towards her.

"Why did you do it? Why did you fuck those girls when your wife was up there?"

John cleared his throat and looked at his shoes before saying, "You must remember that I kept my own company before I met Jason. He's been my only friend for these past two years. I needed someone to talk to—even though I certainly couldn't tell him everything."

"Obviously," I said, sipping my drink.

John continued, "I saw the life he was living. I remembered being a young man and when we had liberty, we would go to the pool halls and the movies near Camp Pendleton. I'd only just made Sergeant when they shipped us to Korea. And, I'd only just turned twenty-two, and married Angelica a short time before that. I had very little time to simply live my life—to have friends, or step outside my own front door just to see a neighborhood and wander. Even in this city," he said, pointing at the window, "I all but hid. I stayed here because Dr. Reynolds provided the house for me, but I never took advantage of my time here.'"

"What did you do for all that time?" she asked.

"Drank," I said.

John said, "Yes, I developed a fondness for liquor. Because of my body's chemistry, after what happened, it doesn't really affect me."

"I'm jealous," I said. Maureen said my name and put her hand on my arm. She wanted to listen, and I kept interrupting.

"I tended to Angelica. I'm in the habit of calling her Maria now, but I attended to her. I read. As I said, I drank. On a trip back from Baton Rouge, I was in an automobile accident. Jason stopped and assisted me. He saw how I remained uninjured. It was difficult to explain myself at that point."

"Jason told me about the accident. You could've just left," Maureen said. "No one would really know, and it's kind of hard to believe."

John sat back in the sofa and stared at the ceiling for a full minute. Maureen and I looked at each other, and waited for him to speak.

Without moving, he finally said, "I needed a ride. The police and a few others were arriving." He paused for a second, and sighed. "Besides, I hadn't known a real friend in many years, Maureen. Jason helped me at the wreck, but he also believed me."

I remembered the events of that night in quick succession. We'd met at the bar. I'd passed his wrecked, flaming car on my way home. I saved him to the extent that he needed it. He explained himself to me. And then, he asked if we might become friends.

And there we sat, two years later—still friends, and still drinking.

Chapter 21

Friday, October 31, 1997

Early Halloween evening around four, well before the Dark Cotillion, Maureen and I started putting on our clothes. Though we planned to catch a murderer, we had to blend in with the crowd. We'd all agreed to abide by the event's dress code and at least wear black. Looking at myself in a hall mirror, I knotted a silk tie around my neck. Maureen rummaged through a tote bag she'd brought filled with makeup, stockings, and a pair of shoes. She decided against wearing heels in favor of a more sensible set of flats. Brad had reminded us we all might have to run at some point. On a hanger over the living room's door, there was a black dress of lace, ruffles, and ornamental silver trinkets, with bats as buckles and stray buttons that held on to nothing. She'd retrieved it from a rack in the storage room of Second Chance. She kept a stash of personal claims from the stream of vintage clothes that passed over her counter.

Finishing with the tie, I looked to see her pull the dress over her head. It slid into place past her bra and over her panties (also black, I noted). She turned to me, still unadorned with any of the objects from her bag.

"What do you think?" she asked. I realized I'd never seen her in a dress.

"You look amazing," I said, walking towards her. I rested my hands on her hips and she looked up at me. "Are you sure you want to go through with this?" She looked down at the cuts on her arms. Flesh-colored bandages sealed them, and she'd brought long gloves to wear.

"Yeah," she said. "I want to know who he is. I want to see him in handcuffs."

"Or, get shot by Brad?" I asked.

She turned and bent over, digging in her bag, and said, "I wouldn't stop him. Whoever he is, he's fucking psychotic and he's just going to do it again. He only let me live because I could get a message to John. The next chick won't be so lucky." She pulled a pair of stockings out of her bag and held them up for a second. She stood and turned to me.

"I know this is a crazy idea," I said, "But, we could've just gone to the real police when he grabbed you. We still could."

She shook her head, and said, "That's not how we do things around here. Plus, NOPD might just grab John and we'd fucking be back where we were before. And then, I'd just end up dead, anyway." She was right, of course. The unofficial New Orleans street code dictated that you took care of things yourself. And, we had no way to stop him from taking her again if we stayed out of it.

Maureen sat on the couch and pulled the stockings up her legs. Standing, she hiked them up under the dress, hopping a few times to fix them in place.

"I think everything's as planned out as it's going to get. He won't do much to John, and Brad will have a fucking gun. I want to end this thing." She turned to me. "I still want to pursue this with you."

"This?" I asked.

She moved closer to me. Looking up, she said, "Yes. I want us to have a relationship, like two fucking adults. I still want to talk about, you know, the thing we talked about." She meant The Question. She hadn't forgotten. I rolled my eyes.

"Don't do that," she said, grabbing my arms. "I only told you all that because I care about you. I'm not your mom. I'm not trying to tell you not to have fun. I know you've started drinking again." She'd seen me drink since Verdilak threw her out of the van and on to her neighbor's grass, so I wondered what she meant.

"Well, yeah," I said. "Doesn't mean I can't stop. You've seen me do it the entire time since the thing."

"That's not what I mean," she said. "You're doing it a lot again. That doesn't mean you have to stop, but I don't know." She trailed off and turned away from me. I rested my hands on her shoulders.

"It's going to be fine," I said. She ducked out from under my hands.

"I'm going to finish getting ready," she said. Before that conversation, I'd planned to offer her a drink. Everyone in New Orleans drank before they stepped out for the evening. A drink at home meant one less to buy at the bar. I glanced behind me, towards the kitchen.

She looked back at me, and I said. "We can talk about it. After, I mean. Let's just get through this."

As soon as I said it, her eyes relaxed slightly, and she softly mouthed "Okay." I walked over to her, and she wrapped her arm around my waist. Leaning over, I kissed her and held her there. When I released her, she smiled slightly.

On my way back to the bedroom, I looked at the darkened kitchen once more. For a second, I imagined the lights on and John standing in the doorway holding two full glasses of bourbon. Shaking my head and closing my eyes, I continued to my room. In there, no bottles rested next to waiting glasses. No ice shuffled and clinked. I closed the door and wondered what might happen next.

From the other side of the door, Maureen asked why I'd shut it. For a moment, I said nothing. And when I answered her, I said just that.

***

At eight o'clock, our group stood around a table with a diagram of the building's thirteenth floor and a pile of grey store-bought radios. We'd all grabbed a drink from the bar, and the glasses of liquor circled the table resting on wet napkins. Maven had picked up the radios earlier, and said they should work inside the building. We all took one, and Brad quickly named a channel. We all dialed in the number and then spoke a few words in them. The test calls echoed from each of them.

"Leave them on at all times, and check in if you're not sure," Brad said.

The Dark Cotillion had yet to begin, but the crew had started to set up the party hours before we arrived.

Chaz looked up and said to the rest of us, "We've only got a couple of minutes. Maven and I have to get back out there and keep an eye on these guys."

Brad looked over at Maven, and asked, "Selling fangs tonight?" Maven laughed a bit, showing his own set of prosthetic caps.

"If we aren't all killed or arrested," he said.

Looking over the group, Brad said, "I wouldn't worry about that. I put in a call to a couple of friends about what's going on tonight. A lot of the guys still see me as a cop. And, if this goes off as planned, it should be really quiet. If I can hold this guy in the chapel, a couple of uniformed officers should come through and grab him right after I make the call." He held up his cell phone for all of us to see. "That's the worst that'll happen. Chaz just has to keep the vampire babies calm, and then y'all can all go back to drinking."

Chaz and Maven had to run the party, but the rest of us had small assignments of our own. Michael Freemont and I would keep watch at the elevator. If anyone looked out of place (and I laughed when Brad explained that), we would radio Brad. He would stand close enough to the chapel to move in when needed. Nearby, John would remain in the side hallway and otherwise lay low. If anyone at the party recognized him, it might unravel the whole plan. Maureen would roam the crowd, looking for any suspiciously young attendees (Fellowship members, perhaps) or anyone else that looked odd. We asked Brad what he meant by odd or out of place at a party full of misfits.

He only said, "You'll know."

At midnight, John would meet Verdilak in the chapel. Brad would follow using the key Chaz had provided. They would bolt the door from the inside and call the police. Verdilak would have nowhere to go, with a real vampire and an armed man between him and the door. All of us agreed to constant radio contact.

A million little things might kill the plan. Verdilak might not even show. He might figure out that we'd set him up and pull the fire alarm. He could bring his own gun and shoot Brad. Our friend swore he'd wear a vest under his black suit, but the lobby had no metal detectors. Anything could happen.

As I considered the particulars, the plan repeatedly fell apart in my mind. But, the alternatives seemed worse. Verdilak might continue killing the people close to John. John must have seen my eyes, downcast, before he said, "Are we absolutely sure we want to go through with this? I never asked any of you to clear my name."

I cleared my throat, and said, "You asked me. Before you left town, you asked me to look around for you."

"I didn't expect it to go this far. I thought the police might find him before we had to," he said.

Brad looked at him and rolled his eyes, and said, "I got sick, okay? I'm doing the best I can."

"Not what I meant," John said.

I raised my glass and stood straight. "I think we can all just hope this works out," I said. "Here's to that." All of us touched glasses with a faint clink and a "here-here" before we sipped. Over the rim of mine, I saw Maureen staring. When she noticed, she looked away. I knew our chat after the ordeal might decide how we'd live—together or not; drunk, sober, or in a place of regal moderation. But right at that moment, I needed it. I wouldn't apologize to anyone, including myself.

***

A few minutes after nine, the brass elevator doors began to open into the corridor as the first of the guests arrived. The four elevators fell and rose, each time unleashing clusters of four and five partygoers. Clad for vampire pageantry, they moved in waves of lace, velvet, and torn fishnets. The air smelled of clove cigarettes and leather. A foppish would-be noble in blue velvet, with blonde hair and dense white makeup on his face, emerged from the same car as a passel of vampire punks. They sported dyed black hair, leather jackets, and band names scrawled across their t-shirts. Fangs flashed in all of their bright pink mouths. Some had applied a trickle of red makeup to the edge of their lips.

Undoubtedly, a few of them had probably tried the real thing before they reached the Dark Cotillion. Chaz leaned on the bar next to me and smiled, rubbing his hands together, as the costumed creatures exited the elevators. A parade of capes, cloaks, claws, and utterly so much black, red, and silver passed us, and Chaz greeted them as they gathered around the bar and entered the main hall. It was like we'd casted a movie with every kind of vampire you could think imagine. Whether they'd fight or fuck remained to be seen. Michael, Chaz, and I leaned against the bar, and I said as much in my large friend's ear.

"Hopefully," Chaz said, then speaking louder, "Hopefully, none of the former and a lot of the latter."

"It is a private party," I said. The sight of them made me wonder if I'd always misunderstood something—if acting like a vampire invoked something more than high fashion and low morals. The lifestyle seemed to draw a wide range of people. Something about the archetype resonated with lawyers and waiters alike. Its power drew them, and some would kill, die, and give up all that made them human in its pursuit.

I shook my head and remembered what might happen later. A killer might enter the chapel and confront two of my friends. The sight of Chaz and Maven's guests had taken me away for a moment. I closed my eyes, and then opened them to see the same thing. But rather than stand in awe, I only worried.

Michael still stood at Chaz's other side, saying nothing. I knew they'd argued before he returned to New Orleans. But, all seemed well enough whenever they were together. I looked over at him, wondering if old resentments had arose in his mind. Ignoring my glance, he stared at the elevators, scowling. He wanted the man who had his half-brother killed. I thought of Rick, and considered how he would have reacted to the web he'd unwittingly spun from prison. Part of me thought he might simply laugh, and take it as one more turn in a game he could play forever. Another believed he might realize how out of control it had become, and perhaps scramble to fix it—more red books, and more cryptic drawings, and letters, and puzzles, and prison visits.

In my mind, I saw Rick Fremont dying—naked and bleeding from his neck in a prison shower. The blood he coveted so much pooled around him, fading with wet distance in a widening gyre. I looked back at Michael. His stare had not left the elevator lobby. Every few seconds, he nodded as each new group entered. I watched with him for a moment, as the black-clad bodies became blurs. It occurred to me again that Verdilak, the Fellowship, and Count-fucking-Dracula could walk by us, and we might never know.

With the ticket-taker stationed downstairs, the guests freely streamed through the lobby and swarmed around us at the bar. Others bypassed us and all but ran to the dance floor in the main auditorium. The pounding of The Sisters of Mercy and Alien Sex Fiend echoed behind Chaz and me as we waited. He turned and waved to the bartender. Clad simply in a black t-shirt and jeans, the young man placed three plastic cups with red straws in front of us. Chaz handed me one, and Michael the other.

"Here's to not getting killed," he said. This time, we did not raise our cups. I moved closer to talk over the rising din as vampire after vampire passed us.

"However this turns out," I said, "I'm glad I brought you in. I don't think we could've come this far without you and Maven. I don't know this crowd like you do." Michael focused, and said nothing. He sipped the drink and swallowed. I waited until he blinked before turning back to Chaz.

"My pleasure," Chaz said. "I'll always be there for you guys. John's the real deal and you're his best friend, so of course." He extended one clawed hand to me, and I shook it.

Maureen stopped in front of us, with her arms crossed.

"See anything?" I asked. She took the red straw in my drink, and placed it to her redder lips. She took a long sip from my cocktail before speaking.

"Nothing," she said. "It's not that crowded yet. And everybody looks the same. I have no fucking idea what I'm looking for."

Even though I could see Brad from where I stood, I unclipped my radio from my belt and said, "Brad, still nothing. Nothing in the lobby, and Maureen hasn't seen anything. Kind of hard to tell with this crowd." I heard my voice in the three radios around me.

Brad spoke into his and said, "That's fine. You'll know something's not right when you see it."

Turning to Michael, Chaz, and Maureen, I said, "He's just assuming his cop sense will finger someone. Fuck."

Michael laughed a bit, and said, "In this place? She's right. It's like picking a flame out of a goddamned fire." He immediately resumed glaring at the lobby.

"Can you switch places with me for a second?" I asked Maureen, touching her arm. "I'll walk around the auditorium and you keep an eye on the elevators?" She nodded and moved to take my drink out of my hand, after already consuming half of it.

I held back, and said, "After. We'll talk about that after." The Question floated between us again, flapping its dead, wet wings, and I knew that it threatened to remain there. I didn't want to—couldn't, really—think about it at that moment. I said as much to her, as she waited in front of me. Again, she'd crossed her arms.

"Fine," she said. "Just don't get too drunk. We can't screw this up. I don't want to get fucking kidnapped again." She paused between each of the last three words and drew them out. I understood, and realized how much it meant that she'd agreed to help.

I nodded and leaned to her ear, whispering, "I know." I felt her relax, and her arms fell to her side. I kissed her ear and moved past her without saying more. To my right, the auditorium waited.

Seats surrounded a great, shining dance floor on three sides and two levels. The fourth, at the front of the room, led to a stage. Scattered throughout the great hall, the children of the night huddled in groups of twos and threes in the seats. Some kissed and touched, and for a few, razors shaped like Egyptian ankhs dangled in the space between them. I looked away, and wondered if they would spill blood there. Others simply talked and drank and laughed, as if they'd found another comfortable party. Nine Inch Nails blared from the speakers mounted from the balcony, and around the room.

I walked down the aisle towards the floor at the center of it all. A great mass of vampiric partygoers moved and swayed to the echoing beats. They had conquered the space and even the stage. Some of the songs I'd heard throughout the evening had come out almost twenty years ago in the dark clubs of London, but I saw them resurrected there as fuel for a youthful black maelstrom. Strobe lights flashed against the clouds of fog emanating from machines at the edge of the dance floor. The lights blinked in time with the beat, and reflected off of the pinpoints of silver jewelry that dotted the crowd. Ankhs, crosses, bats, spiders, and totems of all the meaner things in nature drew into focus as I moved closer. Step by step I walked, with one hand gliding lightly down the rail to my right.

Stopping at the edge of the dance floor, I set my drink down next to my feet. I drew a pack of cigarettes from my jacket pocket. Withdrawing one, I placed it between my lips and lit it with a lighter I'd found buried beneath my keys.

I stood there and inhaled the smoke, watching them dance, as I picked up my drink. It was almost tribal in its own way. Part of me wanted to be among them and feel all that they did. But, just as I had at the bar only minutes before, I reminded myself of all we had left to do. I left my reverie and picked up my drink, before rounding the edge of the dance floor.

Brad had said to look for anything out of the ordinary. He said that something that seemed even slightly out of place might mean everything. Walking the perimeter of the center space, I saw nothing more than I already had. And, no one seemed to see me.

To my left and above me, the stage only showcased the same dance as the one to my right. The auditorium remained quiet of all that we'd hoped to find, and dense and loud with all that we'd expected. I wondered if we were wasting our time.

Leaning against the stage, I pulled the radio from my belt. I set the drink on the ground again and removed the cigarette from my lips.

"Brad?" I said into the small grey box.

Static crackled in return and a voice. I repeated his name, and held the radio to my ear. Faintly, above the noise, I heard "—can't fucking hear!" I looked around me. Of course he couldn't hear me. I saw the DJ on the balcony above me, jumping up and down to the Sex Gang Children track he'd just started. His long hair bounced along with his raised fist. I cursed myself out loud. No one could hear me from the main hall. I grabbed my radio and my drink and walked towards the elevator lobby.

On the other side of the dance floor, a small, black form dashed towards the main hall.

I turned and tried to look through the crowd. Another black streak followed it—not floating or dancing, but running behind the other one. Something bumped against my back and pushed me into the crowd. A few cries of indignation rose as I bumped into some of the crowd on the dancefloor. A couple of voices asked if I was okay. I hadn't hit the floor, but not by much. I stood up straight and realized that I'd lost my drink and cigarette. Anyone I'd bumped into had moved on to dance elsewhere.

Turning to look at the space I'd just occupied, I saw nothing. But behind the seats across from me, I saw another black streak. It moved too fast for me to see anything else. I looked over the room, and stopped long enough to see one more of them weaving through the partygoers towards the lobby.

I cursed again and walked as fast as I could towards the doors. My radio crackled again. Before I could remove it to listen, Maven and Michael ran from the door and down the aisle. I met them in the middle and before I could ask, they both yelled, "Get in there!"

The three of us nearly ran each other over on our way back to the lobby. When we reached the space, I saw Chaz and Maureen near the bar. Brad stood a few yards from the men's room, with the chapel down the hall at his back, breathing hard.

And then, I saw them.

In the center of the lobby stood a formation of youths in black cloaks, with hoods over their heads. They stood in a V-formation, with the point towards the doorway where my friends and I stood. I counted fifteen, and they stood with their backs to us. They faced the windows at the end of the foyer and the night sky beyond them. The other partygoers had cleared a space around them. Some laughed. Others simply watched. They all believed that it was part of the event. The music in the lobby had not stopped, but few spoke. The wall of sound faded to a low buzz. With the attention of everyone in the room, the hooded figure at the point of the "V" raised his fist in the air and yelled something in a language I did not understand. I moved closer to the bar with Maven and Michael behind me. Maureen saw me, and took my arm as we watched.

The other cloaked youths repeated his words. He chanted again, and they said the same. It echoed in the hall, and I only caught the most obvious words—"vampire," "nosferatu," and "undead." But at the utterance of one familiar word, we all winced.

"Verdilak!" they cried.

Chaz leaned over to me, past Maureen. "Jesus, it could be any of them," he said.

"I know," I said. I looked at Brad and pointed at the group, mouthing the words "What do we do?" Even from down the hall, he understood. He held up a single finger, telling me to wait. I looked down at Maureen. Her eyes were wide, and I knew she recalled the anonymous black shapes that had taken her in the van that day.

I looked at my watch. It showed 11:51 p.m., and I wondered if one of their number might finally stand out and walk to the chapel where he would meet John. But, it still seemed too early.

Nearly pounding the bar with my fist, I watched the formation as the chanting continued. It took on rhythmic, melodic tones. The high, adolescent pitch of the young man's voice echoed in the hall. As word spread around the Dark Cotillion about some kind of show in the lobby, others walked out of the auditorium. I realized that the great hall would empty as so many left the dance floor.

They did, and the throng spread throughout the lobby. Eventually, the DJ in the main hall lowered the music to a dull thump.

With nothing to drown him out, the young man—still holding his fist in the air—began his chant again, and the others repeated his words.

Leaning over to Chaz, I asked, "What are they waiting for?"

"I don't know," he said. "I really don't." For the first time, I heard hesitation in his voice. I looked around at my compatriots. Maven and Michael stood nearby, and both looked as confused and frightened as the rest of us. Michael's bravado had faded at the sight of the hooded children. Maven just mumbled a long and drawn out "Holy shit."

By the time they neared the conclusion of their chant, I saw the DJ at the doorway. He looked confused. His eyes met mine, and I only shrugged.

John waited in the chapel.

I looked at my watch, and saw that it was two minutes to midnight.

The formation finished the chant. Then, with almost military precision, the children turned to face the room that watched them so closely. Once they faced the crowd that had gathered around them, they stomped in unison. Their faces shown white-bright beneath their hoods, and they all smiled to reveal vampire fangs. A few had the same bloody trickle as so many of the partygoers. Right at that moment, I wondered if it was real. I wondered if it was all real.

The crowd shifted back against the wall. Faces turned to Chaz and Maven, looking for an explanation. A few of the people around us laughed. Chaz simply held up one clawed hand to calm them. We knew what might come next, and if he broke the spell we would lose everything.

There was one minute to midnight.

The partygoers had fallen silent, and Chaz leaned to my ear and whispered, "The Fellowship." He and Maven had seen them at the coffeehouse. They knew. Verdilak's progeny had assembled to herald his arrival.

The elevator's bell rang. The room turned to face the back-right door, and it opened far too slowly.

The black heel touched the marble lobby floor with a tap. The rest of the tall leather boot followed, and then the knee of legs clad in black velvet. A gloved hand clutching a black cane bearing a silver wolf at the top came next. The ruffles and trim of his long black coat ascended to a face covered by a tight black mask. Atop his head, a great brimmed hat sat low. A single red feather adorned the crown and flopped over its edge.

I knew that the sheer black material across his face meant that he could see us, but we couldn't return the favor. He wanted to remain anonymous until the end. I looked in Brad's direction. He'd left his post near the men's room.

I grabbed Maureen and whispered, "Brad's outside the chapel already." She nodded, but kept her eyes on Verdilak. She hadn't seen him like that—only in the head-to-toe black clothes that hid his identity so well. But, she knew.

Silently, he gave the assembled crowd a great wave with his free hand. He held his cane aloft with the other. He exaggerated each step he took around the formation, extending his long legs and bringing the heel down hard. His arms extended, he looked from side to side with a jerk of his hand. He had waited for this moment for weeks. He'd killed two women, and then drank from Maria. Then, he'd kidnapped Maureen and tortured her. Looking down, I saw that she clutched the places where he'd cut her—all now concealed by the gloves that stretched almost to the tops of her arms.

He continued his promenade past the formation, and, as he reached the corner to the hall where we stood, spun on one heel. He passed the bar, and the crowd remained silent. Fifteen yards ahead, I knew that the chapel waited—and John in it. As quickly as I could, I stole a glance down the corridor to see the narrow hall where, I knew, Brad had concealed himself. When Verdilak entered, our friend would follow and put an end to the entire ordeal.

The partygoers only watched. A few whispers of confusion floated from behind us. Most remained fixated by the man in the black mask that sauntered past them. Past the bar, past the men's room, and down the hall he jaunted. One step followed another, and the crowd all but crawled over each other to see him depart. They pressed at our back, and Chaz spread his great arms to keep them there. The whispers continued, asking the same quiet questions.

Someone hissed, "Amazing."

At the chapel door, Verdilak spun around on his heel once more to face the throng. He offered a deep and grateful bow to the assembly. The crowd hesitated, and then applauded. Verdilak stood up and then bowed a second time. Then, he turned and entered the chapel. The crowd relaxed, and then began to disperse. A member of the Fellowship brushed past me as their formation disappeared into the crowd.

Down the hall, I saw Brad walk from the hall to the chapel door clutching the key. He unlocked the door, and entered with his gun still fixed to the back of his waistband. The door slammed shut behind him. Next to me, Michael pushed his way through the remaining crowd.

"What's happening?" he asked.

And, I could only say that I did not know.

Maven joined us there, so that our whole group—save John and Brad—stood watching the space down the hall. The fluorescent lights reflected on the black marble, shining a trail to the chapel where the three had met inside. We could hear nothing over the din of the party that reconvened behind us. The music returned to full volume. All of them assumed that the presentation had ended—just another one of

Lord Chaz's theatrical showcases—all of it smoke and mirrors and stories in the end. In time, they likely assumed, the dark man would emerge from the chapel with his mask in hand and join the revelry.

"Happy Halloween," they'd say to him. "What a great show that was."

Maven asked what was happening. Again, I replied that I did not know.

Few in the crowd remained there to watch. I drew my cigarettes from my pocket, and a lone smoke from the pack. I lit it and inhaled hard. The seconds passed, and I tried to count them. My watch read 12:03 a.m. Verdilak's dance had only lasted two minutes, and but one had passed since he'd entered the chapel. My heart pounded, and I felt Maureen's through her back as she leaned against me.

Our radios crackled with an echoed burst of words, and all five of us looked down. None of us had called.

John's voice said, five times over, "I always knew."

Maureen looked down at her radio, as the low, guttural voice emerged all around us. She remembered. "If you did, then you could have ended this," it said.

"That's him. That's his fucking voice. It's fucking Verdilak," she whispered. She held the radio in her hand and looked down at it, spitting the words.

Chaz looked around at all of us, and said, "Nobody touch them. John's got his finger on the button."

Another voice broke in—one we did not recognize—and said, "Who are you guys?"

"Is that Brad talking?" I asked. We were all speaking in the same whisper, even though the ranks of partygoers behind us could hear.

Through the radio, John spoke again: "You know how this is going to end, don't you?"

The other man, still growling, replied, "Yes, I do. I'm going to take care of this problem over here. Then, we are going to walk through that door and tell everyone that it's finished. After that, you are going to give me what I want. If you don't, then all the rest of your friends die, and I'll keep doing this until you bleed. This is your fault. You have had so, so many chances to fix this."

"Maybe I did," John said. His normally faint Texas accent emerged full and real. "But, I was never sure. Now that I am, fixing it is exactly what I plan to do.

"Do you have your radio—"

The voices cut out in a burst of static. Michael separated himself from our line and said, "I'm going in there." Chaz reached to stop him, but narrowly missed his shoulder. He walked as fast as a man could without running. We—all of us—broke ranks and followed him, calling out over the emerging music, the laughter, and the dull roar of Halloween.

The loud report of a gun sounded outward from the chapel and echoed through the corridor. We stopped, and I listened for more shots. It wasn't Brad's semiautomatic Beretta. He would've kept shooting, and the rounds would have popped off one after the other. From talking to cops, I knew that much. You didn't just shoot once.

It was a single shot from a much larger weapon. I remembered the .44 I'd found in John's desk. If you hit, you wouldn't need to pull the trigger twice.

The five of us ran towards the door. Chaz turned to face the crowd behind us. The music continued, but the crowd had stopped and looked. A hoard of confused fans gathered near the bar, and we heard "gun" over and over again. He turned and ran to hold them back, yelling, "See what happened!"

The four of us—Maven, Michael, Maureen, and I—ran to the double doors. I pulled at the handle. Brad had locked them from the inside. The stained glass on either side of the door revealed nothing.

We pounded on the door with our fists, and I called out John's name.

***

Chaz found another set of chapel keys in the office before the police arrived.

When the doors finally opened, we nearly knocked one another aside to enter. The same pews led to the same altar we had seen earlier. We walked the short steps to the end of the room to see the man in black lying in the corner of the room. Alive and unharmed, someone had removed his mask.

His cane rested on the altar steps, and he extended one hand to us begging, "Please." Tears ran down his face. He shook his head and simply whispered, over and over again, "I don't know."

Michael reached him first. Grabbing him by the collar of his long black coat, he yelled, "Who are you?" The man only sobbed, still on the ground. Michael asked him again and again.

Finally, he answered, "I'm an actor."

Chaz roared and dragged the young man to his feet, demanding to know who asked him to perform at the Dark Cotillion.

Without saying a word, I stepped around the great wooden altar to find Brad sprawled on his back. A bullet fired at close range had reduced his head to a gaping crevice of brains and gore.

"Oh, Jesus," I said, looking away for a second. "You guys had better come look at this."

Maureen and Maven ran to me and saw his body. On the other side, Chaz continued to interrogate the young man. Maureen cried out when she saw Brad, and covered her eyes. Maven looked away and planted his hand against the wall, as if he might throw up.

Blood pooled around what remained of his head, dotted with fragments of skull and bits tissue. His hand still limply held his Beretta. Across his chest, there was an open copy of the red book. I set it aside, and pressed over his heart to feel the hard surface of his ballistic vest. He'd worn it under his clothes, just as he said he would.

I picked up the red book and opened it to the middle. I saw that, with the only paper he could find in time, John had written three simple words.

"It was Brad."

I called out John's name and begged him to wait. Behind the altar, the wood panels checkered the wall. Jumping over the actor's cane, I touched the corner of the brown, shining surface and pushed. A hidden door gave way and opened into a dark room. As with so many places of worship, it allowed whomever led the service to make a discrete entrance and exit. I found a light switch and flicked it. I saw only a small office. A simple bookcase sat against the same brown walls. A desk waited at the end of the room, with the Masonic emblem above it. John's .44 was waiting there, underneath a white cloth. I knew that he had wiped away his fingerprints with the towel, before departing through an open door on the other side of the room.

From the chapel behind me, I heard police officers yelling for me to come out. I stepped on to the altar, holding up my hands. Brad's corpse remained at my feet. Officers in blue shirts with severe expressions filed into the room. Along with the others, they ordered me to wait in one of the pews. I obeyed and sat next to Maureen, until they questioned each of us. And outside of the chapel doors, they questioned the partygoers. And, the Dark Cotillion ended early on the order of the NOPD. None of us argued the point. I looked at Chaz and saw him resting his head on the pew in front of him. I could only imagine the fallout of having an ex-cop shot at your event.

"Verdilak"—Sam, as it turned out—volunteered the entire series of events to the detective. Wearing a navy blue suit, the officer seemed to understand—almost without our word—that none of us had killed Brad Simoneaux. When Sam emphasized as much, we all relaxed in the pews and waited as the detective removed the young actor from the room.

The story gradually unraveled. The police questioned me—and Maureen, and Chaz, and Maven, and Michael. They knew, at least, that Detective Brad Simoneaux had been suspended following an illness. As to the particulars, they would not say.

They strongly emphasized that, in the future, we should simply call the police and ask for their help—rather than accepting the word of a rogue cop drunk on blood, packing his own gun.

Chapter 22

Wednesday, November 26, 1997

It was Brad.

Those three words stayed with me and played in my mind in the weeks that followed. I tried to make sense of it all, but the NOPD offered little in the way of help. No one could find Sam. John had disappeared, and taken Maria with him. Dr. Reynolds knew as little as I did.

It was Brad.

I sat at my table with a bottle of bourbon near me and wrote what I knew. With each image, the pencil's sharp point scratched across the legal pad—the same one I had used to write about John a few weeks before.

"Detective Brad Simoneaux hands me a stack of photographs in a manila envelope. In them, Raven Cartwright lays dead on the floor of a bar bathroom in the Marigny with her throat cut. He also murders Jenny Dark, knowing that we will find her next to secure John Devereux's alibi. We call, and he arrives just in time and asks us to lie about how we discovered her. But, John was never officially a suspect. We only believed that he was based on Brad's advice. And, by talking to any other police officers, we would cast suspicion on John.

"John leaves town. Brad enters his home using a spare key he knows about. He cuts my friend's invalid wife and consumes some of her blood, believing he will become a vampire. But, the blood only makes him ill, and the symptoms push him to the edge as he becomes obsessed and addicted. We do not know how many times he has bled her like this. Because of his illness and erratic behavior, he is suspended from the police department.

"Maureen and I discover that someone has harmed Maria, and remove the key Brad has accidentally left on the table when he flees John's home. When he can no longer feed, he recovers and reconnects with us. For the entire time we have known him, he has corresponded with Rick Fremont, who is in prison for two murders in Florida and one in Louisiana. Brad uses his newfound mentor to build a vampire cult from prison. Youthful would-be vampires gather in New Orleans at the behest of "Verdilak," who uses the Internet to hold a gathering with the intention of finding John and becoming like him. They pack their bags full of black t-shirts, spikes, and fangs and head to a Southern city they have never seen. John does not know. I do not know. We believe that Radu has committed these acts, but Michael Fremont is innocent. John does not acknowledge the killer's implied demands.

"Brad knows that John will not acquiesce, because he knows us.

"If John had suggested otherwise, Brad would have revealed himself in short order. Instead, Brad kidnaps and tortures Maureen for two days. The entire time, he wears a mask and blindfolds her to send the clearest message: he watches all of us, and it will happen again. Brad answers our phone call for help, as he remains nearby. Removing his black clothes in the back of the van, he attends to us almost immediately. He concocts a plan to confront "Verdilak" at the Dark Cotillion.

"Then, he has Rick Fremont murdered in prison for talking to us.

"For the party, he hires an actor to play Verdilak, whose face we cannot see. In the chapel of the Masonic Temple, on the thirteenth floor of 333 St. Charles Avenue, he reveals himself to John. He demands the blood. He tells John they must leave together. He plans to kill Sam, the actor, and claim that he has finally stopped Verdilak John—Nicholas Marston, former Marine and a veteran of the Korean War—shoots him in the head with his .44 Magnum, that he has concealed on his person. He shoots him to save Sam, to save us, and to stop Brad from hurting anyone else. Then, cleans the revolver and departs the chapel through a nominally hidden door behind the altar. He immediately retrieves his wife and then leaves the City of New Orleans."

I stared at all I had written, with the bottle nearby. Pouring more into the glass, I read it a few more times.

***

Friday, October 31, 2014

Seventeen years have passed since that Halloween. John has never called, nor has he written. The NOPD may still want him for questioning. I do not know, and I have not inquired in years.

In time, Maureen left. She left us. The Question answered itself: "Yes," naturally. She still owns Second Chance, but I avoid the store. From time to time, we pass each other on the street. We nod and say hello, but she understands what I resisted for so long. The weight of John's world drove me to a place from which I will likely never escape. And inevitably, I will remain in those dark spaces in between the drink and myself.

Michael returned to Florida to live with his mother after Rick died. We have not spoken since then. If you ask around the French Quarter, you can find Lord Chaz and Maven. They still live here. But, the ordeal we went through and all that we know now sent us on our separate places.

I live here in mine, alone. The walls of this apartment stare at me as I wait with a bottle, a phone, and a pad of paper. I've written down everything I can remember, and each day I wait for John to call.

Sometimes at night, I sit in the same bar near the corner of Decatur and Ursulines, and I watch the door. And no matter what happens, I am always there on Halloween. Even as I write this, the drinks flow, the music plays, and the maelstrom of costumed revelers turns and dances around me. The bar has changed names and owners more times than I can count. But to me, it will always be the Crypt. It will be where I kept the company of a man unlike any I have ever known.

Once in a great while, a feeling will come upon me—that on that very evening, he will find me. When that happens, I order two drinks. I sip my own, while I hope and pray, to no one in particular, that he will walk through the door. He will shake my hand, he will smile, and he will accept the drink. And then, we will talk again as we did during that bloody October, and all the times that preceded it.

When he returns, perhaps I might ask The Question once more, and the answer will be different.

Until then, I comfort myself with this: I knew Sgt. Nicholas Marston—true and whole—and called him my friend. I have long owed the world his story, and I have written all that I know. Now, I have only to wait—wait and remember.

THE END

Kurt Amacker is a writer from New Orleans, Louisiana. He graduated from Loyola University in 2002. He began writing his first graphic novel miniseries, *Dead Souls*, while recovering from an injury in the United States Marine Corps. After the first issue was published in 2008, he continued writing comics while DJing at several goth nights in the French Quarter. He met Cradle of Filth singer Dani Filth in 2007, and the two ultimately collaborated on the graphic novel, *The Curse of Venus Aversa*. Amacker's work has been publicly praised by Alan Moore, Hart Fisher, and Victor Gischler. He also co-produces the yearly Fangtasia vampire ball with Jyrki 69 of The 69 Eyes. *Bloody October* is his first novel. He continues to live in New Orleans with his wife, Sabrina, and their black cats, Vlad and Erzsebet.

CPSIA information can be obtained at www.ICGtesting.com
Printed in the USA
BVOW06s1950050116

431642BV00009B/43/P

9 780991 571277